SCARLET ODYSSEY

SCARLET ODYSSEY

C. T. RWIZI

Text copyright © 2020 by C. T. Rwizi
All rights reserved.

Published by 47North, Seattle

www.apub.com

Amazon, the Amazon logo, and 47North are trademarks of Amazon.com, Inc., or its affiliates.

ISBN 13: 9781542023825 (hardcover)
ISBN 10: 1542023823 (hardcover)

ISBN-13: 9781542020589 (paperback)
ISBN-10: 1542020581 (paperback)

Cover design by Shasti O'Leary Soudant

Printed in the United States of America

First Edition

For Doreen

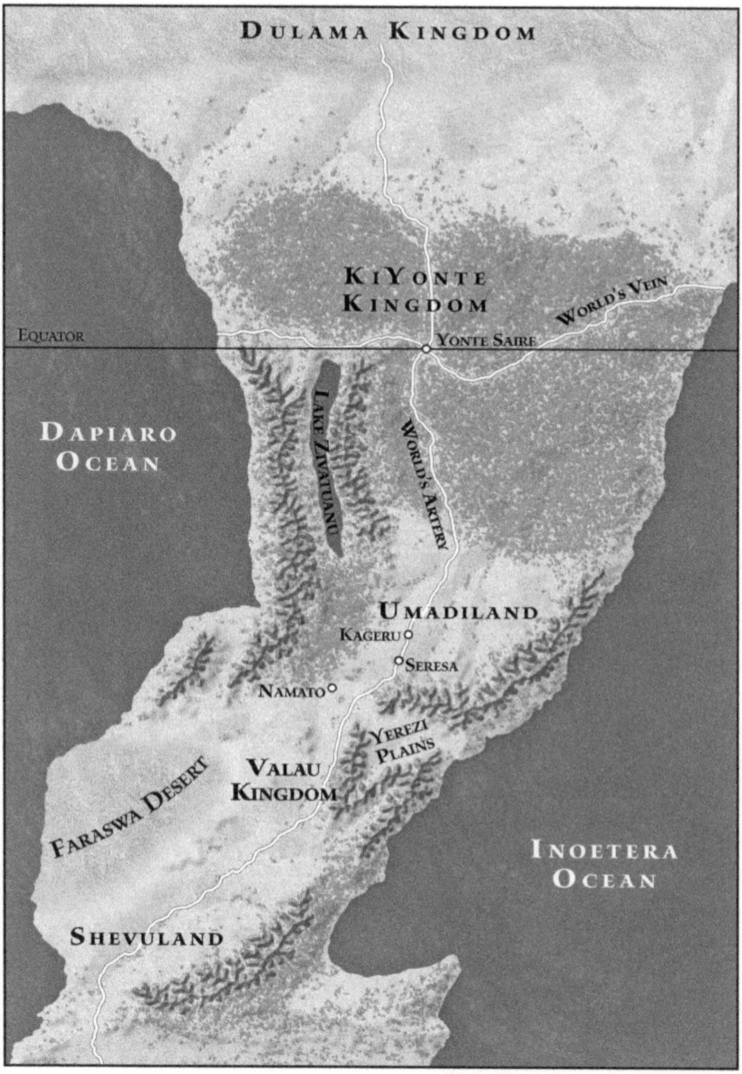

Dulama Kingdom
KiYonte Kingdom
World's Vein
Equator
Yonte Saire
Dapiaro Ocean
Lake Zivatuanu
World's Artery
Umadiland
Kageru
Seresa
Namato
Yerezi Plains
Valau Kingdom
Faraswa Desert
Inoetera Ocean
Shevuland

DRAMATIS PERSONAE

Yerezi Plains

MUSALODI, a young man
MUJIOSERI, his brother, a ranger
MASIBURAI, his brother, a ranger
VASININGWE, his father, chief of Khaya-Siningwe
ABA DEITARI, his uncle, a general
AMA LIRA, his stepmother, a teacher
MONTARI, a young boy
ANENIKO, a ranger
NIMARA, an Asazi
ALINATA, an Asazi
AAKU MALUSI, an old mechanic
IREDITI, queen of the Yerezi Plains
AMASIBERE, mystic of the Sibere clan
AMASIKHOZI, mystic of the Sikhozi clan

Umadiland

ILAPARA, a young mercenary
THE MAIDSERVANT, a mystic and a warlord's disciple
KELAFELO, a young woman

THE ANCHORITE, an old mystic
AKANWA, a young girl
TUKSAAD, a mysterious wanderer
THE DARK SUN, a warlord
BLACK RIVER, his disciple
HUNTER, his disciple
SEAFARER, his disciple
SAND DEVIL, his disciple
NORTHSTAR, his disciple
THE CATARACT, a warlord
BLOODWORM, his disciple
KWASHE, a mercenary
BAMIMVURA, a mercenary boss and money lender
BACHANDO, a general dealer
MHADDISU, a young thief

Kingdom of the Yontai

THE ENCHANTRESS, a mysterious woman
ISA ANDAIYE SAIRE, a princess
KALI, her brother, the crown prince
AYO, her brother
MWENEUGO SAIRE, her father, the king
THE CONSORT, her mother
ZENIA, her cousin
SUYE, her cousin
JOMO SAIRE, a prince, son of the herald
PRINCESS CHIOKO SAIRE, the king's herald
OBE SAAI, a Sentinel, nephew of the Crocodile
DINO SATO, a Sentinel, son of the Impala
IJIRO KATUMBILI, a Sentinel, son of the Bonobo

ITANI FARO, head of the Arc coven, a high mystic
THE SIBYL UNDERGROUND, a clairvoyant mystic

The Ten Headmen

THE CROCODILE
THE BONOBO
THE KESTREL
THE IMPALA
THE LION
THE RHINO
THE BUFFALO
THE CARACAL
THE HARE
THE JACKAL

PROLOGUE

They say that on the day he was to become a man, he cried and wet himself in fear as soon as the uroko bull charged out of its cage in a blur of fury. They say he fled out of the dusty enclosure while his brave peers stayed to take down the bovine monstrosity with nothing but their bare fists.

Their faces were daubed with white earth, their knuckles wrapped in reedfiber. They wore nothing but loincloths as red as the moon and hide skins hanging over their rears. They were there for glory and for manhood.

And what could be more glorious to a Yerezi man than proving himself worthy of a place among the Ajaha rangers, the truest warriors of his people, whose bones are blessed with the power of their clan mystics? What could be more valorous than prevailing over the dreaded uroko, whose hooves could crush skulls, whose muscles ripple like currents in an oily black river, whose horns glint like sabers in the light of the setting suns? What could be worthier than facing this most perilous test of manhood before an audience of four thousand battle-tested Ajaha, whose rowdy cheers make the air itself tremble with fear?

Surely nothing on earth, but Musalodi ran that day. He ran and never looked back, and they called him a coward, and he believed them.

PART 1

MUSALODI

*

ILAPARA

*

THE MAIDSERVANT

Mirror craft—magic of light

Transfiguring the moon's essence into luminous interference patterns to conjure illusions. Used by illusionists to enchant lamps for illumination.

—excerpt from Kelafelo's notes

"Aago, are we not part of the Redlands?"

"Of course we are."

"But we're not like the other tribes, are we? We shut ourselves in, and we don't talk to anyone else."

"There are hyenas out there, my child. When you see hyenas prowling outside your gates, you shut them out so they don't come in and eat your children."

1: Musalodi

"Maybe we should head back."

Near a gushing brook in the central lowvelds of the Yerezi Plains, Salo keeps picking his way through a curtain of tall grasses. The binary suns are high points of light in a clear midmorning sky. Two New Year's Comets have blazed across the heavens since the incident with the uroko bull.

"Did you hear me, Bra Salo?" Monti says as he straggles a few paces behind. "I'm tired, and my aba says there are hyenas this far south of the kraal. What if they find us?"

A rebuke briefly stirs Salo's tongue, but he suppresses it, reminding himself that Monti is still just a child. Exceedingly wise for his age and annoyingly curious at times, but still a child. His fear is understandable. "That's why I brought my bow," Salo says, "and lucky for you, I know how to use it."

The brook comes into view as they emerge from the grasses. Salo leaps across to the other side and keeps going without waiting to see if Monti follows.

"What if it's a tronic hyena?" Monti says behind him. "What would you do then?"

"I'm a fast runner."

"But what about me? I can't run as fast as you."

"You brought your bow, too, didn't you? So you can defend yourself."

"But what if it's a whole pack of them?" Monti says. "Or worse, what if a redhawk comes down and sees us?"

Salo keeps walking, his footfalls silent beneath his worn leather sandals. "Then you should have thought of that before you followed me here."

He left the kraal alone, or so he thought, and by the time he noticed he'd grown a tail in the form of a precocious nine-year-old boy, he'd already gone too far to turn back.

"Please, Bra Salo," Monti whines. "I want to go home."

Salo keeps walking.

"Pleeease?"

Salo sighs deeply and finally stops, pushing his copper-rimmed spectacles farther up his nose. He turns around, intending to scold the boy, but the instant he sees his face, a laugh barrels out of his chest.

Monti's sunset eyes, normally aglow with mischief, blink up at him with betrayal. "What's so funny?"

"The look on your face," Salo says. "Next time, don't follow people around unless you can keep up."

Monti pouts and looks away. "I thought you'd be hunting for mind stones."

"Well, not quite," Salo says. "And you'd have known that had you bothered to ask."

"You came back with a mind stone last time you went out," Monti says with a scowl.

"A happy coincidence. I almost literally stumbled across it."

Deciding he has tormented the boy enough, Salo crouches to bring himself level with Monti's small frame and places a gentle hand around his nape. "Cheer up, little man. I have a secret I'm about to let you in on, but you have to promise not to tell anyone. Can you do that for me?"

"A secret?" Monti says, his eyes widening a little. "What is it?"

"First you promise; then I'll show you."

Monti licks his lips, seeming to weigh his desire to go back home against the prospect of finding out a new secret. Predictably, his curiosity wins out. "I promise."

Salo gives him a gap-toothed grin and rises back up. "Follow me, then. It's just over that hill."

They continue walking south until they crest the hill, then venture into the sun-streaked grove of musuku trees growing on the southward slopes.

They hear it before they see it: first a muffled rustle in the trees, then a high-pitched squeal and a flash of color as the creature pokes its head out of a clump of branches directly ahead. Its reptilian eyes watch them skeptically as they approach, paying special attention to the newcomer, but it must decide he's harmless, because it eventually slinks down the tree in a sinuous motion, clinging to the bark with its clawed, stocky legs.

Upon seeing it, Monti stops and lets out a gasp of surprise. "Imbulu! Bra Salo, it's attacking us!"

"No, she's not," Salo says. "She's just coming to greet us."

The imbulu—a tronic monitor lizard—is as long as a grown man is tall. Its curved little horns shimmer like pure silver; its metallic scales change color depending on the angle of view. As it slowly pads forward, it tastes the air with a forked tongue, swinging its thick tail from side to side.

Monti begins to back away even as it approaches. "I don't know about this."

"Relax," Salo tells him. "She's friendly." He moves forward to meet the creature, going down on one knee so he can scratch the ruffled skin beneath its jaw. The imbulu responds by lifting its head to give him better access, which makes him smile. He looks back at Monti over his shoulder. "See? What did I tell you?"

Monti keeps eyeing the lizard suspiciously. "So *this* is your secret? Is it your pet now?"

"Ha! Can you imagine? A pet imbulu." Salo shakes his head. "No, I'm just helping her. She was badly injured when I found her, and the mind stone inside her head had been corrupted. I've tried to repair it, though. She seems better now. She's actually quite young, if you'll believe it—almost a baby, even."

"A baby? But it's so big!"

"Oh, they get bigger."

While Monti gawks, Salo turns to examine the circular discoloration on the imbulu's head and is satisfied to see that it has continued to diminish. When he first came upon the creature only a week ago, that discoloration was a frightful wound that would have surely proved fatal without his intervention.

"I need to take another look at her mind stone," he says, standing up. "In the meantime, you could feed her if you want. She hunts rodents mostly, but she also loves the taste of milk."

"What if she bites me?" Monti says. "I could get sick. My aba says their bites can infect a whole herd with sickness."

"She won't. She knows I'm helping her. And if you're with me, then she knows you're my friend."

Monti keeps staring at the beast, curiosity and fear once again warring openly on his face. "You have the milk?"

"I do." The quiver on Salo's back is part of a leather harness strapped around his bare chest, to which his bow, waterskin, and utility pouches are fastened. He unfastens the waterskin and offers it to Monti, who warily steps forward to accept it. "Trust me—you'll be best friends by the time that skin is empty."

"If you say so," Monti says.

As he squats down and slowly brings the skin to the lizard's mouth, Salo considers the little serpent bracelet of enchanted red steel curled around his own left wrist: his talisman. Obeying his silent command, the talisman stirs, its crystalline eyes projecting beams of prismatic light that sweep over the lizard's body.

A mirage of superimposed waves subsequently takes shape above the talisman, displaying the energy state of the mind stone inside the imbulu's head. The illusions look somewhat ethereal through the round lenses of his reflective spectacles.

No one knows why, but in the wilds of the Redlands, the arcane essence of the moon can sometimes weave itself into certain life-forms, giving rise to tronic beasts—exotic machine-organic hybrids with met-alloid features and mind stones inside their brains. People figured out long ago that with finesse, these stones could be manipulated to control the beasts and, if recovered intact, could be harnessed as sources of arcane energy potent enough to animate machines or even cast spells.

Salo had been out searching for energy signatures emitted by dead tronic beasts when his talisman detected a faint but live signal. At the end of that signal was the imbulu dying next to a brook, its mind stone thrown so far out of equilibrium that most of its tronic abilities, such as self-healing, had been corrupted. He went on to spend many hours searching for errors in the cipher prose governing the mind stone, trying to repair what he could with his talisman to keep the imbulu alive.

He was reasonably successful, though he'd never repaired the mind stone of a live animal before. In fact, the energy waves shown in the mirage are still somewhat out of sync. But this is nothing the creature won't survive.

He glances away from the mirage and down at Monti, who's now cooing at the imbulu while he strokes its neck. Having guzzled a full skin of cow milk from his hand, it obliges him.

"So," Salo says, trying not to smirk, "what do you think of my secret?"

"I think she's beautiful," Monti gushes, and it's like he's a completely different person. Gone is the frightened boy of minutes earlier; this is the wise and annoyingly curious boy who tailed Salo from the kraal. "Dear Ama, I wish we could take her back with us."

Salo smiles, seeing in Monti the same transformation he felt when he first discovered the creature. He was wary of it at first, but the simple act of feeding it quickly changed his perspective. "That's why you can't tell anyone about her. If you do, they'll kill her."

"I'll tell no one, I swear," Monti promises, and Salo believes him.

Crack.

The loud snap of a twig somewhere off in the distance.

Monti shoots up to his feet. Salo almost gets whiplash when he jerks his head to look, and what he sees makes him temporarily forget not to curse around children.

"Shit."

Monti's wide eyes stare up at him, full of panic. "What do we do?"

"It's too late. He's seen her."

"She could run."

"He'd just catch her, and then she'd die."

The imbulu registers no alarm as it flicks its tongue curiously in the air, perhaps figuring that another one of Salo's friends means more milk for its belly. A wave of protectiveness washes over him, and he sends his talisman to sleep with a thought, snuffing out the illusions. He crouches next to the lizard and hooks a gentle arm around its neck.

"How does he keep finding me?" he complains to Monti. "Do I leave a trail of pheromones and glitter where I walk or something?"

"He's a ranger," Monti says with a shrug. "My aba says a ranger could track a fly across the lowvelds if he set his mind to it."

"How wonderful." Salo pets the imbulu worriedly, praying to the moon to preserve the poor beast. Hasn't it suffered enough?

The moon must not be listening, however, as Aneniko continues to trot down the hill toward them astride the tronic quagga stallion he captured and subdued shortly after becoming a ranger two comets ago.

A ruff of thick fur sits around his bare shoulders. Armor pieces of polished red steel adorn his arms and legs, each piece expertly engraved with magical ciphers. His loincloth—long enough to wrap in loose folds around and between his thighs, reaching down to his knees, as is customary—isn't the ordinary white worn by Salo and most other Yerezi men but the deep-red hue of blood reserved for warriors of the highest caliber, those who carry the blessing of a mystic inside their bones.

He's also holding a long spear in his right hand, burnished to a blinding luster, made entirely of the Yerezi arcane metal.

Because what self-respecting Ajaha ranger would ever be seen outside his kraal without his warmount, his spear, and all the red steel he has earned the right to wear?

Salo might be rangy where Niko is strapping, and Niko might be several shades darker than Salo's coppery complexion, but the two are not completely devoid of similarities. They were born only ten days apart, for example, and have both seen eighteen comets. They both tended the livestock of their respective fathers as young boys, and both grew to be taller than most men in their clan. They both went through Ajaha training and were circumcised in the mountains during the year of their sixteenth birthdays—the same year they met. They even took to cutting their textured hair similarly—sheared low on the sides and left to grow slightly longer on the top.

Similarities indeed, and yet, looking at them now, one would likely fail to guess that Salo was the one born to a warrior chief and Niko to a lowly laborer in a mining village.

A riderless gelding follows timidly behind Niko's tronic stallion. He brings both quaggas to a stop nearby, staring at Salo and the imbulu in that phlegmatic way of his, even though he's probably not happy about what he's seeing.

"Hello, Salo," he says.

Salo keeps petting the imbulu, staring at a spot on the ground. "Niko."

To his side, Monti silently admires the tronic stallion. A handsome beast of lean musculature, it is adorned with the characteristic white and golden stripes of a plains quagga, like the gelding behind it. Unlike the gelding, however, its lower legs, snout, tail, and long spiraling horns all catch the grove's dappled sunlight like steel—the mark of tronic strength. A mount like that will gallop at extraordinary speeds for hours on end before beginning to tire.

"How long have you been hiding this here?" Niko says.

"Three days," Salo replies, perhaps too quickly.

"The truth, please."

Salo grits his jaw, unnerved by the calm in Niko's voice. Insults and an angry outburst would have been easier to defend against. "A week, maybe?"

"So ten whole days."

"Give or take."

"I see."

For Salo, looking at this particular ranger is always an exercise in control. He actually has to force himself to look and not give in to those pesky little instincts urging him to turn away in shame. After a protracted silence, Salo finally lifts his gaze, confused. "That's it? You *see*? No lecture? No outrage? Accusations of witchcraft?"

"What do you want me to say?" Niko asks, the slightest hint of frustration filtering into his voice. "You know what that thing can do to a herd of livestock. Surely you don't need me to tell you. And surely you don't need me to tell you what would happen if you were discovered like this. I mean, you're *fondling* a bloodsucking creature, for Ama's sake."

At that word Salo stops petting the animal, but he keeps his hand where it is. "We can't just kill things because of what they might do.

And not every imbulu drinks blood and milk from oxen. Some are different."

"He's right, Bra Niko," Monti joins in. "This one is good. She's friendly and doesn't bite. Please don't kill her."

Niko scratches his well-groomed beard—yet another thing Salo envies about him, that he can grow a beard like that. The best Salo can do is a fuzzy upper lip.

"I'm not here to fight with you," Niko says. "Either of you."

"Why'd you follow me, then?"

"*Why?*" A flicker of raw emotion in the ranger's eyes. Indignation perhaps, coupled with the sharpening of his voice. "Why d'you think? For the same reason I had to follow you the last time you ran from the kraal, and the fifteen other times before that. Whether you mean to or not, you've made it a hobby of mine, and don't think for a second I don't have better things to do with my time."

Salo almost retaliates with words coated in acid.

I'm sorry, he thinks about saying instead. *I only ever feel like I can breathe when I'm away from the kraal.* But that would be grounds for more criticism, so he settles for: "What's broken this time?"

Niko holds his stare for a moment longer, like he has more grievances to express. "The mill's not working anymore," he says eventually. "I'm told there were lights coming out of the engine or something."

Salo blinks. "Please tell me you're joking."

"I'm not joking."

"Didn't you fix the mill two weeks ago?" Monti says.

For a good few seconds Salo closes his eyes and tips his face heavenward, trying not to fly into a rage. "Those idiot millers probably destroyed another mind stone. I've told them so many times not to overwork the machine, but they won't listen." He scowls at Niko. "Why didn't you ask Aaku Malusi for help? He can fix the mill too."

"We did," Niko says, grim amusement thick in his voice, "but we found him unconscious in that hovel you call a workshop. Again."

Salo shakes his head. "That old man will kill himself if he keeps drinking like this. And it's not a hovel. It's tidier than your Ajaha barracks and definitely smells better."

"I won't argue with you there," Niko says. "Doesn't make it any less of a shack."

"That's what gives it character." Next to him the imbulu nuzzles at the hilt of the witchwood knife sheathed by his side, blissfully oblivious to the danger standing not far away. "So what now?" Salo says to Niko. "You're not going to kill her, are you?"

Any other ranger would have already dispatched the creature with a single throw of his spear. But Niko contemplates the imbulu in silence. "I assume you can give it commands," he finally says.

Admitting to this would mean acknowledging that he has delved deeper into magic than is proper for any self-respecting Yerezi man. But Salo figures that if Niko respected him before today, surely that respect has just turned to dust. "What do you have in mind?"

"Get it to leave the Plains and never come back. Either that or I put it down right now; then you can recycle the mind stone if you want. But I can't let you keep an imbulu here like this." Niko shakes his head. "Too dangerous."

"She's really not, though. And she's not ready to leave just yet. She's still recovering from an injury."

"I'm being reasonable, Salo. You know this."

Salo does, but the sting of disappointment still makes his chest feel heavy. He exhales with resignation, looking down at the creature. "I guess it's time to say goodbye, friend."

Getting the imbulu to leave is the simple matter of changing several lines of the cipher prose running in its mind stone. The talisman projects the prose into the air as a window of luminous arcane scripts—ciphers—that Salo can add to, erase, and change with thoughts and gestures. He proceeds to give the creature instructions to move during the night, avoiding villages and grazing lands, and to keep going until it has traveled two hundred miles north of here—well into Umadiland and out of the Yerezi Plains. When he's done, the mirage winks out of view as the talisman goes dormant.

No ceremony to the creature's departure. It simply turns and slinks away, its scales shifting color so that they seem to melt into the trees. Salo and Monti watch it side by side until it vanishes from sight.

"I wish you'd shown her to me sooner," Monti whispers, a film of tears making his eyes glitter.

Salo gently squeezes his shoulder. "I'll show you my next secret as soon as I get one. That's a promise."

Niko watches them silently from astride his stallion. Eventually, Salo nudges the young boy to the gelding, and together they ride for the kraal.

◆　◆　◆

When he was twelve, Salo broke into his dead mother's vacant hut in the chief's compound and stole her journal. He was a cowherd back then, one of several young boys responsible for the chief's herd of oxen, so he took the journal out with him the next day and opened it only once he was in the privacy of the grazing fields far from the kraal. His hope was to find some sort of closure within its pages, some explanation for why she turned against him during those final months before her death.

The journal's pages, however, were almost black with magical ciphers he did not understand. Indeed, they spoke of things no Yerezi boy had any business understanding. Custom demanded that he let it go.

Yet he knew in his heart that the scripts in that journal were what had corrupted his mother, and his need to understand them burned hotter than his fear of getting caught dallying with the womanly art. So he broke into her hut again and stole something else.

He knew it only as the Carving: an ancient soapstone sculpture his mother had left hidden in plain sight like an ordinary wall ornament. He'd barged in on her once to find her sitting cross-legged before the sculpture, her eyes glazed over as she stared into the mysterious grove of trees it depicted. Later, she would tell him that the Carving whispered secrets into her ears whenever her mind roamed its woods, and that maybe one day it would do the same for him.

She was right. Years after her death, and in the strictest secrecy, Salo began to wander through the Carving's magical grove in search of arcane knowledge. Each visit was an immense risk, and he came close to dying on one occasion, but the Carving ultimately honed his aptitude for ciphers until it cut sharper than a razor, until he could finally read that damned journal and understand why the scripts inside had been so important to his mother—so important that she would betray him in a most profound way.

He did not anticipate everything else the Carving would teach him. He got the answers he wanted, to be sure, exciting, horrifying answers, but the Carving also opened his eyes to the greater world of magic, forever stoking his interest in talismans, mind stones, cosmic shards, and spell theory. And once he'd gotten a taste of *that* world, once he'd seen through that veil, there was no turning back. He became like an addict, a starved prisoner of magic, taking what little he could find wherever he could find it, and still it would never be enough.

Looking back now, more than half a decade later, as he rides to the chief's kraal alongside Niko's stallion, he can't help but wonder how much simpler his life would be had he never set foot into that hut in the first place. Surely he wouldn't be quite so miserable.

"Nursing a bloodsucking tronic creature back to life," Niko says just as the lake appears in the northeast. "Sometimes I think you *want* people to hate you." He looks over at Salo from his warmount. "Is that it? Do you like the way people look at you?"

Salo tightens his grip on the gelding's reins. Monti, sitting in front of him and holding on to the saddle's pommel, says nothing. "Of course I don't like it. Why would you think that?"

"Then help me out here. I'm trying to understand."

The suns have moved past their meridians in the skies, with Isiniso, the whiter sun, hanging slightly lower in the west than Ishungu, its smaller, yellower companion. Their combined light cuts through the low smattering of clouds and strikes the lake so that its waters dance like liquid opals. A few reed rowboats loiter just offshore, carrying silhouettes with straw hats and fishing nets. The chief's enormous herds of uroko and domesticated antelope are a sea of humps and dark muscle in the foreground, grazing along the lakeside. Salo shudders to think what the man himself will do once he finds out what Niko now knows.

"I found the imbulu bleeding out by a brook," he says. "Someone had hit it repeatedly in the head with a rock, I think. But they'd left it alive so it could suffer." Anger stirs inside him. "Nothing deserves that."

They enter a narrow road cutting through a field of millet near ripe for the New Year's harvest. Niko says nothing for a full minute, the silence between them filled by the pitter-patter of hooves on gravel. Then: "I agree with you."

Surprised, Salo tries to read his face, but Niko is staring at the road ahead. "You do?"

"Yes," Niko says. "But Salo, you can't do this again. Maybe your creature wasn't a threat, like you said, but many people have lost livestock to others just like it. You'd only be making enemies by consorting with one. Understand?"

"I guess," Salo says, realizing just now that he never really considered how his clanspeople might have legitimate objections to what he was doing. *But should a whole species be condemned for the actions of a few?* "Will you tell on me, then?"

"Maybe not," Niko says, "but on one condition."

"Extortion, is it? And here I thought the great Aneniko was beyond reproach."

Niko smiles a particularly wicked smile. "What can I say? I see a rare opportunity; I take it. From tomorrow morning onward, you'll come to the glade and train with the Ajaha. And then early next year, you'll enter the bull pen and earn your steel. Those are my terms."

Monti starts laughing, and Salo groans. "Oh, come on. You can't be serious."

"I don't see what the problem is. Most boys get weeded out before the bull pen, but you were right there. You were so close. If you hadn't run, you'd be donning the red right now."

"Maybe I don't want to don the red."

"You're the son of a chief. You can't be tinkering with machines and flirting with magic all your life. It's not worthy of a man of your station."

What if it's me who's unworthy of my station? Salo almost says. *What then?*

"We also need more rangers," Niko goes on. "There are whispers of unusually powerful warlords sweeping across Umadiland. If true, it's only a matter of time before they start testing our borders. We'll need all the help we can get."

"There are five hundred rangers in Khaya-Siningwe alone," Salo objects. "I'd hardly make a difference."

"You are the chief's firstborn. It's important that *you* be one of us. And you *will* be one of us, starting tomorrow. Take it or leave it."

Salo sighs. "Fine. I'll come to your precious glade if it'll buy your silence. Even though I'd rather scrub myself with sandpaper."

"It's about damned time." Another smile breaks on Niko's face, and he spurs his stallion a little faster. "Your aba will be pleased."

Salo doubts that quite a lot, but he keeps his opinion to himself.

The chief's kraal is the largest and most important village in Khaya-Siningwe, sprouting out of a plateau west of the lake. From below the plateau, only its drystone outer walls and conical guard towers are visible, the face of a stronghold as formidable as it is ancient. Behind this face is a vibrant network of compounds—clusters of drystone buildings with reed thatching and a common open space between them. Gravel roads connect these clusters to each other, snaking through gardens and landscaped woodlands. A great circular enclosure at the heart of the kraal houses the chief's herds of livestock.

The quaggas trot toward the plateau across grassy plains, millet and sorghum fields, and musuku groves. Soon they ascend the plateau along a wide road and see the kraal's main gates ahead of them.

As they arrive, Salo's eyes wander up the watchtower rising near the gates. Perched at the top on an overhanging beam is a giant metal sculpture of a leopard with a mane of metal spines flaring out of his neck like a crown.

Mukuni the Conqueror, the Siningwe clan totem.

The totem is inanimate, but every time Salo looks up at him, he can almost imagine the large cat snarling down in distaste.

He looks away with a shudder, urging the gelding to a stop by the gatehouse.

Mujioseri and Masiburai—Jio and Sibu to everyone in the kraal and Salo's younger half brothers by two years—are among the four rangers on sentry duty today. They pause their game of matje to watch as Salo and Monti dismount the gelding, barely concealed sneers stretching their lips.

Salo and his brothers all inherited VaSiningwe's big ears, light complexion, and prominent tooth gap. All three wear little copper hoops on their left ears as a mark of their parentage. But the twins are shorter and brawnier. They didn't run when it was their turn in the bull pen, and they don't need enchanted spectacles just to see because *she* never—

Don't go there, Salo. Don't think about that.

They all got along once upon a time. Then Salo became a disgrace to the family.

Ever the comedian, Jio says, "His Highness finally graces us with his presence," and gets chuckles from the three other rangers seated on low stools around the matje board. "Where did you dig him up, mzi?" he says to Niko, using the affectionate term for *cousin*—what all rangers call each other. "Was he getting high with the cowherds again? Or was he hunting for spirit balls this time?"

Sibu, Jio's right-hand man in all things, says, "He seems to like doing that, doesn't he? Hunting for balls."

More chuckles.

"Lay off him, will you?" Niko says, glaring from his stallion. "What did we say about disrespecting your older brother?"

Niko can talk like that because they actually respect him. He became the de facto leader of the kraal's younger rangers within a moon of moving here.

"We're just joking with him, mzi," Jio says. "No harm done."

"Your jokes are getting stale," Salo tells them. "You should try thinking up new ones."

The twins whisper something to each other and laugh.

Rolling his eyes, Salo starts making his way through the kraal's open gates. He half expects Monti to follow, but the boy is *obsessed* with matje and has already scampered off to inspect the rangers' game board.

"Don't forget your promise," Niko says behind Salo. "I expect you at the glade tomorrow at dawn."

Salo makes a vague motion of the hand.

"Wouldn't that be something," Jio replies loudly enough for his voice to carry. "Four Eyes in the bull pen again. I wonder how long he'll last this time before he wets himself."

Poorly stifled giggles chase after him, but Salo keeps walking.

"For Ama's sake," comes Niko's voice. "Must you be so cruel to him all the time?"

But Salo doesn't expect any different from his brothers, and he certainly doesn't expect Niko's tepid rebukes to result in any lasting changes. This is just the way of things. The sky is blue, the moon is red, and rangers are arrogant bastards.

Well, most of them are, and there's nothing to do about it but adapt.

The mill sits beneath a simple shed not far from the gates so that it is easily accessible to those who live outside the kraal. Normally, its metallic drone can be heard from miles away as its gearwheels turn at the behest of the mind stone inside the engine. But today it's little more than a hulking mass of scrap metal.

Salo finds the millers lounging on old benches next to the shed like a pair of ruminating goats. Their chests are ashen with flour, their conical hats askew on their heads, and they're both chewing blades of grass while they practically drool at the clan's only Asazi, who won't stop pacing in front of them like a restless leopard searching for prey.

She seems too lost in her journal of endless to-do lists to notice their lecherous stares, but she slams the book shut as soon as she spots Salo walking up the road. "Where on Meza have you been? I've been looking for you all day."

You might mistake Nimara for a princess, what with her flowing skirts of patterned kitenges, the confidence with which she wears her beaded bodice and face paints, the intricate spiderlike choker of red steel coiled around her slender neck, and the beaded strings woven into the curls of her bouffant hair like diadems.

But Nimara is no princess. She only looks like one because she's an Asazi, blessed with magical powers by a Yerezi mystic, and just as the Ajaha must embody the masculine virtues, Asazi must always embody the virtues of femininity, which someone long ago decided are artistry, nurturing, intelligence, scholarliness, and, of course, beauty.

Nimara lives up to all of them almost to a fault.

"I went out," Salo says, choosing not to elaborate.

She looks him up and down like she suspects he might have gone swimming in filth. "You were smoking nsango, weren't you."

"I . . . maybe smoked a bit this morning," Salo admits. "Why does it matter?"

"You reek of it."

He sighs. "It's for my headaches, Nimara. You know this. What's with the inquisition?"

She blinks several times like she's just realizing something. "All right, maybe I shouldn't be taking my stress out on you. But the mill broke in a major way, and when you're not here, people come complaining to me. Except I don't do machines, remember? That's your thing."

"Well, I'm here now, so you can relax."

She stares at him, biting her bottom lip. "I may also need your help in an unrelated matter."

Salo watches her for a long moment. "I won't like this, will I."

"Who knows," she says with a coy smile. "You just might. I'll tell you about it once we get to your workshop."

Not one minute inside the kraal, and I'm already wishing I could run off. He releases a heavy breath. "Let me take a look at the mill first."

With the millers watching, he moves to the machine and unlatches the steel casing covering the engine. An old but well-oiled system of gears and cogs stares back at him from within. His gaze immediately lands on the shiny, pebble-size orb of pure tronic bone at the heart of the engine—or at least what was once an orb of tronic bone, with enormous reserves of arcane energy locked inside it, but is now just a useless, deformed husk waiting to be thrown into a rubbish pit.

"Idiots," he says through gritted teeth. "Pure and utter idiots."

"Anyone specific or humanity in general?" Nimara chimes in.

"*Those* idiots over there." Salo points an accusing finger at the millers. "What part of 'Don't overload the machine, or it will overheat and destroy the mind stone' don't they understand? Am I speaking a foreign language here?"

Both millers scowl and stop chewing on their blades of grass. "You can't talk about us like that," says the older of the two. "Just because your aba is chief doesn't mean we have to take shit from you."

"I agree completely," Nimara jumps in before Salo can retaliate with a string of vitriol. "But you *do* have to take shit from him because he's one of two people in this kraal who can fix your mess, and the other one is a hopeless drunk."

The younger miller curls his lip. "He's not good at fixing things, though, is he? Clan Sibere has mills that work all day, and they never break."

"True," Nimara replies, remaining perfectly calm. "But they also have a mystic who can enchant things for them. Things like cooling elements so their machines never overheat. Last I checked, we didn't have that. And last I checked, *I* was in charge of who works here, which means that if I needed to, I could have you replaced for your incompetence. As a matter of fact"—she smiles sweetly and opens her journal, a pen threatening to add another item to her to-do list—"shall I have that arranged?"

The two millers acquire constipated expressions, like boys just scolded by their mother in public. They shake their heads in unison, but Nimara keeps the pen where it is.

"Are you sure?" she says.

"No, Si Nimara," the older one says. "I mean, yes, we're sure. We like working here. Please don't replace us."

"Then this won't happen again, will it?"

"No, Si Nimara. It won't."

"Excellent." Nimara aims her fake smile at Salo. "When can we expect the mill to be functional again?"

Salo glares at the millers, not quite convinced by their sudden contrition, but a nascent headache dulls his will to fight. "I'll have to take the engine apart and assemble it around a new mind stone. If I do it too fast, the spirit won't accept its new home." He shakes his head morosely. "It'll probably take a full day. Maybe two."

"All right, so you can start first thing tomorrow morning and hopefully have the mill working by sundown?"

He hesitates, remembering his promise to Niko. "Maybe?"

"Perfect." Nimara's steel bangles ting pleasantly as she jots something down in her journal. When she's done, she tucks it away in her colorful reedfiber shoulder bag and clasps her hands together. "Now, I have an appointment with that big brain of yours, so why don't I walk you to your shed?"

"Fine. But Nimara, if this is what I think it is—"

"Hush." She takes his arm and starts leading them away from the mill and toward his workshop. "We'll talk about it in private."

2: Ilapara

The World's Artery: an ancient roadway stretching up the Redlands from the southernmost cape of the Shevu tribelands, going up thousands of miles north to Yonte Saire, the heart of the continent, then reaching farther up to the fabled desert city of Ima Jalama, where the Redlands start to give way to the barren dunes of the great Jalama Desert—and the strange lands that lie beyond.

In a shantytown straddling the Artery somewhere in Umadiland, Ilapara treads along a muddy backstreet with quick, determined steps, each one avoiding the rivers of raw sewage oozing down the road. Those boots of hers are high-quality hide, bought for over half her monthly earnings, and she'll be damned if she lets the filthy streets of Kageru muck them up.

Rickety market stalls line the road on either side of her, all waiting for an insistent wind to blow them sideways. As she comes within view of one such structure, the short woman behind the counter ducks down.

At the stall, Ilapara balances the blunt end of her spear on the ground and sighs. "Don't, Mama Shadu. I've already seen you. And even if I hadn't, that's hardly a good place to hide from me."

The woman bites her lips sheepishly as she rises back up. Murky little flasks of medicines are arranged in neat rows on the planks of the makeshift counter in front of her. She wears her dark veil loosely enough to let her rufous dreadlocks spill out.

"Oh, hello, Ilira. I didn't see you there. I was just . . . looking for something I'd dropped." Mama Shadu shows the wooden pestle in her hand, which she was using to grind herbs in the mortar on the counter. "How are you, anyway? Is there something I can help you with? Need a soul charm? Another contraceptive elixir, perhaps?"

Ilira is Ilapara's Umadi alias. She's even dressed like a young Umadi woman, with a crimson veil wound tightly enough around her head to keep all her dreadlocks tucked under. Her leather and aerosteel breastplate, however, worn over billowy crimson robes, might raise an eyebrow or two, since it's not exactly conventional. But it's not entirely unusual, either, so she gets away with it.

"Let's not play this game, Mama Shadu," she says. "You know exactly why I'm here."

"You're right. I do know." Mama Shadu drops the oblivious act and folds her arms, her kohl-ringed eyes flashing with defiance. "The question is, Do you, Ilira?"

"I'm pretty sure it involves you paying me the ten rocks you owe my boss."

"That's not what I mean," Mama Shadu says. "I'm talking about why you're still *here*, in this town, working for a man who chose sides, and worse, the wrong side." She puts her hands on the counter and leans forward so that her yellowed teeth come into view. "It's in the winds, my dear girl. A change of season is upon this town, and when it comes, it'll be swift and bloody, and those who did not plant well will weep. I would not linger if I were you." She leans even closer, speaking in a harsh whisper. "They'll smell your master on your clothes."

An unwelcome tingle begins at the nape of Ilapara's neck. She subdues the urge to rub her silver nose ring, holding the aerosteel shaft of her spear tighter in her grip. The smile she puts on shows too many teeth. "I *really* don't want to have to force you to pay, Mama Shadu. I respect you too much for that. But you are trying what scant reserves of patience I have."

"And I respect you too, Ilira. Actually, I like you. You've been a good customer these last few moons, which is why I'm warning you. Get out before it's too late."

"Thanks for the warning. Now the money you owe, please."

Mama Shadu doesn't move, her expression mulish.

Ilapara holds her gaze, placid but firm as a brick wall.

Finally the woman clucks her tongue and draws a leather purse from beneath the counter. While Ilapara watches, she counts out ten square-shaped silver coins, identical in size but with dissimilar stamps on their faces—in a stopover town along the continent's busiest roadway, every other coin in circulation will have come from a different tribe.

Mama Shadu pushes the coins across with blackened fingers. "Here. Take your damned money."

Ilapara picks up the coins, hides them in one of the pockets of her leather shoulder belt, and turns to leave.

"Wait. Take this too." Seeming reluctant, Mama Shadu slides something else over, a pale circular band of witchwood with esoteric glyphs carved all over its surface. Embedded into the hollow at the center of the band is the silvery orb of a mind stone. "It has the spirit of an inkanyamba. It'll come in handy should you ever need to disappear in a pinch."

Ilapara stares down at the soul charm with narrowed eyes, wondering if the woman really managed to collect the mind stone of a dreaded inkanyamba. She has bought charms from her before, and none have been nearly that impressive. "How much?" she says, not bothering to hide her mistrust.

"Oh no, dear. This one is on me."

"I don't need your charity."

"But I'm doing this for myself, dear girl," Mama Shadu says with an unsettling smile. "I would feel very guilty if you got your head chopped off and I didn't help you when I had the chance."

A chill ripples down Ilapara's spine, but she doesn't let it show. She picks up the soul charm and says, "BaMimvura thanks you for your business." Then she walks away.

"Tell him to enjoy it," Mama Shadu calls behind her. "He won't be in business for much longer."

◆ ◆ ◆

The rules of surviving in an Umadi stopover town: obey the reigning warlords, but don't get too close to them, don't pick sides when they fight, and don't ever get in their way or in the way of their disciples.

Most people ambitious or desperate enough to live in a stopover town know to abide by these all-important rules, but there is no shortage of fools who think the rules don't apply to them. It never ends well.

Case in point: BaMimvura, Ilapara's current employer. Or as most people in the town know him: that greedy moneylender and mercenary boss who joined the Cataract's loyal army of minions in exchange for having his competitors killed or threatened out of business.

She crosses a street and walks past an old monolith with the hypnotic symbol of a gushing waterfall carved onto its faces. That symbol is on banners and plaques all over town, proclaiming to everyone who looks at it the identity of the town's lord and master.

The Cataract.

Mystics of the Umadi tribe have a rather pesky ancestral talent; generally, their arcane power grows with the size of territory under their control, and the more important this territory is perceived to be, the greater the power it provides. As a result, every stopover town along the thousand-mile strip of the Artery running up Umadiland is prime real estate for any Umadi warlord.

For many comets the Cataract was a powerful and well-established warlord with a solid grip on the heart of Umadiland, through which the Artery traverses. His power drank from Kageru and many other stopover towns, and it seemed for a long while that no one would unseat him from his throne. BaMimvura figured, therefore, that the warlord would be able to defend his hold on these lands indefinitely, and that currying favor with him was a worthy risk in the long term.

He was wrong.

Everyone in town is whispering about a new and mysterious warlord they call the Dark Sun. According to what Ilapara has heard, he's been steadily creeping upward from the south, eating away swaths of the heartland from the Cataract. Just recently he took Seresa, the next stopover town south of Kageru, and now there are whispers that Kageru is next.

As she skirts the edge of the town's main market square, Ilapara lets her eyes sweep the muddy streets around her. Travelers from a caravan that stopped over last night can be seen all along the market stalls, buying, selling, bartering. Most are Umadi, the women in colorful veils and billowy robes, men in dashikis and kikois wrapped around their waists, but a number of them are from other, more distant tribes, judging by their foreign garments—boubous, djellabas, kitenges, and capulanas, all sewn in a thousand different styles. Everyone's going about their business as usual. The merchants too. Not at all what would be happening if the town's season was about to change.

Mama Shadu is just being paranoid, Ilapara tells herself. *This town is too important for the Cataract to let fall, and these people know it too.*

All she has wanted since joining Mimvura Company a comet ago is to be part of the company's caravan security crew. The pay is far better for mercenaries who tour the Artery, and their valued experience guarding caravans from raiders and dangerous wildlife makes it easier for them to find other lucrative employment, should they wish to. Leaving now, when she is so close to being chosen, would mean she spent the last comet as a glorified goon for nothing. That won't do.

By the time she reaches the iron gates to the Mimvura premises, she has talked herself out of her anxiety. *Mama Shadu is no sibyl. I can't just leave town because she said so.*

Several stopover towns have a Mimvura office to facilitate the smooth movement of the company's caravans along the Artery from one end of Umadiland to the other. The one in Kageru also doubles as the boss's residence, a walled compound built along a wide street branching off the Artery, larger and steadier than most properties in the town and clearly belonging to a man who has grown comfortable with his position in the order of things.

The main structure, BaMimvura's colorfully painted three-story mud-brick house, is a rejection of the town's aesthetic of utilitarian decrepitude. It has stained glass windows and a roof clad with shingles. A neat driveway of waterworn pebbles leads up to the house, lined by grand outdoor carvings. He even installed an expensive system of tanks and indoor plumbing, all imported from distant tribelands. Gold-feathered peacocks hold court near a spouting rock fountain, and a stable houses the boss's enviable collection of prized tronic antelope and zebroids.

Warlords exist whose homes aren't nearly as splendid.

As she walks past the gatehouse shack, she nods at the guard posted there, a young man with a pronounced overbite dressed in a shiny breastplate over a brightly colored dashiki.

"Hello, Midzi," she says in greeting.

He nods back. "Ilira."

"Is the boss around?"

"They're all in the backyard," Midzi says. "*All* of them."

She slows to a stop and then doubles back. What was that in Midzi's voice? "All of them?" she says, watching him carefully.

His eyes gleam with significance. "Yes. The boss, his whole family, Bloodworm."

Alarmed, Ilapara moves closer and lowers her voice. "Bloodworm is *here*? Why?"

"No clue," Midzi says, eyes wide. "Rode in an hour ago with two servants. You could go look. You have the perfect excuse."

Ilapara was planning to deliver Mama Shadu's debt to the boss or his eldest son, but now she shakes her head. "I take over your shift in twenty minutes. You can go look yourself."

"Kwashe passed by some time ago. He went to look, and he still hasn't come back."

She bristles at the mention of Kwashe in this context. "Why would I care what he does?"

"I thought you'd want to know," Midzi says.

"*Why* would I?"

"Because . . . well, I thought you two had a thing—"

"Had. Past tense. Not that it's any of your business." When Midzi raises his palms, looking genuinely intimidated, Ilapara realizes that she's perhaps being unnecessarily aggressive. *I am not my emotions,* she tells herself, and she takes a calming breath. "Sorry. I'm a bit on edge today."

Midzi drops his arms, offering a weary smile. "I understand. We live in rocky times. I can barely sleep most nights."

Something she understands all too well.

She looks toward the boss's residence, biting her lower lip. Might be her imagination, but the air feels a little too still today. And if Bloodworm is here, whatever's going on behind that house can't be good.

Finally she comes to a decision. "I'll go look," she says to Midzi and leaves her spear leaning against the gatehouse shack.

"Good luck," he says. "Just be back before the shift change. I need to get some of that sleep I've been missing."

The scene in the backyard reveals itself slowly to Ilapara.

It is a reflex she acquired under the tutelage of a beloved uncle in the open wilds of her homeland, a trained but visceral reaction to danger. Her heart beats faster, her senses *sharpen*, and time seems to crawl to a standstill as her mind opens to—

A backyard of barren earth, a latrine in the far corner, an outdoor cooking shed in another, thick smoke billowing from the dying fire beneath its corrugated iron roof. Not far from it, two men in hide skins beating large drums. A dozen people kneeling in a circle, heads bowed. BaMimvura, his protuberant belly hanging bare over a leopard-skin loincloth. His three wives, all bare chested and unveiled. Their children, the youngest a girl of six and the oldest a bearded young man, all with tearstained cheeks. A naked wraith standing in the center, his skin rubbed bone white with chalk, the whiteness marred only by the cosmic shards singed onto his arms, which glow crimson like lit coals, and the putrefying wound on his belly, a ghastly thing boiling with worms, pus, and foul poisons. He looms, with a bloodstained witchwood knife in one hand, over yet another kneeling figure, this one a Faraswa man with the characteristic obsidian skin and curling metal horns of his people. His face is the picture of silent agony, a river of red flowing from where his right ear has just been shorn off—

Ilapara stops next to Kwashe, a silent spectator leaning against a wall a safe distance away, watching the unfolding ritual with his arms crossed. She feels the temperature fall around her, the cold embrace of a harsh truth her mind won't accept.

"What's going on?" she says.

Kwashe was once a carefree young man with a quick smile, and then he went on his first tour up the Artery. Now, whenever she looks into his eyes, she sees only disillusion and anger swimming just beneath the surface.

"The boss got spooked," he says without looking away from the spectacle. "He's paid Bloodworm to perform a muti ritual of protection for his family."

Ilapara feels her stomach churn as she regards the bleeding Faraswa man. "But that's their gardener. He works here."

"For fifteen years," Kwashe says and lifts a shoulder in a half shrug. "Faraswa blood, and all that. And apparently the muti is stronger if there's a bond between victim and perpetrator, so." He shrugs again.

Inside the circle of the kneeling family, standing over the victim, Bloodworm's bony figure sways, trancelike, to the beat of the drums. He is a disciple of the Cataract, the judge and executioner presiding over Kageru in the warlord's name, and is feared by all for his terrible powers over blood and flesh. Even now Ilapara sees trickles of his victim's blood—blood that had fallen to the earth—*crawling* up his legs and thighs like living worms, converging upon the putrid gash on his belly and feeding the poisons brewing there.

He reaches down from behind and cups his docile victim's chin, his manic, bloodshot eyes staring into the east, where the moon will rise in a few hours. "By the power of the Great Woman of the Skies," he shouts in a voice that makes Ilapara shiver, "she who sits upon a throne of blood, we summon you, our ancestors from the Infinite Path, so that you may hear our pleas."

And with a quick motion of the witchwood knife, Bloodworm severs the gardener's other ear.

"I can't watch this." Ilapara turns away in horror, gouged to the depths of her soul.

But Kwashe's arm shoots out to grab her, his nails digging painfully into the skin beneath her crimson robe. "Don't you dare turn away."

She wrests her arm back, tears flinging from her eyes. "Why the devil not?"

His gaze is cold and without mercy, just like his voice. This is not the Kwashe she once knew, the optimist who was always ready to tell a joke; this is a hollow stranger in his body. "That poor man is being tortured to death for the simple crime of being what he is. The least we can do is bear witness. Let his death torment us, drive us to madness if need be. The Blood Woman knows we deserve worse." He looks back at the ritual, eyes hard as stones. "We chose to work for this man."

"No." Ilapara shakes her head vigorously as if to cast the words out of her mind. "I *never* chose this."

"But you knew what he was, didn't you?" Kwashe says. "We all did. And yet here we are, like tsetse to a festering wound. Collecting debts for him, protecting his properties, running his errands. We're no different from him, Ilira. We might even be worse."

Kwashe isn't holding her anymore, but his words keep Ilapara rooted to the ground. She'd like nothing more than to tell him he's wrong, that she's played no part in this atrocity, but she knew going in what kind of man BaMimvura was.

She'd heard the rumors of muti killings. They are not strictly uncommon in Umadiland, despite those who practice them being universally hated and reviled, and there were whispers that BaMimvura was one such individual. But she closed her ears to such talk because she needed coin and a job.

Kwashe is right, she realizes. *I deserve to watch every second of that man's death.* But when Bloodworm reaches into the gardener's compliant mouth and begins to cut out his tongue, she averts her gaze for the last time.

"I have gate duty," she says and can't walk away fast enough.

3: Musalodi

Khaya-Siningwe—Yerezi Plains

Salo and Nimara walk past the kraal's grammar school on their way to his workshop. Several girls in colorful beads and skirts are sitting on reed mats along the school's polished veranda, frowning in concentration at the chalky slates in their hands while a heavily pregnant woman watches with hawkeyed attention.

Both Salo and Nimara wave at her; she smiles and waves back, her copper bangles shimmering reflectively.

"Hello, Ama," he says and smirks at the girls. "A numbers test, I presume? And I'm guessing you didn't warn them."

"They are girls," Ama Lira says unapologetically. "Their minds should be quick, and they should know to be always prepared."

Ama Lira is the chief's wife and Salo's stepmother. She is also one of the grammar school's teachers, with a reputation for testing her students frequently and often without prior notice.

"Go easy on them, Ama Lira," Nimara suggests with a wistful smile. "I remember how much I hated surprise exams."

The girls mumble in agreement, prompting Ama Lira to shake her head at them with both hands on her waist. "Listen to these children. They want things to be easy when they should be begging me to make them harder."

Her students complain in unison.

"We are not playing games here," Ama Lira says. "When Nimara awakens, she'll need Asazi to work with her. But the girls of this clan have lagged behind for too long. You need to be whipped into shape! Now get back to it before I deduct another five minutes from your time."

The girls return to their slates with muted grumbles, and next to Salo, Nimara's smile becomes fixed. "Good luck!" she says. "And don't be nervous."

When they have walked out of earshot, Salo studies the side of her face. "Are you okay?"

She doesn't look at him. "Yeah. I'm fine."

"If you say so," Salo says, deciding not to pry.

The thing about Nimara is that she's practically the only woman in the entire clan still willing to serve in an arcane capacity. In fact, Clan Siningwe hasn't known a mystic in over ten comets.

It is whispered that the last AmaSiningwe cast a curse on the clan before her death, ensuring that any woman who attempted to succeed her would suffer an untimely end. Salo isn't sure he believes this, but a succession of Siningwe women did die at their awakening ceremonies, either accidentally or by the redhawks they had summoned.

The queen was forced to step in so the clan wouldn't remain defenseless, but even she wouldn't go further than blessing Nimara and the clan's Ajaha with her power. She rarely sets foot anywhere near the kraal.

And so, as the first woman in years willing to take her chances and prove the curse a myth, Nimara has become the clan's best and only hope for a clan mystic. So far she's done a fine job of it, but these days her smiles don't come as quickly, and they rarely reach her eyes. A restless energy lingers about her all the time, like she'll explode if she sits still even for a moment. She hasn't complained to him about it, but he can sense her unease. Everyone is looking at her, waiting, expecting, and it's slowly eating at her.

He might have pitied her were she not the most capable person he knows.

The workshop is a lonely drystone shed built within a copse of gum trees at the end of a gravel road, just a stone's throw away from the kraal's northern wall. Practically as far from the gates as is possible to go inside the kraal, and since there's not much else in its vicinity, few people are ever tempted to visit.

Salo likes it that way.

The interior smells of metal and grease. Arrays of tool kits and disassembled rotary machines overrun the tabletops. They find Aaku Malusi dozing with his feet up on one of the worktables, looking mere seconds away from falling off his chair. He jerks as the door creaks on its hinges behind Nimara, which makes her freeze in place. But somehow he keeps defying gravity and starts snoring again a moment later.

"How does he do that?" Nimara asks, still frozen by the threshold.

"Practice." Salo shakes his head with pity. "I better get him out of here." He quietly approaches the sleeping man, grimacing as the stench of musuku wine surrounds him like a cloud. He's relieved to see the man wearing a loincloth beneath the gray fleece blanket swathing his torso. "Thank Ama for small mercies. At least he's not naked today."

While Nimara tries not to laugh, Salo gently shakes him awake. "You must go to your hut, Aaku. You'll be more comfortable there."

Aaku Malusi squints as his eyes flutter open. "Musalodi?" His voice is harsh and croaky. "What time is it?"

"It's past noon, Aaku."

He scratches the bristles on his gaunt cheeks and frowns like there's a bad taste in his mouth. "Past noon, is it? And I had so much work to do."

"Don't worry about it," Salo says. "I'll take care of business here. You go get some rest."

Aaku Malusi blinks around the workshop like he's trying to remember how he got here. "Are you sure? I . . . don't want to burden you with too much work."

If he's even half as confused as he looks, he'll sooner break something than fix it.

"I'll be fine," Salo assures him. "I promise."

A smile briefly animates his haggard face. "You're a good boy, Salo. Thank you."

"Think nothing of it, Aaku."

It takes him a while, but he finally gathers enough wits together to get up on his feet. A current of anxiety runs down Salo's back as he watches him leave.

Take a good look at him, says a cruel voice inside his head. *This is what happens to men who forget their place and chase after things best left to women. Men who've lost the respect of their clan. Is that the future you want? Because that's what will happen to you if you keep walking down this path.*

"I see your education in letters has made you very sharp," his uncle Aba Deitari once said to him. "But I fear you are becoming too much like a woman." They had just finished playing several rounds of matje, all of which Salo had won effortlessly while the older man had struggled to keep up.

"You are crafty and subtle," Aba D continued. "Your mind is like a maze; I can never tell what you're thinking. And you care far too much about books and the mysterious ticking of machines. This is not wholesome behavior for a man."

"I don't see what's so wrong with books and machines," Salo said, trying not to shrink into himself.

"And that's why I worry," his uncle told him. "A man's strength is not in letters written on a page but in his knowledge of the soil and the rivers and the lakes. It's in his herd of cattle and the sweat of laboring in the suns; it's in the arm that wields his spear. Leave books to women;

they are creatures of the mind. You are a man and must be a creature of the flesh."

Books for girls and spears for boys: a creed all Yerezi clans live by, with little room to wiggle. But Salo's aago danced to the beat of her own drums, and if her grandson wanted an education, then he would get it.

And no one, not even her son, the chief, could sway her once her mind was set.

It was her tutelage in languages, scripts, and numbers that gave Salo the skills he needed to read the magical and academic tomes his mother had left behind. By the time Aago passed on two comets ago, he'd learned enough to start making a difference around the kraal, and because they desperately needed a mechanic who wasn't an unreliable drunk, no one made too much noise when he took over much of Aaku Malusi's duties.

The old man, meanwhile, sank deeper into a pit of loneliness and alcoholism.

"Such a shame," Nimara remarks as they both watch him shamble down the gravel road with the aid of a staff. "He looks like he was handsome once."

Salo turns away and walks to a wall-mounted chart listing all his unfinished projects. He was last working on repairing the desynchronized patterns of a mind stone for one of the chief's water pumps—a project due in two days. Given how he'll be stuck at the mill the whole day tomorrow, he doubts he'll be able to meet that deadline.

Just what I need. More blame for someone to lay at my feet. "You said you wanted help?"

"I did." Nimara's shoulders are tense as she drifts past him on her way to the largest worktable in the room, leaving a whiff of her citrusy perfume hanging in the air. While Salo watches, she reaches for the spiderlike choker wrapped around her neck; it unclasps itself, and she places it on the table. That choker is actually her talisman, and he knows what she's about to ask even before she opens her mouth with an imploring look.

"I've hit a wall with my Axiom, and I desperately need a pair of fresh eyes to look it over."

I knew it. Salo immediately shakes his head. "No. Absolutely not."

She tries to work him with an endearing pout. "Please?"

"No, Nimara," he says. "What I do for the clan is one thing. People might turn their noses up at me and Aaku Malusi, but they know they need us. We're useful. But what you're asking? It's not just crossing the line; it's outright sacrilege. I'm not even supposed to know about Axioms, let alone help you with yours."

Nimara stares at him like she thinks he's an idiot. "Everyone knows about Axioms, Salo. You're being paranoid."

"And you are missing the point. I'm not supposed to know enough about them to help you."

"There's no ban on knowing things," Nimara argues. "And all I'm asking for is advice, nothing more. That's not sacrilege."

"It is. It really is. But for the sake of argument, let's say it's not. We still both come out looking bad."

"Only if we tell anyone about it," Nimara says, "which I won't. Not that I'd be ashamed of it, by the way, because unlike you, I don't think there's anything shameful in asking for help from a more informed source, no matter who that source is."

The migraine Salo felt earlier gathers force near his right temple. He pinches his eyes shut beneath his spectacles to soothe the pain, but it makes no difference. He moves to sit across from Nimara, settling down onto a high stool. "Why not consult the librarians at the Queen's Kraal? Helping young Asazi with their Axioms is literally one of their main responsibilities."

"Why bother?" Nimara says. "There's an expert sitting right in front of me."

Salo groans. "Please don't say that."

"I don't need to." She points a playful finger at the talisman curled around his left wrist. "What you've hidden in that little snake of yours says it all."

He sits back, frowning. "Are you blackmailing me?"

The smile Nimara was wearing congeals on her face and then dies. "I'm asking for your help. You can always say no." She begins to gather her things, but Salo motions for her to stop.

"Wait." He subtly tilts his head toward the oldest cabinet in the workroom, where he keeps a particular soapstone carving hidden. "I had help, too, you know. You could have the same help if you wanted it."

Nimara settles back down but gives him a cynical look. "You're joking, right? That thing almost killed you. I was there. You were a mess."

"It's the best teacher you could ever ask for," he says, but she shakes her head.

"Absolutely not. I know my method is slow—"

"Too slow. This clan needs a mystic yesterday."

"—but I'll build my Axiom the conventional way. If it takes me years, fine. When I finally earn my shards, it'll be because I got there the right way. Not because I took shortcuts." Salo sees a crack in Nimara's composure, something vulnerable in her eyes. "I don't want to mess this up, all right? Everyone's counting on me."

He has never been good at saying no to people he likes, and Nimara is one of the few people in his life he can call a true friend. She has certainly kept his secrets, some of which could have gotten him banished many times over. There was also that incident with the Carving when she found him writhing on the floor and saved him from choking on his own vomit.

He pushes up his spectacles and sighs, clasping his hands together on the table. "For your information, not all shortcuts are bad. But fine. Show me what the problem is, and I'll help if I can."

She doesn't need further prompting. Following her silent command, the red steel spider on the table releases a stream of brilliant light from the clear crystal set onto its back, producing a mirage in the air above it.

Nimara gives the image an exasperated glare. "That's the thing. I don't know what I'm doing wrong. I thought I was ready for the next stage, but what am I supposed to do with this? It would take me hours just to summon enough energy to mend basic flesh wounds. Don't get me started on internal injuries and viral infections. What good would I be? I can't use this, Salo. I need your help."

Salo takes a look at the mirage, a monochromatic graph of golden light. He knows that the displayed curves are a measure of how effectively Nimara's cosmic shards will perform given the Axiom she has built for them. Should she proceed to awaken, her shards will behave according to this Axiom, and in general, the better the Axiom, the more finesse she will be able to employ in her spell casting.

Based on the luminous graph in front of him, Salo understands why she's so upset.

"Let's see your prose," he says, and she performs a slight gesture, summoning a different mirage from the spider talisman. This time the vision appears as a projected scroll of green and blue ciphers drawn in neat rows as if on a perfectly transparent window. Flicking his finger sends the ciphers rushing up the scroll. Each row describes an arcane instruction—just one of thousands that collectively make up the prose of an Axiom.

Nimara has explained her steps in the margins, so it's easy for him to follow her reasoning. Her prose is enviably succinct and elegant, keeping simple what could have easily become bloated and dauntingly complex. A cursory inspection tells him she's focusing solely on the disciplines of Blood and Earth craft, a typical combination for an aspiring healer.

Altogether, it would have been an acceptably effective Axiom, were it not for a few major flaws.

"I would definitely hold off on awakening if I were you," Salo says. "This would be a criminal underuse of your shards."

Nimara gives him the look of a predator about to pounce. "Explain yourself."

Shifting on his stool to face her, he says, "The thing is, you're ignoring one vital quality of cosmic shards: they are absolute beasts at multitasking. Literally nothing does it better. But this Axiom of yours would have your shards execute every operation in series, one step at a time, in chronological order—a terribly slow and wasteful way of doing things."

Nimara exhales through her nostrils, clearly frustrated. "What am I missing?"

A pity he can't be detailed in any explanation, since that would only render her Axiom nonviable and likely get her killed during her awakening. That's the first rule of Red magic: the moon does not suffer aspirants who did not devise their Axioms entirely by themselves. He can discuss the broad strokes of her Axiom's architecture with her, but never specific details of her prose. Those are for her and her alone to figure out.

How to explain? "Let's think this through, shall we?" he says. "So casting a spell, any spell, is a multistep process. Correct?"

She frowns like she's thinking it over. "I guess."

"First, your shards assimilate the moon's raw essence from the environment; then they convert this essence into any of the six arcane energies—in your case, just two, which, by the way, I don't know why you've limited yourself to two when you could easily do at least three if you tried—"

"Stay on topic," Nimara cuts in. "We've discussed this. Two disciplines are all I need. They're giving me enough trouble as it is. I don't think I could handle more."

"I disagree completely, but anyway. My point is, the shards take in raw essence, convert it into useful arcane energy according to the rules of your Axiom, then allocate this energy to a particular spell or spells. A process that must be carried out sequentially, one step at a time. Correct?"

"Correct," Nimara agrees.

"Wrong," Salo says, and he has to fight against a crooked smile. He'd never admit it to her, but he enjoys it when they discuss the intricacies of the arcane art. "Shards don't experience time and causality as a linear unidirectional flow, like we do. You can actually have them perform all parts of a multistep process simultaneously by assigning each step to a different operating block. That way, there's virtually no wait between assimilating essence, converting it, and casting spells. They are all performed at the same time."

She begins to drum her fingers on the table, frowning at him in thought. "Huh."

"This is especially useful for multidisciplinary spells," he explains, "where you need to handle multiple forms of arcane energy at the same time. You could even turn the process on its head if you need to. Say it's an emergency, and you need more energy for a spell than your shards can draw. Well, with nonlinear causality you can borrow this energy from the future, a bit like harvesting grain you haven't planted yet. Amazing, isn't it?"

"Borrow from the future?" Nimara studies the ciphers of her Axiom for a bit, then tilts her head toward him with a dubious look. "Is that how most people do it? Because I feel like I'd know if it was."

"It's not," Salo admits. "But to be fair, writing prose for parallel and nonlinear operations isn't exactly easy. Most people just do everything sequentially, relying on clever tricks and tweaks to eke out more efficiency where they can. Use enough of them, and eventually you get something passable. Lucky for us, however"—he beams at Nimara—"*you* are *not* most people, so you won't be doing that."

"Uh-huh," she says, like she was distracted and wasn't listening. "So you're saying I could use these clever tricks and tweaks to improve my current Axiom without *changing its entire structure*. Which took me *months* to figure out."

"That's . . . not even remotely close to what I said."

"Because I know there are good Axioms built the way I've done it."

"Sure, there are *good* ones. There might even be a few *very* good ones. But never *great* ones." Salo folds his arms, lifting an eyebrow. "Which would you rather have?"

Nimara opens her mouth to say something, but a frustrated noise comes out instead. She drops her face into her palms in defeat. "I can't start over, Salo. And what you're suggesting sounds so complicated—"

"It *is* complicated," he says. "But it's by far the better way, and you're more than smart enough to figure it out."

Doubt shows in the pools of her eyes as she raises them to search his face. "You have too much faith in me."

"I have just the right amount of faith. And if you want to speed things up, you could always do what I did."

A pained shadow darkens her face. "Please," she says in a quiet voice, "don't tempt me."

Salo is instantly ashamed of himself. Nimara watched him almost die because of the Carving—he *would* have died had she not found him. And then she had to keep it a secret. Of course she wants nothing to do with any of that. "Sorry," he says. "You don't need it anyway. Take your time, and don't ever underestimate yourself. Just, let's not make a habit of coming here and asking me things that could get me in trouble, okay?"

A slow smile spreads across her face, and Salo catches a glimpse of the young girl who used to chase after him back in the day with sweets and dolls since he was the only boy who would play house with her. That girl grew up way too quickly.

She banishes the mirage with a gesture and picks up her spider talisman. "Thank you, Salo. I'll be back if I have more questions."

He shakes his head and can't help returning her smile. "Why do I even bother?"

◆ ◆ ◆

To the uninitiated, the Carving might seem an innocuous, if particularly detailed, soapstone sculpture of a grove in high relief, something to be hung on a wall and occasionally admired.

Stare at it for long enough, however, and the woods come alive. The leaves rustle with the wind; the branches sway. Paths appear and disappear between the trees, leading to secret places. Keep staring, and the world will finally *vanish* as the mind is sucked into a dreamscape of dense forest. Here the trees are ancient, and the rich crimson soil underfoot is steeped in the knowledge of ciphers and Axioms and the secrets of their power.

During his first excursion into this realm, Salo wandered the woods for what felt like many hours before he understood that the entire grove was a continuously shifting pattern, and that successfully navigating its treacherous twists and turns to the glade at the heart was what imbued the mind with arcane secrets.

And so began his trysts with the Carving and its forbidden knowledge, trysts he managed to keep secret until the day he almost died and Nimara forced him to confess everything.

Salo hasn't used it again since.

He's trying to catch up on the backlog of work an hour after her departure from the workshop when a whirlwind of energy and excitement barrels through the door. "Bra Salo. You owe me a game of matje."

Salo doesn't look away from the patterns of the water pump's unstable mind stone, projected above his worktable from his serpent talisman as a mirage of superimposed waves. Getting the talisman to subtly manipulate the stone's energy and restore it to a state of equilibrium is a delicate task that requires practice and a great deal of patience. One faulty move could ruin the mind stone forever. "Go away," he says. "I'm busy."

Predictably his guest makes himself comfortable on a stool across the table. Salo looks up when he hears the clatter of pebbles; the boy is already setting up the game of matje they didn't finish two days ago.

"What did I tell you about barging in without knocking?" Salo says. "Can't you just knock for once in your life?"

Monti gets an impish look in his eye. "Are you doing something naughty, Bra Salo?"

"What kind of question is that?"

"That's what my ama says. People want others to knock when they're doing something naughty. That way they have time to hide whatever it is they're doing."

Salo rolls his eyes, though he fails to restrain a laugh. "Go away," he says. "I don't have time for your antics right now, and your aba made it clear he doesn't want you spending time with me. I'm probably already in trouble because you followed me this morning."

"He won't find out."

"That's what you said last time; then he almost breathed fire into my face."

"Just one game, Bra Salo. Please?"

"Go play with kids your own age."

"But they aren't any good," Monti whines.

"The rangers on gate duty, then. Ama knows they've got nothing better to do."

"I've already beaten them."

"Then go beat them again."

"I brought these." The boy dips a hand into the leather pouch strapped to his hip and produces a paper-wrapped bundle of stick-shaped toffees. "I'll share them with you if you want."

Salo eyes the toffees despite himself. He never outgrew his fondness for sweet foods, and Monti knows this. "You're the essence of evil," he tells the boy. "All right, one game."

Monti punches the air in excitement. "Yes!"

One game turns into three. By the fourth, the sunlight streaming in through the windows has gained a lazy golden hue, and the glowvines coiled around the shed's exposed rafters have begun to give off a soft yellow light, like embers in a grate.

As they begin to set up the fifth game, a shriek makes both their heads swivel toward the windows.

"What was that?" Monti says.

"I don't know," Salo replies.

Then another elongated scream rattles their ears before ending abruptly.

Feeling the first stirrings of anxiety, Salo rises and walks to the windows but sees nothing untoward beyond the gum trees surrounding his shed. *What's going on out there?*

"Come. I'll walk you back to your compound." The shed's isolation doesn't feel like such a good thing anymore.

"All right." The boy picks up his case while Salo raises a long hand to agitate the glowvines so that they start to dim. He locks up, and they step out of the shed together, chewing on their toffees.

Only to stop dead as soon as they spot it.

There, in the skies above the kraal, a writhing mass of inky patterns that tricks the eye into seeing an infinitely black sphere with a prismatic corona. Salo immediately recognizes it for what it is: a mystic Seal.

Every mystic, upon receiving their cosmic shards and coming into their power, acquires a unique, hypnotic visual signature that can be cast at will—a Seal. To anyone who looks at it, the Seal will announce the nature and identity of its owner. The one above the kraal twists Salo's mind into seeing the outline of a terrible mystic warlord sitting on a throne draped in shadows. His left eye glows scarlet with the intensity of moonfire. His army of disciples has plundered many towns and villages in his name.

A cold wind rustles through the gum trees around the shed. Monti sidles up to Salo, his voice quavering as he speaks. "What's that, Bra Salo? Who is he? Why is he here?"

Salo tries not to let his fear show. "I don't know. Best not to look at it. Come, your ama will be worried about you."

They've reached the main gravel road that meanders toward the gates when, just ahead, a dense, swirling plume of dust begins to rise from the earth as though on the currents of an unnaturally slow whirlwind. Salo and Monti watch it, paralyzed, even as it gathers into a horror straight from a fireside tale. Crouched at first, then slowly rising to stand at almost seven feet tall.

A human skeleton. Human, yes, but its arms are twisted and disproportionately long, and those bony fingers dangling by its sides might as well be talons. A pall of dust lingers about it like a gauzy cloak, effusing from its bones, though never drifting far from them. The reek of loamy earth and decay chokes the air around it, and a white fire suddenly ignites in its skull, flames licking out through the eye sockets.

All vocabulary vanishes from Salo's mind at the sight of it, all except for one word: *tikoloshe*. A devilish creature of Black magic, summoned from one of the underworld's many realms.

Monti makes a feeble noise as the tikoloshe's burning eyes pivot toward them. For the longest second of his life, Salo's heart becomes a still, frozen stone inside his chest. Then he grabs Monti's hand and runs.

4: Ilapara

On a normal day, Ilapara would find standing sentry by the Mimvura gatehouse rather dull and torpid, a chance to let her mind wander to better places. But today something raw keeps nagging at her, a chafing sense of guilt and anxiety that feels like a dog gnawing at her ribs from the inside.

At some point Bloodworm and his two servants ride out the gates on tronic zebroids with metallic hooves that thunder as they strike the pebbles of the driveway. An image of the Faraswa man they used for the muti ritual flashes through her mind—*resigned and helpless on his knees, ears shorn off, rivers of blood on his face*—and she recoils, sickened to her core.

She tries to restrain herself, but her body rebels against her. Her heart pumps like it's preparing for a fight. Her ears listen for signs of trouble. She gets to the point where she's brimming with so much anxious energy she can almost feel her skin vibrating, and it doesn't help matters when the skies grow overcast with the promise of an afternoon storm.

An hour after Bloodworm's departure, one of BaMimvura's house servants brings her a lunch of fermented cassava bread and roasted bush fowl. Her stomach revolts at the thought of food, so she leaves it to the attention of buzzing flies.

Every now and then she'll look toward the residence and shudder at the thought of what might still be going on. Why Kwashe is still here. Why *she* is still here.

She paces in front of the gatehouse. A harsh grating whisper grows inside her mind, becoming louder and harder to ignore.

Get out, it keeps saying. *Get out now!*

Ilapara grits her teeth and picks up her spear, staring at the open gate. She could leave. She could just walk out and never come back. She has no debts and no sworn oaths; no one would waste time coming after her. She would be free of this place and its horrors.

Get out now!

She takes a step forward but stops when she hears the mournful bellow of a battle horn coming from somewhere east of town. At first she thinks she has imagined it, but then three more horns blare out the same alarm ceaselessly.

A chill grips her bones, seeping deeper the longer the horns continue to blare, until she feels like she has dipped herself in ice water. This isn't the kind of warning given when trouble has been spotted hours in advance; this is the warning given when trouble is already here.

A squad of the Cataract's local militiamen streaks past the gates in a clatter of galloping hooves, riding to join the town's defense. BaMimvura's two eldest sons emerge from behind the residence, both now wearing breastplates over their dashikis and carrying expensive pole arms of aerosteel and witchwood. Kwashe trails silently behind them with his own spear.

"Close the gate!" the elder Mimvura shouts, jutting a long finger toward Ilapara. "Close the gate now!"

By reflex Ilapara moves to comply, and as the heavy iron gate slams shut, she catches sight of a glittering shadow sailing past directly overhead. She looks up, and her lips part in awe.

Cutting across the overcast skies is a great flying reptile bearing a rider with a horned helmet. *Kongamato,* her mind supplies, though she did not know that one could grow so big.

Its scales are like silver coins, its wings massive and membranous. The rider sitting astride its long neck has a burning staff in one hand, and Ilapara watches him pull the harness with the other so that the creature banks steeply toward the compound, barely flapping to keep itself afloat. As it swoops by, making a pass along the roadway beyond the gate, Ilapara lives through a horrid, frozen second during which the rider looks down at her and she looks back—and sees that his eyes are red and bright yellow and reptilian and *aware* of her. Then the moment is gone, and her head scarf rustles with the wind of the creature's flight.

She shivers, feeling like she's been marked for death somehow. Beside her, an ashen cast to his skin, the younger Mimvura watches the kongamato carry its rider back into the skies. "How are they already here?" he mutters. "Where the devil is the Cataract?"

Neither Kwashe nor the elder Mimvura has answers for him. Ilapara suspects that they know, like she knows, that if the Dark Sun's forces have come this far, then this battle is already lost.

"If we barricade ourselves in here, we'll at least survive until the Cataract arrives," the elder Mimvura suggests.

A blistering wave of hatred overtakes Ilapara, hatred of him and his whole family, but then she remembers her own choices.

We're no different from him, Ilira. We might even be worse.

"Warlords don't fight their own battles," she tells them. "The Cataract isn't coming. If his disciples can't defend the town, we're on our own." She glances at Kwashe, who blinks emptily at her. "It might be better to make a run for it."

The elder Mimvura gets a dark look on his face. "*No one's* making a run for it. We stay here and defend this gate, all of us."

She ignores him, addressing Kwashe. "We could leave. We don't have to die here."

But Kwashe shakes his head, his spear planted firmly on the ground. "We both made our choices, Ilira. Now it's time to live with them."

She looks away, trying to escape the weight of his gaze, the truth of his words.

A fine rain begins to mist the world, giving the air a biting crispness. She paces the gatehouse while the others patrol along the compound's walls. All around them the sounds of battle intensify. Blaring horns. An uproar of voices. Shrieks of terror. BaMimvura ventures out of his house to take stock of things but cowers back inside as soon as a distant explosion makes the ground quake.

Ilapara frowns, intensely disgusted. Is this the man she should now die for? This miserable pest who would torture and sacrifice a loyal servant to save himself from the consequences of his greed?

Does she really deserve to die for him?

They'll smell your master on your clothes.

Ilapara shivers with revulsion and turns away.

Battle cries from a street nearby. Another explosion rocks the ground, this time accompanied by an intensely bright flash of light that briefly engulfs the east like a third sunrise.

Magic.

She blinks from the afterimage it leaves behind when it dies out, and as her eyes readjust, she sees that the kongamato is on its way back—and that its rider has an orb of crimson moonfire he's preparing to hurl down at them.

"Incoming!" she shouts.

But the orb is surprisingly slow when it launches, like a feather in the wind, and it even arcs away from the compound, falling instead onto the street on the other side of the gates as the kongamato whooshes past.

"He missed," says the younger Mimvura, sounding incredulous and puzzled.

"He didn't," Ilapara says, feeling the blood leaving her cheeks. She has seen this before, spirits unleashed from mind stones in vessels of force, wind, fire, or even light, and sometimes a combination of these. If she had to bet money, she'd say there's a fire spirit now lurking on the other side of the gate.

Sure enough, the gate shudders.

"By the Blood Woman, he's going to force it open," the elder Mimvura says as they all gather in front of the gate.

His younger brother speaks in a trembling voice. "Bloodworm's sacrament will protect us, right?"

"How the devil should I know?"

"*How?* You're the one who suggested it!"

The elder Mimvura steps up to his brother, their foreheads almost touching. "Don't you *dare* put that on me!"

As the brothers start shouting at each other, neither notices the red-hot glow quickly distorting the shape of the gate. Ilapara points and speaks over them. "The gate! It's *melting.*"

Men howl on the street just outside, and the gate's solid iron begins to bubble and warp like molten rock. By silent agreement, Kwashe and the brothers reach into pockets on their shoulder belts and withdraw white disks of witchwood marked with little glyphs, each holding a mind stone at its center—Umadi soul charms. Their eyes briefly glaze over as they palm the disks and possess themselves with whatever spirits were infused into the charms, borrowing some of the abilities the spirits wielded in life.

Ilapara considers using one of her charms, too, but the single jackal spirit in her possession would give her little beyond superior hearing, while the inkanyamba would be best left for a direr situation. Might as well hold on to them.

She braces herself, falling into a defensive stance as the gate trembles on its hinges. Then solid iron gives way like stretched paper before a knife, if the knife were an inferno of pure moonfire in the shape of a dread rhino horn. The beast the horn belongs to is so large its head fills the now-exposed gateway, a monstrosity of magical fire. It emits a ground-shaking screech and charges into the compound, pulsing out waves of unbearable heat.

Ilapara dives out of the way, evading instant death with only inches to spare. She springs back up to her feet just in time to see the fire beast tread over the younger Mimvura, leaving his corpse a charred black thing on the driveway.

The beast keeps going, as unstoppable a force of nature as the winds, rapidly shedding size as it expends itself. Upon reaching BaMimvura's house, it comes to a fiery end in a great explosion that makes the world bloom with heat and light, almost knocking Ilapara off her feet.

Beyond the ruined gate, the Dark Sun's militiamen howl in celebration and begin to pour in.

Ilapara's maternal uncle was a small, quiet hunter most people didn't take seriously, the butt of many jokes who couldn't convince a woman to settle down with him even at thirty years of age—that is, until the night Umadi raiders attacked his hunting party in the open savannas, and he bested six of them with his spear. Alone.

Ilapara had always gotten into spats with anyone who spoke ill of him; after all, he was, and still is, dearer to her than her own father. Yet she'd underestimated him like everyone else and never expected to learn more from him than compassion, human decency, and the art of hunting.

But that night, as she watched him dance with his spear like a moon-blessed ranger, fighting to protect her and the others in their small party, she learned that size and strength in battle were only half as important as pure skill and fast reflexes. She learned that anyone, even a wisp of a man, could hone themselves into a deadly weapon with enough determination. Above all else, she learned that she had the teacher she'd secretly yearned for all along, one who would not refuse to help her become what she truly wanted to be. She needed only to ask.

And so she did, and he taught her all the things he knew whenever they were alone in the wilds, secrets of combat he confessed to having learned from sitting in front of a magical cloth of some kind, an artifact he'd picked up illicitly from an Umadi trader while bartering skins in the borderlands. She wouldn't believe him when he told her, and she still has her doubts, because how could a mere cloth contain such intimate secrets of the body?

What she couldn't doubt, however, was that the secrets were real. Secrets for gaining a deep level of control over the body to draw more strength from each breath and decelerate one's perception of time. Secrets for packing the muscles with latent strength. Secrets that made her a nuisance to all the Clan Sikhozi boys who thought a girl had no place in the Ajaha training pits.

In the split second militiamen with faces painted a ghostly white pour into the compound, Ilapara calls up her training. Time *slows*. Her senses grow keener; her reflexes accelerate.

The spear she wields fits into her grip like it was made for her. High-grade aerosteel from the Yontai with an enchanted witchwood core, it is light as a hollow twig, widening slightly somewhere two-thirds along its length into a thin double-edged blade, tapering sharply at the end into a savage spearpoint. She moves with it just in time to dodge an invading militiaman's spear thrust.

Kwashe yells something over the din. The elder Mimvura roars. Thunder rumbles in the distance, and the rain starts to pour heavily. Ilapara's world narrows down to the militiaman in front of her. The pupils of his wild eyes are dilated like he smoked something. He snarls as he thrusts his weapon, exposing yellowed teeth. She quickly pivots away and whirls her weapon round in a blow that catches him on the collarbone.

A bolt of red lightning arcs along the blade as it makes contact and cuts him, instantly blackening his flesh. He convulses as he falls, electrocuted by the weapon's live charm of Storm craft. But this is just the beginning. A militiaman with a long scar on his right cheek steps over him and rushes her with a sword; she holds her spear like a staff, parries two blows, sidesteps a third, lowers her spear, and strikes.

His blood flows with the rain. The stench of death closes in around Ilapara. She shook and cried herself to sleep on the day she killed her first man, months ago now, but today each kill blurs into the next, her victims leaving only the faintest scars on her soul.

To either side of her, Kwashe and the elder Mimvura move with the savagery of dingoneks, skewering, maiming, and cutting down the militiamen without mercy. Kwashe catches a militiaman in a choke hold and squeezes, and blood erupts between his fingers as he crushes his victim's trachea. Nearby, the elder Mimvura is a flash of movement as he impales a trio of militiamen with a series of rapid-fire thrusts. Whatever charms they used must have been of the highest quality, because they are relentless.

But to what end? Ilapara finds herself wondering when she begins to tire. *What happens when the spirits possessing them expend themselves? Do I really want to fight to my death here?*

Is this really what I deserve?

They have managed to hold the militiamen by the gate so far, but they are beginning to give ground. She thrusts her spearpoint toward a militiaman, intending to electrocute him with her weapon's Storm craft, but he has protective charms on his armor, so the bolt leaves him unscathed. He grins, lifting his weapon, but Kwashe falls upon him before he can charge.

A chance, one Ilapara does not waste. She retreats from the melee and sprints across the compound for the stables, passing the younger Mimvura's charred corpse.

The spirit's explosion blackened much of the main house's facade and shattered every window, and some parts of the wall are still glowing red with embers of moonfire. She passes a clothesline still holding up brightly colored nappies despite the rain. Screams come from inside the house, women and children wailing in grief and fear. Ilapara puts them out of her mind and keeps going.

In the stables she finds only a pair of zebroid mares and a kudu buck with rather fearsome spiraling horns of tronic bone. Each animal is in a separate stall, and the ruckus has left them visibly tense; the zebroids have their ears stiff and pushed forward, and the buck won't stop grunting and tossing his head back and forth. She curses when she notices that he's the only mount already saddled; she's ridden antelope before and managed just fine, but this particular species can be too willful.

He flicks his ears suspiciously when he sees her approaching, so she coos and puts out a placating hand to show that her intentions are peaceful. She is relieved when he allows her to run a gentle hand down his neck.

He's a bit taller than the zebroids, if a little leaner. She knows he's a red kudu, given the size of his horns and the hue of his smooth coat—a rusty red like the temperate woodlands of Valau, the birthplace of his species, where the trees and grasses are said to mimic the colors of a full moon sunset. Several metallic stripes run vertically down his back, and those strong, willowy legs of his, which gradually lose their coat as they terminate in metal hooves, should sustain a swift, loping gait over long distances.

"I want to be your friend," Ilapara says to the buck. "I want to get us out of here, understand?"

She quickly runs her eyes over his tack and tests his stirrups, and once she's confident he won't cast her off, she mounts him, holding her spear tightly in her right hand. He grunts in a manner that might be indignant but seems to accept her as his new rider.

"I'm going to need you to run very fast today," she says to him. "Can you do that for me?"

She doesn't expect an answer, and she doesn't get one, but when she rocks her hips forward, the buck leaps into motion like he's been itching for it all day. She spurs him into a full gallop as soon as the gate comes within sight.

The possessed young men defending the gate are still in the thick of battle, but she can tell that their spirits are beginning to fade. It won't be long before they have lost their inhuman strength, and when that happens, the floodgates will open. As she reaches the fray, a militiaman with bloodshot eyes charges toward the buck's left flank, ready to run it through with his spear. Without hesitating, she thrusts with her right hand, skewering his neck with the tip of her weapon.

Kwashe looks up at Ilapara as she passes the gate, and she glimpses in his eyes something of the young man she once knew, something that rends her heart into little pieces.

Then the buck carries her onward, and that's the last she sees of him.

Fire. Rain. Two militias clashing in a town-wide skirmish. Columns of smoke rising from all over town. Visceral screams, too many to count. The season changing violently in Kageru.

Ilapara doesn't go to the hostel west of town to get her things. She bounds southward on her new mount, following the Artery's wide gravel roadway out of town. A fierce battle is raging in the market square when she passes it, two mystics hurling spells at each other among the smoldering ruins of market stalls. She squints to look and sees the flash of chalk-white skin and glowing cosmic shards, but then her eyes bulge as a stray lance of moonfire shoots out of the smog and toward her.

She ducks. The lance sails over her head, yet she feels a rush of heat so intense it comes close to setting her crimson veil on fire. The lance crashes into a two-story building across the street, and its thatched roof immediately ignites. Ilapara thinks she hears wailing coming from inside.

She spurs her buck faster and keeps going.

In the skies above her, the kongamato is still circling the town, barely visible through the rain. It banks toward her just as she spots it, and she shivers from the chilling memory of its rider's brilliant reptilian eyes—eyes that seemed to look specifically at *her*.

Eyes that will surely see her when the kongamato comes near enough.

With a prayer to the moon, she reaches into one of the pockets on her shoulder belt, takes out the soul charm Mama Shadu gave her earlier this morning, and palms it.

Please don't be a dud, please don't be a dud, please work . . .

Something cold and slippery and intangible rises from the disk and *explodes* into her, suffusing her core, causing her to almost fall off her saddle. A flood of images rushes through her mind, disjointed snippets of a life spent swimming in fast-flowing waters and hunting prey while wrapped in an impenetrable stealth field.

And just like that, the powers of the inkanyamba, dreaded ghost eel of the rivers and freshwater lakes of the Redlands, are hers.

Ilapara has used Mama Shadu's charms before, but she has never felt a merge so intense it demanded she take a moment to recover her balance. She quickly reaches for the stirring of power now sitting at the edge of her mind, waiting to be set loose. As it responds, a cocoon of lies takes shape around her and around the buck, weaving fields of false light and sound so that she becomes a phantom in the street, invisible and inaudible, like a hunting inkanyamba.

From her perspective, little has changed. The sorcery now cloaking her movements creates a mild distortion of her peripheral vision, a shimmer flowing like waves over the ground and making the sky sparkle with false stars. To everyone else, she and the buck are the air itself, nonexistent.

The kongamato darkens the road with its vast shadow as it flies by. Then it banks away, its rider none the wiser.

Ilapara doesn't let herself breathe a sigh of relief; she coaxes her tronic buck into running faster along the roadway, and they hurtle into the rain at speed, leaving the battle and the circling kongamato behind. At the edge of her mind, the inkanyamba frolics and swims, reveling in its new vessel, but she can already feel its power fading.

She could flee north, deeper into the Cataract's fiefdom and away from the Dark Sun. But the north is foreign to her, while the south is where she first established herself in Umadiland three comets ago. She has contacts there, in Seresa in particular, and a modest reputation she could leverage to get herself a job. The region is also closer to home, her *real* home, though she is annoyed that this should be a consideration after all this time away. But the heart wants what it wants, so south she goes.

She rides around the militiamen barricading the town's southern entrance. They don't even look in her direction. She rides until the shacks of Kageru grow fewer and farther between and then vanish behind her altogether. She rides past a caravan that has stopped on the roadway, where it will wait for the season change to run its course before venturing into town.

She keeps going even after the inkanyamba spirit expends its power and its stealth field weakens and fades, and only when she reaches a place miles away, where the Artery begins to dip after having climbed a gentle knoll, does she slow down and bring her buck to a halt. A chill from her rain-soaked garments has begun to work itself into her skin. She shivers and turns to look.

In the distance, the town of Kageru is a hazy smudge. Explosions and black smoke can still be seen even through the rain. She knows they won't continue for much longer.

While she watches, a sphere of black, shimmering light balloons above the town with multiple arcs of color whipping around it in a vengeful cloud. Its rays seem to twist her eyes into seeing a lord of shadows whose power is so glaring it brings tears to her eyes. Many will die beneath its light in retribution today—many have already died, and maybe she deserved to be one of them.

Maybe what she deserves will catch up to her one day.

Ilapara prods her buck into motion and rides southward.

5: Musalodi

Khaya-Siningwe—Yerezi Plains

A shriek from the devil herself trails them, but Salo and Monti do not stop to look back at the thing that emitted it or to find out whether it is pursuing them. They run.

Down a bushy shortcut to the chief's compound. Through a cabbage patch when the shortcut isn't short enough, trampling newly sprouted seedlings with their sandals. Screams come from all over the kraal, rangers shouting at the edge of Salo's hearing. The foreign Seal keeps writhing above the kraal like a black sun. Salo doesn't let go of Monti's hand.

A cloud of dust bursts up from the earth near a borehole to their far left, where a clanswoman has just finished filling a ewer with water. Salo hears a deafening screech, then sees through the dust a skeletal figure heaving itself out of the ground like a rotted corpse from the grave. The woman squeals and starts to run when she sees it, too; like lightning, the thing bolts forward and catches her before she has moved even three feet. It lifts her struggling form toward the Seal like she weighs nothing—only to dig into her flesh with its talons and rip her apart in an explosion of gore.

Shock. The world slows down for a moment, and Salo's ears ring with the echoes of the woman's last screams and of Monti's screams and of his own screams, and the horror of what they've just witnessed almost pulls him down to his knees.

Somehow, he manages to keep running. But Monti trips over the irrigation channel at the edge of the cabbage patch, and his matje case slips from his hand as he falls, rattling to the ground and spilling its contents into the channel and all over the tilled soil. He should leave it be; instead, he crawls to his case and tries to gather his scattered pebbles. With a muttered curse, Salo backtracks, sweeps the child into his arms, and promptly gets back to the business of running.

"My board!" Monti cries.

"Leave it."

Monti squirms in Salo's grip. "Put me down! I can run on my own."

"Not as fast as I can."

By now the suns have dipped beyond those brooding mountains in the west, staining the sky a vibrant ocher that matches the glowvines coming to life all over the kraal. The Seal is a foreign entity above the kraal, a stark black orb against the heavens.

As the large musuku tree just off center of the chief's compound comes into view, its boughs laden with half-ripe yellow fruits and creeping glowvines that make it look like it's on fire, a dense swarm of flies buzzes overhead, and Salo thinks he hears a shrill laugh coming from within the mass.

Then a flash of red in the bushes off to his right makes him freeze. Monti gives a smothered cry as the bushes shake on their stems, but to their relief, three spear-wielding men clad in red loincloths emerge, each bearing an elliptical shield of hide and spears of enchanted red steel.

Ajaha rangers.

Panting, Salo puts Monti down, but the boy clings to his trembling hand. "Aba D," Salo says, addressing the ranger in front. "What's going on? We saw tikoloshe!"

As VaSiningwe's younger brother, and a general who commands the five-hundred-strong regiment of Siningwe rangers, Aba Deitari is the most important member of the chief's council of advisors. He is also quite intimidating, if only because he's always frowning at something. The taller, darker man with him is Aba Akuri, his equally standoffish husband and lieutenant, and the third ranger is a young man Salo knows as Jaliso.

"An Umadi witch flew right past our defenses," Aba D says. "Those creatures are her work." He searches the surrounding forests with his coldly determined gaze. "We'll handle her, though. You should get to shelter. Now."

"Is she alone?" Salo asks. "Are there others?"

Aba D brushes past him without answering. "Get that child to safety, Salo. Don't make me ask you again."

"My name's Monti," Monti says a little petulantly. Aba D isn't listening, though. He and his men are back to searching for something in the woods around them.

"She's here somewhere," he says. "I can feel it."

Instead of running the rest of the way to the chief's compound, Salo and Monti watch with morbid curiosity as the three rangers fan out into the woods, treading softly on their feet like skulking predators. They all stand rigid when the swarm of flies reappears above, moving through the air like no flies Salo has ever seen, like they're of one mind. They hover in place for a wavering moment before they swirl into a funnel and swoop downward.

"Watch out!" Salo cries, but Jaliso doesn't turn around in time to raise his shield. The swarm slams into his side with surprising force, knocking him back several yards. He hits the trunk of a tree with a crack so sickening Salo doubts he'll ever get up again.

While Aba Akuri rushes to check on the fallen ranger, Aba D starts shouting at Salo and Monti to run, which they promptly do, but the swarm veers in their direction and drops right in front of them, reconstituting itself into a woman.

A naked woman. Every inch of her lithe body is a swirling canvas of black tattoos, even her face. But the cosmic shards pulsing on both of her arms, an elaborate network of lines with a metallic sheen, are aglow with the moon's power, and so are her eyes, which burn in the dusk like fluorescent rubies. Her thick braids stand on either side of her head like curved horns. She snarls, exposing an array of teeth sharpened to needle points.

It's Salo's first encounter with a foreign mystic, and he knows just by looking at her that she is a disciple of the one whose Seal is terrorizing the skies, that in fact she is the one who cast it on his behalf.

Salo puts himself in front of Monti, his eyes never leaving the witch, this monster who would harm his people. "Why are you doing this?" he demands in the Umadi tongue, guessing she will understand. "What have we done to you?"

She cocks her head to one side, surprise briefly registering on her heavily marked face. Then her eyes dart behind him, and the next thing he knows, Aba D is slamming into her with his shield.

The Yerezi ancestral talent—awakened exclusively in the blood of Yerezi mystics—is the ability to share with the nonmagical a portion of their arcane power, thereby endowing them with either mental or physical magical abilities. While the former, reserved only for women of the Asazi, turns them into a sort of subordinate mystic, the latter transforms even what would be a warrior of average ability into an unstoppable brute with supernatural strength, exceptional reflexes, and resistance to harmful sorcery.

Aba D is unquestionably Khaya-Siningwe's fiercest Ajaha, with the queen's power thrumming strongly in his bones, and yet when he *slams* into the witch with his enchanted shield, she simply dissipates into a swarm of flies, flows away like air, and reconstitutes in a crouch on a low branch not far away.

She discorporates again as Aba Akuri hurls his spear with the force of a tempest. It explodes into the branch she was perching on with an earsplitting crack, but the witch, again, floats away unharmed, partially reconstituting her upper body so that it looks like she has a vortex of flies where there should be legs.

Salo stares in awe. He takes a closer look at the woman's shards and counts, to his shock, exactly *five* complete rings encircling each forearm—which would make her almost as powerful as the Yerezi queen, who has six rings. She laughs as she drifts between the trees like a whirlwind, her glowing eyes and cosmic shards leaving wisps of trailing red light where they pass in the air. From one outstretched hand she summons a maelstrom of space-bending force; it gathers together into an ornate spear as black as pitch before she hurls it at Aba D with a rabid howl.

Void craft, Salo realizes with dismay. This witch wields power over the fabric of space and time.

The Ajaha general quickly lowers himself into a crouch and raises his shield. The patterns on the shield flash red as the protective magic they hold activates, shattering the Void spear like glass when it hits, a million pieces of cold darkness flaking away into nothingness.

But the witch is not done. She slowly raises her hands with a look of intense concentration, twin clouds of dust and leaves swirling upward from the ground on either side of her. Salo takes an involuntary step back when a skeletal creature emerges from each whirlwind, reeking of compost and rotting things.

The Void spear the witch cast, though deadly, was a pure expression of Red magic, whose eternal source is Ama Vaziishe, the Red Moon. But these tikoloshe can be nothing but the workings of Black magic, the most profane of all sorcery, practiced by those who have corrupted their cosmic shards with the underworld's embrace. If this witch can call upon *that* kind of power, then she must be in league with Arante herself, who is the devil and queen of the underworld.

Too much. Salo finally grabs Monti's hand and runs as he was commanded. The last thing he sees of the battle is Aba D gusting toward the witch and her tikoloshe with his shield raised, his spear throbbing with magic.

All over the kraal, warriors in bloodred loincloths can be seen battling devilish wraiths with their warded spears and shields. Clansmen of all ages have joined them with whatever weapons they could find—machetes, pitchforks, axes. As they race past a peanut field on their way to the chief's compound, Salo sees a middle-aged farmer getting his gut slashed open by a tikoloshe's bony talon while his son tries to skewer the beast from behind with a pike.

Salo looks away, choking back tears. He tries to focus on what's important: getting Monti to safety. Still, the vise of fear clamped around his chest squeezes tighter with each cry he hears.

They reach the chief's compound at last, only to find it silent as death. Aakus and aagos like to come here to smoke their pipes under the musuku tree and complain about today's youth; farmers come to complain about the neighbors' oxen grazing in their fields; neighbors come to accuse each other of jealousy, name-calling, and using malicious rituals to bewitch each other. The compound rarely knows a dull day.

Today it lies empty, a desolate island of stillness amid the sudden storm that has befallen the kraal.

Six drystone buildings surround the compound, the largest being the council house, a giant oval hut with a thatched dome for a roof. If anyone's around, they're probably holed up in there.

Salo makes for the chief's hut, which he knows has powerful defensive wards woven into every brick. The hut's ancient wooden door, engraved with the clan's spike-maned leopard, opens for him without protest as soon as he touches the doorknob. He prods Monti past the barren parlor and into VaSiningwe's chamber, where he shuts and locks the door with shaky hands.

"Okay. We should be safe here. I think." When he notices that the reed curtains aren't drawn, he rushes to the windows and rectifies that quickly. In the ensuing darkness, the glowvines draping the ceiling rafters go active, bathing the chamber in twilight.

Despite their current circumstances, Monti stares around the chamber with undisguised curiosity. Not many people ever get to see where the chief sleeps at night. In fact, Salo hasn't been in here since he was a small boy.

VaSiningwe is a man of simple tastes, so there's not much inside besides a low bed and a wicker chair in the corner, which he sits on during nightly dinners out in the compound. A tapestry on the wall facing the bed shows his genealogy, a proud line of men whose rangers were always the most skillful of the tribe, men whose names Salo could never hope to live up to despite being of their blood.

He moves away from the window and paces the length of the chamber, trying to gather his thoughts. He feels like the fabric of reality is fraying at the seams and tearing away from his grasp.

The witch's marked face flashes through his mind. *By Ama, Black magic and tikoloshe in the kraal. How can this be? Why is she doing this? Could this be a ritual of some kind?*

The killing of humans for magical power was banned from the Plains a long time ago, but Salo knows it is still commonplace in much of the Redlands. Umadi warlords in particular are notorious for raiding villages for slaves and sacrificial victims.

Salo has never heard of them using tikoloshe, however, or any of the other terrible aspects of Black magic, for that matter. That kind of sorcery was supposed to have been rooted out from the Redlands centuries ago, and the Umadi aren't supposed to be sophisticated enough in the arcane to bring it back.

And yet, here is a five-ringed Umadi witch in the heart of the Plains, performing what is likely a ritual of Black magic.

And the speed at which she cast her spells! She summoned those tikoloshe as swiftly as she could breathe. Not to mention her metamorphic abilities, rare even among Void mystics, and how she was completely at ease with the shadowy maelstroms of the craft.

Powerful magic. The kind of thing he'd expect from a Yerezi clan mystic, or even the queen herself.

A chilling cry makes it through the windows, and Monti hugs himself. He sits down with his back against the wall, facing the door. Salo walks over to sit with him.

"What now?" the boy says, his big eyes wide with fear.

Salo tries to put on a brave face for him. "We stay here until it's over."

"What if it's never over?"

"It will be." That's what Salo keeps telling himself.

"But what if it's over in a bad way?" Monti says, a sob breaking into his voice. "What if the witch kills everyone?"

Salo puts an arm around his shoulders and pulls him closer. "She won't, all right? We have the best rangers in the Plains in this kraal, and they all carry the queen's blessing. They'll deal with that witch. You mustn't worry."

Tears pool around Monti's eyes. "She killed them, Bra Salo."

The images are seared in Salo's mind: the woman with the ewer torn apart, Jaliso hitting the tree with so much force it probably cracked his spine, the farmer getting gutted right in front of his own son. Salo wipes his eyes. "When this is over, Nimara will take them to the bonehouse and heal them. You'll see."

"They're dead!" Monti cries. "There's no way she can heal them. You're just saying that because you think I'm a dumb child."

"I don't think you're dumb, Monti, but I'm telling you, I have faith in our rangers. They'll save us. Just you watch."

Monti falls quiet for a while. Salo can almost hear the thoughts churning inside that little brain of his. "Why aren't you out there?" he finally whispers.

The heat of shame works its way up Salo's cheeks. For a child to ask him such a penetrating question, the exact question he's been trying *not* to ask himself this whole time . . . it makes him wonder if maybe his shame is painted all over his face in stark colors.

Niko and my brothers are somewhere out there fighting tikoloshe for their clan while I'm cowering like a child in my aba's bedchamber. Why aren't you out there, Salo? Why aren't you a man?

How to answer? "I'm not a ranger. I wouldn't last a second out there."

"But why aren't you?"

"Why aren't I what?"

"A ranger," Monti says. "Why aren't you?"

"Does it matter?" Salo winces at his own tone. "Look, not all of us can be . . . brave like rangers. Bravery is . . . their talent, I suppose. But some of us have other talents that are just as valuable."

Silence stretches painfully in the chamber, punctuated by rangers shouting in the distance. "So it's true what they say about you," Monti says after a time. "That you are a siratata."

Salo retracts his arm from Monti's shoulders and leans his head against the wall. "That's not a nice word. And just because I'm not a ranger, it doesn't mean I'm . . . *that*."

Salo can't even say it, can barely think it. *Siratata.* The Yerezi term for a man so misguided he does not know his place in the world. An ineffectual man. An impotent man. A worthless, cowardly man. All rolled into one nasty word: *siratata.*

"Lots of men aren't rangers," he goes on. "Matter of fact, most men aren't rangers. Your aba isn't a ranger, is he?"

Monti raises his chin defiantly. "He's a stonemason, but he can fight. And I bet he's out there right now, fighting beside the rangers like the other men. I saw them. They are brave, and so am I." With a determined glint in his eye, Monti rises from the floor. "I'm going."

Salo stares up at him, not believing his ears. "Are you mad? Sit back down! I'm not letting you go out there!"

"I need to make sure my ama is all right," Monti says. "She left the kraal in the morning. I need to know she's safe."

"I'm still not letting you go, Monti. You saw what's out there, didn't you?"

By the way Monti narrows his eyes, Salo knows he's about to say something mean. "I'm not asking for your permission, coward."

Salo represses his rising temper. *Monti is just frightened. That's all. He's a frightened child who has just seen people die. Take a deep breath. Start again.* "Monti, sit down, will you? Please. I'll take you to your ama when this is over, I promise. But I'd be a bad friend if I let you go out there right now. Are we not friends?"

Some of the heat in Monti's expression mellows out, but he scowls as he sits down.

"Thank you," Salo says with genuine relief. A quarter hour passes in silence, the shouts outside getting fewer and farther between.

Then Monti says, "I'm thirsty."

A combination of fear, complacency, and misplaced trust clouds Salo's judgment, and he fails to discern Monti's scheme until it's too late. By the time he returns to the chamber with a half-filled earthenware pitcher of water from the parlor, Monti is gone, with nothing but a yawning window to show that he was ever there.

The pitcher slips from Salo's hands and shatters on the floor, spilling water everywhere. He races for the door and barges out of the hut. "Monti!"

The boy is nowhere to be found. He's probably halfway to his hut by now.

Salo takes off at a sprint, charging across the chief's compound. The mystic Seal has disappeared from the skies, but the sounds of battle have not yet ceased.

Heartbeats later he passes the chief's apiary, now shrouded in darkness beneath the boughs of ancient gum trees. He spots two young Ajaha spinning and twisting around each other amid a party of angry tikoloshe, their spears flashing with red wards as they dance through the air.

The duo moves as one, their bones reinforced with the queen's arcane blessing, their minds and reflexes synced through their red steel. Salo watches a dexterous swing lop off the skeletal arm of a tikoloshe, but the ranger who inflicted the wound is already pivoting to thrust his weapon into the chest of another while his comrade leaps to cleave the first tikoloshe in half. Dusty bones crack and crumble into clouds that disperse with the wind, and the creatures screech, their eyes burning with rage like the white sun.

The rangers are too fast for them, too strong, too brave.

Salo keeps running, and soon the battle is behind him. He flies down the stepped path to the first of two compounds on the way to Monti's hut. Dusk has fallen, so all the huts here are lit like lanterns; their glowvines droop from the thatching and crawl up the brickwork like bioluminescent serpents. Salo doesn't notice the bodies littering the compound until he almost trips over one.

He stops, his throat constricting as he recognizes the corpse as Aago Ruparo, a witty old woman with an easy smile, the clan's most respected beer brewer. Now she's nothing but a bloody sack of newly dead meat wrapped in a dusty kitenge.

Tears blur his vision. His breath comes in strenuous gasps. This isn't supposed to happen. Not in their kraal. Not here.

A shriek to his right brings him crashing back to his senses, and he looks just in time to see a young boy get slashed across the neck and chest by a talon, his small body flung across the compound like a rag doll. He lands gracelessly on his belly yards away, his neck twisted unnaturally so that Salo gets to see his face—and the shock painted onto it in tears and dust, and the vacant eyes that won't blink anymore.

Salo howls and rushes to the boy, crumpling to his knees and cradling him in his arms. Blood slicks them both, its coppery tang thick in the air, mingling with the reek of ruptured bowels, the smell of life tipping irretrievably into death. Salo holds Monti's limp body in his trembling arms and doesn't let go.

He is vaguely aware of a deathly presence drawing nearer, the smell of ruin and burning things. He senses the presence watching him curiously. Hears it growl at him, feels it raise a talon, but he makes no move to escape what's coming—he *can't*.

The two rangers he spotted earlier approach. The tikoloshe shrieks as it turns to face them, a ghastly sound that might as well be the rusty gates of the underworld squeaking open. Rangers and wraith collide in a battle of red steel against bone. The shrieks die out abruptly.

Then one of the rangers speaks. "What the devil are you doing out here? Forget that; just get indoors! Now, brother." Jio or Sibu, one of his brothers, though Salo isn't sure which one. And though he hears the individual words, they don't string together into coherent sentences.

Monti is dead. I let him out of my sight, and now he's dead.

A third ranger approaches. His voice is familiar, but it sounds distant, faint. Unreal, just like the rest of it. It can't be real. "Pits. Is that Monti? Oh, Salo." A hand settles on Salo's shoulder. "I'm so sorry."

Monti is dead. I failed to protect him.

"Salo, we can't leave you out here."

"You can stay with him, if you want," says another voice. "That was the last of them."

"All right. You should go check on your aba and the general. Let me know if they call a meeting."

"Will do."

Salo doesn't know how long he stays in the compound after his brothers leave. Long enough for people to start trickling out of their huts, ululating in grief, covering the bodies with sheets, and carrying them away. Long enough for Monti's tearful parents to come and weep over their son's body. Long enough for Niko to have to pry Salo's hands from Monti so that his parents can take him back to their hut and prepare him for committal.

Once they've left, Niko puts a hand around Salo's nape. Grief shimmers in his earnest brown eyes, as well as cold fury, the kind only vengeance can quench. "I know Monti was like a brother to you. We'll make the Umadi pay for this; do you understand? We'll avenge Monti and all those who died here today. I swear it."

Niko doesn't know yet, but he will soon. They all will. Salo already knows it as well as he knows that he is a coward, yet another stain that will come to define him, the thickest and ugliest to date: *Monti is dead, and it's because I didn't protect him. Monti is dead because of me. I killed Monti.*

6: The Maidservant

Lake Nyasiningwe—Yerezi Plains

Somewhere across the lake, a swarm of flies enters a dank cave and slowly gathers into a vortex from which a woman emerges, a woman who was once someone else before she was the Maidservant.

Black tattoos mark the entirety of her body; she has worn them for years, but the self-inflicted spells they hold ensure that she still feels as much pain as she did on the day they were scored onto her skin. Her every step, her every gesture, sends ripples of agony down her spine, but she embraces the pain, revels in it, for it is the cornerstone of her power, the fuel that feeds the hatred keeping her sane and focused.

Inside the cave, the Maidservant finds a mystic in black garments flipping through the pages of an old book by a slab of rock carved into the shape of a table. A few torches mounted on the walls sputter with flames, casting a trembling light across the range of sorcerous paraphernalia housed in the cave—from alchemical apparatuses to dark shelves overflowing with tomes.

Her pet, a monstrous hyena more metal than flesh, doesn't move from the ledge of rock it is lounging on when it spots the Maidservant. It twitches its three metal horns and gives her a grotesque parody of a smile, complete with a low, rumbling growl. The Maidservant is assessing the threat it poses when the trap springs around her, so quickly she can do nothing but watch.

To the naked eye, nothing has changed, but the wards of Void craft that have suddenly gone up around her—designed specifically to confine a Void mystic—might as well be walls of barbed wire. She can neither touch them nor call upon the Void while trapped inside; if she did either, the Void would warp wrongly around her shards to lethal effect. She stills and waits for her captor to make her next move.

The mystic closes her book and fixes her with a cunning gaze. "I take it you were successful. I could hear the screams from here." She speaks in the Maidservant's native tongue with a thick accent. Her voice is cold, smooth, like a ghost eel in water.

"I've done my part," the Maidservant says, maintaining her composure. "Now it's time to do yours."

"Ah, but loose ends tend to unravel, do they not? And you, my little Umadi witch, are a *very* loose end. Tell me: What would you do in my rather precarious position?"

Hot anger spreads beneath the Maidservant's skin and makes it burn like she has painted herself with fire. She grits her teeth, harnessing the ensuing wave of hatred to bolster the door in her mind—that door only she can see, to a realm of such power it makes her tremble every time even a granule of it flows through her veins.

The door shudders violently and groans from the force battering against it from the other side. Sometimes it'll creak open, and the power will lick out like a flame, blackening her soul with the desire to just let go and become its vessel and thrall.

Maybe I should give in, she thinks now. *I could let the door burst open, let every fell beast from the other side come out and tear the flesh off this presumptuous mystic.*

You will lose yourself to it.

The Maidservant summons her hatred and pushes back against that last stray thought. "If you try to kill me, you'll find that I'm not easy prey. In any case, I took certain measures to make sure you'd pay dearly for betraying me."

The mystic tilts her head, amused. "Measures?"

"One wrong move, and your whole tribe will know about our arrangement, that it was *you* who orchestrated an attack against your own people." An empty threat, but the Maidservant puts enough of a bite in her words to make it sound real enough.

"And just how would you manage that?" the mystic says, her eyes sparkling.

"Make a wrong move, and you'll find out."

On the rock ledge, the hyena emits another low growl. Its master stares at the Maidservant from across the cave for a long time.

The Maidservant doesn't flinch from her gaze. She knows she could die here, and she curses herself for walking so blindly into a trap, but she doesn't flinch. For a moment, the air in the cave seems charged, poised to turn against her.

The mystic smiles. "Well then. I suppose there's no reason for us to part ways on a sour note."

The Maidservant says nothing. Still watching her, the mystic picks up a scorpion pendant lying on her table and approaches. Her skirts sweep the cave's floor as she walks. "Your payment, as agreed. An unbound Yerezi talisman of the highest quality."

She tosses the scorpion talisman into the air, and it slips through the Void wards. The Maidservant catches it effortlessly and holds the object up to the torchlight.

A finely crafted artifact. Red steel and silver, its carapace chased with moongold, a clear crystal serving as the sting. Currents of complex sorcery throb away from it in rhythmic pulses. "How do I get it to answer to me?"

The mystic shows her teeth in a disparaging smile. "How else? You claim it with blood, of course."

"Of course." With a single thought the Maidservant spreads her left palm and causes the tattoos singed there to inch apart and split her skin so that it wells with blood. While the mystic grimaces, the Maidservant relishes the spike of pain. Only after she has rubbed every inch of the scorpion over her bleeding palm does she command her tattoos to knit together again.

Then the scorpion stirs, and lights strobe out from its crystal sting, sweeping the cave. A presence rises from the pendant and tries to enter her mind; she lets it. For a fleeting moment the presence explores her knowledge of ciphers, which it quickly uses to establish a telepathic system of communication that will allow her to control the talisman with her thoughts. Its first message is a ripple of power that reveals to her the extent of its capabilities. The Maidservant allows herself a smile.

"Just out of curiosity," the mystic says, watching her, "why this? You could have asked for anything else. Coin, perhaps. I know how much you Umadi love coin."

The Maidservant commands the talisman to go dormant and clutches it in her bloody palm. "That is no concern of yours."

"I suppose it isn't. Though I should warn you, in case you were planning on deconstructing the talisman to learn its secrets: Don't bother. I took *measures* to ensure you'd never succeed. Those secrets belong to the Yerezi. If the Umadi want to start making talismans, you can figure out how for yourselves."

But I have no intention of deconstructing it . . . "Consider me notified. Now, if you would let me go. Our business is concluded, and I have places to be."

The mystic takes her time to comply, slowly drawing magic into the cosmic shards branded on her forearms. Finally she waves the wards away. "Let our paths never cross again."

Without another word the Maidservant bursts into a cloud of flies and swarms out of the cave and into the twilight skies.

7: Musalodi

Khaya-Siningwe—Yerezi Plains

The day the Carving almost took his life was the first time he encountered the blue apparition.

At first it was just a ghostly outline lurking within the Carving's ancient forest, a cold presence hidden beneath a veil of blue mist, watching him silently. Nothing had ever followed him into this realm before, so he initially dismissed the vision as a product of his nerves; after all, losing track of the Carving's shifting paths could mean being stuck there forever.

But the mist seeped out of the trees, and Salo glimpsed therein an exceedingly tall blue-skinned man wearing only a hide loincloth, like a man from centuries past. He held a long spear of the strangest blue metal in his right hand, and what Salo could see of his face was unnaturally angular and sharp. His eyes, too, were unsettling, old and unforgiving things that shone through the misty haze like enchanted sapphires.

Salo stopped, feeling his heart begin to thud in his chest. "Who are you?" he asked.

Remember. He doubted the apparition had moved his mouth, and yet he heard his voice all the same, something like the whisper of wind or an echo in a vast chasm.

Was this another of the Carving's tests? "I don't understand," he said.

A woman appeared behind the apparition right then, dark skinned and coldly beautiful, with ocher-smeared dreadlocks and a little red snake looped around one wrist. The floral kitenge covering her body was drenched in blood, and so was the glass vial in her right hand. A large feline shape skulked in the trees by her side—all Salo could see of it was a cold metallic gleam and neon-blue eyes.

Fear unlike any he'd ever known took hold of him. He shook his head, taking a step back each time the woman stepped forward. This was a vision lifted straight from his nightmares. "No. It can't be. Not this."

Remember, the apparition whispered, still a distant echo, though it sounded a little closer now.

"No!"

He turned around to flee, but the ground erupted with thick roots that lunged upward to ensnare his arms, pulling him down to his knees. The restraints would not budge no matter how much he struggled.

"Let me go!"

He was helpless as the woman approached, and it was almost exactly like that first time all those years ago, except back then he was a boy and knew nothing of what was to come.

The woman watched him with mournful eyes. Guilt sat in those eyes, too, but her determination weighed heavier, and it was this that pushed her forward.

"No!" Salo thrashed around in his prison. "Please, don't do this!"

Tears flowed down the woman's cheeks, yet she continued to advance. "I have to, my sweet. Don't you see?" Her voice was thunder, making the ground shake. "I have looked to the edge of time, and I know what awaits there, the great and terrible things that will one day part the skies and shatter the world. It is why I must do this." She opened the vial in her hands, and Salo felt roots curling around his neck so that his face tipped upward. "Your pain and your tears, even as they destroy me, will build me anew, and your blood will be my victory over the coming darkness."

Behind the woman, the slinky feline shape finally stalked out of the shadows, its glistening canines bared, eyes gleaming hungrily. Blood stained its metallic leg muscles as it padded around its master.

Salo's eyes brimmed with tears. "Please, Ama. Please don't do this. It will hurt."

The woman's voice became something feeble and broken. "Forgive me," she said. "Forgive me. Forgive me." And then she tipped the vial and poured its acidic contents onto his eyes.

Salo screamed. His eyes became live coals in his skull, and scarlet flames filled his vision. He screamed until his throat tore itself open, until the world shifted around him and the roots disappeared.

Then he could see again, but now he was kneeling in a pool of blood with the woman lying in front of him, trembling in silent pain as she bled out from the mortal wounds on her belly. A witchwood blade lay discarded nearby, stained crimson.

"No."

The sight was like a jagged splinter boring a hole into Salo's skull, another crack in the dam holding back painful memories he did not wish to revisit.

"Ama, no!" He crawled toward the woman and gently cradled her head. "Oh, Ama, what have you done?"

Her head tilted so she could look up into his eyes. "Help me," she said in a weak voice. "Stop the pain."

The blue apparition was still there, standing in the background, watching with his unforgiving eyes. "Why are you doing this?" Salo shouted.

Remember.

He couldn't do this. Salo let the woman go and got up to flee. The apparition's voice echoed behind him, repeating that same word, but he wouldn't stop. He fled across the forest's twisting paths until his feet started to bleed. He fled until he woke up in the workshop to find Nimara hovering above him, trying to resuscitate him. That day he wept in her arms until his eyes ran dry as dust, though she would never understand why.

That was the last time he used the Carving, but the woman and the blue apparition would continue to haunt him in his dreams.

Not until the suns have risen over the kraal the next day does the fog of shock begin to burn away and the scale of loss become clear. The witch came, she fed her lord's Seal with the blood of twenty-seven clanspeople, and then she fled, leaving gaping holes in the lives that survived her onslaught.

The committals are scheduled for the moonrise that day, as is customary, which occurs around high noon for a waxing half moon. Ten of the chief's fattest uroko are slaughtered—an offering of a kind never seen in the Plains before, one not even a chief would merit at his funeral. The Ajaha perform their tribute dance twenty-seven times, honoring all who fell, not just those who donned the red. Twenty-seven burial rafts are carried down to the lake's western shores, not just one. Mourners from the rival Sibere clan across the lake come in their numbers—a first in Salo's memory—and their genuine sorrow surprises him with its intensity. He comes to understand that this was a crime committed not solely against Khaya-Siningwe but against the whole Yerezi tribe.

Monti's aba lets him help carry his son's burial raft down to the lake. The man has never liked Salo, and Salo can see the embers of blame burning hotly in his eyes, but on a day like this, all differences are set aside in honor of the dead. So Salo carries the raft with Monti's aba and two uncles, while Monti's ama trails behind with her only other child—Monti's older sister—and together they lead the procession of mourners toward the clan's place of committal.

The bodies have all been wrapped in hide skins, their rafts covered with white-petaled blossoms. Thousands of voices drift on the wind as the mourners move down to the lake, singing a lament that cuts Salo in half with every note, but he's too numb to cry anymore. Must be all the nsango he smoked throughout the night. It was the only way he knew to dilute the shock and make himself functional again, to stop his hands from shaking, to blunt the scent of Monti's blood in the air. Even now, he can still smell it.

They reach the western lakeshore an hour before moonrise, the suns hanging high just past their zeniths. The clan's sacred island is a rocky granite mound marring the lake's pristine surface in the distance, like a rip in a silky, luminous carpet. Salo and the other three men carrying Monti's body slip out of their sandals and wade into the waist-high shallows, where they wait for the other rafts to arrive. Monti's distraught ama and sister watch from the bank.

It takes a while, but all the dead eventually make it into the shallows, and the sheer number of pallbearers lined up along the lakeside drives a shiver of shock down Salo's numb spine.

Besides Monti's family, he barely registers individual faces in the crowd of mourners. Niko is a silent presence nearby. The queen's towering crown of copper feathers glints somewhere on the lakeshore—her presence was a certainty given the scale of loss. VaSiningwe is next to her, a lean giant in a black loincloth, red steel armor pieces, and a maned leopard headdress. The chief of Khaya-Sibere must be the stocky man in a scaled hyena cloak next to him, and the woman swathed in dark kitenges lurking behind them must be AmaSibere, the Sibere clan mystic. The last time all four of them were here together was for Aago's committal, two years ago.

AmaSikhozi was there, too, that day, and she's here again today to perform the traditional Yerezi honor burial. The totem she flew on from

Khaya-Sikhozi, a great metal eagle with a leather saddle strapped to its neck, can be seen soaring on an updraft to the far south.

The lament goes on for a long while, a mournful song delivered in the full range of voices, and with so many people it sounds like a living thing as it reverberates along the lakeside.

The singing finally dies down as AmaSikhozi steps into the waters with her witchwood staff raised, her crimson cloak billowing out behind her. She stops shin deep in the clear water, facing the lake's eastern horizon, where a rosy tinge has just appeared. Her voice carries to all those present when she speaks.

"Hear us, oh Mother of Sovereigns, oh Great Servant of the Heavens, you who paint the skies in blood and gold. Hear us in our hour of great need, for here lie our beloved kin, who have been torn so violently from our bosoms we will never heal from the wounds of their passing.

"We come to you in tears, Ama who is Queen, for we know not how else to be in the face of such senseless carnage. Our hearts have been torn asunder and left desolate, and we cannot make sense of it. And so we come to you, Ama who is Wise, and we ask that you remind us that this is not the end. Shine your light upon us and grant us the solace we seek. Let us commit our beloved kin into your embrace so that our hearts may be mended in time. Let them ride your first light into the Infinite Path, oh Blessed of the Skies. Serve them in death as they once served you in life."

A flash of light in the east as the half moon begins to rise above the lake's watery horizon. Salo immediately feels an unseen force tugging at Monti's raft as the moon's first rays strike it, and it's a sharp lance cutting straight into the deepest hollow of his chest.

Monti is leaving his life for good.

He thought he'd run out of tears, but now he finds that he has many more to spare. Panic seizes him. He can't let Monti go like this.

There has to be something more he can do, anything, even if it means little.

While the other pallbearers let go of the raft, he holds on to it for just a second longer, just long enough for him to take off his beaded necklace with one hand and place it next to Monti's shrouded head. And when he finally lets go and watches the little raft join all the others as they sail farther into the lake and toward the rising moon, something in his chest breaks, and he weeps like a child.

At that moment, AmaSikhozi raises her hands toward the east, her eyes now glowing like hot coals. The cosmic shards coiling up her arms incandesce like veins of lava as she prepares to complete the burial ritual—a joint spell of Storm and Fire craft. Moon rays pool around the tip of her staff, which becomes a blinding point of white-red light. "Go now, beloved kin of Khaya-Siningwe," she cries, "you who were sons and daughters of the Summer Leopard. Go now and walk the Infinite Path. Remember the lessons of this life so you may triumph in the next. By the power of the queen who reigns eternally, you are released!"

A tempest of moonfire explodes across the lake, engulfing the rafts in brilliant red light. It rages silently for a time, giving the lakeshore a glimpse of the Infinite Path's supreme glory. And then the fires whoosh into nothing, leaving the waters empty and desolate, just like Salo's soul.

A long moment of stillness transpires, thousands of broken hearts beating in silence, and then the mourners begin to drift away. Salo wades out of the water with the other pallbearers, and his chest swells with guilt as he watches Monti's aba bringing his wife and daughter into a tearful embrace.

I caused that sorrow.

Someone puts a hand on his shoulder. When he looks, Niko gives him an understanding nod, but he says nothing. Salo wonders why he's even here, how he can stand the sight of him when he can't stand being inside his own skin.

Monti's ama comes up to them just before they start walking up the bank. She's hugging herself like it's cold, and the pain in her eyes makes Salo gulp with fear and guilt. The emotions go down his throat like bags of needles. Niko watches her warily but remains silent.

"The general told me he saw you with my boy yesterday," she says. "He said he told you to get him to safety. Is that true?"

Tears prickle Salo's eyes. He doesn't wipe them as they flow down his face. "Yes."

She nods like he's just confirmed her suspicions, briefly looking away as she fights off her own tears. She tucks a stray dreadlock behind her ear and composes herself. "I saw you giving him something, so I have something to give you." She extends her right hand and unfurls it, revealing a leather wristband. "This was one of his favorites."

Salo fails to hold in a sob. "I recognize it."

"You do? That's good. Because I want you to have it." She reaches forward and grabs Salo's hand, places the wristband into his palm, and closes his fingers. She traps his closed fist between her hands so tightly it feels like the wristband is biting into his palm. Her eyes blaze with anger and sorrow, her words coming out as a whisper, sharp as jagged glass. "I want you to have it, and I want you to wear it every day until your last breath; do you hear me? I want you to look at it when you wake up and when you go to bed, and I want you to never forget that my son is dead because of you. He loved you like you were his own brother despite what they all said about you. That's how he was, my Monti, quick to see the good in people, didn't matter who, and he loved you, Musalodi, and now he's dead because of it. You let my boy die, and I will never forget it."

"Hey, now," Niko says. "That's not fair—"

"Please, let it go," Salo whispers. "She's right." He puts his free hand on top of hers and squeezes, forcing his words out through trembling lips. "I will wear this until the day I die. I wish I was the one on that raft and not your son, and I will spend the rest of my days wishing it. I will not ask for your forgiveness because I have no right to, but I promise that I will never forget your son."

Tears fill her eyes, and she nods. "Keep your promise, Musalodi." And then she lets go and joins what remains of her family.

"You can't take responsibility for this, Salo," Niko says when she's gone. "It's terrible what happened to Monti, but it's not your fault. You didn't bring that witch here."

Salo twists the wristband between his thumb and forefinger. Monti was wearing it yesterday when he barged into the shed without knocking.

Another sob threatens to burst out of Salo's chest. He covers his mouth, and when he gets himself under control, he wipes his eyes behind his spectacles and joins the trickle of mourners heading back to the kraal. Niko follows silently.

"I may not have brought the witch," Salo says to him in a low voice, "but Monti died because of my weakness, and you have to let me own that."

Worry creases Niko's forehead, but he says nothing for the rest of the walk up to the kraal.

PART 2

KELAFELO
*
MUSALODI

Earth craft—magic of alchemy

Directing the moon's essence toward influencing the alchemies of plant life and organic matter. Used by alchemists to prepare medicines and poisons. Also used to engineer new plant species.

—excerpt from Kelafelo's notes

"How many hours make a year? Be quick with your answer."

"All right, let's see: twenty-four hours, twenty-one minutes a day by ten days a week by four weeks a moon by nine moons a year. Gives me . . . eight thousand seven hundred sixty-six hours."

"Most disappointing."

"Did I get it wrong, Aago?"

"No, it's correct."

"Then what's the problem?"

"That you had to compute it in the first place. Five whole seconds wasted computing something you could have recalled from memory in an instant."

"You mean I should, what, fill my mind with trivial facts like this one? But why would I do that?"

"Why not? Everything you know means less time spent figuring it out when you need it. It might seem trivial now, but who's to say it'll stay that way?"

8: Kelafelo

Namato—Umadiland

For Kelafelo, it begins on the night when militiamen wearing red skulls on their faces descend upon her village and take everything from her—everything but the one thing she later wishes they hadn't spared: her life.

Fire dances like vengeful spirits across the village of Namato as it burns. Mud-brick huts shrouded in flames cough up glowing clouds of smoke and embers that billow like swarming fireflies. Screams rise into the night as bloodstained machetes bite into limbs and slice throats open, and the skull-faced men laugh in drunken bloodlust over the corpses of their victims.

Men, women, children—the people of Namato fall indiscriminately, and it seems to Kelafelo that their cries tear rents into the sky itself, for heavy rain soon breaks, even before the carnage is over. She sees it all from where they left her lying on her back by the threshold of her hut, her belly ripped open through her khanga, the oozing wound turned up to the sky like a screaming maw.

She was trying to block the door so the militiamen wouldn't get inside; she threw herself at their feet and pled with them, but the men in the red skulls are not men at all, with neither hearts nor mercy. They cut her down and defiled her even as she bled, and then, worst of all, they dragged her four-year-old daughter out of her hut and murdered her.

Urura. Oh, by the Blood Woman, Urura. Kelafelo tries to speak the name, but a gasp escapes her lips instead. She stretches a shaking hand toward her daughter, whose motionless body now lies on the bare earth to her side, but her fingers are just out of reach. Blood glues Urura's saffron veil to her head, and the fires consuming the village reflect in the pools of her dead eyes. If she were only a few inches closer, Kelafelo would stroke her cheek, tell her that everything will be fine, that they'll soon be together again on the Infinite Path.

"What good thing could ever come of you, Kela?" her aunts-in-law would taunt her, back when she still lived with her uncle and his many wives, before she became fourth wife to a farmer thrice her age. "You are defective," they would tell her. "Rotten to the core."

But when her daughter was born on the eve of her fifteenth birthday, Kelafelo realized that her aunts had been wrong. If something so precious could come from her womb, then she could not be entirely rotten. Urura was evidence that there was good inside of her.

What is she now that Urura is gone?

Around the village the cries fade into intermittent whimpers, and then those, too, die out. The laughter retreats into the night. The rain douses the fires and peters out. Damaged rafters groan and collapse; thatched roofs cave in; mud-brick walls crumble.

And still, Kelafelo waits for death. But death does not come.

Instead, rage begins to stir inside her. As she lies there with her belly sliced open, waiting to be reunited with her daughter, rage keeps her alive, refusing to let her give up, forcing her to finally confront that thing she has always hidden from, the true reason her aunts despised her, the reason they feared her.

"Do not think yourself special because you are the daughter of a warlord," her uncle would say to her. "Your father was a vile monster who forced himself on my sister. You should have never been born."

And like an obedient niece, Kelafelo kept her head down. She weathered the scorn of her aunts silently, and later the scorn of her sister-wives. She ignored the heritage in her blood and pretended it didn't exist.

Now her rage forces her to acknowledge it, for she will not die this night. Not here. Not like this. Not when Urura's murderers are wiping her blood off their sandals.

This cannot be my end. I have war and fire in my veins. I shall make them pay.

As dawn is breaking in the east, piercing through a silver haze of rain clouds, she sees it: a streak of fire burning across the skies like a comet, making the earth tremble with the thunder of its flight. It is then that she understands what she must do.

It is then that she finally dies and is reborn as something else.

The skull-helmeted men have taken almost everything from her. Their mistake was to leave her with her life.

An old mystic lives in the wilds east of Namato, just a stone's throw away from a wide meandering river. She is neither warlord nor disciple and claims no land as her own but the land on which her hut stands and the vegetable garden growing nearby. Kelafelo's people call her the Anchorite.

In Umadiland, where those brave enough to seek the Blood Woman's power are often ruthless, egocentric men, free agents like the Anchorite are like para-para antelope without herds: they do not remain free or alive for long. Sooner or later they must pledge allegiance to a warlord or be hunted down and killed. Neutrality is not an option; the warlords make sure of it.

But the Anchorite has endured as she is for longer than anyone alive can remember, and no one knows why.

Before the attack she would come to the village on occasion to heal ailments and preside over burial rituals but led an otherwise reclusive life, guarding her privacy with a capriciousness that could be cruel. Villagers who approached her hut in search of healing or divination were often just as likely to wind up cursed with malicious spells as aided free of charge. For the most part, the people of Namato knew to wait for her to come to the village at her own convenience, but sometimes people grew desperate and approached her unbidden. Sometimes they never came back.

As the suns clear the horizon on the morning after the attack, Kelafelo musters up all her hatred and heaves herself off the ground. Too weak to bury Urura, she drags her daughter's body back into their hut and covers her with grass mats.

She can't even cry. The part of her that would have fallen to pieces at the sight of Urura's broken body has been ripped from her chest, leaving nothing but a scalding void of hatred. In a semiconscious daze, she wraps her belly tightly with the torn shreds of a khanga, screaming as the pain lances through her whole body. But she finds the strength to keep moving and trudges through the charred ruins of her village, heading east.

Her wound becomes hot with infection. Nightmares cavort in the fringes of her eyesight as she walks, phantoms wearing the faces of her people, monsters leaping at her from the grasses with teeth meant to tear into her flesh. Still, she keeps walking, each step drawing from the wellspring of darkness that now pervades her.

The suns arc higher into the skies, bringing with them flies that swarm around her wound relentlessly. She has no energy to swat them off, so they feast on the blood seeping through the makeshift dressing. Vultures fly by overhead, drawn westward by the smell of blood and rot. They, too, will feast today. They will feast on Urura.

That last thought is almost Kelafelo's undoing. She sways on her feet, almost tumbling to the ground, knowing that if she falls, she will never rise again. A scream claws at her from the inside. With gasping breaths she holds it in and somehow manages to stay on her feet.

Time distorts itself. The savannas of the wilds stretch and warp, and mirages bleed into her vision, a personal hell that seems to last forever. But she stumbles onward until she is finally there, by the great twisting witchwood tree looming over the Anchorite's old hut, pale and leafless.

Chickens cluck in the coop built next to the hut. A stooped figure leaning on a crooked staff is waiting outside, watching Kelafelo's approach through eyes that long ago clouded over with cataracts.

Standing there draped in a kaross of hide, with a face as weathered as a crag and a thick mane of dreadlocks as white as chalk, she seems carved from stone, like some permanent feature of the landscape, as if she were present when the river was gouged into the land and the mountains raised from it. The people of Namato often whispered that the Anchorite has been an old woman for centuries; she certainly looks like it might be true.

A centipede with metallic legs and an iridescent carapace squirms out of the folds of her hides and perches on her left shoulder, swaying its long chrome-like antennae to the tune of the wind. The Anchorite appears oblivious to its presence, even as it brushes its antennae against her leathery face. Kelafelo might have thought the creature one of her waking nightmares had she not seen it once before, perched on that same shoulder. It is said the centipede is where the Anchorite keeps the spirits she collects, which she uses to cast her darkest spells.

She speaks first, in a croaking voice that seems to come from afar. "Have you come here to die, young one?"

Kelafelo hasn't thought about what she will say to the old woman, yet the words come out on their own. "Teach me," she says. "Teach me so I may find vengeance for what has been done to me."

The Anchorite regards her with those unseeing eyes of hers. The centipede on her shoulder rears up and tastes the air with its antennae. "I owe you nothing," she says at last.

Kelafelo is undeterred. "You will die one day. Are you content to let all the knowledge you've gathered die with you?"

The Anchorite's lips twist into a spiteful smile. "I was here before you were born, dear girl, and I will be here long after you die. You know nothing of the knowledge I possess."

"Nor does anyone else, and that will remain true unless you teach me. Pass your knowledge on to someone who will treasure it."

"I care not for your vengeance."

"And yet I will be all the more eager to learn because of it."

The Anchorite watches her again. "You are wounded. You may be dead by this time tomorrow."

"I will survive."

"What was done to your village was inevitable," the Anchorite says. "A new warlord has risen in these parts. He commands many. You will die if you go against him."

"Then so be it. Vengeance is all I have left in this world. I will have it, or I will die in its pursuit."

Some say the Anchorite can read minds. If she reads Kelafelo's mind right now, she will likely see nothing but a quiet storm.

"If I take you in," she says with a warning seeping into her voice, "there will be a price to pay, and I always collect my debts."

"What is it you want?"

"You will know it when the time comes for you to pay."

Kelafelo doesn't need to think about it. Her daughter is rotting in a shroud of grass while her killers roam the savannas. "I accept your terms," she says, and thus begins her induction into the mystic arts.

9: Musalodi

Life goes on in Khaya-Siningwe. The clanspeople fall back to their usual routines, trying to salvage a modicum of normality from the broken pieces of their lives. Almost convincing if Salo doesn't look too closely at the ghosts haunting their eyes, the strained smiles, the absent stares. As for Salo himself, the days wear on in a dreary haze, like a cloud of soot has fallen around him and leached all the color from the world.

Word spreads about how Monti died, and people start giving him the same looks they used to give him right after his failure at the Queen's Kraal two comets ago. Only this time they aren't laughing, because what he did isn't worthy of simple derision; it's worthy of abhorrence. He let a little boy die.

Even VaSiningwe starts looking at him differently. The specter of disappointment has always lurked behind his eyes where Salo is concerned, though Ama knows the man has done his best not to show too much favoritism among his sons. Now, however, resignation sits openly in his heavy gaze, like he's given up hope that Salo will ever amount to anything worthy of the copper on his left ear.

"A hard lesson learned, dear nephew," Aba D says to him during dinner in the chief's compound.

Every night the compound's dry earth is swept clean of the day's bustle, the lone musuku tree in the center is draped with fresh glowvines and transformed into a towering centerpiece, and three different families from within or without the kraal are invited to come dine with the chief and his family. They all sit in groups on stools or mats and eat communally from large earthenware platters.

"The world isn't going to coddle you," Aba D goes on. "If you don't man up, it'll slit your throat and grind your bones to dust. You have to be strong, son, always. Never, *ever* show weakness, or your life will be nothing but a long string of miseries."

Aba Akuri, sitting next to him, wipes his mouth with the back of his hand, leaving bits of sorghum porridge trapped in his thick beard. "Perhaps now is not the time to speak of such things, dear husband."

"If not now, when?" Aba D says. "There is never a good time for harsh truths."

"You can be so stubborn sometimes," Aba Akuri remarks, shaking his head.

Salo hasn't touched any of the roasted meats and vegetables arrayed in front of him. Instead, he's been idly twisting the new leather band on his right wrist—a recently acquired habit. Now he feels the sting of shame wash over him.

Aba D is right, though, and he certainly knows all there is to know about never showing weakness. Unyielding strength and pure and absolute perfection on the battlefield were the prices he had to pay in order to marry the man he loved without suffering the stigma that often comes with such unions. Anything less, even the slightest slip of the foot or a moment of hesitation, and the stigma would have never left.

An impossible standard to live up to, Salo would say, one he knows he could never achieve in a thousand years. In fact, sometimes he feels like he gathers stigma just by breathing. A walking, living scandal. A blot to be washed clean.

Weak. Useless.

Monti's wristband was too small for him, so he had to sew longer straps onto it to make it fit. Ama Lira is plucking her lyre with calloused fingers beneath the musuku tree to the beat of bowl-shaped drums. The music drifting from the ensemble muffles Aba D's words, so Salo and Aba Akuri are the only ones who hear them. But they sting so intensely the man might as well have shouted them to the whole kraal.

Salo wipes his eyes behind his spectacles and says nothing. And then he stops taking his dinners in the chief's compound altogether.

Life gets no easier, though. The number of crimson loincloths walking around more than doubles in one day when the chief calls almost half the clan's rangers from all over Khaya-Siningwe to come garrison the kraal.

Worse, Niko doesn't forget Salo's promise to train with him and his posse of young Ajaha in the circular glade by the lake, so Salo has to spend whole mornings in the company of people who openly despise everything he is and tolerate him only because their idol tells them to.

More than four times the usual number of aspirants are coming to train with Niko and his crew these days, though this shouldn't be surprising given the legendary status Siningwe Ajaha have recently acquired. Tales of their bravery during the attack have spread across the Plains like a virus, infecting virtually every young man in the tribe with the zeal to prove himself worthy to don the red.

After Salo suffers yet another humiliating defeat to one of these zealous young men in a stick fight, Niko pulls him to the side with a betrayed look on his face. "You promised you'd try," he says.

"I *am* trying," Salo protests, rubbing the painful welts on his arms.

"You're better than this, and you know it. And you've gone through the training before. You should be walking all over them!"

Salo's hackles rise at the criticism. "We can't all be as good as you, all right?"

"No," Niko says with a level stare, "but *you* can. You have your aba's blood in your veins, and your uncle is the greatest warrior this clan has ever seen. Your heart's just not in it."

It doesn't work like that, Salo wants to say, but he holds his tongue. He looks around the forest glade, at the aspirants and rangers sparring for dominance, sticks rattling as they strike each other, faces grimacing, muscles straining. "This isn't me, Niko. I'm trying, but . . . I don't know if I can ever belong here."

Niko's eyes spark with something hot, and he turns around to shout across the glade. "Mujioseri! That log you and your brother are sitting on. Throw it at me with everything you've got."

Jio and Sibu have been presiding over a stick fight between two young aspirants in white loincloths. Now they trade identical looks and lift their eyebrows at Niko. "Are you asking to die, mzi?" Jio says.

"Just do it already."

"If you insist." Jio stands up and pushes his unsuspecting brother off the log, causing a few laughs when Sibu yelps and falls onto his back. The log must weigh more than five men, but Jio slips his hands beneath it and lifts it up like it's a sack of feathers. Insects squirm in the recess of wet earth where it lay. He smirks as the aspirants gawk at him, wallowing in their admiration like a reptile basking in the suns. Then the log flies across the glade and toward Niko like it's been ripped upward by a vicious gale.

Salo sees everything clearly: the way Niko flexes his knees and braces his sandaled feet on the ground, the way strength coils in every muscle of his body, the way his chest glistens with sweat as he thrusts his fist forward. A thunderous crack booms as fist connects with wood, and everyone watches, amazed, as the log splinters into a thousand pieces like it was detonated from within.

Niko slowly walks back to Salo, a fierce blaze burning in eyes that usually hold nothing but kindness. "Do you hate being weak, my friend?"

"You know I do," Salo says in a low whisper, feeling the sting of tears.

"Well, guess what." Niko spreads his arms as if to take in the glade. "*This* is a path to strength. With this you can fight back. With this you'll never have to watch someone you love die in front of you again."

Salo wipes his eyes and nods. "All right. I'll try harder."

"It's all I'm asking," Niko says in a softer voice. "Now go back in there and fight like a leopard."

When the training session ends, Salo wanders to the bonehouse to see if he can't steal something from their stores to quench the fire in his limbs, as well as maybe something to soothe his heavily battered ego.

The bonehouse is actually a circular cluster of five drystone buildings surrounding a well-groomed garden whose focal point is an ancient witchwood tree. Salo finds Nimara brewing tonics in the alchemical workroom attached to the largest building, which has a wraparound timbered porch and recently renewed thatching. She's set her spider talisman on her table and commanded it to display a cascade of semitransparent charts and figures that drift and flicker, feeding her information only she can understand.

She's been busier than usual since the attack. Over a dozen people still require intensive medical care, and while she has several women who help her around the bonehouse, Nimara has the tendency to micromanage everything under her purview. She's barely been seen outside in almost a quarter moon.

Salo quietly wanders into the spacious workroom and sits down on a stool by the west-facing windows. A faint whiff of beeswax floor polish hangs in the air. The place is never anything less than scrupulously spotless, everything arranged in parallel lines, from the glass vials in the cabinets to the journals and sheaves of stacked paper resting on the mahogany work tops, not a lick of dust in sight.

Nimara doesn't take her attention off the alchemical reactor in front of her, a brass apparatus of chuffing pipes and moving cogs, powered by the mind stone from a tronic eland cow. A smoky liquid churns in the glass sphere at the center of the reactor. Salo watches her carefully insert pegs of red steel into slots around the sphere—he knows that each of those pegs has a unique enchantment of alchemical Earth craft. She uses her talisman to keep track of how they influence the smoky liquid over time.

"Are the kraal's harvesters in good shape?" she says after inserting the last peg and wiping her hands with a cloth. "The New Year's harvest starts soon. We should address any problems quickly so we get started on time."

A wave of discontentment rises up from Salo's chest. "You'll have to ask the queen to send an Asazi to help you out with that. I won't be working machines for much longer."

Nimara sighs and returns to tinkering with the little levers on her machine. "She can't force anyone to come, Salo. You know that."

"I'm a man, all right? The son of a chief." He waves a hand around the workshop. "I'm not supposed to know how any of this works. I'm not supposed to *want* to know. I should be a ranger, punching logs with my fists and subduing wild stallions."

"You know what I'm wondering right now?" Nimara says, folding her arms and giving him a hard gaze through a window of information. "I'm wondering when you're going to quit feeling sorry for yourself and finally do what we both know you should have done a long time ago."

Salo flinches. He expected balm for his wounds, not salt. "I'm training with the rangers, aren't I? I'll face the uroko again and earn my steel."

"Not at all what I meant."

"Then what do you want from me?"

Nimara places her palms on the table. "I'm talking about *that thing* you're letting rot inside your talisman."

"Shhh!" Salo gets up and closes in, stopping on the other side of Nimara's worktable. "You don't know what you're talking about! If anyone finds out . . . by Ama, you *can't* tell anyone, Nimara. Promise me you won't."

She stares at him, a challenge in her eyes. "This is exactly what I mean. You have the means to do something—you've had the means for a while now—but you keep choosing to do nothing."

"I can't do anything!"

"Yes, you can!"

The liquid in the sphere suddenly turns blue. With a defeated sigh Nimara grabs a rack of empty vials, places them beneath the sphere, turns a valve, and begins to fill one of the vials with the liquid. "You know the problem with you, Salo? It's never that you can't. Oh, no. It's that you won't even try." She plops a cork stopper onto the vial and proffers it to him. "This'll help you recover from all the running around you're doing."

Salo hesitates, then reaches forward to accept the vial, but she retracts her hand at the last moment. "Have you thought about what difference you could make if you were just brave enough to come out with your secret? What difference you could have made when the witch attacked if you never hid it in the first place? We're defenseless without a mystic, Salo."

"*You* will be our mystic!" he says.

"I'm eighteen," she says. "Statistically, I still have several more years before I achieve an Axiom good enough to live with for the rest of my life. What do we do until then?"

"I can't, all right? I just can't."

She leans forward, her gaze unwavering. "Salo, that witch could return at any time, and she'd still find us defenseless. But we don't have to be! Stop caring about what people think for one second, and you'll know I'm right."

Salo groans, feeling exposed, like he's being attacked. "The queen would never allow it," he says weakly. "It's sacrilege. She'd sooner have me exiled."

"You don't actually know that, do you?"

"Nimara . . ." He looks down at the floor.

"Your fear is depriving this clan of something it desperately needs. Plain and simple." She finally hands him the vial and starts filling another one. "I have fifteen patients to take care of, and these tonics aren't going to make themselves, so."

Taking that as his cue to leave, he thanks her for the tonic and flees the bonehouse. But her words stay with him in his waking hours like painful scalds on his skin and come out in his nightmares through Monti's lifeless lips, accusing him, asking if he knows.

Do you, Bra Salo? Do you know what difference you could have made that day if only you weren't such a coward?

The queen comes to address the clanspeople on the first Onesday after the attack.

The Ajaha welcome her with their lively stick dance, kicking up dust to the powerful beat of barrel-size drums, but the mood is far from festive as the woman rises from a wicker chair to deliver her message.

Her presence seems to thicken the air. Backs are stiffer than usual, brows are creased, and not a single wailing baby can be heard anywhere. In all Salo's years attending clan meetings, he has never once witnessed such a thing.

But this is hardly surprising, considering the vision standing before them.

Salo reckons that if the malaika of dusk came down from the heavens, if she traded the stars and nebulae draping her body for glass beads, copper bangles, and cascading bronze skirts, if she set aside her corona of twilight for a towering crown of copper feathers—if she did these things and her splendor became flesh and she walked the earth as mortals do, she would probably look something like Queen Irediti of the Yerezi Plains.

The queen is a six-ringed mystic—the most powerful sorcerer in the Plains—and cuts a tremendous figure of sharp, imperious beauty so worthy of her station you would never mistake her for anything other than what she is. Her bright umber eyes are oppressive pools of knowledge you would do well to avoid. The copper crown adorning her head doesn't just glint in the encroaching dusk like mundane metal; it *sparkles*, it *coruscates*, it *scintillates,* like something forged in the heart of a star.

Is it any wonder, then, that the clanspeople, who are unaccustomed to such potent blends of beauty and power, should quail when confronted with one such as she?

The suns have just set, while the moon is rising full in the east, partly covered by a blanket of golden clouds. Most people have seated themselves on their mats or stools, though many of the unmarried young men litter the edges of the gathering as they always do. Salo has chosen to stand at the very back of the gathering with a few cowherds, not far from the clan mystic's vacant hut.

The Ajaha are in full regalia today, forming thickets of burnished red steel and glimmering spearpoints all around the compound, each with his best posture since their queen and mystic is in the kraal. VaSiningwe and the ten elders of his council sit on the timbered porch of the council house behind the queen, facing the gathered clanspeople with grim expressions. AmaSibere is among them, too, with a clearly repressed smile, and that is enough to confirm Salo's worst fears about what's about to happen, because nothing that can make a Sibere look that smug can ever be good for a Siningwe.

"When our Foremothers settled the Yerezi Plains centuries ago," the queen says, in a powerful voice that carries across the compound, "they understood one thing many of our sister tribes did not. They understood that mystics are not here to live as demigods but to serve the people on Ama Vaziishe's behalf. We are here to be the vessels of her benevolence, the conduits through which she blesses her children so they may live long and prosperous lives.

"Why else would she have blessed us with knowledge of red steel and an ancestral talent so potent it has made Yerezi mystics the envy of the Redlands? While mystics everywhere else enslave and terrorize their people, we bless and uplift ours. While they extract worship from unwilling lips, we inspire joyous songs of praise.

"We are not just mystics, Yerezi-kin. We are emissaries of the Red Moon. Through us, Ama Vaziishe heals your ailments, powers your machines, irrigates your crops, and shields them from disease. Through us, she gives strength to your Ajaha, warriors so mighty they can prevail over creatures of the underworld. Through us, your Asazi can study the arcane and advance knowledge, and you are protected from callous and destructive uses of magic."

The queen lets her somber gaze roam the rapt compound, and Salo remains still, face impassive, safe in the knowledge that his eyes are hidden behind reflective lenses.

"But ten comets have passed since a mystic last resided in this kraal," the queen continues. "Ten comets since this clan was cut off from Ama's full embrace. While your Ajaha have thrived—and this is in part because the blessing they carry draws from *my* power, a compromise I made to tide you over until a mystic awoke from among you—while their strength is unquestionable, many aspects of your community have suffered. You have failed to retain Asazi in your villages, forcing you to barter for medicines and other basic goods that should be freely available. You have relied too much on bride-price to restock your herds of livestock, which die at a greater rate because they lack the necessary protections from disease."

Unsurprisingly, the old councilmen seated behind the queen, who themselves own sizable herds of oxen, murmur in disagreement.

She doesn't acknowledge them. "And then a quarter moon ago, my beloved kin, a foreign mystic came to Khaya-Siningwe and performed a ritual so evil it took the lives of twenty-seven of your clanspeople. I say twenty-seven, but what does this finite number really mean? Can it truly express the loss we suffered in any meaningful way? The lives cut short? The families torn apart? It cannot, Yerezi-kin, for the lives that were taken from us were each and every one of them infinitely valuable. And do not think that this loss was felt only here in Khaya-Siningwe; we all felt it. This crime was committed against every man, woman, and child with Yerezi blood in their veins.

"Which is why I can no longer sit idly by and watch this continuing decline, for the Yerezi way demands that I intervene. As the Foremothers wisely said: I am, because we are. That is the Yerezi way. First and foremost, above all allegiance to clan, chief, and mystic, we are one people, and it is my responsibility as queen to ensure that we thrive as a whole. While war after war has ravaged much of the Redlands, our unity has kept us safe throughout the centuries, and it will continue to do so as long as we hold it sacred."

The queen glances briefly behind her, first at VaSiningwe, and then at AmaSibere. When she turns back to face the clan, Salo holds his breath.

"Therefore, after considerable deliberation with VaSiningwe and his council, as well as VaSibere and his council, I have come to the decision that your two clans shall become one and the same."

And there it is. The clan's death sentence, the eventuality people have been whispering about for years, though no one ever expected it to actually happen.

Do you know what difference you could have made, Salo?

A defiant murmur rises from somewhere beneath the musuku tree at the center of the compound, low at first, and then it spreads, and then it roils into an uproar as clansman infects clansman with rage and indignation. Enough for most to forget their fear—this is the Siningwe clan, after all, not exactly known for its cowardice.

"We will never join with Sibere, Your Majesty!" comes a voice. "We will burn before we let those hyenas rule us!"

Salo looks and sees that it is Jio who has spoken. Sibu, Niko, and the other young Ajaha around him rattle their spears in agreement, repeatedly striking the ground with their blunt ends. A few of the older men and women shake their heads, but everyone else seems inspired by their bravery. The boys in front of Aba D's hut start to jeer at AmaSibere. Hundreds of voices rise to clamor for attention, and the queen lets them persist for a full minute.

Then a storm of ravens surges from behind her and gathers on either side of her into her two honor guards: an athletic Ajaha warrior with a savage blade clinging to his back, and a dark Asazi maiden, resplendent in pale beads and red steel.

Silence grips the compound. The honor guards need not make any threats; this not-so-subtle reminder of their presence is threat enough, and so is the eerie calm on their youthful faces. Theirs is the calm of trained killers who know that their bones draw deeply from a powerful mystic.

"This is not unprecedented, Yerezi-kin," the queen says without a trace of hesitation or annoyance. Her decision has been made, and her commands carry the force of law. "Those of you learned in history will know that we were once a collection of a hundred small but weak clans, most with no clan mystics to make them viable. But over time we realized that larger clans built around a chief and a clan mystic were far more successful, so we united, until only eight clans remained. The time has come for another unification."

She seems to wait for another uproar; none comes, though fury blazes openly on the faces of many clanspeople. Salo watches from a distant place inside his mind, his limbs rigid as stone.

"I am not blind to the historical rivalry between the Siningwe and Sibere clans," the queen continues. "But this union is critical. This clan needs a mystic's protection, and I am confident AmaSibere will not fail you in her duties. I urge you to put aside your differences at this great juncture and work together with your new clanspeople. Know that I do not make this decision out of malice but from necessity. We face calamitous times ahead, Yerezi-kin. It is clear to those of us who can read the signs: lost rituals of Black magic resurfacing, the Umadi growing more organized, whispers of war between the Great Tribes. If we are to survive these tribulations, if we are to preserve our way of life, we must be watchful and united, now more than ever."

Then Queen Irediti returns to her wicker throne and gives way to the witch AmaSibere, the clan's supposed future mystic, whose long-limbed beauty is as wickedly predatory as a scaled hyena, her clan's totem animal. She even resembles a scaled hyena with those three horns affixed to her copper circlet and the way she laughs with her eyes and shows too many teeth, like a plunderer who's finally clutched her heart's desire. She's never in anything but black: black beads, black skirts, black bangles, black lips, black kohl—an eternal widow. Even the long witch-wood staff in her hands is painted black, save for the lines and circles of inlaid red steel running down its length.

As she takes center stage, the clan's disgust is a wave of heat prickling Salo's skin.

"I know many of you are unhappy with Her Majesty's decision," the witch begins with sympathy as fake as her teeth are white, "and I want you to know that I understand. Truly, I do. Clan Siningwe was once a great clan, and when you lost your mystic ten comets ago, I was deeply saddened, for I knew her quite well."

The clan hisses. She basks in it like a scavenger in carrion. Their hatred is her victory. "I also want you to know that this unification will not mean a loss of your independence," she goes on. "VaSiningwe will remain your chief, and this kraal will remain the center of your administration—for now. We will not enforce any laws upon you, and I speak on VaSibere's behalf. However, in time, the centers of power will have to consolidate into a single coherent whole . . ."

She goes on and on. Pretends that this will be a union of equals when it will be annexation in all but name. Pontificates about unity and togetherness, deliberately fans the flames of indignation around the compound with her glib words.

As she speaks, Salo sinks further into paralyzed panic. What if Nimara was right, and all this could have been avoided if he'd only spoken up about the secret he's keeping? What if he could have saved Monti?

Do you know what difference you could have made?

In the end, what drives him forward is a single thought, an accusation leveled at him by someone who knows better.

The problem with you, Salo, is never that you can't. It's that you won't even try.

"Irediti Ariishe! AmaYerezi who is Queen! I am unworthy, but please, grant me your ear!"

How now, what's this? Who would be so bold as to interrupt a mystic's speech? Murmurs and gasps arrest the compound. Eyes widen; fingers point. At the back of the gathering, in front of AmaSiningwe's old hut, Salo has gone down on one knee, his hands pressed together. He, an unblessed former cowherd in a white loincloth, has *interrupted* a mystic's speech.

"What in the pits is he doing?" says an alarmed voice behind him.

He ignores it. "Irediti Ariishe! Please, have mercy and let me approach!"

Shocked disapproval. Insults muttered under the din. This might be a Sibere mystic, but what Salo is doing is sacrilege.

"What's the meaning of this?" AmaSibere says, peering over the seated clanspeople to get a good look at him. "You wear no steel, and yet

you dare interrupt me? VaSiningwe"—she turns to sneer at the chief—
"what have you been teaching your boys?"

VaSiningwe says nothing; perhaps he is too speechless or too furious, but Salo can't stop now. "Irediti of the stars and the moon! Irediti who is lovelier than a bloodrose at dawn! Irediti who is—"

"You may approach, young man," says a voice that cuts through the air with merciless precision, silencing all others.

Just what Salo was hoping for, but his joints lock in place, and he gapes at the queen like a juvenile hare watching a colorful python slithering toward it. AmaSibere's mouth hangs open just like his, but she rediscovers her tongue first.

"Your Majesty! He is not blessed! He cannot speak before the council. That's sacrilege!"

"It is," the queen says from her wicker throne. "But I am curious. Approach, young man."

Like a lost child, Salo gets up from his knees and stumbles through his clanspeople, making his way to the clearing in front of the council. He can't avoid glancing at Niko and his brothers along the way, and the wide-eyed horror he sees there doesn't surprise him. But this is something he must do.

He reaches the center of the clearing and goes down on one knee again, making an effort to drown out everyone else. He focuses on the queen, this vision of cold beauty who now holds his fate in her hands.

"Thank you for granting me this audience, Your Majesty," he says.

So close, she is simply bewitching. Her flawless bronze skin holds an otherworldly inner glow. Her lips are dusted with flecks of gold so that they glitter. A tiny smile tugs at them now, and it's not friendly.

"Don't thank me just yet," she says. "I haven't done you any favors, and I cannot protect you from the consequences of this sacrilege. I only wish to find out what was so important you couldn't hold your tongue." She motions at him to rise. "Stand up and speak loudly. I'm sure your clanspeople are curious as well."

The first pangs of regret wrap themselves so tightly around Salo's heart he feels like it might explode. What if he faints? What if his bowels loosen and he shits and pisses himself right here, in front of the queen?

The terror of that last thought brings him up to his feet. His arms forget what to do with themselves, so he pushes his spectacles in and clasps his hands together in front of him. The gesture probably looks clumsy.

"Speak, Yerezi-kin," the queen prompts. "We are listening."

And so Salo clears his throat and begins to speak to the most powerful person in the Yerezi Plains.

"Irediti Ariishe," he says in obeisance, "VaSiningwe the Great, AmaSibere who is Chosen, the wise council, and my beloved Siningwe-kin. My name is Musalodi Deitari Siningwe, first son of the Summer Leopard, and I accept responsibility for my clan's plight."

10: Kelafelo

On the afternoon of the first full moon after her arrival at the Anchorite's hut, Kelafelo returns from the river with a ewer of water balanced on her head to find the old mystic sitting on a stool beneath the witch-wood tree. Resting on the ground in front of her is a basket with a lid concealing its contents.

"Bring out a mat and come sit down, young girl," the Anchorite says.

"Yes, Mamakuru." Kelafelo peeks down at the basket as she walks by but learns nothing of what might be inside. Still, her heart begins to race with anticipation; she has been here for a few weeks now, and the Anchorite has yet to begin instructing her in the mystic arts. Perhaps that's about to change.

Inside the hut she sets the ewer down next to the other three she has already filled and takes a mat of woven grass from where it hangs on the mud-plastered walls. Her recovery from the attack on her village was brutal, a feverish hell the Anchorite did little to alleviate. She's much better now, though the scar on her belly still aches when she bends over. Kelafelo has learned to use the pain as her motivation, a constant reminder of why she is still alive.

Back outside the suns are low, casting long superimposed double shadows, and in the east the full moon is a swollen, heavily pockmarked crimson disk emerging from the horizon. Kelafelo spreads the mat and sits on the other side of the basket like a respectful granddaughter, her hands clasped in front of her.

"I am here, Mamakuru," she says, addressing the old woman as her grandmother. If this displeases the Anchorite, she hasn't shown it.

"Tell me why you want to learn magic," she commands, her milky eyes staring into the distance.

For Kelafelo, the answer could not be simpler. "For the power to kill the men who took everything from me."

A sneer twists the Anchorite's leathery face. "And what makes you think yourself worthy of such power, or that your bones could even contain it, when it has broken so many others before you? Speak, girl."

The razor edge in her voice gives Kelafelo pause, and she takes a moment to calculate an appropriate response. *What is she really asking me?* "My hatred burns as hot as the suns, and I have the blood of a warlord in my veins. I will not break."

"The blood of a warlord," the Anchorite repeats, tilting her head to one side in curious amusement.

"My father ruled in the northwest before he was killed in battle," Kelafelo says. "I never knew him, but I am his daughter all the same."

The Anchorite digests this expressionlessly. "I see. And your mother?"

"Died in childbirth. I was raised by my uncle and his wives."

"The daughter of a warlord raised by her aunts." The Anchorite puts on a grim smile. "It is no wonder anger and hatred come so naturally to you."

A hot flash of temper takes control of Kelafelo's mouth before she can stop it. "If you think that upsets me—"

"Don't talk back to me, girl. I have little patience for those who cannot handle the truth when spoken to them."

Kelafelo holds her tongue and looks down at the hands folded in her lap. Right now she hates the old woman more than anything else, but she'll endure her taunts if it means learning the mystic arts. She has endured worse. "Apologies, Mamakuru. The past holds nothing for me but pain."

Just as quickly as she can rise to anger at times, the Anchorite can be surprisingly quick to forgive. "Then let us leave it in the past. In any case, the Blood Woman does not care for your parentage. You could be the daughter of a Dulama god-king, and it would not matter. She cares only for your devotion, the sharpness of your mind, and your willingness to go as far as it takes."

An upwelling of zeal grips Kelafelo, and she can barely stop herself from shaking. "I will go to the ends of the world if need be."

"That is yet to be seen," the Anchorite says. "For now, let us begin with the first obstacle standing in your way: you wish to learn magic, but you lack basic literacy in any script, and I lack the patience to teach it to you."

Something shiny peeks out of the voluminous folds of her hide kaross. Kelafelo is almost surprised when a tronic centipede crawls into view, its long antennae swaying back and forth like blades of grass in the wind. The creature has made so few appearances since Kelafelo's arrival she often forgets that it's there.

"I could simply *give* you the knowledge you need," the Anchorite continues, "but this would inflict on you the most exquisite agony you have ever felt. You might not survive it."

"I have already felt the worst agony of my life," Kelafelo says. "I am not afraid."

For a moment the mystic's opaque eyes seem to stare back, probing her, and Kelafelo gets the impression they see a lot more than she first assumed. "Very well." The Anchorite reaches into her cloak and produces a thick ring of pale wood, holding it out for Kelafelo to see. "Do you know what this is?"

Kelafelo leans forward to examine the ring. Its color is that of bone, like the witchwood tree looming over them. Mysterious symbols have been carved all over its surface. "A soul charm, except the mind stone is missing."

The Anchorite nods in approval. "Anyone can make one of these provided they know what ciphers to carve and in what order. But those who know the secret have wisely kept it within our tribe; should I teach it to you in the future, I will expect you to do the same."

"Yes, Mamakuru," Kelafelo says, though the tronic centipede has stolen her attention again as it crawls up to the Anchorite's shoulder, its carapace shimmering like a film of oil on water. She fails to hold in a gasp when the creature rears up, extends a pair of metal fangs, and bites into the old woman's neck.

The Anchorite doesn't flinch. She holds out her arms as the centipede sinks its fangs deeper into her neck. Then there's a *change* in the air that makes Kelafelo's ears pop, like she has climbed to a place where the air is thinner. The old woman's cosmic shards appear, six rings pulsing scarlet with magic on each arm. Kelafelo watches, mesmerized, as the soul charm lifts off the mystic's palm, floats into the air, and stops to hover above the basket in front of her.

"We all know what these little things can do for a warrior in battle," the Anchorite says, her centipede still lodged in her neck. "But precious few understand that these charms are nothing but vessels of information. Just as they imbue warriors with tronic skills, they can also transfer knowledge from one mind to another."

Particles of dust begin to rise in a circle, lingering in place unnaturally around the witchwood tree. Kelafelo gives the dust a nervous glance as the Anchorite continues to speak.

"With an important limitation, of course. The more complex the knowledge transferred, the higher the risk that attempting to assimilate it will drive you to madness. Literacy in ciphers and multiple scripts will be pushing this limit. Are you still willing to continue?"

Kelafelo looks away from the wall of dust that has risen around them and meets the Anchorite's stonelike gaze. She wants to sound confident, yet this display of power has left her trembling. "Whatever it takes, Mamakuru."

"Then reach forward and accept the soul charm."

Swallowing down her fear, Kelafelo obeys, and as soon as she touches the charm, the dust begins to dissipate with the breeze, and the pressure she felt in the air relents. She notices also that the Anchorite's shards have stopped glowing and that the centipede has finally retracted its fangs. A thin trickle of blood is all the old woman has to show for it, not that it bothers her, judging by the inexpressive look on her face.

"As you noticed," she says, "the charm is missing a mind stone. To access the knowledge I have infused into it, you must place a mind stone into the hollow and possess yourself with its spirit."

Kelafelo frowns at the charm in her hand. "But where am I to find a mind stone?"

A chill in the air. A whisper of the breeze. The slightest of smiles on the Anchorite's face as she drops her gaze onto the basket sitting between them.

Kelafelo looks at it, too, a shiver climbing down her spine. She braces herself and reaches forward to lift the lid, only to fling it away and recoil when a red mamba rears its head from within, hissing at her. Its eyes are soulless voids. Its scales shimmer in the dusk like it was dipped in blood. Kelafelo takes in sharp breaths, wrestling with the instinct to flee, careful not to make any sudden moves.

"You may be wondering why I would place such a trial before you," the Anchorite says. "And you may come to the conclusion that I wish to see you dead. But the first thing you must learn from me is that Red magic is a language of the body and soul. To truly grasp it, one must become acquainted with the most immediate consequence of having both in a chaotic universe. Do you know what that is?"

Kelafelo shakes her head, still staring at the hissing serpent.

"Agony," the Anchorite says. "Intimate knowledge of agony brings you closer to the Blood Woman and the secrets of her magic. It is why I did not ease your recovery when you first arrived. Because of your ordeal, the grief and suffering you have known, you have already begun the path to your Axiom. Now you must face this serpent if you wish to continue."

As though it has understood the Anchorite's words, the red snake lunges at Kelafelo threateningly, forcing her to crawl back a few paces. She shakes her head forcefully. "No, Mamakuru. This is a red mamba. One bite will kill me in seconds."

The old woman shows no sympathy. "Perhaps it will. Perhaps it won't. You said you were willing to go to the ends of the earth. Now we will know the worth of your words. There is a hatchet in the basket; use it to kill the snake and take its mind stone, then possess yourself with its spirit."

The serpent makes as if to strike again, and Kelafelo almost gives this whole thing up right then, an impulse that quickly mutates into scorching anger.

You would give up on vengeance for Urura? You would cower from the first trial thrown at your feet? How dare you even consider it!

A deathly calm settles over her, and her limbs stop shaking. She eyes the serpent and sees through it to the reason her belly aches every time she moves.

The reason she wakes up shouting every night.

The reason she is sitting here right now, in front of this loathsome creature, and not with her daughter.

She needs no further motivation. She takes in a deep breath, gathers all her hatred, and lunges forward.

11: Musalodi

Khaya-Siningwe—Yerezi Plains

Silence. Stillness.

Salo's aago, avid spinner of tales that she was, once told him that when a whole group of people falls silent at the exact same time, it's because the devil has walked by. That is how Salo feels when he announces his guilt to his clanspeople: like Arante herself has drifted by on a gust of wind and planted a deathly kiss upon his cheeks.

As she sits on the wicker throne in front of him, the queen's eyes burn with interest.

He swallows and continues. "My ama, the late AmaSiningwe, killed herself because she thought she was saving me. I don't understand it. Perhaps she was ill—I will not speak of it. All I will say is that her death robbed this clan of a mystic and plunged us into the depths you have spoken of, Your Majesty, and I know that I am to blame."

The words pour out of him from a part of his mind he didn't even know existed, and it shocks him just how much he believes them.

"And I will be the first to admit that I haven't done much to make up for it," he continues. "I have shirked my responsibilities. I have failed to gain entry into the esteemed Ajaha, and I have consistently failed to live up to my aba's name. I am most unworthy, Your Majesty. I know that."

He risks a glance at VaSiningwe. The deep worry he sees there makes him draw in a shuddering breath. The emotions that come with it sting his eyes. Thank Ama no one can see them.

"But this union you have decided on calls me to action, Your Majesty, because accepting it would mean living with the knowledge that I am the reason my clan has fallen to the hyenas." AmaSibere sneers to his side; he ignores her. "But how can I? How can I face my clanspeople knowing I am the cause of their shame? How can I face my own aba?"

Salo shakes his head in answer to his own question. "I cannot, Your Majesty, which is why I have risked sacrilege to stand before you now. And here is what I beg of you, Irediti Ariishe, and I do so for the sake of my clanspeople, for my aba, and for the sake of my own soul. Your Majesty, allow me to commune with the redhawk and receive my shards, and should I be successful, allow me to serve my people as clan mystic."

Laughs abound, all of them mirthless. Salo's clanspeople are laughing in their shock at the temerity, the sheer insolence that he could suggest such a thing.

"Sacrilege!" AmaSibere hisses, baring her teeth like she would rip him to pieces right there.

When his eyes flick to VaSiningwe this time, his blood chills at what he sees. The man's jaw is clenched. His eyes hard as stone.

Salo turns away from him and the queen to face his clan, and the anger he sees on their faces weakens his knees. This is not at all what he was hoping for.

Then he spots Nimara sitting on a reed mat somewhere among the crowds, and she nods at him, the only friendly face in a sea of hostility. "Khaya-Siningwe may be small," he says, finding the courage to continue, "but it is still one of the wealthiest clans in the Plains. Our lands are abundant in iron, gemstones, and moongold. We have rich hunting grounds, a bountiful network of rivers and streams, and fields so fertile we don't need a mystic to keep ourselves fed. Shall we give all this up to the hyenas, who have always coveted our wealth? Shall we betray our forebears, who fought for this land and left it for us as our birthright? Is it not worth a temporary break in tradition to save their legacy?"

Some clanspeople grow silent and thoughtful. Salo presses his point. "I am not putting myself forward as a permanent solution, Siningwe-kin. I only want to buy us more time. Perhaps in a few comets, our own mystic will awaken and take her rightful place. I will gladly step aside. But our clan's integrity is at stake—right now. The hyenas are outside our borders—right now. And if we let them in, they'll destroy us. They'll stamp out any trace of what makes us Siningwe, and the Yerezi will be weaker for it."

AmaSibere raises a long finger in warning. "Remember, Yerezi-kin! Our Foremothers barred men from sorcery for a reason. Men do not possess the control and poise necessary to safely wield such power. They are too susceptible to their passions and their pride and their desire to dominate. Allow him to awaken, and he would soon become a tyrant. Just look at the rest of the Redlands. Was it not a man's Seal that burned in your skies only a week ago? Male sorcerers are abominations. We must not allow one within our borders."

Many shout in agreement. Salo can't think of a defense against her words except to say, "I have no will to dominate, AmaSibere, only the will to see my clan free of your clutch." A few cheers arise.

AmaSibere smiles dangerously. "You say that now, but once you've tasted power, you will want more. It is in your nature; you cannot escape it."

"With all due respect, you don't know me. You can't tell me what my nature is and what it isn't."

"That may be so, but what you ask for is still sacrilegious. More to the point, it is impossible. You cannot just commune with a redhawk and become a mystic. You need at least a decade of schooling in the language of ciphers. You need to discover your own key to the moon's power. You need years of experience as an Asazi apprentice. You have none of these."

"Why don't we let Ama be the judge of my worthiness? I'm prepared to take that risk." Salo turns back to the queen, whose little smile is somewhere between wry and cruelly amused. "Your Majesty, would you say that someone who has derived an Axiom is ready to face the redhawk?"

Now the smile wanes, her head tilts, her eyes narrow in suspicion. "Perhaps," she says.

"Could I press you for a more definite answer, Your Majesty?"

The queen sits back in her throne and crosses one leg over the other. "All right," she says. "Yes, I would agree with that claim. But why do you ask?"

"Because I derived an Axiom, Your Majesty."

Gasps. Whispers. AmaSibere laughs. "Take him for flogging. The boy lies."

"I speak the truth," Salo says.

"Explain yourself," says the queen. No amusement now, only intense scrutiny.

"My ama . . . AmaSiningwe wrote about a certain Axiom before she died," Salo says. "I used her teachings to devise it."

The queen rises to her feet, and the rest of the world seems to disappear, like she's sucked all the light from the compound and spooled it around her crown. The shock on her face is so terrifying Salo finds his knees buckling to the ground. He bows his head and braces for the worst.

"*You* derived your mother's Axiom? The Elusive Cube?"

It takes him a moment to recover from the fact that the queen knows about the Axiom, then another to shudder at the implications of this, and then he finally says, "I did, Your Majesty."

"You lie!"

"I tell the truth! By Ama I swear!"

"Look at me," the queen commands. Salo looks up and is awed once more by the wondrous sight before him, this malaika made flesh. What foolishness to think that he could ever be anything like her. What utter madness.

In the compound's tense silence, she walks down the porch toward him, the long train of her skirts trailing behind her. The metalloid shards on her arms begin to glow a furious red as they fill up with the moon's essence, and even more terrifying are the six complete rings encircling either forearm—the indisputable proof of her power and preeminence.

"I will rip the truth from your mind if I have to," she says and then splays a hand toward him, and suddenly—

Pain. Intense, unholy pain like a fire burning just beneath his skin. Salo crumples to the hard earth and curls into a fetal position. The world goes dark. He can't cry out because his throat won't let him, so all he does is choke and wheeze.

He knows the pain isn't real, nothing but a distraction. The queen is a powerful Blood mystic with the ability to read thoughts, but to reach them she has to flood his senses with pain so that his mind is powerless to resist her intrusions. Indeed, his mind opens up to her like the pages of a book.

In the distant background, he feels her sift through his memories with an aggressive searching spell. His mind is cut in half, then those halves into halves, on and on until eighteen years' worth of memories yield the one truth she's looking for.

Surprise blooms in her mind as she plunges deeper into his; he senses this. She's shocked at the nature and structure of it, the deep pathways reordered for pattern manipulation and mental multitasking. This is so far from the mind of an ordinary boy she spends entire seconds wandering through its restructured synapses, aghast.

Here is the mind of a boy so foolish, so thoroughly reckless, he spent years—years!—gambling with a high-risk mental artifact, a *forbidden* artifact, and so stupidly lucky that he survived every encounter with it. His mental pathways even offer minor resistance to her probes, and while he should be delirious with pain, he's actually *aware* of what she's doing.

Still, his mind yields to hers, and she sees, and she sees, and she sees . . .

And when she mind-touches the memory of a certain cache of ciphers locked within the red steel core of his talisman, and when she follows the memory all the way to its root, she recoils from it like a hand from boiling acid. She retreats from his mind altogether, so quickly it leaves him convulsing and temporarily paralyzed.

The pain goes away slowly, like fog clearing away from the lake at first sunrise. When he struggles to pick himself up from the ground and return to a kneeling position, he finds the queen standing with a hand pressed against her chest. Shock, disgust, and *fear* wrestle on her face. Behind her, VaSiningwe has risen to his feet. His eyes are wide, and he seems, rather uncharacteristically, at a loss for what to do.

"Abomination," the queen breathes. "Fool. What have you done? I . . . I didn't think it was possible. I thought she was mad . . ."

"Your Majesty," AmaSibere says, and the urgency in her voice scares Salo more than anything else right now. "Asanda's work was evil. She was in league with darkness. If he recreated it . . ." Her staff begins to pulse with cold energy. She eyes Salo with murderous intent. "We can't risk him bringing it into this world. He must die."

"Don't even think of it." VaSiningwe takes a step toward the hyena. He's one of the tallest men in the kraal, and his spine-maned leopard headdress turns him into a giant. He looms over her. "How dare you!" The anger in his voice is almost a physical force.

"VaSiningwe," she says, standing her ground, "you of all people know I do not speak lightly. You know firsthand the wickedness of Asanda's work."

His jaw ripples with anger, but he has nothing to say to that. To Salo this feels like splinters of glass slicing straight through his heart.

"Aba?" he says.

The man faces him, endless anger in his eyes. "What the devil were you thinking, boy? I should have barred you from that cursed shed a long time ago. I have been far too lenient with you." Endless anger and guilt and contempt.

For him.

"But Aba, I—"

"Silence! Don't make things worse than you've already made them."

Salo bows his head to hide the rivers of shame flowing down his cheeks.

The queen, though, takes things along a different tangent. "This changes everything," she says, more to herself than to anyone else. The world spins on her words like a ceramic ewer and then stops by the edge, waiting for the wind to tip it either way.

She addresses the chief. "VaSiningwe, your clan's sacred altar. It is on the island in the lake, is it not?"

"It is, Iredifi Ariishe," he answers, looking visibly confused.

"Tonight, at Heaven's Intermission," the queen announces to the whole compound, "you, Musalodi Siningwe, will commune with the redhawk and receive your shards if Ama deems you worthy." Her eyes glint with a grave warning. "But if not, then you shall die. That is the risk you have taken."

Not a peep from the whole compound.

Salo looks up in shock. Not because of the death—that goes without saying—but because the queen has actually granted him his impossible request.

"You cannot be serious, Your Majesty!" AmaSibere cries. Her staff might snap in half if she grips it any tighter. "Your Majesty, you cannot entertain this sacrilege! You cannot—"

The queen's eyes slit and cut to the hyena, silencing the woman. "Do not presume to tell me what I can and cannot do, AmaSibere. This is my decision." She returns to addressing the clanspeople. "I am putting the clan union on hold until further notice. All of you here will be at your sacred island by Intermission. This is not a request."

Silence rings all over. Salo surprises himself by breaking it. "I thank you, Your Majesty. You are most generous."

"Don't," the queen says, moving a little closer, "think I'm doing this for you." She comes near enough to lift his chin with a slender finger. Her smile is cruel and lovely at once. She smells like power and bloodrose essence. "You are an abomination," she whispers, "but if you succeed, you'll be more useful to the Plains than any clan mystic could ever be." Her finger traces his chin, then leaves, and he almost bemoans the absence of her touch. In a louder voice she says, "This meeting is concluded. You are dismissed."

Then Queen Irediti of the Yerezi Plains disappears into the council house, cascading skirts flowing behind her, honor guard in tow.

He flees the compound soon afterward, hoping to find refuge in the silence of the workshop because he's not quite ready to look anyone in the eye right now. But Aaku Malusi is already there, nursing a gourd of musuku wine by the largest table.

His eyes glisten in the dim light of the shed's glowvines. "You're still alive," he says, like he's half-surprised by this fact.

Salo's heart feels like it's about to beat right out of his chest. He drifts closer to the old man, pulls up a chair, and sits across from him. He breathes in deeply, lets it out slowly. "You saw?"

Aaku Malusi nods. He pushes the gourd Salo's way. "I left when she cast that spell on you. I . . . couldn't watch."

Grateful for the offer, Salo reaches for the gourd and takes several desperate gulps of the cloying wine. As he sets the gourd down, he notices the wet streaks on the old man's cheeks. He is at once deeply moved and saddened.

"I'm fine, Aaku," he says. "The queen is letting me awaken. Tonight! I can hardly believe it."

He thought Aaku Malusi might share in his joy. Instead, the old man shakes his head, despair deepening the lines on his weathered face. "Oh, you stupid boy. You stupid, foolish boy. Why did you have to tell them your secret? Why, my child?"

For a second Salo watches him in stunned silence. "You knew about it?"

"Of course I knew! I'm not blind. I notice things." He points a frail finger at the old cabinet in the room. "And I know what's hidden inside there and how you used it."

Salo doesn't know what to say. He thought he was careful in all his dealings with the forbidden. He used his talisman for all his work, never writing anything down on paper, and he only ever used the Carving when he was alone. Aaku Malusi certainly never hinted that he knew what was going on under his nose. "Then . . . why didn't you say something?"

The old man sighs. "Because I thought you were smart enough to keep it to yourself."

Salo looks down at the gourd on the table, the wine turning sour in his mouth. "I take it you don't approve."

"I'm worried about you, Musalodi. What you did today marked you forever as a man who doesn't know his place. I'm worried this will be a stain you won't ever wash off."

"But don't you see?" Salo says. "I did it for the clan. I averted the hyenas taking over and undermining my aba's rule. I'm sure everyone will understand. They have to. Don't they?"

The old man regards him with pity. "I think you overestimate their capacity for understanding and acceptance. I would die for this clan, my child; I would die for my tribe, but I know all too well that my people aren't kind to those of us who are different." Tears gather in his eyes again, and his voice wavers. "I just don't want to see you become like me. That's all."

"I . . ." Salo's voice dies in his mouth, and he finds no words worthy to speak. What can he even say to this?

"Musalodi!"

A loud, angry voice coming from outside draws their attention to the door. Salo blinks, wondering why whoever it is has chosen to yell rather than knock.

"Musalodi! Come out here and face us!"

He stills as he recognizes the voice, cold dread settling into the pit of his stomach. "I think those are my brothers out there."

"Don't move a muscle." Aaku Malusi's lips press together into a thin line as he rises and picks up the staff leaning against the table. He walks over to the door and opens it, stretching his normally stooped figure to its full height. When he stands erect, he is almost as tall as the chief.

"What do you want?" he demands. "Why do you shout like this when the suns have gone down? Have you no respect?"

"We're not here for you, old man," says the voice from outside. "We're here for the siratata you're hiding, or is he too much of a coward to face us?"

That's it.

Salo shoots up to his feet and strides for the door, where Aaku Malusi is still facing down the visitors.

"Is that any way to speak to an elder, young man? Have you no respect?"

"We won't leave until he comes out. Musalodi!"

"I'm right here," Salo says behind Aaku Malusi, intending to slip past him and out the door, but the old man blocks the way forward with his arm.

"You don't have to do this," he says over his shoulder, his eyes imploring. "This is all very silly. It's foolish."

"What's the worst they could do? Beat me? If that's their plan, then they'll do it anyway, so I might as well get it over with."

Aaku Malusi holds his gaze and doesn't move. "You don't have to do this," he says again.

"You can't protect me forever, Aaku."

His eyes fall to the floor, and he shakes his head in sorrow. Finally he steps aside. "I'll be right here."

Salo nods in gratitude and proceeds to step through the doorway, bracing himself for the worst.

Night has fallen outside, but the full moon and the outdoor glowvines provide more than enough light. What Salo sees makes him instantly realize that a beating is probably not the worst thing that could happen to him after all.

No, what's about to happen is much worse.

He surveys the scene before him silently—they let him take a good long look. He has taken off his sandals, so he's barefoot. He doesn't venture too far from the door.

Around fifty boys are standing in front of him, each with a woody reed in one hand and a steely glint in his eye. The bulk of them are among the clan's younger rangers, though Salo spots a few white loincloths in their midst.

His two brothers are at the front of the gang.

Apprehension makes his limbs start to tremble. He folds his arms and puts on a stolid mask. "I'm flattered," he says. "Truly. All this, just for me? You really shouldn't have."

Sibu, the more quick-tempered of the twins, glowers with murder in his eyes, like it's taking everything in his bones to keep his rage on a leash. "I told you this is all just a joke to him."

"Calm, brother," Jio says to him. "We're not here to fight."

"Are you really going to do this?" Salo says. "Are you really going to toss those things at my feet? I know you're upset, but—"

"*Upset?*" Sibu snarls. "That doesn't even *begin* to describe how I feel. You're a disgrace, Salo. You've disgraced our aba, and you've disgraced this clan."

His anger is like a field of dry grass just waiting for a bolt of lightning to strike it and set it on fire. Still, it's the calm in Jio's voice that Salo finds more disconcerting.

"Do you remember that time Aba sent us to Khaya-Nyati?" Jio says. "I think it was three comets ago. The suns had set, and we were riding in the open wilds, just the three of us, and from out of nowhere comes this massive kerit with a mouth full of drool and teeth like daggers. Do you remember?"

Salo says nothing, knowing that he is but a spectator to a performance.

"Now, me," Jio continues, "I thought we were done for, but you? Oh, you were like a devil unleashed with your bow." He shakes his head as he looks Salo over, and his mouth twists with disgust. "What happened to that warrior? Who is this soft, weak, pathetic shadow of a man standing in front of me?"

Defend yourself, damn it, Salo thinks. But he sees that he is teetering at the lip of a chasm and that saying the wrong thing could tip him over.

Jio turns his head slightly to include the other boys in his speech. "I'll be the first to admit it—I know we've been unkind to you these last few years, but a part of me always held out hope that the brother I saw that night would return to us. Now *there* was someone I could respect." He looks back at Salo, and the betrayal shining in his eyes is surprisingly genuine. "Shows me what a fool I am."

I hurt them, Salo realizes. *I hurt my brothers. But how can they be so blind?* "Did I really do such a terrible thing?" he finally says. "The queen was about to hand our clan over to the hyenas. Am I the only one who remembers this? You seemed pretty opposed to it, brother. You shouted in defiance at the queen, your own mystic. You all did. But I stopped it. I bought us more time."

"To what end?" Sibu says. "So we can have *you* as our mystic? *You?*" He spits on the ground. "You've turned our clan into a laughingstock. I can hear the Sibere cackling at us as we speak. And for what? Just so you can satisfy your *sick* desires to have what should belong to women?"

Salo can already see himself tipping over and falling, and a part of him recognizes that he has already lost. He tries to catch himself anyway. He takes off his spectacles and lets his brothers see his unnatural eyes, hoping that maybe this will convince them of the sincerity of his words. The world grows too bright and blurry without the magic of his spectacles correcting his vision, yet he can still see Jio's and Sibu's outlines etched against the false brightness.

"I didn't do this for myself, brothers," he says. "You have to believe me. I did it for the clan and for the people we lost when that witch attacked."

"Lies!" Sibu says. "This is what you've *always* wanted, and when you saw the opportunity, you seized it. Ama as my witness, I will flay myself and jump into a cauldron of moonfire before I *ever* accept your blessing."

"We'll never bow to you," Jio says. "Stranger." And then he tosses his prematurely cut reed at Salo's feet. Salo doesn't see it, but he hears the reed's dull thud as it hits the ground.

A Yerezi reed, severed before it has reached its gainful potential, hitting the dry earth unceremoniously: this is the sound of disownment, a brotherhood coming to a permanent end.

Sibu's reed follows. "Stranger," he says.

Yet another reed hits the ground, and another after it. One by one the boys come forward to sever any bonds of brotherhood that may have existed between them or could have existed in the future, each time declaring him a stranger.

He puts on his spectacles to find that his brothers have already walked away. Meanwhile each thud of the reed is like a knife in the gut, tearing up a howling void. But he doesn't let it take him, not in front of these boys. He stands in silence until they've all made their points, the reeds piling up before him. Even the young cowherds he smoked with on occasion are there, and they don't quite meet Salo's gaze as they toss their reeds.

"Stranger," the last one says before walking away. And then it is over.

A hand comes to rest on his shoulder from behind him. "I'm so sorry," Aaku Malusi whispers. "I'm so sorry, my child."

Salo wipes his cheeks and speaks without turning to face the old man. "You've been here before, haven't you?"

A pause. "I have."

"Then you know I need to be alone right now."

The hand squeezes his shoulder once, then lets go. "I'll be there at your awakening tonight. I'll be praying for your success."

"Thank you, Aaku."

Back in the shed, Salo sits in the lonely stillness for a long while. At some point, however, the stinging in his eyes overwhelms him, and he hunches up in a corner, convulsing. He hates himself for being so weak, so *soft*, for crying so much lately it feels like he's almost always on the verge of tears. What kind of man is he? Is he even a man?

Maybe they're right about him. Maybe they've always been right.

12: Kelafelo

In her nightmares, a crimson serpent watches from the shadows as men wearing red skulls on their faces push into her body while she bleeds from her stomach, violating her until she thinks they'll split her in half.

The snake watches while the men drag her screaming daughter out of her hut and cut her down like a rabid hound before leaving her broken corpse on the hard earth for the vultures and scavengers to devour. It watches as her entire world goes up in flames, as she relives that horrid night over and over again. She wakes up crying every time.

She is still alive only because the Anchorite weakened the red mamba's venom before asking her to kill it beneath the witchwood tree and take its mind stone. The venom still burned like sulfur through her body, leaving her writhing on the ground and screaming in pain for a whole day—one of the prices she had to pay for the spirit's gift, a torrent of knowledge she would have needed years to acquire naturally. She can already read and write in ciphers just days after that afternoon.

The nightmares were the other price. Sometimes they're so overpowering she toys with the idea of finding relief via one of the poison vials on the Anchorite's medicine rack.

On one such occasion she goes as far as getting up from her pallet, tiptoeing across the hut toward the rack, and lifting a jet-black vial of deadly root essence. She doesn't drink it in the end, but she keeps the vial anyway, and on subsequent nights, whenever she wakes in a cold sweat, she studies it in the starlight coming through the shutters above her pallet. She imagines herself pouring its contents down her throat, her insides turning to liquid and her blood congealing in her veins. She imagines herself gasping for her last breath. Somehow, this makes her feel a little better, and eventually she falls into a dreamless sleep.

If the Anchorite notices the missing vial or hears Kelafelo screaming in the night, she makes no mention of it.

They spend their mornings performing their daily chores. Kelafelo sweeps, washes, cooks, fetches water, and forages for firewood while the Anchorite feeds the chickens and tends her garden with a hoe. After high noon they sit in the yard outside, and the mystic passes on her arcane knowledge. Kelafelo struggles at first to take down everything on paper, still not quite used to the sensation of holding a quill and dipping it into a gourd of ink, but her muscle memory catches up, and soon she acquires a wealth of notes on multiple arcane subject areas.

She learns about the six crafts of Red magic, how casting spells revolves around converting the Blood Woman's essence into one or more of these crafts. She learns that this conversion is performed in the shards by a great pattern called an Axiom, which she must devise entirely by herself before she meets the redhawk. She learns about mind stones and their uses beyond soul charms, including the conjuring of spirits that can manifest as lightning or fire. Her mind expands with each new thing she learns, and she waits impatiently every day for the suns to arc past their zeniths so that her lessons can begin.

Nightfall, though, brings only dread as she frets about the horrors that will visit her in her sleep. She despises herself for it, for fearing the skull-faced men so much that the thought of closing her eyes makes her shudder. She wishes she could look at them in her nightmares with nothing but the hatred she feels so intensely for them.

She wishes she felt nothing but hatred.

The Anchorite sits her down one day and confronts her. "Your progress is satisfactory, young girl, but I am concerned that you are cutting yourself off from your emotions."

"I don't understand, Mamakuru," Kelafelo deflects. "What do you mean?"

"You are having unpleasant dreams, are you not? I sense you numbing yourself against them. You are shutting out your humanity to make the nightmares easier to bear."

A surge of self-loathing sours Kelafelo's expression. "My humanity weakens me, Mamakuru. I cannot be emotional. I need to detach myself from what happened to my daughter, or I will never be strong enough to kill her murderers."

Kelafelo's frown deepens as the Anchorite begins to chuckle, hoarse and throaty like a crow.

"That is where you are wrong," the woman says. "To become a true master of Red magic, you need your humanity. Did I not tell you that agony feeds your understanding of it?"

Kelafelo's anger gathers and redirects itself toward the Anchorite. "I am not afraid of pain. I will scarify my whole body—flay myself if I have to—but I cannot be weakened by sentiment. I will not."

The Anchorite is unmoved. "You speak only of agony of the flesh. That can be powerful, to be sure, but far more powerful is the agony that visits you in your sleep, for this is the kind that will reveal to you the greatest secrets of sorcery, secrets you could never hope to grasp with a hollow heart. The powerful emotions that come from spiritual anguish are crucibles of transformation; embrace them and let them forge you anew."

"I am filled to the brim with hatred. Why is that not powerful enough?"

"Because hatred alone is not agony. Hatred is the burnt husk that agony leaves behind when it is done with you. It cannot offer you any insights into the universe. But grief and guilt—the things you feel because you have a soul—now that is where the truth lies, and with it, power."

"I cannot accept that. The men who killed my daughter and defiled me laughed while they did it. I saw it in their eyes. They had no humanity. They felt no remorse for what they were doing. You can't tell me they weren't stronger for it."

"Silly girl. Men such as those who attacked your village deny their humanity not because they are strong but because they are cowards."

"I find that hard to believe, Mamakuru."

"It is true. They fear unraveling under the crushing weight of their guilt, their love, compassion, so they scour themselves free of these attributes to make what they do easier. But this is not strength! It is weakness masquerading as strength! Those who are truly strong *embrace* their humanity; they shoulder the weight of it and then persevere *in spite* of it."

Now Kelafelo tilts her head, defiance slipping into confusion. Why embrace something one must then persevere in spite of?

"The strong face their guilt, the consequences of their actions, the sorrow they've caused, and they weep over it, and yet, if it will further their own ends, they will readily shed rivers of blood," the Anchorite explains. "To torture and sacrifice another soul while feeling the full weight of the crime upon your shoulders, and then to do it again, and again: now *that* is strength. Use your hatred, yes, but don't kill your humanity. The spiritual agony of defying it is what will lead you to your greatest Axiom."

Kelafelo has never feared the Anchorite before. Not truly. But now she feels something disquieting stir in her core. The men who attacked her village and killed Urura were evil, but their evil was mindless in its intensity, bestial. Far more terrifying is the evil that knows *exactly* what it is, that contemplates itself, philosophizes its own nature, an evil that Kelafelo can now see for the first time behind the Anchorite's milky eyes.

How did she miss it?

"I will think on what you've said, Mamakuru."

The Anchorite gives her a knowing smile. "You do that. In the meantime, I think you are ready for the next stage of your learning."

Kelafelo fails to conceal her surprise. "I am?"

"Indeed. There is something we must collect before you begin." With the aid of her walking stick, the Anchorite rises from her stool and gestures for Kelafelo to do the same. "Come. Let us take a walk down to the river."

The calm and coppery waters of the River Fulamungu can be seen glittering from the Anchorite's hut through a copse of tall shrubs. The river is navigable almost as far inland as the World's Artery, so it's not uncommon to see boats and the occasional ship gliding by.

While Kelafelo stands next to her along the riverbank, the Anchorite starts to chew on a dry stick of licorice root, as is her wont when she's in a philosophical mood. That's how Kelafelo knows she's about to be tested.

"The Blood Woman blessed Umadiland with arguably one of the most powerful ancestral talents in the Redlands," she begins. "No other tribe can rival our capacity to grow our powers. It takes *years* of meditation, study, or ritual sacrifice for every other mystic to achieve the same growth in power we can achieve in mere weeks by simply rooting our cosmic shards to our lands." The Anchorite spits out a chunk of desiccated root. "Now, given this incredible advantage, tell me why Umadiland is not an empire with dominion over all the Redlands."

Deciding that the lecture will probably be yet another polemic against the tribe—the Anchorite is fond of these—Kelafelo responds accordingly. "Because our mystics don't build strong Axioms, Mamakuru."

"Explain."

She takes a moment to consider everything she's learned and proceeds with caution, thinking over every word. "While it is true that the number of rings on your cosmic shards determines how much essence you can draw per unit time, the quality of your Axiom is a far more significant factor in determining the speed and efficacy of spell casting and charm creation. Fundamentally, the Axiom dictates how much of this raw essence is converted into useful magic and how fast. So even if your shards provide you with a stream of essence as forceful as this river, if your Axiom is rubbish, then little of that power will ever be usable."

The Anchorite acquires a distant look as she mulls over the answer. Eventually, she tosses her root into the river. "That answers why you might want a good Axiom, but not why Umadiland is where it is today."

Kelafelo hesitates. "I guess . . . I'm not sure I know."

"It is quite simple. Instead of using our ancestral talent to uplift ourselves, we have used it as an excuse to get away with rubbish, as you've so accurately described it. Why slave over an Axiom when rooting yourself to even a small piece of land can add a whole ring to your cosmic shards? All you need is an Axiom that works, and then you can make up for its deficiencies by conquering more and more land. A solid plan, yes?"

Kelafelo takes some time to think. "There is a fatal flaw to that logic, Mamakuru. Spellwork with inefficient Axioms is vastly more taxing to the mind, and you can forget about casting charms."

A little smile appears on the Anchorite's weathered face. "Then you understand something many of our tribe's young men do not. From the day they are born, they dream of becoming warlords. They teach themselves the art of death and violence but do not bother to master the language that underpins the art of magic. And why? Because that would require that they actually use their brains—a waste of time in their eyes. They want the Blood Woman's power but are too lazy or stupid to apply themselves."

Kelafelo's attention is slightly drawn away from the Anchorite when a rowboat appears upstream. She can make out two men inside, one shirtless with his back toward her—the rower—and the other in an olive-green robe. A third, much smaller passenger sits next to this second man. A veil covers her hair as is customary for young Umadi women and girls, turquoise as the sky on a clear day.

The Anchorite continues with her lecture, as if oblivious to their approach. "Do you know how most of them discover their Axioms? Not through hard work and effort, I can tell you that much."

The boat is steadily approaching, and Kelafelo can now make out the rower's shoulder muscles as they bulge and the water pouring down the blades of his moving oars. She answers the Anchorite without taking her eyes off them. "I saw a man awaken once, back when I still lived in my uncle's village. He'd never read a book in his life, but one day he drank an elixir that made him see visions, and two days later he faced the redhawk. Last I heard he was a disciple somewhere in the south."

"A cheap trick. Those elixirs force the mind to string together random ciphers along predetermined pathways. The result can sometimes be unique and workable enough to survive an encounter with a red-hawk—but not always, which is why so many of our young men die at their awakenings." The Anchorite shakes her head with disgust. "No intellect required, no scholarship, no effort whatsoever. And people have the audacity to call such a thing an Axiom."

The boat has now completely captured Kelafelo's interest because the rower seems intent on navigating toward them. He's looking over his shoulder as he powers the vessel closer and closer toward the river-bank. Kelafelo looks at the Anchorite with a question on her lips. The woman continues her lecture.

"Is it any wonder that Umadiland is the poorest and weakest of the Great Tribes? We are so weak we cannot even conquer a tiny tribe of bone charmers with no more than nine mystics to their name."

Kelafelo's head swivels back to the Anchorite. "Bone charmers? Do you speak of the Yerezi?"

"They never have more than nine mystics," the Anchorite says. "Yet we have hundreds. But because they value erudition over expediency, those nine mystics are too powerful even for a whole tribe of warlords. That is the worth of a well-devised Axiom. Nine learned mystics standing against an entire tribe of illiterate fools."

The Anchorite's milky eyes take on a chilling fierceness. "I have gifted you with knowledge that has accelerated your learning, but do not mistake my intentions. All I have done is give you the bricks and mortar. *You* will design and build the edifice. You will sweat over it, bleed, cry. You will be broken. Even if it takes you ten comets, you will derive an Axiom worthy of the name, or you will die trying. Is that clear?"

A tremor runs through Kelafelo, and her throat bobs. "Yes, Mamakuru."

By now the boat is close enough for her to clearly make out the faces of those onboard. Her eyes lock on the robed man, whose bald pate glistens with sweat in the suns. As soon as he comes within earshot, he puts on an oily smile and addresses the Anchorite. "Greetings, great healer. We have brought your parcel, as you requested."

From the array of golden rings poking out of his ears and the many bones attached to his necklace, Kelafelo guesses he's a merchant from somewhere along the World's Artery.

"Bring her to me," the Anchorite says, and the merchant makes a motion to his rower. Kelafelo watches anxiously as the khanga-wearing rower beaches the front of the boat on the riverbank, rises to his feet, and picks up the girl in the turquoise veil. She lets herself be handled like a docile lamb.

Once on dry land the rower places the girl in front of the Anchorite and presents her with a flourish.

Her eyes are crimson. They gravitate to the ground, and she fidgets with her hands in palpable fear. Kelafelo is struck by just how young she is, not more than six.

The Anchorite steps forward and grasps the girl's shoulder, turning her around slowly so she can inspect her as one would inspect livestock on sale. The eyes, the obsidian complexion, the slight bulge in her veil, like it's hiding a pair of curling horns—all confirming what Kelafelo already suspects: that the girl is Faraswa. The idea that the Anchorite has purchased her makes Kelafelo more than a little sick. In Umadiland and beyond, the word *Faraswa* is practically interchangeable with *slave*.

The Anchorite steps back and gives her verdict. "She is older than what I requested."

Still on the boat, the merchant—a slaver, apparently—spreads his hands and gives a vulpine smile. "Supply is limited, great healer. I did the best I could given the time frame."

The Anchorite regards the girl once more and purses her lips. "Not ideal, but I suppose she'll have to do."

"I'm glad to hear that," the slaver says with a flash of teeth, the avarice behind them obvious. "I assume you have the payment we discussed?"

From the folds of her hide kaross, the Anchorite produces a vial of cloudy liquid and hands it to the rower. "Any woman who drinks a thimbleful of this will conceive multiple offspring for the rest of her life."

The slaver eyes the vial with undisguised hunger as the rower walks back toward him. When it is finally in his hands, he holds it up to the suns briefly before it disappears into his robe. He smiles again. "Thank you for your business, great healer. This will be most helpful. Call on me again should you need my services."

The two men row away, leaving the young Faraswa girl alone with two strangers. Dread raises the hairs on Kelafelo's nape. "Mamakuru, what is going on? Who is this girl?"

The old woman turns around and begins to shuffle back toward the hut. "Name her whatever you wish. You will care for her. Bathe her, feed her. You will be affectionate toward her as you would be to your own daughter."

Kelafelo had started to follow the Anchorite, but at the mention of her daughter, she stops dead. "*What?* Why? That child is not my daughter, and I will *never*—"

She silences herself when the Anchorite spins around with surprising nimbleness, leveling a warning finger at her chest. "You will do as you are told, girl, and you will not question me. Are we clear?"

She wants to strangle the old woman, but she fights the urge by reminding herself why she is here. After a few deep breaths through flared nostrils, she gives in.

"As you wish, Mamakuru." She looks back toward the riverbank, where the Faraswa girl is still waiting with her eyes downcast. A wave of disgust washes over Kelafelo, but she hides it behind gentle words. "Come, young one. Let's go home."

And the girl follows.

13: Musalodi

Heaven's Intermission, or the last twenty-one minutes of the day—a day being twenty-four hours and twenty-one minutes long—is supposedly a time when the heavens lean closer to the world to oversee the death of an old day and the birth of a new one. It is during this time that an aspiring mystic must appeal to their chosen patron in the skies and hope that they are found worthy.

As midnight approaches, Salo makes his way down to the small jetty by the lake, figuring that if he borrows one of the boats moored there and rows himself to the clan's sacred island, he'll avoid any potentially acrimonious encounters with angry clanspeople. He doesn't need to take a lamp. The moon is full overhead, and the spirals of the Devil's Eye constellation have come out to play, hanging over the south like a distant whirlpool of luminous milk.

As he approaches the lake, he sees that someone is already there, a broad-shouldered figure sitting at the end of the jetty with his legs dangling over the edge, staring at the waters in pensive silence. Several boats are moored on either side of him, large, narrow shapes floating quietly in the gloom. He has no armor tonight, no necklaces or furs, just his crimson loincloth.

He must sense Salo's presence but doesn't look over his shoulder.

Salo hesitates and stops, frozen by a terrifying thought.

What if he hates me now?

Niko was not among the rangers who tossed the reed at him earlier tonight, but are they still friends? It's entirely possible that when he turns his face to look at Salo, those kind brown eyes of his will instead be filled with rage and contempt.

Salo realizes right then just how much this would kill him. It would kill him more completely than the crushing void he felt when his brothers disowned him. He would not survive.

"You're here," he says, treading forward with the caution of a condemned man to the executioner.

Niko still doesn't turn away from the lake. "It's a good place to think," he says. Then: "Is it time already?"

"Almost."

His shoulders rise as he draws in a deep breath. "You're really doing this, huh?"

"I guess," Salo says after a pause.

"Think you'll make it?"

"I hope so."

"You sound calm."

"Honestly, there hasn't been enough time for me to worry."

"I guess not." Finally Niko gets up, dusting himself off. "Come on, then. I'll row you there."

A wave of relief washes over Salo. It is short lived. Niko won't meet his eyes when he undoes the moorings attached to one of the boats or when they sit facing each other and he begins to row toward the island in strong, regular motions. The silence thickens and stretches in the space between them, until Salo begins to feel that Niko is pulling further away from him by the second.

"My brothers threw the reed at me," he says.

Niko keeps his eyes on the floor separating their feet. "I know."

"I noticed you weren't there."

He pulls hard on the oars, and they creak in their oarlocks. He still won't look at Salo. "It was stupid, what they did. I get why they're angry, I really do, but they didn't have to take it that far."

Salo doesn't miss the emphasis on how much he gets their anger. "Are you angry with me?"

"I don't know what I feel."

"What do you want to feel?"

"Not confused."

"About whether to be angry with me?"

"About everything, Salo! About you. You confuse me. A lot. I know you can't help it, but sometimes I wish you were just . . . normal. Life would be easier for everyone."

He looks away, and they say nothing more after that, the air between them much too charged for words.

I'm not normal, Salo thinks. *Have I always been like this, or was there a point where I went from normal to not normal?*

Eventually they arrive at the island on its west-facing bank. Salo holds his sandals as he carefully steps out into the shallows, where the cold water bites into his legs.

"Thanks for rowing me," he says, and Niko acknowledges his gratitude with a simple nod. He's gone back to not looking at him.

"I assume you have to go back," Salo says, peering at the lakefront from whence they came. A procession of rowboats and oil lamps is already gliding toward them.

"There'll be others who don't have boats," Niko says. "You'll be fine here, right?"

"I think so."

For a moment Niko looks like he wants to say something. But then he starts turning the boat around with his oars. "Good luck," he says. "Stand strong and fearless."

Strong and fearless are the last things Salo will be today, or any other day for that matter, but he thanks Niko anyway and wades to shore, holding his sandals in one hand.

◆　◆　◆

The altar at the island's center is a raised slab of granite whose sides are engraved with esoteric figures that glow a furious red, as if an inferno of moonfire were raging within the rock's interior.

Memories of the last time he was here inundate Salo's mind as he approaches it: his ama, a striking woman in scarlet and copper, plunging a witchwood knife into a hapless ewe over the altar as the New Year's Comet burned like a blue streak of fire across the heavens. He didn't know it back then, but people were terrified of her.

She was secretive. Her smiles were cold, enigmatic. She was frosty with most people, though she lavished him with uncritical affection. He wonders what she would think seeing him here now, about to face his awakening.

Remember.

A cold shiver makes him turn from the altar and sit on a patch of grass while he waits for everyone else to arrive.

The boats form a floating crescent in the shallows around the island's western bank. None of the clanspeople come ashore—as with all awakenings, they will watch from their boats. About sixty or more boats are present by the time a string of darkness shoots up from the kraal on the plateau in the distance. *Ravens.*

Everyone watches them cut across the starlit skies at great speed, only to descend upon the island and swirl down in front of the altar. Salo rises to his feet as the queen emerges from the black maelstrom like a ghostly puzzle coming together, feathers becoming flesh and copper, honor guards flanking her.

With four disciplines of Red magic at her command and a well of power as boundless as the skies, the queen is the most fearsome mystic any Yerezi will ever encounter and the only metamorph in the Plains. Witnessing her sorcery with one's own eyes is something of a privilege.

Her discerning gaze quickly finds Salo standing nearby. He bows to her in deference. "Irediti Ariishe."

"It is the full moon tonight," she says. "An auspicious time to awaken. There can be no turning back once we begin."

He briefly wonders if she's actually giving him a way out, and if so, if it wouldn't be wise to take her up on her offer. These thoughts must be playing out on his face, because the brawny Ajaha on her left curls a lip in muted disgust. The Asazi's expression remains impenetrable.

"I am ready, Your Majesty." He'd never redeem himself if he gave up now.

"Then come closer and face your clanspeople. One way or another, tonight you will make history."

He stands with the queen and her honor guards, the four facing the clan with their backs to the altar. His stomach does a flip when he notices the earthen bowl of clear, oily liquid in the Asazi's hand. She catches him staring, and her eyes gleam at him with something unreadable.

Averting his gaze, he lets his eyes roam the sixty-odd rowboats floating in the shallows. He catches VaSiningwe's looming silhouette, back-lit against an oil lamp burning somewhere behind him. And if that's VaSiningwe, then Aba D must be the man in the boat with him. Jio and Sibu aren't with them, though, which they would be if they'd come at all. Nimara probably couldn't leave the bonehouse, and Niko might not have returned after their exchange on the boat.

Salo is annoyed with himself when his eyes begin to sting. He slams them shut until the wave of emotions ebbs away.

"Behold Musalodi, your clansman!" The queen juts a finger toward Salo, and all eyes follow it. "He has gazed upon Ama Vaziishe and coveted her embrace, and against all tradition, he has asked us to let him reach for it. There are good reasons, Yerezi-kin, to condemn him for this aberration. After all, our people have thrived for centuries by knowing their allotted places in society, and it would seem that Musalodi does not know his.

"But what, Yerezi-kin, are convictions, if not blind dogma, unless they are tested against fact? We know as a matter of course that no men are suited to serve as Ama's intercessors, that they are not nurturing enough, that they are too prone to tyranny to wield her power, but how much of this knowledge is preconception, and how much of it is based on objective observations of our world?"

The queen scans her audience, perhaps waiting for someone to answer her questions. No one does.

"Some of you might point me to the Umadi warlords and the Dulama god-kings and say, *Here is objective evidence for the unsuitability of mankind,* but how can we be certain that their manhood is the true problem? Could their tyranny not simply be a by-product of their flawed but extrinsic understandings of Ama's will? Would that not explain why so many women sorcerers throughout the Redlands turn to tyranny as well? How do we know that a man raised in Yerezi tradition, who has seen firsthand the warmth and benevolence of Ama at work—how do we know that such a man would not be different, as his Foremothers were different from their tyrannical sisters?

"Musalodi poses all these questions, Yerezi-kin," the queen continues, "and I believe that we must answer them sooner rather than later, lest they fester in our minds and destroy the fabric of our society. Let his success or failure be the test of our convictions; let us know that we believe what we believe because it is true, not because we want it to be true—starting now."

She motions to her Asazi honor guard, who nods and makes for the altar with her earthen bowl. Salo is pretty certain the liquid inside is an alchemical solution of false fire. While the queen continues her speech, the Asazi begins to sprinkle the altar with the liquid.

"For every Red mystic," the queen says, "the path to Ama Vaziishe begins with a simple question: Can your mind prevail over agony? The answer will determine whether you are worthy to continue, or whether your journey must end before it has begun."

The altar dramatically increases in brightness as it erupts into a blaze of crimson false fire, illuminating all the faces watching from the boats with a red glow. Salo has known what was coming all along, and he's tried to harden himself, but now he finds his limbs so crippled by fear he can barely breathe.

The queen turns to face him and infuses an unforgiving bite into her voice. "I assume you are satisfied with your Axiom and that it is an original work of your mind. If not, this is your last chance to say so."

Unconsciously he rubs the red steel serpent clinging to his left wrist. "I am satisfied, Your Majesty."

"Then the time has come for you to call down your redhawk." She gestures at the altar. "Place your arms into the fire and prove yourself worthy before your clan and before Ama herself."

Salo might have asked to call the whole thing off were it not for the queen. His fear of her is the only thing that gets him moving toward the burning altar.

False fire is an ingenious blend of Earth, Mirror, and Blood craft—alchemy, illusion, and sensory manipulation—and now the altar has become a shadowy outline wreathed in its red flames. A forbidding wall of heat presses against Salo as he approaches.

A mirage, he tells himself. *A hollow imitation of the real thing. Can't hurt you. Just do it.*

So he forces himself to stop thinking. With a shout he steps up to the altar and thrusts his arms *into* the inferno.

◆ ◆ ◆

An old tome of magical theory Salo once read claimed that the deepest truths of the world can often be glimpsed at the height of agony.

But in the first few excruciating heartbeats after he touches the fire, heartbeats that each seem to stretch to infinity, Salo gleans no truths from his agony but that of his own stupidity and imminent death, for there is no possible way he can survive such consuming heat.

His shout rises several octaves into a full-blown scream. The stench of burning meat fills the air around him, his vision clouds over, and the sum total of his existence condenses down to a sensation of pure, unadulterated torment.

By some miracle, however, he finds a fragment of sobriety floating somewhere in the deepest recesses of his mind, a place conditioned through years of gambling with a mental artifact. With every ounce of willpower he can summon, he gathers all his thoughts onto this fragment, clinging to it like a drowning victim to a piece of driftwood.

The world is immeasurably old, he tells himself. *Larger than I can ever imagine. What is my pain to such a world? What is my agony when it isn't even real? I am insignificant, and so is my pain.*

And yet he can *see* his flesh sizzling and smoking, and every part of him wants to pull out before the fire consumes him.

His whole body trembles. Tears pour down his face. Bone appears beneath the ruins of his burnt flesh, and still he keeps his arms in the flames. He's about to reach the absolute limit of what he can take when something *stirs* in his blood. Then a slow explosion of ecstasy spreads from his core to the rest of his body, joining the pain to overload his senses.

He instantly knows in a way he could not have known before, he *knows*, that this risen thing, this intangible spark, is what gives mystics the ability to draw power from the heavens and unleash it upon the world as magic. The spark was dormant in his blood, but now that he has come face-to-face with it, now that his agony has pierced the veil of his ignorance, it has *awakened.*

Salo feels the altar, though he does not know how—he feels it reaching up into the heavens and announcing his presence, his awoken power, and he feels something responding to this call, something that catches fire as it begins to descend . . .

The pain abates while the euphoric sensation spreads to his extremities. He gasps like a newborn taking its first breath.

"You may retract your arms from the flames, Musalodi," the queen says behind him, and Salo slowly obeys, inspecting his hands with speechless wonder. They are tingly and cold to the touch but otherwise unharmed.

The island stews in crushing silence, save for the waves breaking on the rocky shore. As he rejoins the queen to face his clan, she gives him the barest nod of approval, just the slightest incline of her head that, from someone like her, might as well be glowing praise. An unfamiliar wave of pride makes him stand taller before his clanspeople.

"A young redhawk learns to fly when its mother casts it into a ravine or over a precipice," the queen shouts, "where, faced with impending doom, it must quickly come to terms with its true nature or perish. And many do perish. Those who fail to challenge themselves are dashed upon the rocks and forgotten, their carcasses left for maggots and scavengers."

She raises a finger and smiles. "But those who succeed, Yerezi-kin, those become undisputed rulers of the skies, ferocious and fearsome, because they have met death and survived. It is said that the great Empire of Light, those sun worshippers beyond the endless seas of the Dapiaro, have buildings and machines that can defy gravity, but not even they can soar as high as the redhawk. Not even they can reach the heights it surpasses as easily as it breathes.

"And so it is with those who claim kinship with Ama Vaziishe. Greatness awaits in the folds of her embrace, but the path there is treacherous. Musalodi, your clansman, must now be judged by the redhawk. If he has been honest in his work, he will receive his cosmic shards. If he has not, then he shall die, as many others have died before him. But none of you here shall pity him, for he has made his choice freely. Ajaha, into positions. Everyone else, remain still and silent. You will not move without my permission."

The armed Ajaha who are present start wading to shore with their heavy shields and shiny spears in hand, faces grim, red steel secure and shimmery. It's Salo's first visual reminder of what's coming, and he knows that if the Ajaha end up having to use those weapons, he'll already be dead.

"A word of caution," the queen says for his ears alone. "Run, and you shall surely die; but look death in the eye, and you might just live to see another day. Now wade into the water, and keep going until I tell you to stop."

They say he's a coward, and he thinks they might be right, but he knows he's no fool. He knows that the queen speaks the truth: to run now would be suicide.

So he does as he's told, and the cold water is up to his knees when the queen finally commands him to stop. Then the longest wait of his life begins.

When the redhawk first appears on the horizon, it is little more than a brilliant point of light, a falling star advancing from the east.

Then the star becomes a streak of red fire and smoke descending with a terrible rumbling that grows and grows until Salo can barely hear the gasps and cries of shock behind him. The approaching entity soon resolves into a definite shape shrouded in a red glow and lowers itself to almost skim the surface of the Nyasiningwe, parting the waters beneath it in a turbulent wake.

The first thing he makes out as it draws nearer is a wingspan as broad as a house. Then a maliciously hooked bill and a crest tapering into a horn. And then the redhawk arrests its flight with a mighty flap of its four wings and is suddenly *there*.

But what is it, this extraordinary beast? The malaika of rage, perhaps, come down on his chariot of fire and smoke? Or maybe a wrathful spirit of pure evil sent by Arante herself?

Looking up at the redhawk, Salo finds it almost impossible to believe that the beast isn't some such metaphysical being, even though he knows that it is actually just a species of astrobird—one of those inexplicable creatures with plumage that can burn so fiercely they can propel themselves in and out of the world's atmosphere. They live in the clusters of floating rock in low orbit around the world, in the deep black void beyond the skies, and come down in dazzling balls of fire to breed or to pillage livestock and inattentive cowherds. The terrible boom of their hypersonic flight is often a warning to seek shelter, or, for those not wise enough to do so, a portent of a grisly end.

In the silence just after the redhawk lands in the water in front of him, Salo envisions his clan watching as the bird devours him. He imagines the horrified looks on their faces—or maybe they'd just cluck their tongues and say, *Most unfortunate, but he did ask for it.*

In the silence and stillness when he first looks death in the eyes, these thoughts are what keep his feet rooted in the water when his instincts are begging him to run.

The beast before him stands at nine feet tall, peering down its beak with the pride of an emperor, as if the whole world is its domain. Upon closer inspection, much of its body is metallic, even its feathers, which aren't feathers at all but scaly red plates burning with an inner fire. They give its four wings a nefarious serrated look about them, as if the bird could cut through the toughest bone with a well-placed swipe.

It probably could.

Salo kneels down before the beast, shivering as the water rises up to his waist. Its pupils are red points of light in whirlpools of darkness. Their inhuman gaze enthralls him, because if death has a pair of eyes, then surely they must look like this—*deathful* eyes, shining with startling intelligence.

The redhawk cocks its head curiously, then takes a step toward him on equally deathful black talons, creating ripples in the water that make him shiver as they lap against him. Another step, and then another, until its massive hooked bill is so close it could probably take Salo's head off in one motion.

Total silence. Unnatural stillness.

The redhawk bends its long neck and lowers its head. Salo feels heat as its scales brush against the side of his face, but strangely, the heat doesn't burn him. Stranger still is the powerful wave of calm that pervades him. He closes his eyes and waits for his cosmic shards to appear on his arms.

But an intruding presence uncoils from some corner of his mind like a serpent lunging to strike. He could not have known that he harbored such a thing inside him; now it pours out of him and into the redhawk. Salo feels the bird's mounting confusion and then anger, and then it raises its head and belches out a horrible screech right into his face.

Smothered cries come from somewhere behind him, but Salo ignores them—rather, his whole body has grown so rigid he can't even breathe, let alone flinch. All the calm he felt before recedes, and warmth spreads down his groin. They stare at each other, beast and man—or beast and coward, because a man certainly wouldn't piss himself so quickly.

The redhawk shrieks like Salo has personally offended it. The next thing he knows, it's raising a talon out of the water. He falls back with a cry, but not fast enough to escape the pain.

Drowning, thrashing pain. Salo's chest is transfixed upon three long claws and pinned down to the lake bed. The cold water rushes into his mouth and nostrils. The pain is infinite.

Commotion erupts behind him. Cries. Shouts. Screeches from the angry god impaling his chest. None of it changes the fact that he's *dying*.

How peculiar, then, that while he chokes on the bloodied water around him, he still has the presence of mind to wonder what he could have done differently during his short life. Maybe he could have tried harder to be more like Niko instead of just giving up. Maybe he should have never opened his ama's journal all those years ago. Maybe he should have . . .

Maybe he could have . . .

Oh, but what does it matter now? The time for maybes is over. The world around him blackens, and that's the end of it.

Except for a glade somewhere in the middle of a grove, where the sky is a lavender canvas spattered with many suns and ringed moons. Salo opens his eyes to find that he is standing barefoot in the glade on crimson earth, hemmed in by old gnarled trees with darkly luxuriant foliage. Their branches droop with their own weight; their thick roots twist into the ground in strangely familiar patterns.

Recognition strikes him like a ray of light. As sure as fate, this place is the realm of the Carving. And yet . . . something is different. A dreamlike essence always colored the Carving's woods, an amorphous not-quite-there-ness he couldn't put his finger on. But these trees, this here and now, it feels all too real.

There is great power here, something tells him, though what, he cannot say. He only knows that this is the same intrusion he felt earlier, and when he quests after it with his thoughts, searching the trees, whatever it is retreats deeper into the shadows.

How long I have waited, it says from the darkness, its voice like the hiss of a biting wind. *How long I have hoped. And now, to finally be here . . . I shall not squander this chance. This time, things will be different.*

"Who are you?" Salo says to the trees, but he thinks he knows. That voice is unmistakable. Cold and cavernous and unfathomably distant. He has heard it before. "Please, tell me who you are."

The thing ignores him, flowing like smoke in the shadows around the glade. He tries to track its motion, but it continues to elude him. Then he looks down at himself. He has three bloody punctures on his chest, but when he touches them, he feels no pain. Still, his trembling fingers come away stained crimson. "Am I dead?" he wonders aloud.

Look up, the thing says. *Behind you.*

Startled, he turns around, and there, descending from above the glade, is a great sphere of red fire. Unexpectedly it flares with a brilliance so glaring he has to raise an arm to shield his eyes. As the light washes over his face, he thinks he glimpses a thousand sunsets all at once, a panorama of fiery red suns sinking over myriad horizons.

Something whispers into his ear that this burning globe is the fire at the heart of the moon, the source of all Red magic, and that it is actually a star—no, *thousands* of stars scattered across the deep black.

But how can this be? What does it mean?

So much has been lost. So much forgotten. You must remember.

Salo turns sharply around to face the thing that spoke. He could swear the voice came from just behind him, that he felt the breath on his nape. There is nothing there now. His bones tingle with awe and wonder and sheer terror. "What do you mean?" he demands of the trees. "What is this place? What's happening?"

Look again.

He turns around once more and comes face-to-face with a great cube of pure crystal rotating in the air on multiple axes. The sphere of fire hangs above it like a crown jewel, infusing its crystal interior with an ethereal red light.

Years ago, when he could finally understand the writings in his dead mother's journal, he realized that what he was looking at was the framework for an Axiom so extraordinary it warranted its own name: the

Elusive Cube. The writings described radical arcane theories and ingenious methods of cipher manipulation and prose construction—all the tools an inventive reader might need to carve their way to this Axiom.

And now it is spinning in front of him. The Elusive Cube, supposedly the ultimate Axiom, the *impossible* Axiom, capable of accessing *all six* disciplines of Red magic, unparalleled in efficiency. *This* is the culmination of years of work, the thing his mother died for, the thing for which she betrayed him.

He can feel each of its six sides vibrating strongly with a different arcane energy. One side burns with red flames: *Fire craft*. Another side churns with winds, frost, and lightning: *Storm craft*. Yet another glitters with illusions and light bending: *Mirror craft*. A fourth side is the color of flesh: *Blood craft*. A fifth side has thick roots spreading across its surface: *Earth craft*.

As for the sixth side . . . a vortex of malleable force. Space and time warping around it, threatening to suck him in and crush him with its many secrets. *Void craft*.

For a long time Salo watches the Axiom, appreciating how terrifying and undeniably powerful it is. Some people would kill to wield such a thing, but he starts to wonder if this is all there is to his mother's obsession.

Is this enough to turn a loving mother against her own son?

He thought he'd found the answer to the mystery of her betrayal, but now, looking at the Cube, he realizes that his search never ended. Surely there has to be more to the story.

"Why am I here?" he says.

You must remember. Wisps of blue smoke drift within the trees, following the voice. *Gaze upon the source and know the fires that warmed your ancestors. Sink your feet into the earth and know the soils that hold their bones. Remember.*

"What are you?" he asks the moving smoke, and then more reverently, "Are you a malaika? A servant of the heavens?"

The trees rumble in displeasure. *I have been called many things—I have been many things to many peoples—but never a servant.*

Salo turns around, following the voice. "Then what are you? What am I *doing* here?"

You are here to begin.

"To begin what?"

To remember. Pledge yourself to this source, and your eyes shall be opened.

"But how do I—"

The answer slips into his head, and in an instant he knows. He feels himself going down on his knees in the glade and turning his face up to the burning sphere above the Cube, the source that will grant him its power, and his lips seem to speak on their own. "I pledge myself to these fires, which warmed the faces of my forgotten ancestors." He grabs a fistful of the red earth underfoot. "I pledge myself to these soils, which hold their bones. I pledge myself to . . ."

The words that he knew not a moment ago slip away from him like water sluicing off the blade of an oar, leaving nothing but the trace of an incipient migraine. He winces, grasping for the words with his mind, but they vanish into oblivion.

That will have to do, the apparition says. *For now. The pledge cannot be spoken in full. Not yet. Not here. Not until you remember.*

Salo doesn't know what any of that means, but something is different. Somehow, he now feels *connected* to everything in this forest—the soil, the trees, the source, the Cube. Strangely, though, he senses that the connection isn't nearly as deep as it could be. A substantial blockage is in the way, like a film covering his eyes so that he views the world only in blurry detail. Pain lances through him when he tries to focus on the blockage, so he lets it be.

Then his arms change. He watches as they acquire elaborate networks of metallic lines that meander from his elbows to the tips of his fingers, throbbing red with power from the source—his cosmic shards.

Halfway along either forearm is a single ring, conspicuous in that it encircles the arm and is thicker than all the other lines. He will have to acquire more of those rings to become more powerful, through meditation, spellwork, and lunar rituals. But he feels that his shards are exquisite all the same, that having them is like seeing more colors than he knew existed, like tasting things no ordinary tongue can taste.

To his side, the apparition finally steps out of the trees, once again wearing a loincloth of hide and wielding an embellished spear of blue metal—a bright cobalt blue similar to the hue of his skin. For all Salo knows, this strangely beautiful specter might have once been a warrior chief. His angular face is a living sculpture hewed from the finest lapis lazuli. His eyes catch the light like sapphires one moment, then clear diamonds the next, changing as if on a whim. They bear an aspect of timelessness, and when they lock on Salo, he feels he is staring into the face of a god.

He has never seen those eyes quite so clearly, but he has definitely seen them before.

"You," he breathes, staying where he's kneeling on the ground. "You were in the Carving."

Something hidden gleams in the apparition's gemlike eyes. Somehow he speaks without moving his mouth, and Salo nearly shudders at the sound of his voice, so clear and yet so distant and cold. *A part of me was. Just a small part, but enough.*

A troubling thought occurs to Salo. "Did you . . . did you *possess* me?"

I needed you to bring me here.

"But why?"

I cannot tell you that here. You must find me elsewhere. You must remember, and then you must find me.

Movement in the trees catches Salo's eye. When he looks, he sees a pall of black smoke drifting into the clearing, growing thicker by the second. Gripped by urgency, he looks back up at the apparition, this entity whose presence feels as old as the stars. "What am I to do, great one? What do you want from me?"

Our time here is at an end, the apparition says. *Find me elsewhere. Remember.*

"But *where* should I find you?"

The smoke has engulfed much of the glade, though the apparition's arresting eyes still shine at him with unnatural brilliance. *Somewhere along a scarlet road, past a gateway beneath a red star. It shines far beyond your horizons. Your path there has been set; now you must walk it.*

Salo tries to speak, to tell the apparition that none of this makes sense, but the smoke swallows his words before they leave his mouth. The glade is already becoming a distant memory. His dwindling awareness coalesces around the apparition's voice.

Time is not on our side. You must walk the path your mother would have walked. She was to be my last chance; now, my hope is with you. Find me. Remember.

And all becomes dark.

PART 3

THE ENCHANTRESS

*

ISA

*

MUSALODI

Storm craft—magic of the elements

Channeling the moon's essence into artificially inducing weather phenomena, such as winds, frost, and lightning. Used by rainmakers to irrigate fields.

—excerpt from Kelafelo's notes

"Ah, daylight. Beautiful, isn't it?"

"It is, Aago."

"Even so, it is a lie."

"A lie? But how can it be a lie?"

"Because now the stars are hidden from you, an illusion that might tempt you to think you're bigger and more important than you really are. The stars put things into perspective."

14: The Enchantress

The Enchantress is entertaining a textile merchant in her parlor when the crimson jewel on her necklace vibrates. Casually, she rests a hand on the jewel. *I'll be there in a moment,* she thinks to it, and the vibrations still.

She goes on to take a sip of shaah from a porcelain cup, all the while watching her guest from above the teacup's rim. He's perusing the squares of different fabrics laid out on the table sitting between them. The look in his eye is the kind a starving man might inflict on a roasted sirloin steak he suspects might be poisoned.

The Enchantress smirks inwardly and takes another sip of her spiced tea. The merchant, a member of the Yontai's jackal clan—one of the kingdom's eleven clans of KiYonte-speaking people—is an insider in his headman's court. She lured him here on the pretext of discussing possible cooperation in a new business venture; judging from the wariness with which he examines the cloths in front of him, he's likely realized that there's considerably more at stake than money.

Finally he lifts his gaze off the table and slowly shakes his head. "I have been in the textile industry for three decades, but I have never seen anything like this."

He caresses one of the sample fabrics, a square of pearlescent silk with subtle fractal patterns that move and pulse with light. Each of the samples in front of him, in a range of different textiles, has its own design of moving patterns—spinning flowers and geometric shapes, birds in flight and animals on the hunt. No such cloths have ever been seen on this side of the Jalama. Not until now.

"Truly, it's like they're woven of light," the merchant breathes, but then he retracts his hand from the table with an astute look in his eye. "Forgive me, Your Highness. I struggle to believe you'll simply hand me the blueprints for the looms. Surely you'll want something in return."

The Enchantress waves his concern away. "I'm only indulging my curiosity, nothing more. I adore your textiles, you see—the patterns, the textures. I'm excited to see what you'll do with this technology." She has mastered the art of speaking the local language like a woman from a northern tribe, so her accent is appropriately guttural.

"But why choose me?" the merchant says. "I'm not the biggest player in this industry. I only sell locally. My biggest competitors, on the other hand, export to all the Redlands. Why not go to them?"

She is not surprised that he should ask her this. He's a smart man and an even smarter merchant, and men like that see everything in the binary of give-and-take; one without the other is either a fraudulent scheme or, worse, charity. "Your biggest competitor is Saire owned, is it not?"

The merchant grunts. "The elephants own all the banks, so it's easy for them to raise capital. But they're not as generous to everyone else. Doesn't make it easy to compete with them."

"No, it does not." The Enchantress gently sets her teacup on the table. "But don't you think it's time that changed? In fact, I suspect the winds of change are already stirring, and who knows: perhaps an intelligent man like yourself could stand to gain if he positioned himself correctly."

By his smile and the sharpness that briefly flashes across his eyes, the merchant reads the subtext loud and clear. "I'd welcome such a change with open arms, Your Highness, but I'm a practical man, and as any practical man would tell you, not even the strongest winds can move mountains." *The ruling clan is well protected, and so long as that protection remains, nothing anyone does will make a difference.*

"You'd be surprised," the Enchantress says, making sure to meet the merchant's eyes. *Do my bidding, and you won't have to worry.* "But we digress." Breaking eye contact, she picks up her shaah and sips. "I'd like to get this technology out there, and I think your firm would be a great place to start. Of course, it would require a significant investment on your part, at least at first. I know how costly it can be to procure enchanting services from the House of Axles, and the charms these looms will require are especially complex. But with some guts and perseverance"—the Enchantress smiles—"I think this could be quite lucrative for you in the long run." And then she lets her smile falter slightly for effect. "However, if you feel you're not up for the challenge . . ."

"Nonsense." The textile merchant sits up straighter, and the look in his eye says, *I will do anything you want.* "No one is more up for it than I, Your Highness."

"Then it's settled. I'll have the blueprints delivered to you and you alone." With that, she rises to her feet. "Now I must beg your pardon. I'd walk you out, but I have an urgent matter to attend to."

He is all smiles as he gets up from his sofa. "It's no worry at all, Your Highness." He bows graciously. "I'll see myself out."

She leaves him in the parlor, feeling satisfied with how the meeting progressed.

He isn't the first merchant she has offered a significant edge over a competitor of the ruling clan; she has offered designs for superior climate control, superior refrigeration, carriages with superior suspension—all in strict secrecy and to well-established merchants who hold sway in the courts of the headmen she seeks to influence. The textile merchant, for example, will now be an indirect but powerful link to the Jackal, whom she knows harbors no love for the elephants.

The groundwork is almost complete, but the merchant was right. I cannot change things if I have mountains standing in my way.

Even if she breaks the ruling clan's hold on the kingdom's economy, it won't matter unless the true source of their power is also pulled from underneath their feet. *And that is why I need help.*

She wanted to do this on her own, to prove to herself and to everyone who's ever underestimated her that she is far from the victim she once was. But her pride cannot blind her from the greater objective. In the end, winning the Great War must supersede every other concern.

The train of her carmine-and-indigo robe sweeps the patterned marble floors as she makes her way through the halls of her palace. Lush interior gardens fill the air with their earthy scent, like stolen pieces of the jungle. She is still amazed that such luxury can exist here, in what should be—at least according to what she thought she knew about the so-called Red Wilds—a squalid cultural vacuum inhabited by a primitive people. Indeed, she has had to renounce her preconceptions in the face of evidence to the contrary. They may not be as advanced in technology as the rest of the world, but this city alone has demonstrated an architectural sophistication and a mastery of pure magic that has at times left her speechless.

The world is right to fear this place, she thinks, *for there is great power here.*

Inside her private chambers the Enchantress reclines on a lounge chair and prods the centerpiece of her golden necklace with her thoughts. The crimson jewel—a synthetic quartz stone saturated to the atom with the moon's essence—thrums in response, and she lets herself relax, closing her eyes.

Instantly, the metaform operating in the crystal's high-speed lattices responds and begins to weave her consciousness into a mental construct that takes shape around her from the ground up, rising like a vivid dream. Soon she finds that the lounge chair has been transported into an open circular pavilion built on the highest peak of the tallest mountain range in the world.

Balls of fire are raining from the twilight skies, thousands upon thousands, each leaving a stream of smoke and flame in its wake. A man stands silhouetted against the skies in the foreground, leaning against one of the pillars encircling the pavilion with his back toward the Enchantress. His is the kind of stillness that suggests he could wait for a thousand years.

A shiver of worry runs through the Enchantress, and she briefly second-guesses herself, but then she remembers her priorities.

I need his support if I'm going to move mountains.

She gets up from the chair and slowly walks to the edge of the pavilion, where the world drops into steep, jagged snow-covered slopes that spread away into the slight curvature of the distant horizon. The sight still leaves her queasy, even though she knows it is only a construct.

"So. You've finally decided to remember me."

In such constructs, where minds can be entangled even across great distances, communication is by thought. But the metaform running the construct can be directed to vocalize this communication. What the Enchantress hears as the man's voice sounds like something that might belong to a cold-blooded monster if it could speak.

The Enchantress reminds herself not to be afraid. "Hello, Prophet. Thank you for agreeing to meet me."

"But how could I not? I was worried when I heard my favorite prodigy had gone missing." Prophet finally looks at her. "Imagine my surprise when I learned you'd snuck off to the world's back end. I'm interested to hear what tale you will spin for me."

While the Enchantress has manifested in the construct as she is, Prophet is a god-king in a white hooded robe over a full suit of gold-plated armor. Atop the hood sits a golden crown, with two horns like those of a young ram curling out on either side. His face is an empty void. The Enchantress knows he's interfacing with a metaformic jewel just like hers wherever he is.

"I couldn't risk telling anyone I was coming here."

"And why not?"

"You would have tried to stop me."

"For good reason, Enchantress. The law is clear: there is to be no contact between the hinterlands and the outside world. If you are caught, I will not be able to protect you from the consequences."

The Enchantress stares at the fires raining ruin upon the world far below. "If the Veil fell today, the world would unite against our Master, and all would be lost. But with your help, I can brew a war that will shake the foundations of the earth and crack the heavens open. That's what I'm doing here."

Prophet chuckles, and it comes out as a bloodcurdling roar. "Ah. So you want my help. I should have known."

"I can't do it on my own."

"But what can you possibly accomplish there? And I'd better like your explanation, or this will be the last time we speak."

"An analogy, if you will."

"Proceed."

"Say there is a contested swath of land that all the great powers of the world have agreed to leave alone."

The Enchantress can almost feel his amusement. "An analogy, you said?"

"Bear with me."

With a magnanimous gesture he permits her to continue.

"Say this land, though exceedingly rich and fertile, is fraught with danger, and the indigenous peoples are . . . problematic. In fact, you might think of this place as a giant hornet's nest no one wants to poke—so long as everyone else stays away. Are you with me so far?"

"Carry on."

"Moreover, everyone knows that breaching the agreement to stay away would trigger a scramble so vicious there would be no victors, only losers. No one wants this, so the treaty holds. Now, if you want to start a war, how do you use this to your advantage?"

"If these were the only pertinent facts, then you would pour your efforts into persuading one of the world powers to break the treaty. The question is how."

The Enchantress feels a modest surge of hope. She has Prophet's attention now. "A good question. Let us suppose, then, that one of these world powers once had an enemy so terrible that the mere mention of its name could get you imprisoned indefinitely. Suppose they vanquished this enemy at immense cost to themselves and upon their victory vowed to do everything in their power to ensure that this enemy would never again rear its head. Do you see where I'm taking this?"

Prophet's monstrous voice is suddenly subdued. "Not exactly, but you are treading on dangerous ground. Explain yourself."

Ah, the mighty Prophet, afraid of a long-dead ghost. The Enchantress continues. "What you do, Prophet, is raise the specter of that vanquished enemy in the hornet's nest. Then you will have your war."

He watches her, stunned, but quickly finds his voice. "You cannot be serious."

The Enchantress gives him the rest of her pitch. "This specter wouldn't be the real thing, of course—it can't be and wouldn't need to be. It would only need to be convincing enough. Let this great power think that their old enemy is resurfacing in the heart of this contested land, and they'll break any treaty to quash them. And once the treaty has been broken, there will be no incentive to hold anyone back. War will break on so many fronts it'll crack the world like an eggshell."

Prophet turns back to the burning skies, his broad armored chest rising and falling in a slow rhythm. "I must admit it sounds . . . feasible in theory, but raising this specter would be no simple matter. And the consequences of failure . . ."

"I will not fail, not with your support. I have already infiltrated the most powerful tribe on the continent and will soon restructure it as I see fit. In my hands it will be a weapon that will deliver us the war we've always wanted."

"There are too many variables in this plan of yours, too many moving parts that may break." Prophet turns to face her, dark emptiness where his eyes should be. "Worse, I worry you will unleash a monster you cannot control. Even as a pale shadow of what it is imitating, in the Red Wilds for that matter, this specter would be tremendously dangerous and unpredictable."

"All the better to serve our ends. Time is not on our side, Prophet. The Veil will fall soon, and this may be the last chance we have to clinch our victory once and for all. Don't you think we need to at least try?"

He thinks for a long time, and the Enchantress holds her breath.

"What would you need in this scenario?"

She keeps her smile to herself. "I need to buy the support of a group of powerful individuals. This means offering them something they don't already have: Higher technology. I need blueprints for metaformic crystals and ciphermetric machines. I need access to your information network. If they are to become a convincing specter, they must look the part."

Predictably, Prophet shakes his head. "The law of zero contact was created specifically to prevent Higher technology from falling into their hands. Now you want to *hand* it to them? *Teach* them how to work it and create it? You're asking for trouble."

"I am trying to start a war. Your apprehension only proves why this will work. The world has always feared the Red Wilds, but from a place of ignorance. Let us give them a better reason to be afraid."

Prophet stares at the Enchantress, calculating. Eventually he looks away and turns his gaze to the fiery skies. "You may leave now, Enchantress. I have heard your case, and I will think on it."

This time she allows herself a brief smile. He won't admit it just yet, but she has won him over to her cause. She looks out to the skies as well, hugging herself. "Please, let me watch for a while longer."

"Isn't it beautiful? I wonder if we will live to see it with our own eyes."

"That is the hope, my dear Prophet."

They stand there together for a while, in the pavilion above the world. Prophet is still watching the skies when she finally leaves.

15: Isa

"Your Highness? Your Highness, are you listening?"

"Yes. Sure. Inviting the Valausi ambassador is an excellent idea."

Only when she hears a snort of laughter coming from her left does Princess Isa Andaiye Saire finally lift her gaze from the book in her lap. Cousin Zenia, lounging on the white velvet couch nearby, won't stop giggling.

"Oh, Isa." Eyes flashing with amusement, Zenia idly caresses the gems on her silver-and-diamond necklace, perfectly at home in the milk-white opulence of the Ivory Drawing Room. The stones contrast beautifully with the clan tattoos rising up her long neck, elegant lines and motifs of the elephant clan. "We moved on from the guest list ten minutes ago," she says.

"Oh." Across the room, Chief Steward Maumo has gotten that pinched look on his wrinkled face, the one that visits him whenever he tries hard not to show just how annoyed he is. Isa has been getting that look from him quite a lot lately.

A plush rug of white-leopard skin stretches across the floor between their legs, and on top of it sits a glass-paneled table whose clawed feet are pure ivory. Isa closes her book and gently places it on the table. She straightens her skirts of patterned silver brocade and attempts a look of contrition. "I'm sorry," she says. "I'm a bit distracted today. Where were we?"

The chief steward's lips grow thinner. "Your Highness, forgive me for saying so, but you seem disinterested of late. Perhaps event planning isn't stimulating enough for you?"

Her mother would hound her into the underworld if she abandoned yet another princess-worthy responsibility, so Isa lies without a second thought. "Not at all, Chief Steward." *Of course I'm fond of the endless minutiae of planning feasts and celebrations.* "I just became engrossed in this book, that's all. The city's architectural history is simply fascinating. Did you know that the undertown warrens have never been fully mapped?"

"But is that really where your mind was, Isa?" Zenia says from her couch. "In the undercity warrens? Or was it perhaps with a certain Sentinel—" She giggles and covers her mouth with a bejeweled hand when Isa cuts her a freezing glare.

"Chief Steward Maumo," Isa says, turning back to the long-suffering man. "I will look over all your proposals before the end of the day tomorrow. Perhaps we can continue our planning then? I promise I'll be less distracted."

Isa would rather do anything else. The New Year's Feast happens every comet; why can't the guest list and the menu and every other wearisome detail just be the same as it was during the last feast?

With a resigned shake of his head, the chief steward gathers his pens and papers, and his white grand boubou makes a swishing sound as he gets up from his divan. "Very well, Your Highness. Shall we meet in the Turquoise Drawing Room, same time tomorrow?"

Isa peers down at her ivory bangles and silver-encrusted nails. Meeting in any of the Summit's other themed private drawing rooms would require changing her look, which is simply more fuss than she's willing to subject herself to right now. "We'll meet here," she says.

His pursed lips suggest the steward has an opinion on the matter, but he manages to keep his thoughts to himself. "As you wish." He bows. "Your Highnesses." And then he shuffles out the door and into the hallway beyond.

As soon as he disappears, Zenia turns to Isa with a gleeful smile. "So? What does it say?"

Isa pretends not to know what she's talking about. She casually picks up her book from the table and flips through its pages. "What does what say?"

"The mirrorgram you've been staring at all day."

"For your information, I was using it as a bookmark. I *was* actually reading."

"Of course you were." Zenia reaches over and wiggles the fingers of an open hand. "The note, if you please."

Isa sighs and pulls the little white note out of her book. A single line of uniformly printed red script runs across its center. "If you really must know . . ."

"I must." Zenia plucks the mirrorgram from Isa's hand and reads it out loud. "'I am writing to tell you I'll be on palace duty in a week's time.' Signed, Obe." She wrinkles her nose. "A bit dry, isn't it? This is hardly a suitable love note to a princess."

"Not a love note, Zenia. Just a note. Chaste, like our relationship."

Zenia rolls her eyes with a huff, returning the note. "You know you can't fool me, so I'm baffled why you even try."

Isa once again wonders why she took Zenia into her confidence. They might be the same age, at seventeen, and Zenia is probably the most like Isa among the princesses of the rather large extended royal family, but she's a pathological chatterbox. Certain people who were never supposed to know about the secret behind the little white note now know about it, and Isa suspects Zenia is the one to blame.

She considers confronting her, but then a young girl with a white dress and silver threads in her braids rushes into the drawing room, panting like she's been running for some time.

Isa frowns at her in worry. "Suye, what's wrong?"

"Cousin Isa!" Suye says excitedly. She bends over, bracing her hands on her knees as she tries to catch her breath. "You said to announce when your mother was coming."

"And?"

"She's coming!"

Isa curses under her breath.

"Why is that significant?" Zenia asks. Then her eyes slit with suspicion. "And why do you suddenly look like you expect a ninki nanka to rush in through the door?"

If only it were a ninki nanka. Quickly, Isa slips the white note back into the book and closes it. "I've got to go. Come, Suye."

Zenia's confused gaze tracks Isa as she leads Suye toward the wide exit opening out into the White Lily Garden with its gushing marble fountains. "Isa, what's going on? Why the devil are you avoiding your mother?"

Isa turns around. "Because, Zenia, it turns out she knows about *him*. She heard a rumor somehow, and now it's all she'll talk about. I wonder who babbled."

"Oh." At least Zenia has the decency to look abashed. "Go on, then. I'll cover for you."

That's what I thought. Shoving down a spike of annoyance, Isa brushes past the filmy curtains by the threshold and into the lushness of the garden beyond. Suye's laughter trails behind her as they hurry along a stone path through well-kept beds of white lilies glistening with droplets from an earlier cloudburst. The Summit's brightly painted limestone walls and glazed bamboo domes loom largely all around them, pregnant with the history of the thousands who've walked its halls before, reminding Isa, as they always do, that she is but a footnote, an insignificant player, in the story of a dynasty that has endured for centuries.

Faraswa gardeners and patrolling Sentinels in patterned green tunics and aerosteel armor bow to the duo along the way. As they turn onto a marble-columned gallery, Suye races to catch up, her little silver sandals pitter-pattering on the tiled floors. "Cousin Isa, where are we going?"

"Somewhere my mother won't find us."

"Oh. *Oh.*" Suye slows down, hesitating. "Cousin Isa, I don't know . . ."

"It'll be fine." Isa keeps walking determinedly, giving the girl no choice but to follow.

A minute later they sweep up a flight of winding stairs, through a glazed bamboo rotunda, past a pair of silent guards in aerosteel armor and blue tunics patterned with elephant motifs, and then into a grandly appointed study. The four people already inside—the king, his two sons, and his herald—give them only passing glances before returning to their animated conversation.

"Don't mind us," Isa says, even though she knows she'll be ignored. "We're just here to join the furniture."

A set of coal-black couches takes up the center of the oval room, and beyond it a pair of open doors leads out to a balcony with a view fit for a king. A gold-leafed colossus of a young warrior can be seen rising on the far side of the palace's manicured lawns and palm trees, and in the distance, the twin waterfalls gushing beneath the Red Temple appear as turbulent white ribbons. Isa pulls Suye to the couches, almost wincing as the impossible red jewel hovering above the distant temple briefly glares, its facets catching the afternoon sunlight. The Ruby Paragon seems almost like a star where it hangs, caught in an eternal lateral spin between the thin black towers of the temple's Shrouded Pylon.

Suye's wide eyes slowly take in the study and then fix nervously on its four occupants, who are seated around a mahogany table at the front of the room. She isn't a shy girl by any means, but for some reason the king makes her nervous, and the crown prince even more so. Isa suspects a girlhood crush might be the culprit for that last one.

She smiles in amusement and begins to tug idly at Suye's braids while she picks up the threads of the conversation she intruded on. Technically, the king's study is no place for a young princess, but the king has always been permissive with his children, and he's never once complained about Isa coming and going as she pleases. Her mother, on the other hand, never sets foot in here, which makes it the perfect hiding place.

"What about the reports of increasing violence against our clans-people in the crocodile province?" Kali, the crown prince, says. "Some of the things I've heard, the language being used against us—it's out-right genocidal propaganda."

The crown prince, Isa would say, is far too serious for his own good, certainly more serious than any twenty-one-year-old man has any right to be. Unlike the typical Saire prince, Kali served with the King's Sentinels and dresses in the blue tunics of the Saire Royal Guard, with nothing but a single golden chain to indicate his princely rank. Isa misses the much less austere brother she knew growing up.

Prince Ayo—a better-looking if slighter version of the crown prince, possessing all of the ego and none of the humility, in emerald robes as princely as his brother's are plain—leans back in his chair with a smirk. "That's nothing new, though, is it? And I doubt it's restricted to the crocodile province. Every other clan has always hated us, and why wouldn't they? The Saires own all the banks, the entire transport infra-structure, not to mention stakes in practically every mine and grainfield in the kingdom. On top of that, we get to be kings." Ayo shrugs unwor-riedly. "Resentment is inevitable, but it's nothing we can't handle."

Isa rolls her eyes. Trust Ayo to be smug about Saire predominance and absolutely blind to why that might not be such a good thing.

"Your overconfidence concerns me, brother," Kali says to Ayo, then turns to the man across the table. "And it's especially concerning that you're not more worried about this, Great Elephant. Kola Saai is con-scripting every young crocodile into his legion. He's almost doubled his forces just this last comet. How can you not wonder what he's up to?"

King Mweneugo Saire, portly in his middle age, with eyes that can be as soft as they can be unyielding, strokes his thick beard. The many gold and ivory chains of his office seem to add more bulk to his chest, glittering in tandem with the gilded elephant mounted on the wall behind his large chair. "I can wonder and worry until I'm a wrinkled corpse, my son," he says, "but at the end of the day what matters is what I can prove. Can you prove the Crocodile is up to no good?"

"Well, he did just marry that foreign woman," Ayo says. "Dulama, I think, or from somewhere else up north. I heard he had to put her up in his Skytown palace because she found his clanlands too, and I quote, 'rustic.' Isn't that a little strange? A woman who won't live in her own husband's princedom because it's too 'rustic'?"

"Strange, maybe," the king says, "but some people find it hard to part with the comforts of this city. I can't say I see any malice there."

"Neither do I," Kali says, "and all of that is irrelevant in any case." He briefly shoots his brother an irritated look. "I'm talking about the size of the crocodile legion. Specifically, why Kola Saai has doubled it."

The herald, Princess Chioko Saire, a shrewd woman in a matching golden caftan and head wrap whose eyes always seem to twinkle like she knows everyone's secrets, chimes in with her characteristically diplomatic voice. "I suspect he'd remind you that Umadiland kisses the southern edge of his province. To anyone looking, he's only doing what needs to be done to secure his borders. We all know how rapacious those southern warlords can be. More so now than ever."

"I get that," Kali says, "but why so many men?"

"I think you are right to be concerned, Your Highness," the herald says, "but perhaps your focus is a little misplaced."

"How so?"

"It's not so much the expansion of his legion that should catch your eye as the fact that he's done it largely without consulting His Majesty. A clear challenge to the mask-crown's authority. Your larger point remains, however. The headmen need a firmer hand."

Isa smiles. This is why the herald is one of her favorite members of her father's court. Her ability to subtly influence the minds of princes and kings while flattering their egos is matchless.

"Exactly," Kali says. "Kola Saai is a subject prince—*your* subject prince, Great Elephant. He shouldn't get to make these types of moves without your permission. I say you rein him in. Remind him that while he's headman of his clan, you are king of the Yontai."

"Being king is a delicate balancing act," the king says. "The other clans let us rule over them because we respect their internal sovereignty. Every headman has the right to administer his legion as he sees fit. I can order them to march and fight for me if there is a need for it, but I cannot—I *must not*—tell them how to organize themselves. That is not our way."

"That's where you're wrong, Father."

Isa raises her eyebrows, and next to her Suye covers her gaping mouth with a hand, her eyes wide with shock. The king might be an indulgent father, but challenging him so openly is pushing things too far.

"They let us rule because it is our divine right," Kali continues, "and if you keep giving them leeway, they'll abuse it until the mask-crown means nothing."

"I think what His Highness means to say, Great Elephant," the herald interjects, "is that you've been a kind and generous king thus far, and it has served you well. But now it's time to be firm. Kola Saai's ambitions must be curbed before drastic measures need to be taken against him."

"I say you send a high mystic and a contingent of Jasiri to pay him a visit," Ayo suggests. "The Spiral or the Fractal, perhaps. Ooh, maybe even the Arc. I guarantee you'll see him fall back into line very quickly."

This idea is so asinine Isa fails to keep her mouth shut. "Yes, Father. Behaving like a common thug will really get the headmen to respect you. And I'm sure the Shirika will just *love* being used as your personal goons."

Ayo turns in his chair to face her. "That's pretty much what they are, Isa."

"Ayo." The king frowns at his younger son. "You will not speak ill of the divine Shirika, understood?"

Ayo raises his palms. "My sincerest apologies; I recant my statement." He comically addresses the richly tapestried walls of the study as though they might have ears. "The Shirika are holy and infallible, and I repent of my blasphemy." He drops his arms, not looking penitent at all. "In any case, it's obvious what the Crocodile is doing if you think about it."

Isa rolls her eyes again, and Kali smiles without humor. "Then enlighten us, little brother."

"He's clearly preparing for a southward expansion into Umadiland," Ayo says. "I bet he'll raise the issue for discussion at the next Mkutano. He's always had a stiffy for empire."

While the king shakes his head, and the herald masks a chuckle as a cough, the crown prince glares at his younger brother. "Don't be crass."

"And to be honest," Ayo goes on, "I don't think empire is such a terrible idea."

"Now you're being daft," Kali says.

"Am I? The Yontai has never been stronger. If Father took the reins of the ten legions and marched south, we could take all of Umadiland within the month. Not only would that give us control over a vital section of the World's Artery, I'm willing to bet they'd welcome us with open arms for ridding them of their blighted warlords. Imagine the economic possibilities, the new resources to exploit. It makes complete economic sense."

Oh, Ayo, Isa thinks. *Consistently proving yourself to be nothing but a pampered prince eager to expend lives in your quest for power, with no thought for the human cost.*

"The kingdom's fine just the way it is," the crown prince says, and Isa silently thanks the Mother for him. "We don't need an empire. What we need is more cohesion. The headmen need to know who's in charge, and Father needs to take a harder line with them."

"I know one way you could do it." When Ayo looks back at Isa with a sneer, she knows the gist of what he's about to say. "Make the Sentinels serve for ten comets instead of six."

"Perhaps we need not go so far," the herald says. "The logistics alone would be a nightmare."

But this was an indirect barb meant for Isa, so she doesn't shy away from it. "The Sentinels are a barbaric, outmoded tradition that has no place in civilized society." Magically binding your own citizens in obedience to the crown on pain of instant death for six years of their youth? They might as well be slaves.

Ayo scoffs and turns away from her. "Says the bored princess with no functional understanding of the real world. Good thing the kingdom will never be in your hands."

Isa feels her blood run frigid. "And it's just as good it won't ever be in the hands of a covetous spare heir with a massive chip on his shoulder. Must be an awfully cold existence living under the permanent shadow of your betters."

"They go straight for the jugular, don't they?" Kali remarks.

"He started it," Isa points out.

"Children . . . ," the king cautions as Ayo turns around again, this time with his lips twisted in a snarl.

"Why are you even here, Isa? Don't you have dresses or something to try on? Or better yet, a crocodile to consort with?"

Isa's nails bite into her palms. *I am absolutely going to kill Zenia.*

The king abruptly straightens in his chair. "Heh? What's this about consorting with a crocodile?"

Ayo's snarl turns into a cruel smile. "He's a Sentinel, isn't he? Tell them, little sister. What *is* it about the crocodile?"

"That's none of your business," she says.

"Not according to what I've heard."

"And what have you heard?" the king says, his worried eyes darting back and forth between Ayo and Isa.

Ayo turns to his father, looking smug and triumphant. "I've heard we might have bride-price negotiations to prepare for in the near future."

"With a crocodile?" The king and the crown prince both look at Isa like they just found out she's contracted a particularly disgusting, virulent plague. The herald, on the other hand, looks at Isa like she already knew and the knowledge amuses her. Isa squirms in her seat next to Suye and says nothing, suddenly regretting her choice of hideout.

"A Sentinel?" Kali demands. "Who is it? I'd like to have a word with him."

Isa thanks the Mother when a guard in the crisp blue tunic and aerosteel armor pieces of the Saire Royal Guard enters the study and executes a bow. "Great Elephant, His Worship the Arc is here to see you."

"And not a moment too soon." The king sighs. "Go ahead and show him in." Sitting back in his chair like he's weary, he shakes his head. "Perhaps a visit with the Sibyl Underground is long overdue, otherwise I swear by the Mother you children will send me to an early grave. Herald, we will continue this discussion at dinner tonight. As for you, my deeply troublesome progeny"—he wags a finger at Ayo and Isa—"I will want an explanation about this crocodile business."

Kali scowls and folds his arms. "And so will I, quite frankly."

On their way out of the study, Isa gives Ayo the evil eye, which only makes him smirk. "I swear I will get you for this," she whispers to him. "Don't forget I know your secrets too."

"I'm quaking in my boots," he says before walking off with Kali and the herald, leaving Isa in the glazed rotunda with Suye and the silent pair of guards.

She glares at their retreating backs until she sees them stopping to bow to a tall figure walking toward the study with the same guard who announced his arrival. Long, layered crimson robes hang from his lean frame, and a moongold half mask covers the left side of his face, though it isn't enough to dim the brightness of his deep-set eyes.

The high mystics of the Shirika have always frightened Isa with their power, this one in particular. Before he comes close enough that they have to acknowledge him, Isa grabs Suye's hand and drags her out of the rotunda, praying to the moon that they don't run into her mother.

16: Musalodi

In the depths of an insensate slumber, Salo watches as a witchwood blade thrusts repeatedly into soft flesh, coating itself with red, violent slickness and flinging drops of it into the air. The blade thrusts and thrusts, and the blood falls like rain, until he, like the blade, is drenched to the bone. All the while, a feline shadow watches from a corner.

Help me; stop the pain, a voice says.

She was to be my last chance, says another. *Now, my hope is with you. Find me. Remember.*

Nimara wakes him up when she knocks once on his door and enters, bearing yet another wooden tray with gourds of acrid tonics and broths. Salo shifts on the bed, propping his back against a mountain of downy pillows and doing his best to shake off the nightmare. Since he awakened, his dreams have acquired a particularly vicious lucidness, and it's a struggle not to let them eat away at his sanity.

A pungent smell wafts from the tray, and he tries not to grimace. Nimara has been taking good care of him ever since they fished his mangled body out of the lake over a week ago and delivered him to the bonehouse. Despite the excellent care, she's been merciless about keeping him on a strict diet of slop so bitter he's probably gained permanent wrinkles just from frowning at it.

And judging by the smell alone, the slop she's come with now doesn't bode well for his future.

She smirks when she notices his expression. "Yes, you're going to eat every last drop. No negotiations."

"But I said nothing," he complains.

"Your face said everything." She sets the tray on the little table beside his bed and lowers herself onto a chair. She's smiling, though her expression is worn around the edges. "By the way, I bring news. An emissary of the queen will be visiting tomorrow."

The windows in the room are yellow stained glass, so there's always a sunset glow refracting onto the polished floor and the bare drystone walls. Salo thinks it's early afternoon outside, though after several days of mandatory bed rest, time no longer seems to make a difference to him.

"You're worried," he says, studying Nimara's face in the room's gold-filtered light. "Why?"

Her eyes glimmer anxiously at him. "I happen to know that this particular emissary is the one the queen sends to deliver bad news."

"Huh," Salo says. Bad news from the queen. What might it be? *If you succeed,* she said to him on the night of his awakening, *you'll be more useful to the Plains than any clan mystic could ever be.* Now that Salo has had time to think about it, he sees plainly what she was really telling him: *There's a price you'll pay for this, and I will come to collect.*

"I guess I'm about to learn what Her Majesty has in store for me," he says. "Whatever it is, at least I'll be finally getting the devil off this bed."

A sketch pad sits on the bedside table, with strings of cipher prose scribbled all over its front page. He picks it up, along with the pencil on top of it, and tries to continue where he left off, but there's a traitorous tremor now pestering his hands.

"I don't like this," Nimara says, watching him. "Your awakening shouldn't be used to extort favors from you. And you're definitely not ready to leave the bonehouse. You were a lump of blood and guts not a quarter moon ago."

"I look fine, considering, don't you think?" Salo points to his chest, where not even a scratch remains of his encounter with the redhawk. "I feel fine too." At least he *sort of* feels fine, but she doesn't need to know this.

Nimara seems troubled as she regards his chest. "Looks can be deceiving. I mean, I might be a competent healer, but your recovery has been a little *too* miraculous for my liking. There could be complications we haven't detected yet."

"Maybe, but nothing good can come from worrying about things we can't control."

"Easier said than done."

"Have you seen Niko lately?" Salo says, changing the subject. He hasn't seen the ranger once since awakening, though Niko was supposedly here every day when he was still unconscious. Aaku Malusi, on the other hand, visits once a day; Ama Lira, Salo's stepmother, has visited a few times; and VaSiningwe came by just once, though he didn't stay long and spoke barely ten words.

"He's . . . been on patrol duty this whole week," Nimara says, fidgeting with her steel bangles. "I'm sure he'll drop by as soon as he can."

"Right."

"What are you working on?"

Salo looks down at his sketch pad with a self-mocking smile. "Oh, this? Nothing interesting. I'm trying to design my first spell."

A smirk touches her lips, and she peers at the sketch pad. "And how's that working for you?"

"Not well, to be honest. Take a look."

She is warily amused as he places the pencil on his lap and stretches out his hands, palms facing each other. The moon might be far off in the heavens, but he now understands, in a way he couldn't have before, that its reach is boundless; he could be anywhere in the universe, and his shards could still drink from its reservoir.

As his shards come alive on his arms, pulsing with raw essence, he begins to feel a light drizzle on his skin—no, not exactly a drizzle but an echo. No, not quite that either. He's already drawn essence a few times before, but he still can't compare the sensation to anything he's ever experienced.

Like drinking liquid light. Like soaring on an electric cloud or kissing the dawn. This isn't theory anymore, the secret fantasies of a boy who knows things he should not. This is real, powerful.

His shards begin to crackle with red sparks, but he doesn't release the power as it is—that would accomplish nothing beyond a pretty light show. Raw essence is indefinite potential, like a piece of steel yet to be shaped by the smith's hand. It needs an Axiom to harness it as useful energy, and then a spell to direct that energy toward a specific magical goal.

So he commands his shards to harness the essence as Storm craft. Then, using the patterns of the spell he has created and memorized, he releases the magic.

A tiny cloud forms between his palms, air condensing into liquid. Then the cloud compresses into a crystal of ice that grows outward from the center, branching off into increasingly complex arrangements. His Axiom provides the necessary Storm craft so effortlessly he suffers very little mental strain.

Too bad the spell doesn't quite work the way he wants it to.

The yellow window beside his bed shudders ominously. With a sigh he cuts off the flow of power and watches the ice crystal fall onto his quilt, where it melts and disappears. His shards vanish back into his skin.

"This is frustrating," he says. "At this rate it'll be ages before I come up with something that won't explode in my face. I need a spell book."

Only now does he look at Nimara and notice her open-mouthed stare. "What?"

"Nothing," she says. "It's just . . . the spell needs work, sure, but the fact that you're making windows shake with *one* ring . . . how are you doing it? I thought any kind of Storm craft required at least two rings."

He smiles, relaxing into his pillows. "It's what I was telling you the other day. A well-built Axiom will stretch every ounce of essence as far as it can go."

"Huh," Nimara says, a thoughtful look in her eye. "So how does it feel?"

How does it feel to see? is what she's really asking. *To have power coursing through your veins?*

Salo flicks his tongue in the gap between his teeth, the right words eluding him. "It's . . . magical. I don't know how else to describe it. And the strangest thing is, I feel some kind of . . . block on my shards."

"A block?" she repeats, her forehead creasing with concern.

"Right now they only respond to Storm craft, but I know I should be able to do more because of the way my Axiom is built. Something is blocking my access to the other crafts, and I'm not sure what it is."

"I told you your recovery was too miraculous," she says gravely. "This is probably a side effect."

Salo shakes his head. "I don't think so."

"What makes you so sure?"

"Call it a hunch."

"Meditation might help," she says.

"Mm. You know what else would help? If I got my hands on, say, a spell book, maybe that would speed up my recovery."

She smiles like she can see right through him. "I wasn't aware learning spells had curative effects."

"Please, Nimara," he begs. "I need to start building my repertoire, and right now I have nothing that actually works. There aren't any spell books in the kraal; I know because I checked. But I can't be expected to design everything for myself, can I? I'd never get anything done."

She bites her lower lip in thought. Finally her eyes twinkle, and she reaches for the bowl on the tray. "Tell you what—if you eat your lunch without a fuss, I'll ask a friend of mine at the Queen's Kraal and see if she can't send a falcon over with a spell book or two. Storm craft, is it?"

Salo forces himself to smother his resentment and accept the bowl. "Fine. But just so you know—"

"I said no fuss."

He keeps quiet and scoops up broth with a spoon, failing not to grimace as he slips the concoction into his mouth. The taste is so harrowing it almost brings tears to his eyes.

She laughs. "Oh, Salo, you make this too much fun."

"Glad you're enjoying my misery."

"Maybe just a little," she admits. "But as much as I would love to keep watching, you're not my only patient."

"What a pity," Salo quips.

"I'm sure you'll manage." She gets up from her chair and makes to leave, but at the door she pauses, looking sideways at him. "Salo, I probably shouldn't ask, but . . ."

"But?" he prompts her when her voice trails off.

"What happened when you were under? I mean, you were down there for a *long* time. What did you see?"

With his free hand Salo picks absently at a frill on his quilt. The motif of a blue flower repeats all over it, blue like lapis lazuli, like the hard planes of the apparition's face. *Remember.* "It was strange. So strange. In fact, I'm still not sure I didn't hallucinate the whole thing. I met some kind of spirit or being, and it told me to find it somewhere beneath a red star—"

"I'm sorry. Did you say something?"

Salo snaps out of his reverie. Nimara is massaging her temples by the door and squinting her eyes like she's fighting a headache. "You asked me what I saw when I was . . . you know, under," he says, "and I told you I met this old spirit and—are you all right? You look like you're about to swoon."

"Just a headache." Nimara grimaces and pinches the bridge of her nose. "Might be lack of sleep." She shakes her head like she's trying to wake herself. "What were you saying?"

"Uh . . . huh. I was telling you how much I appreciate what you're doing for me. It must be a chore watching over a grown man all day."

Nimara smiles. "Believe it or not, I like fixing broken people as much as you like fixing broken machines. All right, Salo. That bowl better be empty when I come back."

Then she leaves Salo to his bitter slop and to the uncanny feeling, now spreading inside his chest like a cancer, that he might not be alone in the room.

◆ ◆ ◆

The emissary rides into the kraal the next morning on a majestic quagga charger with white stripes over a chestnut coat. Salo is summoned to the council house not long after.

With a sick feeling in his gut, he slings a crimson blanket cloak over his shoulders and makes his way to the chief's compound using slow, measured steps. No need for anyone to know he's still feeling somewhat weak kneed and light headed.

His clanspeople react just as badly as he expects them to. Conversations stop whenever he walks by; eyes swivel and stare. As he reaches the chief's compound, he passes an old clansman walking the other way. Salo smiles at him as harmlessly as he can, but the man's eyes widen, and he takes off his straw hat anyway.

"Good day to you, Aaku," Salo says.

The man clutches his hat for dear life. "Yes, yes, good day, young leopard," he says, clearly not sure if he should bow or run or say something else. In the end, he chooses to keep walking, albeit rather briskly.

A bitter taste develops in Salo's mouth. *You'd think I'd sprouted a pair of horns. Or a beak. Or grown hideous warts all over my face.*

Upon entering the council house, he takes off his sandals and leaves them by the door, then makes his way through the stone archway leading from the antechamber into the main hall.

The walls beyond are lined with tapestries that tell the clan's entire history, and the waxed floors are carpeted in colorful reed mats and grids of light and shadow—patterns formed by sunlight spilling in through the strategically placed slits all around the walls. A network of exposed beams supports the thatched oval dome.

Five people are already waiting for him inside: VaSiningwe, sitting on his big wicker chair; a pipe-smoking Aba Deitari sitting on the chief's right; an Asazi Salo has never seen before on his left; and then, surprisingly, Jio and Sibu, both in full Ajaha regalia.

The presence of the last two makes Salo's skin tingle with a flurry of conflicting emotions. He supposes the two boys are here in their capacities as the chief's only eligible heirs. Ama knows he could never be chief now—not that he's ever wanted to be.

They all fall silent when they notice him. He greets them politely and sits on the wicker chair between Jio and Sibu, completing a circle of six.

Sibu gives him a little curl of the lips. Jio won't look at him.

Aba D pulls his pipe out of his mouth long enough to say, "It is good to see you up and about, Musalodi. Ama be praised."

Salo manages a weak smile. "Thank you, Aba."

VaSiningwe, on the other hand, never one to waste time with small talk, goes on to introduce the emissary and welcome her officially to the clanlands, and when that's done with, he lets her take over.

"First things first, Musalodi—may I call you Musalodi? I'm not sure how to address you without being disrespectful. This is an unprecedented situation, after all."

She wears a towering orange head wrap and a quick, beguiling smile that says, *Let's be friends,* and in the same breath, *I'm a better human than you.*

"Musalodi is fine," he says, raking his family with his eyes. He suspects they already know what she's about to tell him, but they give nothing away.

She smiles again, instantly stealing back his attention. "Thank you, Musalodi. Now, as I was saying, allow me to congratulate you on your successful awakening. I heard it was a close one."

"It was," Salo says, "but I feel much better now."

"Well, I'm glad you pulled through, least of all because your awakening has come at an opportune time." The emissary frowns a little so that he knows she's about to be serious. "In fact, this brings me to the point of my visit. You see, certain . . . political winds blowing in the north have caught the queen's eye, and she's worried about the real possibility that these winds will evolve into existential threats to our tribe in the not-too-distant future. As to the specific nature of these potential threats, she remains uncertain due to a lack of reliable, up-to-date information—and that's a significant problem. You can't prepare for a threat unless you know what it is."

She gestures at Salo. "Your recent awakening, however, presents a favorable opportunity to rectify this. If Her Majesty can have someone close to these calamitous winds, collecting information and reporting to her on a regular basis, she will be better able to build a picture of the threats we might face in the future. And so, after careful consideration, the queen has decided that *you* are the best person suited for this task, Musalodi. It is a great honor, if I may say so myself."

Salo blinks at the emissary, then at the other four men in the hall. His world has stopped making sense. "I don't understand. Can you please explain? Because it sounds like you're sending me away."

"In a manner of speaking," the emissary says. "Tell me, have you ever heard of the Bloodway?"

He goes very still. *This can't be happening.* "Yes," he forces himself to say. "It is a pilgrimage to the Red Temple of Yonte Saire in the Kingdom of the Yontai. Every three decades a mystic is chosen to walk it with the hope that they'll bring back a magical treasure for the tribe."

The tiniest smile moves the emissary's gold-painted lips. "Indeed," she says. "The Bloodway is a tradition practiced by every tribe of the Redlands. Knowledge gifted to worthy pilgrims upon reaching the temple's inner sanctum often becomes lucrative for their tribes. Red steel, talismans, totems—these are some of the gifts Yerezi pilgrims have earned in the sanctum." She tilts her head curiously. "In fact, your mother was the last Yerezi mystic to walk the Bloodway. Did you know?"

She's trying to unsettle you, Salo thinks. *Don't let her succeed.* "I did," he says as calmly as he can. "She returned with designs for an alchemical reactor."

"And what a boon it was for us. It completely revolutionized the way we brew our medicines."

"Forgive me for stating the obvious," Salo says, deciding it's time to defend himself, "but that was twenty-seven comets ago. Three years short of the waiting period."

"True. However, the thirty-year period is merely a guideline based on the average shortest interval between highly fruitful pilgrimages. It is not enforceable, and three years is an acceptable deviation."

This isn't happening.

This isn't happening.

I can't breathe.

"Now, as I was saying, you will travel to—and stay in—Yonte Saire as a Bloodway pilgrim, but in truth, you'll be there as Her Majesty's eyes and ears and, if necessary, the hand with which she will influence the course of events unfolding there. And to give you the leeway you need to operate without rousing too much suspicion, the queen has bestowed on you the title of emissary. Your extended pilgrimage will appear as an overture to the Kingdom of the Yontai, our tribe finally opening up to the rest of the Redlands, and what better place to start than the political heart of the continent?"

Salo finds himself laughing. Not the loud sort of laugh, either, but the silent, choking kind, where it's not clear to others whether he's laughing or on the verge of tears.

"Contain yourself," VaSiningwe growls. "There's nothing funny about this."

"I know," Salo says in between breaths. His chest stings. He can feel tears brimming in his eyes. "Not funny at all. It's *absurd*." To the emissary, he says, "Let me see if I understand what you're telling me. I'm being exiled to Yonte Saire—"

"This isn't exile at all," she chimes in.

"I'm being exiled to Yonte Saire," Salo says, "on the pretext of becoming what is essentially a spy, a job I'm *hideously* unqualified for. I mean, seriously, *me*, an emissary, operating—no, *spying*—in the capital of the most powerful tribe on the continent? *I'm* the best person for this task? Am I really supposed to believe that? I've barely just awoken! Why not send *any* of the tribe's other mystics?"

The emissary leans back in her chair, smiles like she's reassessing her strategy, like maybe he isn't quite what she was expecting. But she is the queen's emissary, and that means she's quick to find another way to work him. "May I be blunt with you, Musalodi?"

"Be my guest."

"Very well. The simple fact is no other mystic in this tribe is dispensable. You, on the other hand, could leave the Plains for many moons, or even years, and we would not suffer."

Salo grins, though he feels the sting of bitterness in his heart. "All right, I'll give you that much. But still, if it's a spy you want, there are Asazi in the Queen's Kraal trained specifically for infiltration and espionage. *You* are probably one of them. So why don't *you* go?"

"Oh, but Musalodi," the emissary says, reflecting his smile, "I am only an Asazi. The power I wield isn't truly mine. And in a city like Yonte Saire, where power is the only currency that matters, this would define me. I'd be lucky to get an audience with even one of the KiYonte princes; you can forget about the king and the high sorcerers. You, however, are a mystic, powerful in your own right. Moreover, as a pilgrim of the Bloodway and a royal emissary to boot, you would carry significant diplomatic clout and enjoy easy access to the social circles that matter. So when I say there is no one better to send, I truly mean it."

Flattery. It shouldn't work. It really shouldn't. "What about my clan?" Salo says. "I confessed to sacrilege—I risked my life—in service to my clan. Are you telling me it was all for nothing?"

"Not at all," the emissary says. "But I must inform you that the queen will not allow a man to hold the mantle of clan mystic, as this would go against the philosophy of the Foremothers. I'm afraid this is not negotiable."

The ensuing silence is such that Salo can hear the thud of his heartbeat just behind his ears.

"That said," the emissary continues, "in acknowledgment of your service to the tribe, the queen will allow one of her promising apprentices to awaken and serve this clan in a limited capacity until the Asazi Nimara is ready to take over. Rest assured, your clan will want for nothing."

He can barely believe his ears. A clan mystic must be a member—by blood—of the clan she serves, or the totem will not answer to her. Even so, if the queen can do this now, then why the devil didn't she do it before?

Salo looks to his family for some clarity but finds only shifting eyes.

But of course. This is what they want, isn't it? They would rather have him exiled to a foreign land than have him stay and serve as clan mystic. To think he'd actually convinced himself that they would one day come around to the idea. *I'm such a fool.*

He takes a deep breath to center himself and keep the tears at bay. They probably expect him to cry. All the more reason not to.

"What time frame are we talking about here?" he says. "How long am I expected to be away?"

"The time frame is indefinite for now."

"Indefinite," Salo repeats, incredulous and indignant. "Even though there are dangers I know nothing about brewing there. I'm supposed to stay there indefinitely. Is my life so worthless there should be no concern for it whatsoever?"

To either side of him, Jio and Sibu trade meaningful looks and shake their heads. "Something to say, brothers?" Salo says. "But where are my manners; I don't get to call you that anymore, do I?"

Sibu replies with silent smugness. Jio's temples ripple as he tightens his jaw and looks away. This only makes Salo more furious. "I mean, who knew a brother could be so expendable? Like an old loincloth you can just toss aside when it gets too smelly."

"Calm yourself, Musalodi," VaSiningwe cautions. "This is no place for harsh words."

"Why don't you say what you obviously want to say? I'm all ears. Speak, damn it!"

"Musalodi, calm yourself!"

Salo slips two fingers beneath his spectacles to wipe his eyes. Aba D shakes his head and mutters something under his breath. Jio has shrunk deeper into his chair, but he still won't look at Salo. Sibu has clenched his fists and tensed up like a compressed spring.

"Apologies, Aba," Salo says, but it's still anger that moves his lips.

The chief maintains his glare for a lengthy second until at last he sits back in his chair and sighs. He massages his stubbled jaw with a hand, looking like a man twice his age. "Please, Asazi, tell my son what resources you're giving him."

"Of course, VaSiningwe." The emissary reaches down into her reedfiber shoulder bag and retrieves several items: a folder bound with strings, an ornate wooden case, a leather pouch making the telltale clinking sounds of coins, and a red steel medallion.

First, she hands him the medallion. As he brings it close to his eyes to inspect it, his dormant shards detect morsels of power trapped inside, organized into specific patterns. Both sides are emblazoned with a mystic Seal: a tangle of lines and triangles that fools his eyes into seeing two psychedelic suns sinking into a plain of golden grass. Their multicolored rays assault his thoughts like a blast of wind to tell him exactly whom this disk belongs to: a queen.

He draws the medallion away from his face and sets it onto his lap.

Clearly amused, the emissary says, "You are to present that medallion as identification, if necessary. It contains your credentials and proves that you are both a royal emissary and an official Bloodway pilgrim chosen by Her Majesty. I'm told it will grant you access to the money vault she keeps in the city, among other things. It will also be the link between her talisman and yours to facilitate long-distance communication. I don't have to explain how that works, do I?"

Salo has to smother a groan at the idea of regular communications with the queen. "No."

"Excellent."

Next, the emissary hands him the bag of coins. He takes it hesitantly, never having held money before.

"This will be more than enough for your journey," she says. "Moongold is extremely valuable out there, so be very careful. There will be even more of it waiting for you when you arrive in Yonte Saire. Accommodation, house staff, local security: that has also been arranged."

Salo knows that moongold is a naturally occurring ore of essence-infused gold, valued for its ability to hold enchantments of Red magic. The arrival of red steel—a physically stronger, significantly cheaper, and much more abundant alternative—largely meant that the Yerezi could build up hefty stockpiles of the mineral, which they use almost exclusively in their dealings with other tribes.

Next, the emissary hands him the folder. "Take your time with these reports. You'll know a whole lot more about the Kingdom of the Yontai and your mission there once you've read them. I think they will answer many of the questions you have."

And finally she hands him the wooden case. When he opens it, a set of redhawk scales shimmers up at him, each one like a tongue of moonfire trapped in an ellipsoid of crystal glass.

They say a single active redhawk scale is worth an entire palace of gold and silver. There are seven scales in the case.

"That is the gift you will present to the king when you arrive," the emissary says. "Keep it safe; it would be highly undignified for you to arrive empty handed. You will be a representative of our people, after all. We can't have them think us poor and uncivilized."

Salo considers what she has given him, and he decides that it's not enough. "Am I supposed to travel alone?"

"You are free to make travel arrangements as you see fit."

"No, I meant, am I going to stay in Yonte Saire on my own, with no one else from home? A clan mystic always travels with at least two Ajaha."

"You're not a clan mystic," Sibu reminds him and gets a furious look from VaSiningwe for it. Sibu shrinks back and shrugs as if to say, *Hey, it's true.*

The emissary ignores the comment. "Use your discretion, Musalodi. Remember: this is your pilgrimage. Tradition dictates that whoever accompanies you does so willingly. Neither the queen nor I can compel anyone to do so. But if you can convince two Ajaha to take your blessing and assist you on the journey, so be it."

Salo glances at his brothers. They both look away. He opens his mouth with an acidic rebuke, but VaSiningwe beats him to it.

"You will not be alone."

Aba D nods, so he must know what his older brother is talking about. The emissary watches silently. So do the other two boys.

"I don't understand," Salo says.

"You are Siningwe. You have successfully awoken, and there is no other mystic of Siningwe blood alive right now. That makes you the rightful master of the clan totem and staff. I have decided that you will claim them."

Jio's eyes go wide. He moves his lips like he wants to say something, but then he shuts his mouth and grits his jaw. Sibu's face gains a reddish tinge, his nostrils flaring with shock. "But Aba, you can't! He's not our mystic!"

"It is his right, Masiburai," the chief says. "Were it not for him, our clan would be in ruins. This is the least we can do. Now leave it be."

Sibu fumes while Salo flounders, not knowing what to say. VaSiningwe is a chief; before that he was a great warrior of the Queen's Regiment. He is the epitome of what it means to be a Yerezi man: strong, courageous, honorable, stoic, and loyal to a fault.

Salo never realized that at least some of this loyalty would also extend to him.

Charged silence pervades the hall. The emissary clears her throat. "I suppose that settles it." She gives Salo a fixed, professional smile, betraying nothing of her thoughts. "I wish you all the best. I imagine you're quite anxious, but you'll be helping to keep the Plains safe in a way no one else can. That's something, isn't it?"

Salo weighs the folder and the bag of coins in his hands. "I guess it is," he says, and he sounds defeated even to his own ears.

A flicker of something pained crosses VaSiningwe's stern face, but the man knows to be stoic at all times, so it's only a flicker. "I know you'll do well, my son," he says and leaves it at that.

17: The Enchantress

Yonte Saire, the Jungle City—Kingdom of the Yontai

In a terraced garden overlooking a great city in the jungle, the Enchantress sits down with a Faro—a high mystic of immense power—and together they speak of treasonous things.

"When will it happen?" says the Faro.

The Enchantress has burned psychotropic incense around the garden to confuse any prying ears, yet she takes a moment to look around before she leans across the side table between them and says, "In the coming days, Your Worship."

The Faro crosses one leg over the other in a gesture that shows a complete lack of unease. Then again, fear and unease might as well not exist in a high mystic's vocabulary. "You should know that I intend to disrupt your plans."

The Enchantress blinks, alarmed, and for a second she sees all of her carefully constructed schemes and plots falling apart right before her eyes. She speaks carefully. "But I presumed we had an understanding, Your Worship. The advancements I'm offering you would transform this kingdom. You would be centuries ahead of the rest of the Redlands. And with ciphermetric machines it would be easier for you to train and induct new mystics. Your covens would fill to bursting—and that would just be a start."

This is why the Enchantress knew the high mystics would be receptive to her advances. Their ancestral talent, unique to the KiYonte tribe, lets them share their Axioms with other mystics—their acolytes—a process that also makes them more powerful with every new recruit. Ciphermetric machines would drastically reduce the difficulties associated with awakening, which would only increase the number of potential new acolytes and thus deepen their pools of power.

So why the change of heart?

"I am aware of all of that," the Faro says, "but the agreement no longer suits my purposes. I have found something more . . . compelling, and I wish for us to come to a new understanding." The Faro's expression reveals nothing. No anger, no emotion, like a metaform simply following its directives.

What was it Prophet said to her when they last spoke? *Your plan has too many moving parts.* Maybe he was right. Hard to play a game when the pieces are playing games of their own. What could be more compelling than Higher technology delivered on a gilded platter?

"And your colleagues?" the Enchantress ventures to ask, watching the Faro closely. "Do they know how you feel?"

"I'd rather keep them in the dark," the Faro says. "In fact, I'd rather . . . remove them from the picture, so to speak. They are ineffectual, too caught up in their own divinity and power. But that is a discussion for another time."

This conversation was treasonous before; now it has become blasphemous. The Enchantress brings a hand to rest on her crimson jewel and slows her breathing. This makes no sense. Of all the Faros of the Shirika, the seven men and women who serve the KiYonte tribe as gods on earth, this one struck her as the most pragmatic. "But why, Your Worship?"

The Faro seems thoughtful for a while, eyes distant, fingers steepled. "Power is a duplicitous friend, is it not? All my life I have watched it turn the best of people into fools, liars, and degenerates. And yet its pursuit must be the logical corollary of being good in a chaotic universe, for when the forces of entropy can crush the innocent and reward the wicked, being good has little to do with feelings of kindness or sympathy, only one's ability to defeat injustice—and this, my dear girl, demands power. But I wonder: Am I letting myself become a fool?"

To this illogical soliloquy, the Enchantress says nothing, and the Faro gives her a piercing look. "I know not what ambitions have brought you here, why an outworlder would seek to meddle in our affairs, but I see an opportunity in your presence. You seek to revive the Ascendancy, do you not?"

"I do," the Enchantress says cautiously. Playing games with high mystics is perilous, requiring a deft tongue.

The Faro nods, mulling this over. "And you seek to make this tribe the center of the Ascendancy."

"It is the only thing that makes sense. This city is the world's beating heart, after all."

"Then you will understand why I must renege on our agreement. I appreciate your devotion to the cause, but let us face the facts: What you are aiming to build would only be a travesty of the true Ascendancy. It would be a laughable mockery pretending to be something infinitely superior. A farce."

The Enchantress tucks a strand of dark hair behind her ear, trying to hide how exposed she feels. She thought she'd moved the mountains that were in her way, but now her success is slipping from her fingers.

"Do you know why the Hegemons of the Ascendancy never conquered any part of this continent?" the Faro asks.

"It was hallowed ground to them," she says, wondering where this conversation is headed.

"Indeed. Every Hegemon came to the Redlands at least once before rising to power. It was here that they found themselves and their purpose. They might not have been Red of blood, but they recognized that this was the Mother's true land and the only place they could forge the strongest connections with her. You people of the outside world have allowed yourselves to forget the Hegemons and their history, but some of us here have not forgotten. We know things about them—about the Ascendancy—that you do not. Things that would shock you."

The Faro's eyes flash with unspoken secrets. "Suffice it to say, you will find no better home for a resurgent Ascendancy than the heart of the Redlands, but at present, you lack the key to its true power. Furthermore, this so-called Ascendancy would not stand the test of war with external forces. How could it, when the center is divided against itself? You would be better off removing all divisions first, reuniting the central tribe under one king, with no clans and no headmen, as it was in the days of old."

A wave of anxiety threatens to overwhelm the Enchantress, but she doesn't falter. She is not the weak little mouse she once was. "The KiYonte clans can never be united, Your Worship," she says evenly. "They were writ in blood a long time ago." *And your predecessors cast the curse.*

"Then what was writ in blood must be erased by blood," the Faro says. "It is the only way forward."

She sits back in her chair, frowning in thought. The Faro clearly knows something she doesn't. But what?

She decides to test the waters. "As far as I'm aware," she says, "erasing the clans, if possible at all, would require an artifact that might not even exist anymore."

"Oh, it exists," the Faro says confidently. "It is just hidden very well."

"Yes, in a place no one can enter." The Enchantress looks toward the Red Temple and its gleaming Paragon, the red jewel hanging above it like a star. "Not unless they have . . ." She falls silent as it hits her: *Not unless they have the key to the Ascendancy's power. Could it be?*

The Faro smiles, seeming to have read her thoughts.

"I fear to ask, Your Worship," the Enchantress says, so quietly she can almost hear her heart racing inside her chest, "but you don't mean to suggest that you have one of the lost keys of the Ascendancy in your possession, do you?"

The Faro's eyes glint with satisfaction. "Not quite in my possession, but close enough. A recent discovery, brought to my attention by an old acquaintance of mine. She will be sending the key to me soon."

The Enchantress loses control of her expression and feels her mouth falling open. Could it really be? But the Faro would not lie about such a thing.

She knows Prophet would quail at the idea, but this is beyond her wildest dreams, beyond anything she could have hoped for. She sought to raise a mere specter, a puppet to scare the world into the fires of war, but to resurrect the *real* thing? In the Red Wilds, no less?

The world will tremble, and its foundations will fracture. Humanity will be left weak and divided, and when the Veil falls, my Master will sweep in to claim Her victory. Surely it is no coincidence that this should fall into my lap now, just as my plans come to fruition.

Biting down on the excitement now simmering in her chest, the Enchantress exhales a shaky breath. "I assume your colleagues aren't aware of this discovery of yours," she says.

"They are not," the Faro says, "and I'd prefer to keep it that way. If we work together, it will strictly be between you and me, and they need not know that you have betrayed them. I will take the blame, and you will appear as confused by my actions as they are."

To fool six high mystics will be quite the task, but the Enchantress knows she is up to the challenge. "What do you wish of me, Your Worship?"

The Faro raises an eyebrow. "Do we have an understanding?"

"Our goals are aligned. We both serve the Mother, and we both wish to see her Ascendancy restored. It would be foolish of me to oppose you, especially now that you have found such a vital piece of the puzzle." The Enchantress traces a finger across her heart and bows her head. "I am at your disposal."

"Ah. I thought you'd be reasonable." The Faro gives her the faintest of smiles, gone with the wind a second later. "Now listen closely. You will continue as planned: a complete wipeout of the palace. The king, the herald, the Royal Guard—everyone. But with one small change . . ."

18: Isa

As the Ruby Paragon flashes ten times across Yonte Saire's night sky, signifying the turn of the tenth hour after high noon, a knock comes on the door to Isa's private chamber in the Summit, two quick raps, then four, then three.

"I'll be right there," she says, and with a smile she rises from her reclining chair, setting down the book she was reading onto the side table nearby.

She pads barefoot across a thick Dulama rug toward the door and pauses as she catches her reflection in a full-length mirror.

Maybe I should make myself more presentable, she thinks, noticing how immodestly her silken emerald slip clings to her body. A good princess would never let herself be seen in such a state. *But I've never been a good princess, have I. Besides, more clothes would be counterproductive.*

She unclips her butterfly hairpin, set with emeralds across its golden wings, and lets her thin braids fall to her back. Only then does she proceed to open the door.

A pair of dark eyes meets hers from across the threshold. The young man they belong to, dressed in the Sentinels' patterned green tunic and black trousers, gives her a shy smile. "Your Highness."

Her return smile is crooked and full of mischief. Without giving him a warning, she grabs the warrior by the elbow and drags him into her chamber, kissing him as soon as she locks the door. A languid kiss, lingering, like a lazy day in the suns. When it is over, they smile at each other, their foreheads touching.

"Hi," she says.

"Hi yourself."

Obe Saai of the crocodile clan, nephew of the headman himself, isn't handsome, exactly; his jaw is too strong, and his nose has been broken so many times it's a little bent. And yet he is striking. Whatever he lacks in classic charm he makes up for with his sensuous intensity—when he looks at Isa, she knows she has his full attention.

Isa's smile softens, and she reaches up to run a finger over the black patterns twisting down his neck, not very different from the marks on her own neck, though the motifs on his are those of the crocodile, while hers are of the elephant. Those marks say that he should be her enemy, for the crocodiles and the elephants of the Yontai have never gotten along, but on his skin, she finds that they are beautiful.

"Did my guard give you trouble?" she says.

Obe's face creases with concern. "I was going to ask you about that. Why did he let me through without any questions? That can't be safe for you."

Isa hooks her arms around his neck, bringing his lips closer. "I appreciate you worrying about my safety, but I was tired of broom closets. This will be so much better." She leans up to kiss him, but he draws back, going completely rigid.

"You told him about us?"

She raises an eyebrow. "Do you think he'd have let you in if I hadn't? But you mustn't worry, Obe. Manchiri has been with me for a long time. I trust him." Obe begins to pull away from her, but she doesn't let him. "It'll be fine. I promise."

His worried eyes gleam down at her. "Your Highness . . . Isa, we have to be careful. If your father . . ."

"I don't want to talk about him. I don't want to talk at all. You're not here to talk, are you?"

The heat in his eyes is unmistakable, but Isa can almost see the restraint keeping it in check. "I don't care how we spend time together," he says. "I've told you this. We don't have to do anything. Just being in your company is enough. But Isa—"

She cuts him off by rising onto her toes and kissing him again. He is hesitant at first, but soon his self-control melts away in the heat, and he kisses her until she is breathless.

"No more talking," she says when they surface for air. "You can talk my ears off later, but not right now."

This time Obe gives in completely, and they lose themselves in each other.

Isa began their secret trysts for the thrill of them, for the scandal it would cause if it was ever discovered that the young Saire princess, the Great Elephant's own flesh and blood, cavorted with a Sentinel—the Crocodile's nephew, no less—in the halls of the palace.

He was forbidden fruit, and she was seduced by the taboo of him.

What she didn't anticipate was discovering that he's far more than the brusque and sullen warrior he appears to be. He proved rather well read and introspective for a man raised for the legions, and surprisingly innocent and trusting. Far too quick to assume that people are good. Despite being four years his junior, she felt like *she* was corrupting *him*.

And yet she couldn't stop. His emotional intensity left her gasping for breath during their first time together, and the way his eyes worshipped her, the way she could see into his soul and feel the power she held over him—intoxicating.

Does it make me deviant that I want more of this? Does it make me wanton? Does it make me a bad person?

Isa decided that she didn't care. Obe Saai is a choice she made for herself, and only she will get to decide if and when to let go.

They hear the first screams just as they fall into a heated rhythm on the chamber's large bed, their fingers intertwined like vines, their toes curling into the silken sheets beneath them, breaths mingling as they kiss, bodies edging closer and closer to release.

The screams don't quite jolt them out of their ecstasy, but the loud thump on the door is harder to ignore. They stop when they hear it again and stare at the door, still entangled in each other. When the noise comes for the third time, Obe pulls out of her and moves to sit at the foot of the bed, where he begins to put on his trousers.

With a frown Isa sits up on the bed and pulls up a sheet to cover her chest. Obe's back is turned to her, and the muscles of his shoulders are glistening with sweat. "What are you doing?" she asks him.

"Something is off. I need to see what's going on." He ties the drawstrings of his trousers and gets up.

"Maybe I should open the door," Isa suggests. It would not go well for either of them if the person on the other side turned out to be the crown prince or, worse, her mother.

But Obe is determined. "No. You stay here."

At the door, he listens. The thumps have since intensified to insistent bangs, except no one is demanding entry, which is odd. Slowly, Obe unlocks the door, perhaps intending to peer outside, but before he can stick his head out, the door bursts open, striking him in the face. He staggers backward with a groan.

"Obe!" Isa cries from the bed. "Are you all right?"

He groans again, clutching what must be a busted nose, and in front of him a bulky figure fills the doorway.

Anger and mortification make Isa's cheeks burn as she recognizes the figure, and she holds her sheet tighter across her chest. "What do you think you're doing, Manchiri? I told you I was not to be disturbed."

"Bastard broke my nose." Obe tilts his head up, trying in vain to stem the gushing blood.

The royal guardsman, a Saire who served in the Sentinels during his younger years, slowly stalks into the chamber, armed with a spear, and something about his eyes looks *wrong* to Isa.

Creeping fear joins the swirl of emotions roiling in her belly, and she unconsciously shifts back on the bed. "Answer me, Manchiri, or the king will know of this."

He has been her personal guard for over five comets, and she has known him to be stolid and taciturn, a dependable pillar who lets her have her way so long as he knows she's safe. But this man in her room . . . she doesn't recognize him at all, nor the feral hunger in his eyes.

She shivers when a shriek comes in through the door behind him. He takes another step closer, and his spearpoint glistens in the chamber's dim light like it's coated in a layer of wetness.

Blood. Spattered all over his blue tunic as well.

Isa shifts farther back on the bed. "Obe."

Her lover is so preoccupied with looking for something to stanch the blood from his nose he hasn't noticed Manchiri's menacing advance.

"Obe!"

"What?" He looks up just as Manchiri decides to lunge for the bed, and what happens next is a blur.

It involves a shirtless Obe leaping several feet and tackling the guardsman so that they crash to the floor. It involves a battle for the guardsman's spear, both men growling like wild animals as they roll and tumble on the Dulama rug by the foot of Isa's bed. It involves Isa getting a grip and unsticking herself from her paralysis. She climbs out of the bed and rushes to the dresser across the chamber, where she unearths a sheathed dagger from the top drawer. She wills her hands to stop shaking as she grabs the diamond-studded hilt and pulls, freeing the smooth aerosteel blade from its gilded scabbard.

When she turns around, she sees to her horror how the battle between royal guardsman and Sentinel will be decided if she does nothing: The spear has been forgotten, cast to the side with its blunt end now sticking out from underneath her bed, but Manchiri has overpowered the younger warrior and has his big hands curled around Obe's neck. Trapped beneath his considerable bulk, Obe kicks and thrashes wildly.

"Manchiri, stop!" Isa screams.

But the guardsman keeps strangling the Sentinel.

What happens next involves Isa doing something that will destroy her. It involves Isa crossing to the warriors and crying out in anguish before she thrusts into the guardsman's left side with all her strength, feeling the sickening give of flesh and bone at the blade's sharp point.

Manchiri arches his back as he howls in pain, an almost beastly roar, and the brutality of what she's done shocks Isa so much she immediately steps back, covering her mouth with her trembling hands and leaving the dagger where it is.

Obe reaches for the dagger's hilt and pulls, only to plunge the blade back into the guardsman's side, not once but over and over again, until the bleeding guardsman falls silent and becomes a limp weight on top of him.

Isa's eyes cloud with tears so thickly she barely sees Obe freeing himself of Manchiri's corpse—*corpse*. Manchiri. The guardsman she has known for the last five comets. A *corpse*, made by her dagger. "I don't know what's going on." Her voice is a shattered thing, a quavering whimper. She claws at her braids because she doesn't understand. *Dear Mother above, a corpse.* "Why did he try to kill me?"

Obe is already pulling his tunic over his head. Despite his broken nose and blood-spattered face, his voice is steady, solid as rock. "We have to get out of here. This might be a plot. There could be more coming. We need to hide you." He steps over Manchiri's body to pick up the bloodied dagger from the floor where he left it, then goes on to do the same to Isa's emerald slip, which they discarded in their passion not minutes ago. "Get dressed." He presents the slip to her. "I'll take you to the Sentinels' quarters. You'll be safe there."

Isa blinks at him, her mind looping around a single word he spoke. "A plot? *What* plot? Manchiri was a Saire, for the Mother's sake! What plot could drive him to this?"

"I don't know," Obe says, "but I hear screams out there. This is clearly part of a larger attack. Now get dressed."

"My family—"

"Will be fine, I'm sure." Obe comes close enough to pull her into an embrace so tight it squeezes the breath right out of her lungs. Still not tight enough. "Isa, I'm with you. All the way to hell and back. I promise. Now please, get dressed."

What happens next involves Obe taking Isa's hand and dragging her out of the chamber. It involves skulking down tapestried hallways with high ceilings and brightly patterned pillars. It involves coming upon a body at the entrance to the domed hall connecting the palace's private and state wings. They freeze.

A framework of bamboo rises from the floors all around the hall, meeting at the dome's apex, where an oversize coconut-shaped crystal lamp droops from a cord so thin it's almost invisible. In front of them a young man, a Sentinel, is lying facedown in a lake of blood with his right hand inches away from a spear.

Obe lets go of Isa's hand and crouches next to him, his expression unreadable. He makes a gesture with his left hand, running a finger across his heart. "Find peace on the Infinite Path, my brother."

More bodies await farther in. Another Sentinel in green. A guardsman in blue. A figure in nightclothes slumped awkwardly at the foot of a large bamboo strut, like she was struck from behind while trying to escape. Whatever happened here happened quickly, and then whoever did it probably left to go find something else to kill.

A piercing cry from somewhere out of sight makes Isa shiver, and she hugs herself, battling the urge to vomit. Or curl into a ball and weep. Or pinch herself until she wakes up.

"Come on." Obe takes her hand again. "We've got to keep moving."

◆ ◆ ◆

They see more corpses. A cousin of hers was cut down by the entrance to the principal reception room. His green dashiki is blood soaked. His kufi cap must have fallen off during a struggle, because it's on the tiled floor a few feet away from him. They weren't particularly close, but Isa's eyes blur, and she feels a rasping howl rising up her throat.

Obe mutters a curse, the first sign he's shown that this might be getting to him too. "Dear Mother, it's a bloodbath."

He keeps leading her toward the Sentinels' quarters in the Summit's south wing, where the Sentinels on palace duty are barracked. The Saire Royal Guard might be the king's most trusted guards, being Saires themselves, but the Sentinels are bound by ancient sorcery to serve the crown on pain of death; whatever is happening here, they will die before they see the king and his kin harmed.

Isa tries to tell herself that her mother is fine. Her father and brothers too. Zenia. Suye. She says a silent prayer to the moon, willing them all to be safe, because she can't bear the thought of anything else.

As they approach a foyer with a grand staircase, Obe stops dead so abruptly Isa almost runs into his back. Just as abruptly he turns around and tries to push her back the way they came. "Move!"

Isa remains stuck on her feet long enough to see a guardsman in blue and aerosteel skewering another guardsman with a spear in the thigh, both of their faces twisted with wild rage, but his victim doesn't fold over as he should. Instead, he somehow finds the strength to raise his sword and slash his foe in the face, cleaving off a lump of flesh from his cheek. They are still at it by the time Obe manages to pull Isa away.

By the Mother, it's like . . . like they're possessed.

"Change of plan," Obe half whispers. "We won't make it to the south wing. We need to find a place to hole up until whatever the devil this is blows over."

An idea strikes Isa, and with it comes an unexpected fount of courage. She grips Obe's hand a little harder and quickens her pace, leading him for a change. "This way." He doesn't fight her.

They slink down the halls of the Summit for a full minute without event, silently threading their way through a trail of bodies—palace officials, liveried servants, Faraswa workers. Isa recognizes many of them but keeps going. One step after the next. Survival first, if only to know that her family is safe.

Just as her eyes settle on a body partially hidden behind a thick pillar, a growl and a flash of blue to her right make Obe shout her name. From out of the darkness comes a guardsman with a missing ear and frightful cuts oozing all over his body. He lunges for her, but Obe pushes her out of the way and springs forward with her jeweled dagger, knifing the guardsman in the chest. The guardsman wielded a spear; now the weapon rattles to the ground, and Obe lets him slump onto him like they are embracing, the dagger still lodged where it struck.

Looking over Obe's shoulders, Isa thinks she sees a glimmer of lucidity enter the guardsman's eyes, but then it is gone, along with everything he ever was. Obe lays him gently on the ground and pulls out the dagger.

"Obe?"

He releases a shaky breath. "I'm all right. Keep moving."

Isa numbly obeys, and soon they make it to an inconspicuous door not far from the kitchens.

"A broom closet?" Obe says rather dubiously as she pulls the door open. They have both been here before, during a happier time.

"No one ever comes here," Isa says. "Come on."

It is gloomy inside, and an unpleasantly sour stench hangs thickly in the air. The darkness becomes total when Obe shuts the door behind them, making Isa almost regret her decision. But Obe takes her hand again, and that's a small comfort. She looks where she thinks his face is. "Now what?"

Obe is silent, like he's thinking. "Now we wait," he finally says.

"What's going on, Obe?"

"I don't know, but it reeks of sorcery." His voice becomes throaty, like he's fighting back tears. "My brothers aren't prepared for this, Isa. We're not as experienced as the Guard. They'll be butchered." He means the Sentinels. *Brother* is what they call each other, even though they might be from different clans. "I should be out there with them, but your safety must come first."

He surrounds her with his warmth by pulling her into his arms.

"My family, Obe."

"I wish I could say what you want to hear. But I can't. All I can tell you is that I'm here, and I'll die before I leave."

Such an earnest expression of devotion should make her feel better, but she can't stop thinking about all those bodies she saw and wondering if one of them was—

No. She doesn't let herself complete that thought. She buries her face in Obe's chest and keeps it there for so long she loses track of time.

"It smells like vomit in here," Obe says eventually. Shouts are still coming from outside.

Succumbing to a wave of weariness, Isa finally disentangles herself from him and moves to sit down on the floor, only to freeze when her foot brushes against something.

She crouches and feels with her hand. A boot. And it's attached to a leg wearing brocade pants. "There's a body in here," she says distantly, numbly. But then her fingers slide over metal, and her breath stills. Quickly, she brings both hands to trace the contours of the smooth metal contraption, and yes, it's wrapped around the leg. A leg brace. "Jomo?"

Jomo Saire, the herald's son and Isa's rake of a cousin, crippled by the bite of a ninki nanka as a child and the only person she knows who needs a leg brace and a cane to walk about—this leg has to be his.

"Isa, what are you doing?" Obe says. "Is that really Prince Jomo? Is he dead?"

Fighting off the edges of blind panic, Isa pats the rest of Jomo's body, frantically searching for the wet slickness of blood. When she doesn't find it, she places her hand on his chest. A strong, regular thud rises to meet her palm. The relief is so heavy it almost makes her head spin. "He's all right." She leans closer to take a whiff of him and grimaces at the stench of palm wine and vomit. "But he's drunk and unconscious."

"Why the devil is he in a broom closet?"

"He probably needed a place to retch and pass out in private. He does this all the time."

Obe grunts. "So it's true what they say about him. But I guess it probably saved his life tonight."

That remains to be seen. "We need to wake him up. In case we need to run."

Isa feels around for his face, and when the bristles of his beard prick her fingers, she lightly slaps his rounded cheeks. "Jomo, wake up. Jomo?" She slaps him a few more times until he emits a groan and slurs something unintelligible.

"Get up, Jomo. It's Isa. We're in danger."

It takes a while, but she feels him attempt to sit up; then he slumps back to the floor. *"Isa?"*

"He sounds out of it," Obe remarks.

"Jomo, our family is under attack," Isa says, a little desperate now. "The guardsmen . . . they're killing everyone. Obe and I came here to hide. Our family . . ." She chokes on her words, feeling like a ghostly pair of hands is constricting her throat. *Inhale, exhale. Keep going.* "I need you to try to get up, Jomo. Something terrible is happening."

Still on the floor, Jomo groans again. *"The devil is Obe?"*

"Obe Saai. He's a Sentinel. He's here too."

"Wait, I don't . . . *what?*" Jomo tries to sit up again, and his leg brace makes a squeaking sound. Isa reaches for his shoulders to steady him. She has to work because he's somewhat hefty, but soon he's sitting up on his own, so she lets go. "What are you talking about, Isa?"

He suddenly sounds sober, which is a relief to Isa because Jomo is someone who will understand how she feels. His immediate family lives in the palace too. "The guardsmen are killing everyone," she tells him and goes on to relate everything that has happened, everything except the part about Obe being in her chambers when the attack began.

"That makes no sense," Jomo says. "They are Saires. Why would they attack their own?"

"Obe thinks magic's involved."

Jomo seems to think about this, and after a moment he says, "The Crocodile. It must be."

Isa almost feels a flash of heat coming from behind her.

"You don't know what you're talking about," Obe says. "My uncle is no sorcerer."

Jomo scoffs. "Sorcerers can be hired, you nitwit. This city is crawling with independents and foreign mystics who can be bought for the right price."

"My uncle would never."

"Ha! Your uncle would skin every Saire alive if it meant he could sit on the throne." Jomo's slur returns, becoming more pronounced in his anger. "In fact, my mother was talking about it just the other day . . . oh no. Isa, my mother! My family! Isa, you have to help me find them."

"We're not going out there until this is over," Obe says.

"I wasn't talking to you, crocodile."

Isa finds Jomo's hand and squeezes gently. "Obe is right, cousin. I've seen what's out there. It's not safe, but you need to be ready in case we need to run."

Jomo falls quiet and feeble, and then: "How bad is it?"

Tears instantly fill Isa's eyes. "Bad, Jomo."

"We should probably stay quiet," Obe suggests, in a softer voice now, and this time Jomo doesn't object.

In the silent blackness, Isa's thoughts spiral into panic, and time becomes deceitful, stretching the seconds to feel like hours. And when the shouts from outside, which had waned some time ago, resume with force, she brings her knees to her chest and tries to fold into herself and disappear.

The door yawns open.

Isa winces at the unwelcome light that floods in, and she barely sees Obe getting up to put himself between the closet's interior and whatever's outside.

She expects another battle, more blood and bodies; she expects death, which is why the deep voice that addresses her throws her off completely.

"Your Highness, you are safe now."

She squints into the brightness and sees beyond the door an imposing figure in grand red robes.

Around him are Sentinels armed with spears and swords, in various states of injury and dishevelment. She also counts at least three spear-wielding members of the Jasiri order of warrior mystics, recognizable in their horned aerosteel masks, which have no eye slits, as if sight is a base form of perception their wearers long ago transcended.

Isa takes another look at the central figure. Like all members of the rare magical caste of the KiYonte tribe, who do not answer to any clan, he was born with two simple vertical lines running up his neck in place of clan tattoos. He stands tall and lank, spry for his advanced age and somewhat severe of countenance—probably because of the ordered maze of scarified lines covering the expanse of his dark face. And his eyes, though black as tar, seem to hold a flickering light of their own.

"Your Worship," she breathes, for this man can be no one but Itani Faro, master of the Arc coven and high priest of the Red Temple.

The Shirika have come to save us.

"Please, Your Highness," the high mystic says, "you must come with us immediately."

◆ ◆ ◆

The high mystic of the Arc, his trio of Jasiri warriors, and over twenty Sentinels all watch solemnly as Isa emerges from the broom closet in nothing but her emerald slip, with a bloodied Obe Saai helping her drunken cousin limp out, one of Jomo's arms slung over his shoulders. She immediately notices what's deeply wrong about this arrangement.

In the event of an attack on the royal family, all the Sentinels on palace duty must cluster around the king. It is why they are called the King's Sentinels. They should not be here.

Touching a high mystic is not wise, not even for royalty, for the Shirika are divinity in mortal flesh, but Isa steps forward and reaches for the Arc's right hand, gripping it between hers as though her life depended on it. "Your Worship, my family. The king." *My mother and brothers. Suye. Zenia.*

Not a question but a prayer. She is begging this man to tell her what she needs to hear for her soul to be at peace. She is begging him not to shatter her world.

The Arc remains grim. "Some of the servants survived, Your Highness." His eyes flick to Jomo, who is still using Obe for support. "But the two of you are all that is left of the royal family. This was a targeted assault. That you survived is nothing short of a miracle."

The world seems to fall away from Isa's feet, and this time it is the high mystic who grips her by the arms so that she doesn't collapse. "I cannot accept that," she says.

Behind her Jomo begins to sob. "No. No. Please. Isa, no. I had a fight with my parents this morning. And my brother. They can't be dead, can they?"

Isa clutches onto the Arc even tighter. "Your Worship, tell me you are wrong."

The man speaks bluntly. "I'm afraid I cannot, Your Highness. The Royal Guard attacked everyone in sight, and when they could find no one else, they turned on each other." He pauses, and Isa could swear he's being hesitant. "I must confess . . . I suspected treachery was afoot, which was why my Jasiri and I were in the vicinity, but evidently I underestimated the scope of the attack. I assumed an external threat and never once considered that the threat would emerge from within the palace. It is a personal failure I will never forgive and a burden I will carry to my grave."

Isa's ears ring with this revelation. "What are you saying, Your Worship?"

"It will dismay you to hear this, but the other high mystics of the Shirika have forsaken your clan and withdrawn their protection. I believe the Crocodile has taken this as permission to move for the throne. I, however, am not of one mind with them, and so long as I live, a Saire will be king, and so long as *you* live, Your Highness, he who orchestrated this treason will have failed."

"I told you it was him!" In a rage Jomo frees himself of Obe. Another Sentinel has to rush forward to help him stay on his feet. He stabs the air with an accusing finger. "Stay the devil away from me, crocodile filth! Your uncle did this! Your clan did this! I swear I'll kill every one of you if it's the last thing I do."

Obe's shoulders flex as he fumes, glaring death at Jomo. "My uncle would never. You're jumping to conclusions."

"I'm afraid the facts suggest otherwise," the Arc says. "I do not doubt your devotion to the crown, young man. You are a Sentinel, after all, and I suspect we have you to thank for Her Highness's survival. But I have received intelligence via mirrorgram; Kola Saai is on his way to the capital as we speak, bringing with him a significant contingent of his legion."

Isa looks to Obe, who looks back like his world has just been turned onto its side. Isa doesn't know what to think. She feels angry tears pouring down her face.

"Isa . . ." Obe takes a step closer, then seems to remember that there is an audience. "Your Highness, I had nothing to do with this. You have to believe me."

She wants to—she *does*—but her whole family is dead, and his uncle is responsible. How can she ever look at him in the same way again?

"Your Highness," the high mystic says. "You must take refuge in the Red Temple. Once you are safe inside, I will summon the ancient protections. No one will be able to safely enter the citadel unless I allow it."

"To what end?" Isa hears herself say. "The Crocodile has already won. If I fled to the temple, what difference would it make?"

"The mask-crown is still in this palace," the Arc says. "So long as it exists, and so long as there is a Saire of royal blood fit to wear it, the Shirika cannot crown another king. It is the pact that founded this kingdom. Take refuge in the Red Temple; claim the mask-crown. Let us thwart the Crocodile before his hold over this kingdom grows stronger."

Isa stares at her audience of Sentinels, who stare back expectantly. Without the king, she and Jomo are now the Sentinels' sole responsibility. The young warriors are bound by death oaths to be absolutely loyal to whichever one of them ends up wearing the mask-crown.

Isa does not want that person to be her. "But I am a woman, Your Worship. My cousin Jomo is a Saire prince. He is the one you must crown."

"No." Jomo shakes his head so vigorously he almost brings himself and the Sentinel propping him up crashing to the ground. "I cannot. Please, Isa. I cannot. I *will* not."

The Arc does not appear surprised by Jomo's reaction. "Women have worn the mask-crown when circumstances required departure from tradition," he says. "This is one of those times. It is what your father would want."

Isa covers her face and forces herself to take deep breaths. Falling apart in front of so many people would not do. When she has found her composure, she wipes the tears off her cheeks. "I want to see my family before I leave."

For the second time tonight, the high mystic hesitates. "Your Highness, I wouldn't recommend it."

"I have to see my family." A troubling thought occurs to her. "Who will see to their committals if I'm hiding in the temple?"

"I will see to the arrangements," the Arc says, "but I'm afraid your presence would incur too much risk. Your enemies will stop at nothing to see you dead; we must not give them another chance."

"Then I need to see my family. I need to say goodbye." Isa's voice cracks in her throat. "Please."

The Arc considers her silently for a moment, then relents with a nod. "But be prepared, Your Highness. What you're about to see will stay with you forever."

A tremor of fear racks Isa's body and almost proves her a coward, but she weathers it.

And then she goes to see her family.

19: Musalodi

As morning comes on the day he is set to leave the kraal, Salo sits cross-legged beneath the pale, leafless branches of the witchwood tree growing in the bonehouse garden. With his back against the trunk, he places his hands on his knees, palms facing upward. Then he *ignites* his shards.

Essence rushes into them from the environment, transformed therein by arcane logic into the energy of Storm craft. The energy grows denser and denser until the shards crackle with dancing sparks of red static, and only now does he release it, sending it out along the set of predetermined patterns he learned from a spell book.

Nimara kept her promise, and over the last few days Salo has spent hours with his nose buried inside the spell book she procured for him, imprinting its patterns into the pathways of his mind. To the layperson, the little book is no more than a few pages of meaningless angular scripts. But to those who can read ciphers, it is a precise description of how Storm craft can be harnessed as jets of wind. A basic spell compared to what he could find in the library at the Queen's Kraal if he were ever given the chance, but a far better one than what he attempted to design himself.

At his command the pressure changes in the garden, and the air begins to stir as he tests the boundaries, a slight breeze at first, then a whirlwind that gathers force and whips around the tree, cocooning him in a fast-moving funnel of twigs and leaves.

He smiles. The spell is flirting with the limit of what his single ring can handle, but the conversion of essence in his shards is so effortless he can direct individual microcurrents or the entire swirling mass.

I have always wanted this, says a quiet voice in his mind. He's always known this, of course, always felt it in his soul. He just couldn't admit such a thing to himself, for to do so would have been to prove what they all said about him right: that he wanted things meant for women and was therefore questionable as a man. Now, though, with the power of magic flowing through his veins, he feels like he has looked at himself in the mirror for the first time in his life.

This is who I am. My true self.

Still, he's not certain he likes this reflection, as he feels a tingle of shame for being so much of a deviation from what is expected of a Yerezi man, let alone the firstborn son of a chief.

"And you told me you weren't ready to leave the bonehouse," says a voice, and when Salo shifts his focus beyond the funnel of debris, he sees Nimara shaking her head with her arms folded. "I should have known you were lying and kicked you out days ago."

With a smirk he slows down the currents and lets the spell die. The air stills, and the leaves drift to the ground. "This place has everything I could possibly want. A lovely garden. Privacy. No chores. Why would I leave?"

"Because the bonehouse is for sick people, which you're clearly not."

"True, and it's thanks to you."

"You'd better not forget it."

"I'm serious, Nimara," Salo says. "I owe you. Not just for the spell book, mind you, but for everything. For giving me the push I needed, for saving my life afterward. For being a good friend."

She smiles, uncharacteristically bashful, but her smile wanes as something sad enters her eyes. "Are you done packing?"

"Mostly," Salo says.

"Even the supplies I left in your room?"

"I'll be able to treat an army if I ever have to."

Nimara shrugs. "When it comes to preparation, over is better than under."

"Actually, I was hoping I could ask you one more favor," Salo says.

"What do you need?"

"You know where the totem staff is, right?"

Nimara peers at him with suspicion. "I do, and I'm certain you do too."

"Yes, but can you please get it for me anyway? As well as the other totem-related items. I'm sure it's all there."

She keeps watching him, studying him, then comes to some hidden conclusion. "One day you'll have to stop being so weird about that hut. But yes, I'll get it for you."

And with those words a great deal of anxiety ebbs away from Salo's chest. That's one unpleasant task avoided. "Again, I owe you, Nimara. For this and a whole lot more."

A twinkle briefly lights up her eyes. "You can pay me back by bringing me something nice from the Jungle City. And it better be good, Salo. Nothing cheap, or you'll have to go back for something better. Got it?"

He doesn't know when he'll come back or even if he'll come back, so he shouldn't be making promises. But he smiles and says, "It'll be the biggest and best gift you've ever seen."

◆　◆　◆

He goes to say goodbye to his stepmother.

Ama Lira is in the middle of teaching a calligraphy class to a group of young girls sitting on little desks arranged beneath a tree outside the grammar school. A yellow kitenge with white patterns covers her body, haltered over her neck and falling down to her knees. She smiles when she sees him approach, a chalky hand falling onto her swollen belly. Ama Lira is still graceful even in the late stages of her pregnancy.

The story goes that a young VaSiningwe fell so in love with his clan mystic he was prepared to flout the rules of propriety by taking her as his wife. But she would not have him, for a clan mystic must be married only to her clan.

To console him, she bore him a son, whom she named after him. And when that only exacerbated his attentions, she found him a young woman and convinced him to marry her. That woman was Ama Lira, and a year after their wedding the twins were born.

Some whisper to this day that the chief never really stopped pursuing the mystic. Some whisper that she was in fact the villain and had bewitched him so he could love no one else. Either way, Salo would not have blamed Ama Lira if she hated the sight of him.

As it is, she has always been kind to him, if a little demure.

They don't talk much when he pulls her aside to say goodbye—they rarely do—but she tells him she finally learned the sex of her unborn child—or children, it turns out.

"Girls," she tells him, rubbing her bulbous belly, and she glows with so much motherly pride it makes him smile. "You'll be a big brother to two beautiful girls. That is why I will pray every day for your return—so they don't miss you too much."

Salo has always wanted a little sister, and now he'll have two. His heart breaks to know he won't be there to greet them when they come into the world. "I'll think about them every day," he promises.

Ama Lira smiles and places a gentle hand on his arm. "Check the kitchens before you go. I've packed a little parcel for you."

He thanks her and hopes that she knows it's not just for the parcel, or for being one of the few people who visited him in the bonehouse, but also for never making him feel unwanted.

◆ ◆ ◆

He doesn't find Aaku Malusi anywhere in the kraal, so he decides to walk down to the Ajaha training glade, driven by an impulse he doesn't probe too much.

At first no one notices him come to a stop in the trees at the edge of the glade, where he silently watches Niko sparring with a would-be ranger, both of them wielding blunt swords and elliptical hide shields. Niko has strength that can turn brutish at a moment's notice, but he holds it in check. He's neither cocky nor domineering, just confident in a way that can't be overlooked. His sparring partner, on the other hand, a tall weedy boy in a white loincloth, is inexperienced, though light footed like a dancer. Agility is his answer to strength, improvisation to experience.

"Stance," Niko keeps telling him whenever he improvises too much. "Nice one," whenever he lands a solid hit on Niko's shield.

Then the grunts die down, the sticks and swords stop rattling, and suddenly everyone's looking Salo's way. Niko pauses midstrike, noticing that something is off. When he turns around to look, his eyes widen slightly with surprise. It's been a while since they last spoke, and seeing Niko now, Salo realizes he doesn't want to leave without at least saying goodbye.

In the training glade, Niko glances at Salo's brothers; they both frown and shake their heads slightly. He twists the hilt of the sword in his hand, seeming to consider their advice, but in the end he drops the sword and starts to walk over, telling the rangers to keep sparring in his absence.

Salo feels a nervous tingle in his stomach as he watches him approach. He once resented everything about the young man and couldn't stand to look him in the eye. Now he is beginning to understand that it wasn't resentment he felt but something else entirely.

Something perhaps more complicated.

The sunlight strikes Niko's red steel greaves and vambraces so that they glitter. As he comes to a stop in front of Salo, he smiles for the briefest moment like he has forgotten everything that has happened these last few weeks, but the smile loses its shine, and his gaze falls to the ground. "Hello, Salo."

"Hello, Niko." *I wanted to see you before I left, but now that you're here, I'm not sure what I want to say to you.*

Niko shifts uncomfortably on his feet. "I'm glad you recovered. You look well."

"I'll be leaving for Yonte Saire this afternoon."

Niko's eyes lift, flashing with surprise, but he masks it quickly. "I see."

"I'd ask you to come with me, but—"

"I can't, Salo."

It shouldn't hurt to hear. There could have been no other answer. Still feels like a knife to the heart. "I know."

"Not that I don't want to—"

"But what would people say, right?"

Niko turns his face away.

"Don't worry. I understand." Salo really does, but his voice grows bitter anyway. "You're risking a lot even talking to me right now."

He might as well have slapped Niko in the face. "I'm here, aren't I?"

Dear Ama, I'm messing this up. Salo looks heavenward and curses under his breath. "I know," he sighs. "I shouldn't have said that." *Compose yourself and start again.* "Look, I came here to thank you. You've never said a harsh word to me, even when I deserved it. You've defended me from scorn, even at the risk of your reputation. You were there for me when Monti died, and you took my side when everyone else blamed me. You're a good man, Niko. Better than most, and I hope that one day I'll earn back your friendship. That's all I wanted to say."

Salo turns and starts walking away, trying to escape the riptide of emotions, and he gets several paces away before Niko calls his name.

"Salo."

He stops. Waits. He knows what he wishes Niko would say, and he knows just how unlikely he is to hear it, but as the silence stretches, he holds his breath, and hope fills the cavity of his chest.

"Come back to us in one piece."

Salo doesn't turn around. He doesn't trust that his face won't betray too much of the emptiness, the sheer desolation, he feels from having his hopes crushed. He nods and keeps walking.

For the first eight years of his life, one of Salo's best friends was a giant metal cat. While most people feared it, often more than they feared its master, Salo knew the beast would never turn on him, given whom it answered to.

At least until the night its master betrayed him and set in motion the events that would culminate in her death. Then the cat returned to its post by the kraal's gates, where it would lie in wait for the next clan mystic to rouse it from its slumber.

The suns are high when Salo walks out of the kraal, lugging the sack of belongings he's packed for his journey. He has worn his leather harness and fastened to it his bow, a half-filled quiver, and a hatchet. He has filled his waterskins, honed his steel hunting knife, and rubbed his witchwood knife with an alchemical preservative.

Nimara follows him out carrying the clan's totem staff, which she unearthed for him from some shadowy corner of AmaSiningwe's vacant hut, along with the totem's ancient leather saddlery. A young boy she recruited is hauling the saddlery in a wheelbarrow; apparently, no one else wanted to touch anything that came out of the hut.

Word travels quickly around the kraal, so a crowd is waiting for them at the gates, with expressions ranging from curious to incensed. A quick scan tells Salo his brothers and a small group of young Ajaha are among the latter. *Figures.*

Mutters of "witch" and "siratata" ripple across the crowd as he unburdens himself of his luggage. He feigns indifference, but the whispers are like barbs digging into his heart. How will he ever win these people over?

Next to him Nimara proffers the staff. "Don't mind them. They'll get over it."

He doesn't believe her, but he reaches for the staff anyway, only to freeze when he sees VaSiningwe, Aba D, and a contingent of the chief's council looking joyless as they walk out of the gates in a group.

"Ignore them," Nimara says. "Actually, it's good that you have so many witnesses. It'll be harder for them to reject you once the totem responds positively. Now claim it already, or I'll do it for you."

"Okay, okay." Salo finally accepts the staff from her, and a strange tingle ripples down his whole body when he touches it. He ignores the surge of unwelcome memories that follows, focusing instead on the feel of the staff in his hands. An old thing, this staff, a serpentine affair of twisting witchwood and red steel, just a little longer than he is tall, though light as air. Like the totem connected to it, the staff has served every Siningwe mystic since the clan's inception. And now it is his.

"Don't keep us in suspense," Nimara goads him. "You know what to do, don't you?"

He does, or at least he has a general idea.

Shutting the rest of the world from his senses, he walks toward the watchtower overlooking the gates, where the totem sits on an overhanging beam, looking down at the gathered clanspeople like a proud king. He was named Mukuni the Conqueror after the leopard constellation of the high summer skies, and whatever sorcery that made him and all the other Yerezi totems is a secret guarded in the most impenetrable vaults of the Queen's Kraal.

A breeze whistles by, and Salo gets the sensation of a shadow stalking him from behind, the cold glint of metal and sharp teeth. He forces himself not to look over his shoulder. *He will not harm you if he responds to you.*

First, Salo claims the staff. Just one push of essence, and it becomes *his*, connected to him by an intangible tendril that settles at the back of his mind. The staff's secrets immediately unravel before him, and he sees that it is actually a mental lens of a kind, with the power to focus the mind onto a single task, thus greatly augmenting spell-casting ability.

He takes a long, uneven breath, trying not to be overwhelmed.

Next, he extends his free hand toward the totem and casts his mystic Seal for the very first time in his life.

The patterns erupt into the skies from his cosmic shards, knitting together before the watchtower into a dazzling arrangement of lines and flickering shapes that quickly resolves into something distinct: a cube of pure diamond spinning rapidly beneath a twinkling red star. Its hypnotic rays reach out to everyone looking at it to tell them of a young mystic born to a house of leopards.

For a fleeting instant the star flares to an almost blinding degree as something rises from the bowels of a deep slumber to answer its call, and when the Seal winks out of existence a second later, the metal cat on the beam has *opened* his neon-blue eyes.

Gasps and murmurs from the gathered clanspeople. Instant awareness glitters in those eyes. Even the way the cat abruptly rises to his feet is graceful.

He is alive, but the totem is no ordinary tronic beast. He has no flesh to speak of and is completely metalloid. Yet in the blink of an eye, most of his exterior transforms through sorcery from exposed silvery musculature to a glossy pelt as white as soured milk, with spots the color of burnished copper. The cat's underlying metalloid structure remains visible on his face and legs, however, which, next to his spotted pelt, gives him a rather striking appearance.

All eyes watch as he rustles the mane of sharp erectile metal spines encircling his neck. Then he leaps off his high perch to land on the ground with unnatural grace.

Those watching Salo probably think he's paralyzed with fear as he stands motionless while the arcane leopard makes for him, stalking around him with his long sinuous tail dancing fluidly in the air. What Salo is actually feeling, in fact, is shock.

Shock because he, Salo, is the cat.

Mukuni might be capable of independent motion, like Salo's beating heart, and even a little independent thought, like his subconscious mind, but the totem is still him, an extension of his will. He doesn't have to think much to get him to move—in fact, he doesn't have to think at all. The cat knows what Salo wants even before he knows it himself.

Silence thickens in the air as the totem brings his metallic snout close to Salo's face. Salo sees himself through the totem's eyes, and it's like looking into a strange mirror. Even after all the growing Salo has done, Mukuni still stands taller, as tall as any quagga stallion, though infinitely more terrifying.

"Hello, old friend." Salo raises a hand to stroke the fur beneath Mukuni's right ear. "It is good to see you again." For a beast with no flesh, the fur is surprisingly soft, just as soft as Salo remembers, and Mukuni purrs just like he used to when Salo was a child. The sound triggers a flood of bittersweet memories.

Purring again, the cat lies down on his belly in an unmistakable show of submission.

Murmurs of dissent. Muted arguments. But a hush descends as VaSiningwe steps forward with a raised hand. Before he speaks, he gives Mukuni a long wary glance laden with emotion. Seeing AmaSiningwe's pet alive again can't be easy for him, not when he saw him last on the night of her death.

"We are honored that our totem has returned to us," he says to the clanspeople. "This kraal is as much his home as it is ours, and it is always an honor to have him among us. As chief of the people who claim his name, I bid him welcome."

He preempts the brewing clamor with a raised hand. "This is not a debate, Siningwe-kin. The totem has always chosen whom he serves, and if he has chosen my son, we must respect that decision." His eyes burn into one particularly vociferous young man in a red loincloth. "You *will* respect that decision. That is an order."

Fury seethes on the young man's face, but he says no more.

"I am glad that Mukuni has chosen this moment to return," the chief continues, "for my son faces a journey to lands far beyond our borders in service to this clan—in service to *our* clan. I was worried he would have to go alone, but now I shall sleep better knowing he has found a formidable companion to accompany him." The chief's expression softens as he turns to Salo, and his voice too. "I wish you well, Musalodi. Know with every step you take that you are in our hearts and prayers—always."

"VaSiningwe." Salo goes down on one knee, his eyes filling with moisture. "I thank you," he says, and he means it, more than he's ever meant anything in his life.

Soon the totem is saddled up and ready to go. Salo's plan is to ride northwest into Khaya-Sikhozi and spend the night at the chief's kraal there. He will likely receive a cold and awkward reception, but it would be rude for him to sleep in their grazing lands without paying them a visit. Then, first thing tomorrow morning, he will cross the borderlands and ride toward the World's Artery.

He fastens the staff to a harness and straps his belongings to the back of the saddle. He's about to climb onto the cat's back when Aaku Malusi walks up to him. The sight of the old man drives a pang of shame and guilt into his heart. He really was about to leave without bidding him farewell.

"Aaku," he says, unable to meet his friendly gaze. "I came by your hut to say goodbye, but you weren't there." The truth, but still. Besides Nimara, no one visited him in the bonehouse as frequently as Aaku Malusi. He deserves better.

The old man smiles, no sign of hurt or offense in his expression. Instead, an unusually lucid glimmer dances in his eyes, and he's not leaning on his walking staff. Salo hasn't seen him look this hale in a long time.

"All is well, my child," he says. "You had many other things to worry about, and in any case, I knew I'd be seeing you off now." He looks around to make sure he won't be overheard before leaning closer. "Listen, Musalodi. I wanted to give you this." Almost timidly, Aaku Malusi unfurls the fingers of his free hand to reveal a ring of twined, rough-hewed witchwood set with a round little stone of citrine quartz. "I've had this ring since I was a boy but never the courage to wear it. I would be honored if you took it."

Salo hesitates, but the expectant look on the old man's face forces him to accept the ring. The witchwood flexes ever so slightly as he slips it onto his right middle finger, making a perfect fit. He feels its fibers humming with patterns that will come to life should he feed them essence. A dormant enchantment, perhaps?

He tests this by pushing just the slightest bit of essence into the ring and is amazed when a small yellow star ignites inside the citrine rock, bathing his face in a brilliant glow. A ring of Mirror light.

"May it brighten your way in your darkest hour," Aaku Malusi says, his eyes shining with emotion. "Go well, my child, and may Ama guide your steps."

Salo feels his own eyes begin to water. "I don't know what to say, Aaku. Thank you."

"No, my child. It is I who must thank you, for you have given a hopeless old man something to believe in. Now go, and make sure you come back."

People are still watching, people who have ill-treated and scorned Aaku Malusi for longer than Salo has been alive, but he doesn't care. He embraces the old man, hoping the contact will convey what words cannot express. A tear rolls down his cheek when he lets go, and he doesn't bother wiping it.

He has to force himself to climb onto the totem's saddle, to keep moving, to leave everything he's ever known behind. It's all he can do not to turn back and beg for everything to go back to the way it used to be.

The cat begins to move, and Salo is almost shocked to be reminded of how smoothly he stalks upon the ground, how silently, like a boat rocking gently on the waves of a calm lake.

He's a good twenty paces down the road when he can finally handle looking back and waving his last goodbye at the people he's leaving behind. Nimara, the friend who's never turned her back on him. Aaku Malusi, the friend he took for granted. The chief, a father who has always tried to do his best for a son he doesn't understand. His clanspeople, many of whom will never accept him. And a familiar silhouette watching him from atop the now-vacant watchtower, wearing armor pieces that glint like stars against the blue sky.

Perhaps in another world, in a different time, Salo would have stopped right there and then and said to the figure, *Come with me,* and it would have been so.

But now, as they stare at each other for the last time in a long time, all he can do is wave once and look away.

20: Isa

In an ancient temple at the heart of a continent, in a chamber awash with the torpid light of glowing rubies, before an audience of temple votaries, Jasiri guardians, clanspeople, young Sentinels, and a high mystic, a king wears the mask-crown for the first time.

This is no throne room—far from it, in fact—but she sits upon a high wooden chair on a dais, raised so she can overlook the small crowded chamber and see the anxiety and fear sketched onto the faces of all those present.

She knows how they feel. The gold and ivory chains of her forefathers burden her shoulders; sweat drenches her brow behind the mask-crown. She is afraid, just like the people looking up at her, but she is king now, and a king must never show his fear. So she swallows it up and projects an outward vision of calm and resolve, just as her father would have done.

The mask-crown is a heavy thing, a moongold artifact enchanted to give its wearer the head of a four-tusked elephant with a lofty crown of spikes, overlarge on her face because it was designed long ago to be worn by imposing, battle-tested men, not girls nearing the cusp of womanhood. Still, it clings to her face, failing to dent her posture if only because she cannot allow it to, as if by conquering the mask-crown, she will conquer the horrifying reality that it now sits upon her face.

The horrifying reality that *she* is now king.

The mask is clean today, burnished so that it gleams brightly in the ruby light, but when she last saw it, it was bathed in blood, askew on a marble floor next to the face of a dead king.

"All hail Isa Andaiye Saire!" cries the high mystic. "King of Chains, Great Elephant of the Yontai, she who straddles the center of the world and rules its beating heart! Long may she reign!"

Empty titles; she knows this. She no more rules the world's beating heart than she rules the temple that now holds her prisoner. Her father always used to say that the mask-crown is greater than its wearer. This has never been truer than it is today.

All around the chamber, those present bow their heads low in obeisance. It is against convention, but the old sorcerer who has just crowned her bows, too, even though his blood is divine and hers is not. Then again, of the seven high mystics of the Shirika, Itani Faro of the Arc has always been the most contrary. It is why Isa is still alive.

He remains by her side when she exits the makeshift throne room to forced cheers and applause. Two young warriors in the light-green tunics of the King's Sentinels follow solemnly with their ceremonial hide shields and spears—warriors of the King's Sentinels, because the entire Royal Guard was wiped out when . . . when . . .

Inside the antechamber to the throne room, Isa takes the mask-crown off her face, and it collapses into itself, becoming static and somewhat less remarkable in appearance. Anxious to part with it, she extends the mask-crown to Obe Saai, but the Sentinel draws back, aghast.

"Please," she says, proffering the thing to him. "My neck hurts, and I'd like to take a walk."

Obe's eyes swivel to Itani Faro, who gives a subtle nod. "It's a great sign of trust, young man," the Arc says. "You should be honored."

"Yes, Your Worship." Obe accepts the mask-crown with a shaky hand. "You honor me, Great Elephant."

She trusts him, yes, more than anyone else still drawing breath, but this is no honor.

Except that's not quite how it looks to Dino Sato, Isa's other honor guard. Certainly not by the way he tightens his jaw in unexpressed displeasure. Dino was at one point Obe's rival for her affections; she knows the two warriors have no love lost between them and belatedly realizes now that she's probably made things worse by so obviously choosing one over the other.

Only minutes after being crowned king, and she's already sown enmity between her two most trusted guards. But that's what it means to be king, isn't it? Sowing enmity with every breath.

"Will you walk with me?" she asks the Arc.

His height and his scarified face are intimidating, but it's his divinity that terrifies her. His power, his gravity. As the high priest of the Red Temple, Itani Faro is possibly the most powerful high mystic of them all. And yet she finds comfort in his company, this god in mortal flesh, who remained true when the rest of the Shirika turned their backs on her father and her family. He was there for her when it would have been prudent to turn away.

And even now, he bows to her. "Of course, Your Majesty."

The four of them walk along the temple's bamboo arcades in grim silence, a fresh wind buffeting their robes. Rivulets from the recent storm drip from trees and rooftops into the ponds dotting the gardens. The skies remain gray and somber, like a mirror of her soul.

Jasiri temple guardians pledged to the Arc's coven have been patrolling the bamboo cloisters in silent pairs since Isa got here. There probably aren't more than a dozen of them in the whole temple citadel—tall, forbidding figures who keep to themselves, all of them as striking as their coven master—but Isa knows that even if her enemies ever made it past the lightning barrier the Arc erected around the citadel, those dozen Jasiri would be a more than adequate defense of the temple.

Isa's retinue crosses paths with such a pair along the arcade, two barefoot young men with large shoulder muscles peeking from beneath the folds of shimmering red brocade and aerosteel armor pieces chased with moongold. White tattoos run in thin lines down their necks—the marks of the magical caste. Charmed spears gleam brilliantly in their right hands, and their faces are hidden behind horned masks with no eye slits.

Isa inclines her head to them in respect. They acknowledge her with deep bows of their own and then proceed without a word. Isa and her companions do the same.

Minutes later a tall figure clad in blue appears along the arcade, hobbling toward them with his face set in a crestfallen glower. A squeaky gilded leg brace clings to his left leg, which he favors as he walks, leaning on a cane with a golden knob for support. The other hand holds the herald's scepter, which belonged to his mother until a few nights ago.

A small part of Isa resents Jomo for refusing the mask-crown, in essence forcing her to accept it. The rest of her, though, is infinitely grateful for his presence. He has been a pillar of courage she would have crumbled without.

Today, for example. While Isa was being crowned, Kola Saai, head-man of the crocodile clan, was holding an emergency meeting with the headmen in the Summit; Jomo was brave enough to leave the safety of the temple and attend the meeting in his capacity as Isa's herald.

It is more than a big relief to see that he has returned safely.

They all stop when they come face-to-face. He bows to the Arc first. "Your Worship." Then he bows to Isa. "I apologize, Great Elephant, for missing your coronation. I have only just returned from the Summit."

"You were doing something much more important, cousin," she says. "You were serving me as herald. What news do you bring?"

Jomo's expression grows darker. "The headmen have elected the Crocodile as their regent. You should have seen the smug look on the bastard's face." Jomo seems to remember his company, and his light-complexioned cheeks gain a reddish tinge. "Excuse my language, Your Worship."

"They moved quickly, didn't they," the high mystic remarks with a slight sneer.

"He claims he's simply stepping in to bring stability back to the kingdom, but he says he'll step down as soon as Her Majesty decides to leave the temple."

"So he can have me killed," Isa says.

Jomo grunts. "The filth denies any involvement in the Royal Massacre, and that's not even the worst part."

Isa raises an eyebrow. "There's worse?"

"Oh yes. Right after reminding me of the mortal peril our clan now faces since we're deeply resented and unprotected, he had the gall to propose a marriage of equals. He claims you'd rule as king and queen in your own rights, except that the mask-crown would have to be destroyed—you know, since he can't be crowned king so long as it exists."

Isa feels Obe Saai going tense behind her. It takes everything she has not to look his way. The Arc, meanwhile, glares in her direction. "This is madness, Your Majesty. You cannot possibly consider the proposal."

She wanders to the edge of the arcade, a hand braced upon her chest. The colorful minnows in the pond below scurry away from her reflection. She can't stand the fear she sees on her own face, so she looks away. "But what other choice do I have?" she says to the men around her. "I may be safe from him in this temple, but our people are still out there. Anti-Saire sentiment has been on the rise throughout the kingdom. If I don't give him what he wants, he could orchestrate a genocide, and no one would stop it."

A memory flashes through her right then: her brother Kali warning their father about the Crocodile's growing ambitions. She balls the trembling hand on her chest into a fist, locking her kingly chains in a tight grip. "This has been his plan all along," she says, thinking aloud. "He has stoked hatred against us to prepare himself for this."

"The King's Sentinels still stand, Your Majesty," the Arc says. "So long as that remains true, Kola Saai's hand will be stayed. We have time to find another way out of this."

Jomo snorts, his eyes red rimmed with misery and anger. "With all due respect, Your Worship, I don't want my cousin to marry that excretion of a human being, but what help could the Sentinels offer us? They're whelps as green as their tunics." He scowls at the warriors standing stiffly nearby. A fire sparks in his eyes when he sees Obe Saai—specifically, when he sees what Obe Saai is holding in one hand. "And what in the pits is *he* doing here? He's a Saai, for the Mother's sake. Kola's own nephew! He could be spying for his traitor prince!"

Obe seethes visibly but dares not speak.

Jomo hobbles closer to him, squaring his broad shoulders. "Something to say, crocodile filth?" Jomo has always been the most dissolute and academic of the Saire princes, but he has never been accused of lacking a spine. And one of the first things people often learn about him is that he has a quick temper.

"Cousin, this is unseemly." Isa places a gentle hand on his arm, then bows to the high mystic. "Forgive him, Your Worship. It is a deeply emotional time for all of us. Might I have a word with him in private?"

The old sorcerer gives Jomo a disapproving glare, then nods to Isa. "Of course, Your Majesty. We will not go far." And then he leads Obe Saai and Dino Sato down the arcade and out of sight. Elsewhere, she might have begun to fear for her safety, but not in this citadel, not with a dozen Jasiri guardians and the temple's high priest only yards away.

"I know you're hurting," she says to Jomo when they're alone, in as gentle a voice as she can manage. "Believe me, I know, but Obe has proven his loyalty, and he saved my life. You haven't forgotten that, have you?"

Jomo's round cheeks flush with shame, and then he looks skyward, eyes heavy with unshed tears. "I'm so sorry, Isa. Dear Mother, what has gotten into me?"

"Nothing you don't have the right to feel."

He lowers his eyes to study her and sniffs. "How do you do it? You're so calm and strong when I feel like my head will explode any second now."

She wonders why no one can see her trembling hands, hear her racing heart. She's inches away from pulling her hair out with her bare hands, and yet he sees strength when he looks at her. "I feel the same way. I guess . . . I'm just a better liar."

"No," Jomo says. "You're the King of Chains, dear cousin. You're Mweneugo's daughter. You're brave and strong, and you'll be a great king."

She smiles, and even though it's feeble, the emotion behind it comes from the little corner of her heart where hope still shines. "And you will be as great a herald as your mother was."

He smiles, too, but the gloom soon returns to his face like rain clouds obscuring the suns. "What are we going to do about this, Isa? We're the only clan without a legion. We didn't need one with the Shirika on our side, but the Crocodile bought them off somehow, and now he's taken control of the City Guard. I've been out in the city, Isa, and many Saires aren't leaving their homes out of fear. It's madness, I tell you."

Isa walks to stare down into the pond again. The gold and ivory chains woven into her blue robes seem to mock her reflection. She looks like a girl playing dress up, not a king.

"How's the palace?" she asks.

Jomo lets out a harsh laugh. "The bastard's turned it into a moth-erforsaken whorehouse. You should have seen the way he welcomed me like a guest—into my own home! The filth already fancies himself king."

Just as well, a part of Isa says, the part that never wants to see the palace again, not after what happened there, what she saw there . . .

. . . blood on the floors, blood drenching the tapestries. Her mother slumped by the wall like she was taking a rest, except for her dry, vacant eyes; the grimace; and the congealed blood from the mortal gash on her temple. Kali sprawled on the floor with his head halfway severed, Ayo gutted in his own bed, Zenia floating in a bloody bathing pool, Suye's little golden shoe upside down by her cot, a shape lying facedown on the crimson-stained sheets. Isa didn't look; she couldn't . . .

Isa shuts her eyes. They say that when her father was enthroned, years before her birth, the Mother sent slow, gentle rains to shower the city for an entire week, signifying that his would be a peaceful, prosperous reign. Today a violent storm tore through the sullen skies, rattling the temple's shutters and threatening to tear them off their hinges.

She has never been one for omens, but Isa needs no omens to know that the mask-crown will kill her. She knew it the moment she saw her father lying dead in his own blood.

"His Worship might be right, you know," she says. "The Sentinels are a thorn in Kola's side. He can't touch our people so long as they stand."

"What's to stop him? The Shirika are on his side. The City Guard won't obey me anymore. He has the Bonobo in his pocket, and together they command the kingdom's two most powerful legions—and by the way, those legionnaires are all older, far more experienced, and a lot more committed to the cause than our dear Sentinels. What chance do we have?"

"It's not about strength or numbers, cousin." She turns to face him. "Yes, if it came to a fight, the Sentinels would perish, and us along with them. But every headman, including Kola himself, has sons and nephews bound to the Sentinels. Heirs, future vassals, young men who'll command and fill the ranks of their clan legions in the future. He'd be foolish to risk a confrontation that could kill them off. The other headmen would soon turn against him, even those who've stayed neutral thus far."

Jomo sighs. "I understand that, Great Elephant, but you're operating on the assumption that Kola Saai is a rational man."

"I *know* he's a rational man," Isa says with enough venom to surprise herself. "Coldly rational. A man who can turn high mystics—*gods*—to such a bloody cause can't be anything else." She takes a deep breath and slowly exhales. She can't allow herself to lose control. "Kola Saai is chipping away at our power to force my abdication. He has taken the Shirika from us. Now he'll seek to disband the Sentinels so he can put pressure on our people. It has to be his next move."

The irony. Isa has always hated the Sentinels, what she's always seen as hostage taking disguised as military training. Every year hundreds of sixteen-year-old boys are plucked from their homes and brought to the capital, where a curse is cast on them so they can barely even think a traitorous thought without suffering extreme pain. The Sentinels are a stick the Saires have always held over their sister clans: *Play nice, because we have the Shirika on our side and death bonds coiled around your young men. Start a war with us, and it's their blood you'll be spilling.*

She used to argue with her brothers about the injustice of the custom, how it only bred further hatred for the Saires and didn't guarantee continued loyalty once the curse was lifted. And yet here she is, making plans to preserve it. She feels covered in dirt she can't ever wash off.

"I suspect he'll petition the Shirika to vote on the matter," she says. "If and when they agree, he'll need the support of at least five other headmen for the vote to go his way. We mustn't let that happen."

Jomo scratches the bristles on his cheeks and shakes his head slowly. "But he has the support, Isa. They elected him regent, didn't they?"

"Only because no one else wanted to contest the position."

"Even so, you know as well as I do that they've always hated the Sentinels. How hard do you think it'll be for Kola to convince them to vote his way?"

"Kola has enemies among the headmen, cousin. We need to capitalize on that. We'll have to appeal to them. Buy their allegiance if we must. So long as the Sentinels stand, we'll . . ."

They'll what? The Crocodile won't be going away without bloodshed, and if it comes to bloodshed, he has every conceivable advantage on his side.

"We'll have hope," Isa finishes, covering the hand on Jomo's cane with her own. "We'll have time to find another way, and we *will* find another way. You and I, we'll make it out of this; do you understand me?" Isa knows that these words are as good as lies, but they're what Jomo needs to hear, so she speaks them without compunction.

Jomo blinks away the moisture in his eyes and nods. "I won't give up so long as you keep fighting, Isa. You're all I've got left."

Above the towering pylon of the innermost courtyard, peeking over the temple's bamboo rooftops like a small red sun, the Ruby Paragon begins to strobe brilliantly, signaling the turn of the hour. Isa and Jomo bask in its cold light, hand in hand, until it strobes six times and then falls silent.

"Come." She forces another smile. "I won't have us be miserable at my coronation feast. After all, there'll be no one to tell us we can't drink the cider."

His laugh is sad and gravelly, but his shoulders seem lighter as they walk to rejoin Itani Faro and the two Sentinels. Isa counts this as a minor victory, the first of her reign.

PART 4

THE MAIDSERVANT
*
ILAPARA
*
MUSALODI

Blood craft—magic of the flesh

Converting the moon's essence into the energies of life to manipulate flesh and minds, both living and dead. Wielded by healers, hypnotists, beast masters, necromancers, and monster makers.

—excerpt from Kelafelo's notes

"Aago, why do so many bad things happen in the world?"

"A very difficult question, my child, and the sad truth is that no one really knows. The way I see it, we are creatures who thrive on order and predictability living in an inherently chaotic universe. That leaves us exposed to any forces beyond our ability to control, and in such a universe, there are an infinite number of these."

"So . . . if we controlled more things, then less bad things would happen?"

"Perhaps. But it would depend on who wields this control, for in the wrong hands, control—power—can be a greater agent of evil than chaos."

21: The Maidservant

Southeast Umadiland

Agony. Hatred. Whorls of fire dancing across her skin. A door shaking violently until it bursts into a million splinters, revealing a yawning abyss that sucks her in while letting terrible things rush out and take over her body, monsters with gnashing teeth.

You will lose yourself to it.

In a cold sweat the Maidservant emerges from a fitful dream to the sound of an old wooden door creaking in its frame as the wind beats softly against it. A raw stench clings to the air, faint but sickly, like bile and dried blood.

She sits up in her pallet, letting the woolen blanket covering her fall away from her naked body. The soft glow of dawn has leaked in through the gap beneath the door and around the rickety shutters, casting a diffuse light on a starkly appointed room with an earthen floor and walls covered with grass tapestries.

A hut. Somewhere in a remote valley of the southeastern Umadi savannas, if memory serves her right. A body too. Not the warm, hefty one curled up on the pallet next to her, snoring like a veldboar, but the crumpled lifeless form across the hut. That body is the source of the stench.

You will lose yourself to it.

The Maidservant quietly rises from the pallet, suppressing a groan when waves of searing pain lap and purl across her body: her tattoos bidding her a good morning. She doesn't fight the pain; she lets it wash over her. The agony chases away every vestige of sleep and fills her to bursting with hatred, which she uses to fortify the rattling door in her mind.

Enough of this weakness.

She drifts to the table across the room, draws up a chair for herself, and sits down.

After a glance at the slumbering form on the pallet, she draws magic to reach into her Voidspace and summon two items: a scorpion pendant on a beaded string and a shiny spherical mind stone. She places both gently on the table.

Like a key lying just out of the reach of a caged prisoner, the mind stone has tormented her for years with the things she knows it holds, truths that would break the mental shackles binding her if she could only access them. But no more. Now those truths will be hers, and she will finally be free.

Free to bathe the world in blood until her hatred is sated.

With a thought she awakens the talisman; it responds immediately, curling its tail and setting its crystal sting alight with multihued beams that sweep over the mind stone. An illusion of Mirror craft appears above the crystal a moment later, displaying to the Maidservant an image of the mind stone. In this image a thick layer of protection surrounds the stone, an enchantment that manifests as countless lines of semitransparent neon-green cipher prose, each line swarming around the stone along a different orbital path, like insects around a crystal lamp. Together the ciphers bar access to the information stored within the stone's lattices.

The Maidservant sits back in her chair, staring intently at the mirage. The secret to her freedom is buried somewhere behind that moving layer of prose. She has tried to break through with her mind, but the prose mends itself so quickly she can't keep up, not even with spells that slow her perception of time or elixirs that speed up her thoughts.

But now, with this Yerezi talisman and its vastly accelerated logic, she will be able to analyze the prose and chip away at it, widening the cracks until the enchantment collapses. This is only her third session with the talisman, and fractures have already appeared. She focuses on such a place now, unraveling the prose faster than it can self-repair, and several minutes pass in silent productiveness.

Then a hoarse male voice calls to her from the pallet across the room. "Come back to bed, my little fly."

Everyone else calls him Black River, for he shed a river of blood upon his awakening with spear and magic to prove his allegiance to their warlord. She just calls him River, or the man with whom she sometimes spends the night. A diversion, really. A constant nuisance.

At the sound of his voice, a strong current of distaste makes her wonder why she tolerates him at all. She returns her attention to the mirage. "I have work to do."

River collapses back onto the pallet and sighs. "You're always tinkering with that stupid thing these days."

"If by 'stupid thing' you mean one of the most valuable repositories of arcane knowledge in existence, and if by 'tinkering' you mean inching closer toward breaking the powerful charms protecting it, then yes, I'm tinkering with the stupid thing."

Anyone else, and she would have had to kill him after divulging such information, but the man across the room, mystic though he may be, is an idiot. He wouldn't know true magic if it exploded in his face.

"That's a flashy new spell," he says dreamily. "I didn't know you could work illusions too."

"I can't."

"No? Then what am I looking at?"

"Something you wouldn't understand if I explained it to you a thousand times."

River snorts with low-pitched laughter. "You're probably right."

The Maidservant isn't looking his way, but she can picture him relaxing on his back with his head resting on interlaced hands, staring up at the rafters with a crooked grin while his chest heaves with laughter. A tingle of arousal and something else stirs inside her at the image, but she kills it quickly with a well-aimed spike of hatred. "You should get rid of the body."

"What body?" River asks from the pallet.

"The old man you killed last night. I believe this was his hut. The stench of him offends me."

"*I* killed him? Huh. That's not how I remember it. Then again, we did have a bit of a wild night, didn't we?"

You will lose yourself to it.

The smugness in River's voice irritates the Maidservant, and she grits her teeth. "Get rid of him."

"Why bother? It's not like we'll be coming back here again."

"Just do it, River."

The man emits a loud groan before fumbling around the pallet for his kikoi. "As you wish, my little fly." She hears him get up, wrap the kikoi around his waist, and pad toward the old man's body.

He must study it because he's quiet for a while. "Why'd we kill him again?"

"Why d'you think?"

"Can't remember. I'm guessing we had to torture him for information on our free agent. But are you sure it's *me* who killed him, because . . . you know what? Never mind. Doesn't matter anyway."

While she continues deciphering the mind stone's protections, River hauls the body out of the hut and returns minutes later with the whiff of smoke and burnt flesh hanging about his person.

He's a man of simple dress for a warlord's disciple. Nothing ever covers his heavily tattooed torso save for a cascading necklace of beads and bones, and he's always in a red-and-black kikoi.

He's a broad-shouldered silhouette when he stands by the door, blocking the light from the rising suns. "Speaking of our free agent, I say we pay him a visit soon. The big man hasn't summoned us in more than a month, and I have a feeling he'll do it today. I don't want this assignment delaying us."

The Maidservant tenses up in her seat. River might not know why, but he has a knack for knowing when the "big man" is about to summon them. Sure enough, he has no sooner finished speaking than a tremor of power ripples across the ground beneath their feet.

No one but a mystic with the Umadi ancestral talent in their blood would sense this tremor—though it isn't quite a tremor, more like a shadow blanketing the earth as a storm cloud floats by. Either way, it's a clear message from the man who rules the land from which she and River and many other disciples draw their strength, and it says: *Come.*

A command the Maidservant could never defy even if she wanted to.

River gives her a self-congratulatory grin, teeth showing through a thick beard. "See? What did I tell you?"

Uttering a curse, she waves a glowing arm over the table, banishing both talisman and mind stone back into her Voidspace. "I'm so close," she mutters. "Closer than I've ever been. I can feel the walls cracking and giving way. I just need more time."

River frowns at her in concentration. He scratches his beard, seeming to weigh the words in his mouth before he speaks them. "You know, little fly, I have no idea what you're up to, and I really don't care that you haven't told me, but . . . you know I'm with you to the end of the world, right?"

The Maidservant blinks at him, this stupid walking conundrum of a man. She has seen firsthand how ruthless and cruel he can be, how callously he can kill, how black his heart is. She has seen him slaughter countless innocent souls. And yet he can stand there and feel genuine concern for her?

How is he not a howling, hateful void? How is it that he expects her to *feel* something as he does? How *dare* he expect this from her. Who does he think he is?

She gives him an icy smile. "You're not going soft on me, are you, River?"

He lifts his open palms in a gesture of appeasement. "Point taken." And without another word he moves into the hut to collect his spear of tronic bone where he left it balanced against the wall. "We should get going."

For some reason the Maidservant is annoyed that he doesn't say more or try harder; she cleanses herself of that useless sentiment by focusing on the lingering pain of her tattoos, inviting a purifying torrent of hatred to wash over her. Instantly sobering.

A minute later she whisks them both into the Void, and they sweep toward the village in the valley in a cloud of swiftly moving flies, leaving the hut forever.

The secluded village is a group of thatched mud huts surrounding a central compound. The Maidservant and River materialize from the Void in a recently cultivated field just south of the village and watch for a time as it slowly wakes up to the morning.

A woman with a baby swaddled on her back is bent over as she sweeps the dry earth around her hut with a brush of twigs, stirring up clouds of dust. Not far from her, two young boys in brightly colored kikois enter a pen and start herding a group of bleating goats out of it. A trio of teenage girls moving in procession walks up a well-beaten path from the river, balancing earthen jars on their veiled heads. Distastefully quaint, how these people seem to take their peace for granted.

"I like this part," River says, idly twisting his metalloid spear.

The Maidservant studies him and notes the predatory glint in his deep-set eyes. This is the River she understands, the bloodthirsty brute. "What part?" she says.

His teeth show as he practically salivates at the village. "Watching while they're still going about their lives. They have no idea what's about to happen to them."

The Maidservant looks back at the village. Some part of her prods itself to see what she feels about what she must do here; as usual, it comes up empty. "Then let's change that."

Stretching his neck muscles and grinning a feral grin, River ignites his three-ringed shards with the moon's power. And then they attack.

River is a Fire mystic, and though his sorcery might not be particularly skillful or powerful, his deadliest spell can enshroud an unwarded victim in devouring moonfire.

He's also quite lethal with his spear. While he skewers and burns everything in his path, the Maidservant shapes the Void into sharp projectiles that she launches at doors and windows all around the village to catch everyone's attention and draw them out.

The door in her mind, however, the one that always rattles more fiercely whenever she commits violence, demanding that she open it and use its dark power: that one she keeps shut. No need for it just yet.

Screams disturb the peaceful skies. A startled man runs out of a hut with a machete; she launches a Void spear at him, and he goes down with a cry, his chest split in half. River clenches a pulsing fist, and a woman goes up in flames. They kill for a full minute before an old woman kneels behind the Maidservant with her hands thrown up.

"Please!" she cries. "By the Blood Woman, stop!"

Both the Maidservant and River stop their killing to consider her. By the kaross of hide draped over her shoulders, they know she's one of the village elders.

"Where is he?" the Maidservant asks her, knowing she doesn't need to elaborate.

Anger twists the old woman's face, tears trickling down her wizened cheeks. "How could you be so evil? Have you no heart? We are peaceful people, and yet you butcher us like swine."

"You can't say I didn't give you a chance." The Maidservant finally opens the door in her mind, and her shards flare with dark energy.

She almost sways at the staggering force that pushes against the door in response, a throng of profane spirits attempting to rush out of that other realm all at once, but she remains outwardly calm. Beneath the surface, her whole body vibrates from the tremendous effort of bracing her will against the door and allowing only one entity to come through, a particular fiend in the form of a malignant web of black slime.

She shuts the door as soon as the fiend leaps from her hands and straight onto the old woman's face, where it immediately crawls into her eyes, nostrils, and ears, burrowing into her head. The old woman lets out a cry as she claws at her face, but she is powerless to stop the webs as they begin to consume her mind, stealing the information the Maidservant wants.

Eventually she falls to the earth as a deadened husk. The other villagers scream.

Ignoring them, the Maidservant calls back the inky webs. They flow into her shards from the woman like streams of oil, and she closes her eyes as she feeds on the knowledge they acquired. Then her eyes fling open, and she points to one of the larger huts. "He's in there."

With a throw of his burning hand, River releases a blast of moonfire that collapses a third of the hut's round wall. A figure coated in dust emerges seconds later with his palms raised in surrender. "Please, stop! Why are you doing this?"

The free agent. He is young and somewhat fat, and the Maidservant discerns his whole story just by looking at him. Probably a disciple's bastard who's been treated like a prince his whole life. It all went to his head, making him think he could awaken and rule his people as some sort of mystic chief. Now many of them are dead because of his folly.

Idiot.

She can sense the way he has rooted his shards to the land beneath their feet, like he's a tree drinking arcane sustenance from the earth. Unfortunately for him, there's another power rooted to this village and to a great swath of the Umadi savannas, and it demands a steep price for sharing even the smallest square foot of its land: complete and unquestioning fealty.

"You have claimed land that belongs to the Dark Sun without his permission," the Maidservant tells the mystic.

His lips tremble with fear, and he stutters. "B-but this is my home! The land of my forefathers, and rooting myself to it doesn't affect the warlord's power at all!"

River leans on his spear, crosses one foot in front of the other ankle, and smiles like he thinks the young mystic is an idiot. "But this is the Dark Sun's land, you see, and he only shares it with those who pledge allegiance to him, which you have not, hence our presence here." He looks at the Maidservant, his face comically incredulous. "You'd think everyone would understand this by now, what with all the killing and burning we do to drive the point home."

"What do you want from me?" the free agent says. By now all the villagers who are still alive have gathered behind him to listen, a wretched crowd of shocked and tearful people huddled together like terrified sheep around their shepherd.

The Maidservant scours their faces before her gaze falls back onto the young mystic, who presses his palms together.

"Please. How can I fix this?"

She is blunt with him, and as she speaks, his eyes grow progressively wider. "Offer a gift of blood to the Dark Sun as penance for your transgression, and a second as proof of your allegiance to him. Once that is done, we will leave you be."

"*Two* blood offerings?" He casts an apprehensive glance over his shoulder at the people behind him, two of whom he must now kill if he is to save what's left of his village. When he looks back at the Maidservant, she sees a fragile glimmer of defiance in his eyes. "And if I don't?"

The Maidservant crushes that glimmer with her next words: "Then we kill everyone here, burn down the village, and take your head back to our lord, who will keep it as a trophy."

The villagers gasp. Some of them wail. The free agent starts to stutter again, making floundering gestures. "B-but I only wanted to help my people! I-it's why I awoke! We're far from any other settlements, and we don't have a healer—"

River blessedly interrupts him with a raised hand. "I'm going to stop you right there. Your sob story? We've heard it all before. 'Oh, we have no healer, and my mother was dying.' 'Oh, we needed to protect our families from raiders.' Well, guess what: No one told you to root yourself to the land. You could have healed or protected or whatever without taking what isn't yours."

"And you'd have just left me alone?" the mystic bursts. "I doubt that very much! Everyone knows the warlords don't leave free agents alone."

River smiles. "Ah, so you laid your roots anyway, knowing that if we *did* come for you, we'd come whether you laid roots or not. Which means you knew exactly what you were doing." He raises a bushy eyebrow at the Maidservant. "Can I kill him now?"

"Make your choice," she says, ignoring River. "Two blood offerings and allegiance to the Dark Sun, or death for you and all your people."

Tears are now pouring down the young mystic's face. "That isn't really a choice."

River rolls his eyes. "Devil's tits, boy. We're not here to mother you."

"My patience is at an end," the Maidservant says, "and destroying your little village would mean nothing to me. But whether that happens is up to you. So what will it be?"

Covering a sob with a hand, the young mystic turns around to face his people. "I'm sorry. I thought I could do this without bowing to a warlord, but such is our fate." His shoulders start to shake, and his voice breaks. "Please don't ask me to choose who dies. I can't! I need two people to offer themselves for the sake of the rest."

"How typical," River mutters with a cynical shake of his head. "A free agent asking others to make things easier for him so he doesn't have to live with the consequences of his decisions. I'm tempted to gut him just for that alone."

"Easy," the Maidservant cautions him. "No killing unless he fails."

River doesn't hide his disappointment, but he obeys.

While the free agent settles things with his people, she reaches into her Voidspace and withdraws a medallion of witchwood infused with the ciphers of her lord's mystic Seal. Palming the medallion, she fills it with essence from her shards until it is saturated, then keeps filling it until the power arcs out of the medallion and manifests above the village as a black sphere bounded by a brilliant halo of colorful light, almost like the moon during a solar eclipse.

At the sight of the orb, the villagers gasp, many falling to their knees. Even if they have never seen it before, they now know that this vision is the Dark Sun's mystic Seal, his symbol of authority and power. When the free agent spills the blood of his own people beneath its light, their agony will feed the warlord's power. Marginally so, but what matters is that he will know it happened, and he will be pleased.

Intense hatred briefly blinds the Maidservant's vision. She rides it out by remembering how close she is to her freedom. Soon there'll be nothing holding her back, and she will spit on his bloody corpse.

She banishes the medallion back to the Void and replaces it with a ritual witchwood dagger, turning her attention back to the villagers. Two elderly men with defeated postures are now flanking the tearful mystic, all three staring up at the Seal like they think it might swallow them whole.

"Will these be your victims?" the Maidservant asks, and the mystic sobs his assent.

"Why is it always two old men?" River mumbles to the side.

Ignoring him again, the Maidservant says: "While they still draw breath, you will take their ears, lips, tongues, and finally hearts. You will speak your pledge to the Dark Sun both times. Do this incorrectly, and you'll have to repeat, which means another victim. Understood?"

Broken and distraught, the mystic falls to his knees.

She proffers him the dagger. "Now choose who goes first."

22: Ilapara

Seresa, along the World's Artery—Umadiland

The hovel Ilapara steps into on her way to work is the Vuriro Transporters office here in Seresa, though *office* is very generous, considering the lack of a floor and the lingering stench of wet mud and goat shit.

Nothing much in the way of furniture inside, just a rickety old table, behind which sits a gaunt, pipe-smoking foreman drowning in paperwork and the folds of his oversize dashiki. A hand-painted sign hanging perilously above him tells potential customers to **Be Safe! Be Smart! Travel with Vuriro Transporters!** and then proceeds to list the exorbitant destination-based prices for doing so, all in bright-yellow standard script.

Once upon a time, Vuriro Transporters was her old employer's biggest rival. Now, with Mimvura Company effectively extinct, Vuriro is the biggest mercenary company in the heartland of Umadiland. Business has been splendid for them of late, which is why she is here.

Despite the ill-favored atmosphere, quite a lot of money changes hands in this hovel, so there's a younger man standing next to the table like an overgrown guard dog. Looking at his brawny arms and the ax clinging to his back, one would likely think twice about trying anything funny in here.

But Ilapara happens to know that those muscles are purely cosmetic, so she has no qualms about approaching the table and clearing her throat. For one thing, she has a long shiny spear in her right hand.

"Foreman Jijima," she says in greeting. She keeps her expression polite and nods at his guard. "Rufa."

Rufa flashes his pearly teeth and winks knowingly at her. A pang of regret cuts her so sharply she has to fight off a grimace. *I'm never getting drunk again.*

The foreman finally raises his baggy, bleary eyes from his paperwork. "What do you want now?" he says, mumbling around his burning pipe.

Far from the greeting she was hoping for, but Ilapara has never gotten a job by being thin skinned. She keeps her voice level, professional, politely expectant. "You told me to come check this morning. Has anything opened up?"

"Sorry, girl, but I've got enough lackeys on my payroll." And with that dismissal, the foreman returns to his paperwork. Just morning, and he's already in a surly mood. Not promising at all.

After three comets scraping a living in stopover towns, insistence has become Ilapara's default. "You hired Rufa, Foreman Jijima," she says with a little more steel in her voice. "He can't swing a blade to save his life." She shrugs at Rufa. "No offense, but it's true."

Rufa grins and returns the shrug. "I still got the job."

"Which is what confuses me," she says to the foreman. "If you can take him on, why can't you take me too? You know I'm worth it, and the whole thing with Mimvura Company blew over a half moon ago. I'm in the clear."

Foreman Jijima drags deeply on his pipe and pulls it out. He shakes his head as he exhales. "What does a man have to do for some peace around here?" He seems to be addressing Rufa, but the boy's smart enough to know the question's rhetorical.

"You want to know why I hired him and not you?" Jijima says to Ilapara. "I'll tell you." He leans back in his chair and jerks his pipe toward Rufa. "I look at him, and I see a big boy no one wants to mess with. See those arms? They win fights without doing anything. You and I know they're worthless, but see, our clients don't. He scares the shit out of people. That's what they want to see—it's what makes them feel safe." He points at Ilapara. "You, on the other hand—they take one look at you, and they see a pretty girl trying to prove something."

"I have experience. I have fought and even killed. I would be a real asset to your company, Foreman."

"*I* know your record. I know it, all right? I've heard lots of good things about you, but here's the thing: This job is as much protection as perception. Our clients don't just want to *be* safe; they also want to *feel* safe." He points at Rufa again. "That feels safe. You feel like a risk—or worse, a stunt, and stunts invite the wrong kind of attention. Sorry, girl, but I'll have to pass." Jijima slips his pipe back between his lips, returns to his work.

All right. Time to try a different tack. Ilapara breathes in deeply. She was hoping not to have to resort to this, but it worked the last time she wanted a job, so . . . "I'll take two-thirds pay if you sign me on," she says.

That catches Jijima's attention. Something slithers behind his eyes as he seems to consider the idea for a second, but then he smiles and shakes his head. "That would be criminal."

She grits her teeth. "Half pay, then. You won't get a better deal anywhere else."

He wheezes out a laugh this time. "Tell you what—get a few tours under your belt, and maybe we'll talk."

"That's exactly what I'm trying to do, Foreman." The words come out with a little more frustration than she intends.

"With some other company," he says.

A lost cause, then. Ilapara could scream at the injustice. But that kind of emotional display in this town would be tantamount to professional suicide, so she nods instead. "You know where to find me if you change your mind."

She starts to leave but stops when Jijima says, "Are you working at the general dealer's again?"

"The one and only."

"He's not paying you enough, is he?"

"He pays me well for the work I do for him." Ilapara knows never to badmouth an employer—past, present, or prospective. No need to burn bridges that might come in handy in the future.

"I see. Well, if there's nothing else . . ." And Jijima returns to his work, as complete a dismissal as any.

"Good day, Foreman," she says. "Rufa."

"Drinks later?" Rufa says as she leaves.

She suppresses a shudder. "Maybe some other time."

BaChando, Seresa's general dealer, was the first person to offer her a job when she arrived in Umadiland three comets ago with nothing but a sack of clothes and a cheap spear to her name.

A series of carts and wagons had driven her along seemingly endless dirt roads stretching from the Yerezi borderlands in the southeast and joining the World's Artery just south of the stopover town. She already knew the local language, having learned it back home, but she quickly taught herself to speak exactly like a native so she could convince someone to give her a job without asking too many questions. And when BaChando hired her and she finally had the coin to spare, she taught herself to paint her face and dress like a native too.

It was supposed to be a mere disguise, but to Ilapara it became a way to remake herself in her own image, without anyone's input on what was proper and what was not. Now her crimson Umadi veils and robes and her leather and aerosteel armor are the truest garments she could ever don, and Izumadi rolls off her tongue like she was born to it.

BaChando gladly rehired her when she fled back to Seresa after narrowly escaping Kageru with her life. The work's a big step down from a mercenary company, and BaChando is as cold blooded as a snake, but at least the pittance he pays her keeps her fed, leaving just enough for her buck's extortionate livery fees, a daily bath, and a bunk at the hostels in the town's river district. All things considered, she can't complain too much.

His store is one of those two-story buildings built along the Artery. Because of her detour to the Vuriro office, Ilapara has to meander through the meat market to get there.

She usually avoids Seresa's meat market if she can, but she's almost late for her morning shift, so there's nothing else for it. *Keep your head down, your eyes forward,* she tells herself. *Walk quickly; don't look in the cages. Mind your own business. It's a harsh world out there, and it's not like you can do anything about it.*

Ilapara is good at minding her own business—that's a habit one quickly learns in Umadiland—but there's something about the meat market that makes it hard for her not to look . . .

Like now. As she passes one of the caged wagons butting into the muddy road, she can't help but sneak a look inside at the wraithlike Faraswa woman slumped against the iron bars—*about my age, covered in layers of grime. The filthy dress clinging to her bones might have once been bright yellow; it's a sooty brown now, brown like disease and old vomit. Her dark hair might be shoulder length, but it's all matted to her scalp. And her tensor appendages, so spotless in her filthy prison, curling out of her temples like twin snakes of polished bronze. Ritual bed slave or muti sacrifice? Which one is worse?*

Most people new to Seresa assume the meat market is named thus because of the wide selection of meats sold there—meats sourced from every corner of the Redlands and brought in enchanted frostboxes so it's as fresh as the day it was killed.

Most people new to Seresa are wrong.

By far, the most lucrative meat sold at the meat market is the living, breathing, *human* kind. The Faraswa kind in particular, who are treasured as slaves and victims of muti rituals for their essence-rich blood. Those who don't sell get hauled up the World's Artery and displayed at every town on the way until a buyer comes along.

The girl in the caged wagon quickly looks up, as if she can sense the weight of Ilapara's gaze, and her vivid crimson eyes choke Ilapara with the weight of the suffering they've seen and the suffering they have yet to see. They are devoid of hope, dead to this world.

Behind the wagon, a gray banner hangs with the Seal of an infinitely black sphere that seems to blink at her. Ilapara looks away and minds her own business.

When you're in the trade of buying things from money-strapped travelers—anything, really, from clothes to dried foods to charmed trinkets—at a quarter of the price they are actually worth, only to make a hefty profit when you resell them in that same store, you are bound to make some people very angry, perhaps angry enough to get violent.

Ilapara's job at the general dealer's, put simply, is to discourage any malcontented travelers from physically expressing their grievances with BaChando. The few instances she had to use her spear when she first worked here earned her a reputation in the town, enough for her to walk into a mercenary office and not get laughed out of the room when she asked for a job.

She hasn't had cause to put her new armor and weapon to use, though, not since BaChando rehired her two weeks ago. A good thing, of course, but sometimes she wishes the job entailed a little more risk and excitement. The riskiest thing she's seen so far was an old woman who pelted BaChando with her sandals and stormed out barefoot. Certainly a duller job than watching the comings and goings at the gates of the Mimvura compound.

A caravan is leaving town this morning. Ilapara watches it longingly from her post at the door, wishing she could join the mercenaries escorting it. Perhaps if she traveled more of the world, if she saw what else could be in store for her out there, perhaps she would finally understand what it is she wants for herself, whether to go back home or seek a life elsewhere.

Her thoughts engross her so completely that she's uncharacteristically startled when, like a ghost from her past, a bespectacled young man walks into the store and greets her in the Umadi tongue. She barely manages to respond before he continues inward to browse around the shelves.

She gapes at him, perplexed.

He is Yerezi. A Yerezi tribesman is here, in Seresa, here in this store.

Besides his uniquely Yerezi straw hat, she knows he's Yerezi from his white loincloth and the bow and quiver harnessed to his back—that and his distinct beaded necklace, and the numerous leather bands wrapped like tiny snakes around his wrists, and that earring that says he's a copperborn princeling, and his indescribable *homeness,* so unexpected in this place of vice it makes her ache for the peace of her motherland.

She smothers those annoying feelings before they catch fire. It's easy: all she does is remember why she left.

Still, there's something fundamentally wrong about seeing a Yerezi tribesman *here* in Seresa, *in this store,* walking around like it's the most normal thing in the world. She knows there are Yerezi who brave Umadiland for trade, but they don't usually venture beyond the tamer towns and villages of the borderlands—far from the Artery.

They certainly don't come *here.*

Ilapara watches him from the door while he peruses the aisles of stuff with visible interest. He's tall and lithe, and his skin is a few shades lighter than her own russet brown. *Oblivious* is the first word that pops into her mind; the boy has caught the dealer's hawkish attention—the man's practically leering at him from behind his counter—but the boy seems completely unaware. At one point he stops, lifts a fluffy-looking plaything off the shelves, sniffs it, grimaces, and puts it back.

A village boy comes to town.

Ilapara shakes her head. What on Meza is he doing here? And what's with those spectacles? Eye defects are the sort of thing Yerezi clan mystics treat regularly—and for free. Some sort of personal statement of individuality, perhaps? Certainly not implausible, not with a princeling.

But then . . . where is the red steel? A princeling his age would never leave his kraal without wearing all the Yerezi arcane metal he could fit onto his body. And why the devil is he wearing *white*? The more she watches him, the more he confuses her. Yes, he is Yerezi, but he makes no sense.

"Looking for something, friend?" BaChando says to him in a clipped mercenary voice. He doesn't like loiterers in his store, especially if said loiterers look as . . . well, rural and rustic as this boy.

A brazen gewgaw has caught the boy's attention. He doesn't take his eyes off it when he says, "Nothing specific, no." He takes a moment longer to grasp the question's true import, then finally straightens and looks at BaChando. "You don't mind me looking around, do you?"

It shouldn't be, but his Izumadi is faultless, bespeaking years of education—not exactly what Yerezi men are known for.

BaChando contains his surprise very well; Ilapara sees it only because he starts tapping his fat bejeweled fingers on his counter. "Not at all," he says with a prompt smile. "Just let me know if you need any help."

"Thank you." The boy returns to studying the brass gewgaw. "I've never been inside a store before."

BaChando's smile grows strained, and he flashes Ilapara a glance that says, *Watch him.* She nods to assuage his concerns; the man might be a callous reptile, but nervousness is his natural disposition. Nursing it is only part of the job.

The princeling takes his time going up and down the aisles, touching, sniffing, feeling the miscellaneous articles on sale. The clothes don't interest him much. He avoids any other fluffy things, grimaces at most of the dried foods, lingers near the herbs and medicines, marvels at one of the smoking pipes.

Only as he returns to the brass ornament thingy does Ilapara realize what he's been doing all along, what she couldn't see him do because of those spectacles of his, and it exacerbates her suspicions about him: while she's been watching him from the door, he's been watching *her*.

He came into this shop *specifically* to watch her.

That means he knows who she is.

She has no idea who he is, but *he* knows who *she* is.

An unacceptable imbalance.

Ilapara strides toward him, fixing her expression into calm, professional curiosity, and in a voice low enough to die before it reaches BaChando, she says to him in Sirezi, "Who are you, and what do you want?"

He freezes where he stands, and a slow smile creeps onto his face. A shy smile, and he doesn't quite turn away from the brass ornament to face her, but it's still one of those smiles that tugs at the corners of your lips, like you already know each other and share a joke just between the two of you, the kind of smile that lulls you into trusting.

Ilapara has had a lot of practice mastering her body language—an invaluable skill in her line of work—so the smile slides right off her and leaves her unscathed.

"I apologize." He pushes his strange spectacles up his nose, finally facing her. "I didn't quite know how to approach you. I wasn't sure how you'd react."

A soft-spoken tenor voice. Mellow, polite. His ears are a bit too large. A big gap between his upper incisors. She has to look up at him, but everything else about him invites her to relax, and yet . . . *what* is it?

"Well, this is awkward," he says when she says nothing.

"Probably because you still haven't answered my questions."

BaChando clears his throat by his counter. "Do we have a problem, Ilira?"

"Not at all, boss," she tells him in Izumadi, then arches an eyebrow at the boy. "Well?"

For a moment he seems taken aback by her forwardness—*good*—but his words come out confidently when he speaks. "All right. I suppose I should be forthright with you. My name's Musalodi, and I hail from the western shores of the Nyasiningwe. I heard about you from your cousin Biro—Birosei? He tends VaSikhozi's sheep at the—"

"I know who Biro is," she cuts in, and her voice is a little curt and tetchy because the two worlds she's worked hard to keep separate are suddenly coming together, all because of this strange boy.

"Of course you do," the boy says, keeping his cool. "Well, he said I might find you here when I told him I'd be passing through town. As it happens, I need to get to Yonte Saire, but I'm not sure how to go about it. I've been led to believe it's not a matter of simply riding up the Artery."

Ilapara almost laughs. "No, it's not."

"Exactly, so I came here hoping I could pick your brains, so to speak. Biro said no other Yerezi would know this town better than you." The boy hastens to add, "If you don't mind, of course. I'll understand if you're too busy. Maybe if you just point me in the right direction, I'm sure I'll find my way."

Ilapara lets herself study him unashamedly. The ornate staff in his hand looks like something AmaSikhozi carries around. One of those pouches tied to his waist is definitely a coin purse—reckless. Not a lick of red steel on him, and yet he's definitely copperborn; it's in his bearing, the way he looks and talks, though he obviously tries to hide it beneath a veneer of politeness.

She feels a sudden and rather belated flash of annoyance that he managed to find her. What betrayed her to him?

She has worked hard to cultivate the image of a streetwise Umadi girl, from the way she speaks to the way she dresses: her silver nose ring, her black Umadi kohl and lip paint, her flowing red veil. He shouldn't have been able to know her by sight.

"Why on Meza are you going to Yonte Saire?" she asks him. "What's there for someone like you?"

He winces at the note of disdain in her voice, and she immediately feels guilty, but she decides an apology isn't necessary.

"I'm running an important errand for Her Majesty Queen Irediti," he says.

Ilapara blinks at him, then smiles, and then the smile bubbles up into laughter. She has to place a hand on her chest to stop it from heaving so much. "This is rich," she says when she can speak. "Musalodi, is it?"

He shifts where he stands, though he seems amused by her reaction. "You can call me Salo."

"You have tall tales, Salo."

"I know," he says, "but in this case they happen to be true."

Though she can't see his eyes, the trace of bitterness in his response makes her wonder. She lists her head, studies him some more. "You're serious."

He nods.

"But that makes no sense."

BaChando clears his throat again. "Ilira?"

"One minute, boss." Ilapara grabs Salo's arm and pulls him out of the aisles. They stop by the door, and BaChando's nervous eyes track them the whole way. She ignores him. "Why would the queen send *you* anywhere? Let alone halfway up the continent. You're no Ajaha, are you?"

The boy's shoulders droop a little. "No."

"And I know you're no Asazi, either, hence my confusion."

His jaw clenches almost imperceptibly, but he keeps his voice polite. "Look, I'm sure you have many questions about me, but trust me when I say that any answer I give you right now will only bring up more questions. Then we'll be here all day. The fact is, I need to get to the Yontai. Can you help me?" He looks around and leans closer, lowering his voice. "I could make it worth your while."

Ilapara tries not to take offense. She has no need for his charity. "How much money do you have?"

"Enough, I think. I'm not sure. It's moongold."

So trusting, so unwary. Why offer her such dangerous information? She could be anyone, a criminal.

She smooths out any reaction from her face and drops her gaze to his waist. "I assume that's what's clinking in that purse of yours." Crime is dangerous in this town, but the boy is just begging to be mugged, walking around with his money in such an obvious place. And if it's moongold, then it's a fortune.

The boy looks down at his purse. "That's some of it, yeah."

"Some? Where's the rest of it?"

"Oh, I left it with my other possessions."

"You . . . you just *left* your money somewhere, in this town?" By Ama, such naivety. He's a naive village boy, and he's going to get himself killed. Ilapara shakes her head. "I won't even ask."

"Don't worry," he says with a grin. "I'm sure it's safe."

"Uh-huh. How are you traveling?"

"I—uh, I have a mount."

"A mount," Ilapara repeats, and she knows the smile growing on her face isn't nice. "Of course you do. For your sake I hope it's a good mount. Yonte Saire is half a continent away."

"I think he'll manage."

"Right. Well, you might want to consider getting a berth in a wheelhouse. It'll cost you, but at least you won't have to worry about that mount of yours dying on you along the way, because then it'll *really* cost you."

"Ilira, a word."

Ilapara suppresses a sigh. "One moment," she says to Salo, then heads over to BaChando. The man's trying so hard to hide his smoldering anger behind a thin smile it's almost hilarious. The smile mutates into a scowl as soon as he can hide behind Ilapara.

"Ilira, this is a place of business, not a lounge for wanderers. I want him out of here, now."

"Yes, boss. He was just lost, that's all. I'm giving him directions."

"Then be quick about it."

"Yes, boss." She returns to Salo and finds him watching as a tronic dread rhino with a giant metal horn drags a two-story wheelhouse along the Artery. She can't see his eyes, but his lips are slightly agape. She reckons he's just as overwhelmed as she was when she first arrived here. "Look, Musalodi," she says.

"Salo, please."

"I'm working right now, Salo," she says, "but my lunch break is in an hour. If you can wait that long, I'll take you to the best caravan company in town. I think their next convoy sets off later tonight, so you won't have to stay here for long. I wouldn't stay here overnight if I were you."

"Oh? I guess I'll defer to your wisdom on that front." He steals a glance at a scowling BaChando. "I'll wait for you outside, or maybe I'll take a walk around town. There's so much to see."

"It's your prerogative," Ilapara says. "Just . . . be careful."

He nods and leaves the store, and she shakes her head, watching him go. A creature like him should be hunting antelope in the tranquil Plains, not wandering the sordid streets of Seresa, just a stone's throw away from the meat market.

Still, she can't quite shake off the sense that there's something . . . not quite right with him.

23: Musalodi

For a time he wanders due south, staff in hand, drinking in the foreign sights and smells. Being so close to the World's Artery feels like standing at the edge of the Redlands and watching them spin like thread on a reel.

Over there, a behemoth of the wild, a colossal four-tusked elephant, pulling an impossible wooden fortress on wheels. Faces peer out from within, and as it passes by, a child with flowers in her braids leans out to wave down at him; he waves back like a man in a waking dream.

Behind it a clunky, rusty, slow-moving machine drives past on articulated tracks, and by Ama, it's moving on its own accord. Salo senses multiple spirits possessing its gears, tronic oxen and buffalo, and together they draw a train of wagons piled high with timber, sacks of grain, and other mysterious goods.

He sees riders on creatures both familiar and strange: fast-running ostriches; muscular zebroid creatures with glossy ivory horns and flowing manes; nimble tronic antelope; ponderous mules; humped, long-necked beasts with braying calls; giant lizard creatures with fat, stocky legs; and the occasional predator for the bold.

As he watches, a company of proud riders in hide skins passes by on thickset feline beasts, each with massive protruding upper canines.

A woman whose short hair is dyed the color of gold rides at the fore, and who knows, she might be a warrior or the daughter of a chieftain; she takes a passing glance down at him and gifts him a smile so haughty and worldly it seems to say: *What are you to us, oh wanderer, oh coward of the Plains? We come from lands far beyond your tiny horizon of oxen, kraals, and grainfields. We have seen things you cannot dream of.*

It's one thing to know that the world is bigger than you could ever comprehend. Quite another to see it with your own eyes. Marvelous and terrifying—terrifyingly marvelous—and the blend is intoxicating.

Salo turns onto a dusty byroad when his nose catches the wafting scent of grilled meat and his stomach growls in response. He figures he might as well grab something to eat while he waits.

He smiles, thinking about his encounter with Ilapara. He wasn't quite honest with her. Yes, he heard about her from her cousin Birosei when he stopped over for the night at the Sikhozi kraal, but he didn't seek her out for help finding a caravan—he could do that on his own if he wanted to. He sought her out for another reason entirely.

Biro was one of the few Sikhozi boys who would talk to him without curling his lip, an outcast of sorts who bonded with him over their mutual love of nsango and matje. They smoked well into the early hours of the morning, and at some point during their time together Biro leaned closer and whispered about the kraal's renegade daughter who had run away to live alone in the Umadi town of Seresa. Apparently she'd done so because VaSikhozi wouldn't let her go to the Queen's Kraal to earn her steel and become an Ajaha.

"She's a bit like you, no?" Biro said, and Salo nodded quietly, even though he vehemently disagreed, because this girl sounded incredibly brave and self-motivated, not at all like him. He vowed to find her and see her for himself—because what would a girl so brave be like in person?

Like a smoldering fire, it turns out. Seething passion wrapped in a steely red exterior. Burnt umber eyes hidden beneath kohl like torrid mysteries. She tries to disguise what she is, but Salo knows an Ajaha when he sees one, and what he saw guarding the entrance of the general dealer's was an Ajaha far from her clanlands.

She wears no red steel, but the training is there in her posture, in the way she assesses her surroundings and carries that spear of hers. Definitely no Asazi dagger; that's an Ajaha's weapon, unwieldy in untrained hands.

She is everything he was hoping for and more. Now he just has to figure out how to convince her to come with him.

The merchants and buyers on the byroads are lurid rivers of color and textiles fashioned into all manner of clothing, very much in contrast to the desperation clinging like a miasma to the rows of decrepit shacks and the vile waters muddying the streets. A lively place, to be sure, but certainly no place of leisure or peace. This is a cradle of money, its pursuit the town's heartbeat.

"Two pebbles for a cold beer," cries an Umadi woman in a bright, flowing veil and a nose ring that invites his eyes to linger.

"Come, my friend, the finest hides and leather you've ever seen, starting at two stones each." That's a gruff, thickly bearded man in a blue tunic, with red dreadlocks so long they reach down to his waist.

Salo keeps going until he reaches a rickety stall displaying a selection of spicy grilled meats on skewers. He stops to inspect them.

"Are you hungry, my child?" says the bright-eyed vendor behind the grill, and she's already preparing a leaf to dish onto. "Four pebbles for one, but just for you, I'll make it six pebbles if you take two."

The cubes of skewered meats sizzle with fat and aromatic spices. Salo's mouth waters at the sight. "These look delicious," he says to the vendor, "but I don't have pebbles with me. Do you have change for a mountain?"

By the way her eyebrows shoot up, one would think she has just watched his brain crawl out of his skull. "Change for a mountain, my child! But where would I find so much money?"

He's about to tell her to forget about it when someone brushes past him so violently he almost bumps into the grill. He whirls around to look, anticipating an apology, but his assailant has already slinked away.

The vendor gasps. "Thief!" She points at a figure retreating into the bustling crowds.

Salo rights the skewed spectacles on his face and looks again. "What? Where?"

She wags her finger furiously. "There! He's getting away! I saw him steal your purse!"

Salo looks down and sees that his leather purse is gone. A complete stranger has singled him out from the crowds for exploitation and *robbed* him. Instantly the most galling thing that has ever happened to him.

"Hey, you!" Salo shouts at the thief. "Stop!"

No such luck. The thief is a light-footed teenage boy in dirty rags scuttling away on bare feet. His hair is hidden beneath a threadbare woolen hat. For a split second Salo considers letting him go—it's not like he doesn't have more money stashed away—but indignation prevails, and he decides that no, he won't be victimized in this town, and starts chasing after the boy, shouting at him to stop.

The boy is a fast runner. He weaves through the busy streets like he knows them well, keeping up a good pace despite the heavy foot traffic.

Too bad for him he picked an even better runner to steal from. Salo might not be much of a warrior, but he was a cowherd of the Plains: running is in his blood. So he closes in on his quarry, eating up the distance between them with a swift, easy gallop.

The boy tries to lose him by taking a series of confusing turns, but it's not hard for Salo to keep him in sight. Moongold is a little like red steel in the way it radiates faint ripples of power; the coins shine to Salo's shards like mirrors catching sunlight.

He pays no heed to the worsening character of the streets as they race away from the World's Artery—the thickening stench of raw meat, the sudden change in what's inside the caged wagons parked by the way-side, from livestock and tronic beasts to human . . . to human beings?

He stops. He looks around. He turns, he blinks, he sees.

Wrongness is like grease or tar. It washes over you slowly and thickly, and when you try to rub it off, it only clings harder. Salo blinks his eyes as if to rub off the nightmare that has reared its ugly head all around him, but the sights burrow deeper into his mind. They take root and solidify, and he knows that they will haunt him until the day he breathes his last.

Locked inside these cages like wild animals are actual human beings. Dirty, filthy human beings, some naked, some young, some haggard, some strapping, some crammed together like swine, some alone—all of them looking out of their cages like ghosts, people who know they are already dead.

Most are lithe and swarthy, with eye colors ranging from startling sunset ambers to full moon crimsons, and all of them have tubular metallic-looking appendages curling out of their temples . . .

By Ama, these are Faraswa people. It is said they were once a deeply spiritual tribe who relied on magic in almost every aspect of their lives, much more adept than average at drawing and manipulating the crafts of Red magic due to their ancestral talent, which gave them tensor appendages and eyes that could see magic. It is said that during their golden age, their empire extended across much of the continent's western seaboard, and the inflow of tribute from their conquered lands allowed them to build great cities across the arid regions of the Faraswa Desert.

That was, so the legend goes, until they grew proud and allowed many of their number to forsake the moon and practice solar magic. The moon forsook them in turn, and soon they began to lose their ability to awaken, gradually and irreversibly.

Now ruins are all that is left of their once-glorious empire, and their people are hunted and enslaved throughout the Redlands for their essence-rich blood, which supposedly offers stronger effects when used in blood sacraments.

The wagon directly in front of Salo holds an emaciated Faraswa girl in a dirty brown habit leaning limply against the iron bars. He would think she were dead could he not feel the faint glimmer of her soul with his shards, so faint the slightest wind could snuff it out. The wagon next to hers holds even more tensored figures in various stages of frailty, some so gaunt he can't tell whether they are male or female.

A pair of olive-skinned men in orange robes is standing next to the wagon. One of them says something to Salo in Izumadi, but whatever it is fails to pierce through the fog of horror that has clouded his mind.

By Ama, this is the true face of the Redlands, isn't it? This is why the Yerezi Foremothers isolated themselves in the Plains. It finally makes sense to him, grotesque, horrible sense. Oh, these poor people.

"Two pounds of human liver for a silver rock. Six pounds of lung for the same. It raises an interesting question, doesn't it? How much is a human life truly worth?"

A young man of short stature has sidled up to Salo unnoticed. He's chewing on a pastry, looking at the slaves in the wagon like they are curiosities on display. Not knowing what else to do, Salo blinks at him.

The young man stuffs the rest of his pastry into his mouth and says, "I just purchased this tasty treat for two copper pebbles, and it says here that each of these Faraswa slaves is priced at—let's see . . ." He leans forward briefly to better read the placard affixed to the wagon. "The penmanship leaves much to be desired, but I believe this says one mountain, or four golden hills, which I know is equivalent to a thousand pebbles, so that means each of these slaves is worth, what, five hundred pastries?" He turns his dark eyes on Salo, one cheek dimpling in a lopsided smile. "Think about it: five hundred fried balls of dough will get you your own sentient being to do with as you please. Isn't that something?"

His skin is the color of pale river sand, suggesting he might hail from a tribe in the distant north. Dark shoulder-length hair frames his lightly stubbled face. Save for the rather conspicuous silver gauntlet gleaming on his left hand, he is dressed entirely in black, from his form-fitting sleeveless dashiki to his pants and boots to the leather knapsack clinging to his back.

For whatever reason, it takes Salo a moment of blank staring for the stranger's words to register, and then a hundred questions spring to his mind as sense returns to him, the most pressing being: "How is it you speak my tongue?"

"I speak many tongues," the young man says, once again in perfect if slightly accented Sirezi. He extends a hand for a handshake. "Tuksaad at your service."

Salo stares at the hand, doesn't take it. "But you are not Yerezi."

The young man keeps the hand there a moment longer before he retracts it with a shrug, his eyes twinkling with amusement. They are actually a mossy shade of green, not dark, as Salo first thought. "One need not belong to a tongue to speak it," he says.

"That's not what I meant."

"I know. Your tribe isn't exactly one of the big five, but I'm on a pilgrimage of sorts, you see. My mission is to speak to people from as many Red tribes as possible, and you are the first Yerezi tribesman I've ever met. When I saw you running past, I knew I had to come and speak with you." The young man named Tuksaad tilts his head when he notices Salo's earring. "Forgive me if I'm being rude, but you are a prince, are you not? I know that copper is a signifier of royalty among your people—or am I mistaken?"

A strange man in an even stranger place. But before Salo can think up an appropriate reply, sudden commotion up the street draws his attention, and when he looks, he feels his grip tightening around his staff.

The thief. Except now he's caught between two armed men in black dashikis, and he's wailing and struggling against their iron grips as they haul him down the street by his shoulders. A third man leads the party, and it seems they are headed Salo's way.

"You there," says the leader when they stop several paces away from him. The man uses a deliberately loud voice to attract attention, presenting a leather pouch held solidly in one meaty hand. "Is this yours?"

Distracted by the horror of the meat market, Salo had forgotten all about the thief. He feels a small flicker of anger seeing him now, but more than anything he feels pity. The boy's face is now covered in a sheen of snot and tears. "Yes, that's mine," Salo says, albeit cautiously. "It was . . . taken from me a short while ago."

Tuksaad's eyes have dimmed again. He's maneuvered himself next to Salo so that they look like they are traveling together. Salo finds that he doesn't mind too much.

"The victim has confirmed that this is his coin purse," the guard says, raising the purse for all to see, and again his voice is loud enough for the whole meat market to hear. Salo notices with unease that a crowd is gathering around them. "The stolen purse will now be returned to its owner."

The guard tosses the purse at Salo, and he catches it. He doesn't have to open it to know that all his money is still there.

"As for our little thief . . ." With a malicious smirk the guard walks to the weeping boy and unceremoniously divests him of his tattered woolen hat. Salo's heart lurches when he sees the bronze-like tensors growing out of the boy's temples. "Faraswa filth," the guard spits. He reaches down and pulls the boy's hair back so that his face is upturned. "How did you escape the pens, filth? No matter. We will put you to good use now."

To the watching crowds he shouts: "By the Dark Sun's decree, the punishment for the crime of theft is death by dismemberment. All thieves are to be immediately offered to the Blood Woman in our lord's name, in payment for the injury done to him, for all theft in this town is theft from him." With callous ease the guard unlimbers the machete tied to his belt—and offers it to Salo.

At the same time, his two comrades shove the Faraswa boy to his knees and stretch his right arm so that it is taut and ready for butchering. Salo's breath pauses momentarily.

"As the wronged party," the guard says, "you have the right to exact punishment. Will you exercise this right?"

"Absolutely not!"

"Very well." The guard turns to face the boy, whose wails have become spine chilling.

"Wait!"

The guard stops. Turns around. A heavy frown darkens his face. "Would you like to exact the punishment?"

"No! I mean, I don't want *any* punishment exacted. Certainly not this."

Next to Salo, Tuksaad steps close enough to whisper. "What are you doing, friend? It is not wise to interrupt them."

"Your coin purse was found in the Faraswa thief's possession," the guard says. "A witness reported the incident, and you have confirmed that the coin purse is yours. The law is clear: he must be dismembered."

The crowd is thicker now. The slavers are watching with ghoulish curiosity next to their wares. Salo's words come out as a stutter. "B-but . . . you can't just kill him! Not for money!"

The guard shares puzzled frowns with his comrades, like Salo has said something nonsensical. That's when his new friend steps in. "What he means to say, my good man, is that the boy is no thief."

"I don't follow," says the guard, and neither does Salo, but he nods in agreement anyway.

"All just a misunderstanding," Tuksaad explains with a smile and his palms raised in a gesture of peace. "They were playing a game, you see. My friend here"—he gestures at Salo—"gave the boy his purse and told him to run so he could catch him. It's a variation of hide-and-seek, a popular game where he comes from."

"Very popular," Salo says, nodding in fervent agreement. "We play it *all* the time."

"Exactly." Tuksaad gives a cheerful laugh. "He just wanted the challenge of playing it in a crowded place for once. So you see, just a misunderstanding. There has been no theft here."

"We're terribly sorry for the trouble it's caused." Salo looks at the boy in desperation. "Tell them, friend. We were playing a game, weren't we?"

The Faraswa boy nods the way one nods when one's life depends on it.

"See? Please, Red-kin. Let my friend go."

"And we'll buy you a cold beer each for the inconvenience," Tuksaad adds with his dimpled smile.

For a moment the guard appears inclined to accept Tuksaad's offer, but then he looks at Salo, and he must see right through him to the dread beneath, because he firms his expression and shakes his head. "I'm afraid that's not how we do things around here. When a thief steals from the people of this town, he steals from our lord. He must be punished to deter others from following his example. I understand your sympathy, but the law is clear."

The anticipation in the air is almost thick enough to touch as the guard faces the boy, his machete dangling in one hand. "You have been judged guilty, filth, and now your life shall be offered to the Blood Woman in the name of our Muchinda, the great Dark Sun. May he be blessed with a thousand years of life and good health."

Salo is about to fall on his knees and beg for the boy's life when, hanging from a bitumen-coated pole behind a wagon nearby, a gray banner flutters in the breeze, flattening out just enough for him to make out the rather unsettling web of curves and circles printed onto it. Then the shapes reach out and twist his eyes into seeing a black sphere with a glaring corona.

Time stops.

Tikoloshe. The smell of compost and Monti's blood in the air. Monti died in his arms because a witch came to their kraal to kill in her lord's name, and her lord is the same man who owns this Seal.

The same man who owns this town.

This town belongs to Monti's murderer.

These men are about to sacrifice this boy to Monti's murderer.

A red mist settles around Salo, and he sets his shards ablaze with raw essence. Before he knows what he's doing, he's reaching forward with his left hand, reaching forward and *unleashing* his power.

The air pressure abruptly changes in a pocket of space surrounding the executioner. A powerful whirlwind rises in response, a serpent of dust and Storm craft coiling itself around him and lifting him yards off the ground, where it holds him prisoner. His machete careers away as his hands fly to his throat. He wheezes, desperate to draw in breath, but the air will not obey him. His eyes bulge as he suffocates, veins appearing on his temples like they're about to pop.

"Murderers!" Salo's voice sucks every other sound right out of the air. His heart's beating so hard he can feel it at the base of his tongue. "I should kill you all!"

It would be so easy. He could command the air and starve them of breath, steal it right out of their lungs—the least these people deserve for what they did to Monti.

A woman screams. Her screams beget more screams. The floating executioner is still choking helplessly, inching ever closer to death, and the sight of him in this state hammers a wedge of sobriety into Salo's mind.

What am I doing? Am I really going to kill *this man?*

He aborts the spell, letting the executioner plummet to the ground in a cloud of dust. He didn't really think through his actions, so he's not sure what to expect—he's not sure of anything right now—but it's probably not for the executioner to struggle onto his hands and knees, coughing, while he lifts a shaking finger at Salo. "Kill him!" he wheezes at his comrades, who were up until now patently dumbstruck. "In the name of our lord, kill him!"

The two men trade looks, perhaps to bolster each other's confidence, and then together they charge with their machetes raised high.

They don't get far. Earth and red light erupt on the road, bringing them to an alarmed stop. Another such explosion close to their feet makes them jump back with cries of surprise.

Salo looks to his side and sees Tuksaad pointing a silver gauntlet at the guards, his fist clenched and his palm facing downward. A slender barrel has appeared above the wrist by some telescoping mechanism, and the inside of it throbs with a nefarious nimbus of red light.

Gasps and murmurs come from those still watching. One of the guards looks like he wants to charge again, so Tuksaad releases another blast of energy at the man's feet from his gauntlet, making him dance back. He shies away, gawking at the strangely powerful weapon.

"How about we leave it at that, my friends?" Tuksaad says to them. "Let's not interrupt business any further. What do you say?"

The three guards exchange wide-eyed looks with each other, then turn around and flee, leaving the Faraswa boy cowering on the ground.

The rush is already underway. Surprisingly quiet but hasty. Vendors near the meat market are packing their wares. Customers have forgotten their purchases on the stalls. An anxious tattoo of pattering feet spreading outward like the shock waves of an earthquake, with Salo and Tuksaad at the epicenter. What was once a bustling marketplace quickly becomes desolate, save for the living ghosts trapped in the cages around them, as well as their slavers, standing stiffly, stubbornly next to their wares.

And the boy, the terrified Faraswa thief, who presses his forehead into the earth when Salo looks at him, seemingly more terrified now than he was when the guards were about to butcher him. "Mercy, my lord! Mercy!"

Salo walks closer and crouches in front of him. "What's your name, friend?"

"Mhaddisu, my lord," the boy says without lifting his face.

Salo's skin crawls unpleasantly to see someone so terrified of him. He grabs the boy by his shoulders and helps him up to his feet. "Come on, Mhaddisu, get up. I won't have anyone groveling in the mud on my account." The boy flinches and cowers, but Salo is insistent.

"Mercy, my lord!"

"Relax. I won't hurt you." A residual flicker of indignation compels Salo to add, "But why did you steal from me?"

The boy's eyes dart back and forth, and he stammers, "I . . . I just saw the purse, and . . . I'm just really hungry. I . . . oh, mercy!"

"You reek of kindness and naivety," says the brown-eyed stranger named Tuksaad—and yes, his eyes are now a light shade of brown as they search the market for further threats. "Do you even know the danger you've drawn to yourself by saving this thief? A Faraswa, no less."

"Stay here, Mhaddisu," Salo says to the boy. "And you . . ." Salo frowns at Tuksaad as he takes a good look at him. "*What* are you exactly, Tuksaad?"

He says *what* and not *who* because now that he's paying attention to his shards, he senses an unusual energy surrounding this stranger. He looks like a man, but he feels . . . *made* to Salo, in the same way a machine or a weapon feels made. His bones pulsate with the signatures of steel, copper, moongold, and several other mysterious metals. And his eyes—

His eyes! They were brown not a moment ago, but Salo sees them acquire a greenish hue that brightens considerably over the next heartbeat.

"Please, call me Tuk," the young man says, "and what I am is the man who just saved your life." He looks around again. "But it is unwise for us to linger here. We must go."

"We? What makes you think I'm going anywhere with you?"

Tuk smiles, and there's far too much guile in his eyes. "Because you owe me. And because you're a Yerezi mystic in the flesh. I would be foolish to let you out of my sight now, after being so lucky."

Salo frowns at the stranger; he's not about to be taken advantage of again. "Whatever you think you'll get from me, I assure you, you won't."

"You misunderstand," Tuk says. "You are walking the Bloodway, are you not? You must be. A mystic of your tribe would not be out here otherwise."

"What of it?"

"I can make sure you reach the Jungle City in one piece."

"Why?"

"For your blessing, of course. I know of your people's ancestral gift. I know the strength you could give me if you chose to. I am exceptional as I am, but with your blessing I'd be magnificent. Transcendent, complete."

Salo flounders, temporarily speechless. Then he shakes his head. "That's definitely not going to happen. For one, I don't know who the devil you are. For another, you are not Yerezi. Blessing you would get me into all sorts of trouble back home."

Tuk doesn't seem to hear that. "I'd owe you a debt of gratitude so large it would take me a lifetime to repay you."

"If you want payment for your assistance, I have money."

"I don't need or want your money." Tuk glances at the thief. "Here's the thing, Yerezi prince—"

"I'm not really a prince, and you can call me Salo."

"Look here, Salo. You can't travel up the World's Artery anymore. Not after this." Tuk points out the empty streets. "In case you didn't know, this town belongs to the Dark Sun, and the disciple responsible for it will be coming for you when he learns what you've done."

Salo represses a nervous gulp. "I can protect myself."

"From a warlord's disciple and his militiamen?" Tuk smiles like he can see right through that lie. "I've heard Yerezi mystics are talented, but you must be newly awoken if you're on your pilgrimage. Talent alone will not be enough to save you."

"I doubt I'd be any safer with you around," Salo quips.

Tuk lifts his gauntleted hand to show it off. "Know anyone else with this, do you?"

Salo eyes the weapon and is forced to admit its power. What he would give to analyze its charms with his talisman. "I suppose not."

"And do you know another way to Yonte Saire?"

Salo sighs. "Not really."

"Well then." Tuk spreads his hands. "That's why you need me, because I can take you. We'll even visit a Primeval Spirit along the way if you want. And you don't have to bless me until we reach your destination. In fact, I insist that you don't. Not until you're sure you can trust me."

Salo stares at him ambivalently.

"Either this or you head back home, my friend," Tuk says. "You go up the Artery, and you might as well chain yourself to that post over there and wait for the Dark Sun's disciple to come flay you alive, because that's what he'll do when he catches you—if you're lucky. And I'm not just saying this to scare you."

"Well, it's working." Salo searches the empty streets of the meat market, feeling out of place. How the devil did he end up in this nightmare? He breathes out and makes a decision. "We get to Yonte Saire first."

Tuk's eyes turn very blue, and his face lights up with excitement, but he keeps it out of his voice. He extends a hand, and this time Salo takes it. "Your wish is my command."

"And if you try anything funny, the deal's off."

They end the handshake, and Tuk raises his palms. "No funny business. I swear it on my life."

Salo lets himself stare at the young man. Those eyes of his are terribly disarming, and despite himself, Salo finds that he is drawn to this stranger.

"I . . . guess we have a deal, then. But how are you traveling? Because I'm not walking."

"I've traveled by wheelhouse thus far," Tuk says, "but I can purchase a mount at the livery yard west of town. I have the money for it. We can go there right now."

"Uh . . . all right." A pang of sorrow cuts Salo deep as he takes another look at his surroundings: the Faraswa slaves in their cages, the slavers watching carefully, the thief trembling nearby. "But what about these people? Can I really just walk away?"

"There's something you could do," Tuk says, following his gaze, "but it'd depend on how much money you're willing to part with. You'd have to act quickly, though."

Salo flicks his tongue over his teeth in thought, weighing his choices. "Better to do something than nothing at all." He nods at his new friend. "All right, Tuk. Tell me this idea of yours."

24: Ilapara

Seresa, along the World's Artery—Umadiland

Her lunch hour is fast approaching when the brewer from the shebeen next door hurries into the general dealer's in a racket of clinking bangles.

"BaChando, didn't you hear?"

"Hear what, Mama?" Behind his counter, BaChando's eyes are already wide with alarm.

"A magic man attacked the town guards just minutes ago!"

"Oh, by the Blood Woman. Please tell me he serves the Dark Sun."

"No, they say they've never seen this one before," the brewer says, then adds in a panicked whisper, "What if the Cataract is moving to take back the town? I can't afford to pay tribute again!"

At her post by the door, Ilapara curses under her breath. This is the last thing she needs right now. Another power struggle for the town will force BaChando to shut down his store, which means no work for her, which means no pay. She's scraping by as it is.

BaChando moans, heaving himself up to his feet. "Thank you for telling me, Mama. I must . . . I must close immediately. Ilira!"

Ilapara sighs. "Coming, boss."

They close up minutes later, and BaChando retreats upstairs, where he lives with his wife and two young daughters. Outside, Ilapara stares morosely at the handful of copper coins in her palm—her wages for the half day. It'll be enough for her kudu's daily livery fees. She'll have to use her savings for food and rent. She exhales, leaning against the dealer's mud-brick facade.

The Artery is quiet. Which isn't strange for the time of day as such—caravans usually come and go at the extremities of daylight—but it's a little too quiet. The stillness feels eerily deliberate rather than natural. Shops have closed down. Not a single hawker can be heard peddling her wares at the top of her voice.

Ilapara wouldn't call herself jumpy, but seeing such a lively town frozen to stillness always perturbs some deep-rooted part of her, and it's at times like these that she's most tempted to just give up and go back home. Because this shouldn't be the norm. No one should have to live in such a constant state of fear. She knows this in her bones and in the depths of her soul.

But she also knows the freedom of living her life the way she wants to, and that's always enough to make her stay.

She starts pacing the length of the dealer's facade, wondering why the Yerezi princeling hasn't shown up already. It wouldn't be wise for him to be traipsing the streets with a warlord making a move on the town.

After another five minutes of waiting, she decides that he's not coming, so she heads to the river district, taking the shortcut through the meat market.

Most of the market is as dead as she expects, but as she walks round a bend, she comes upon a surprising flurry of activity centered on two wagons lined up on the street, ready to go.

She slows down, resisting the urge to grip her spear with both hands. No need to get defensive, no need to get noticed. Besides, these people don't look like attacking militiamen—*a group of slavers gathered next to a wagon still parked aslant by the wayside. Looks like they're dividing money among themselves, payday smiles all around. Must be one mother of a payday. Armed mercenaries loading slaves onto the two wagons on the road. One buyer? But why so many slaves? Buyer must be one of the five figures standing next to the wagons. By Ama, is that the princeling?*

Ilapara moves briskly, ignoring the mud making her boots squelch. Whatever he's gotten himself into, she can still extricate him from it. Preferably without violence. *Preferably,* but it's an option if it becomes necessary. No way her tribesman is getting into trouble in this town under her watch.

But the closer she gets to the figures by the wagon, the less confident she feels about what's happening. One of the slavers is smiling at the princeling unctuously. By the subtle twist of his lips, the princeling seems repulsed by the man, yet they are nodding at each other. They shake hands, and the slaver walks away, leaving the princeling with the other three strangers.

She swallows her rising apprehension, walks past the wagons, tries not to look inside. The princeling notices her only when she's close enough to touch him—or strike.

His face brightens. "Ilapara! I'm glad you found me. I'm so sorry I couldn't make it back to the store."

She quickly assesses the three strangers around him and decides they're not immediate threats. Then she slits her eyes at Salo. "What's happening here?" she demands, and when he tells her, it takes every ounce of self-control just to keep her eyes from bulging in shock and horror.

Because apparently the princeling is the buyer. He's purchased *every slave in the meat market*—that's thirty-two Faraswa in total. And he's also purchased two of the wagons they came in, along with the mules drawing them.

I am calm, she tells herself. *I am not my emotions.* Even so, she fails to douse the fire in her words. "Why? Why the devil would you do such a thing?"

"To be honest?" he says. "I'm not sure I know myself, but I have all this money I don't need and can help these people with it, so."

She almost sighs in relief, almost, but common sense stifles it in her chest. "Where are you taking them?"

"Oh, I'm not going with them. He is." Salo points at the olive-skinned man next to him, the one wearing orange robes and a reptilian smile on his face. A few of his teeth are golden, one ear looks like it was partially bitten off, and his beard is a perfect tapering goatee. A mercenary. Probably Dulama. "I'm told he carries a recognized transporter's license," Salo says. "Whatever that means. Anyway, I hired him to take these people home. Most of them don't even know where they are or what's happening to them. If I freed them here, they'd just get enslaved again. They need help, rehabilitation. I don't know."

Ilapara keeps her expression level. "When you say home, you mean home as in the Yerezi Plains."

"Yes." Salo bites his lips like he knows how crazy that sounds.

"They'll never be allowed to cross the borderlands," she tells him.

"I'll give them these." He opens his right palm to reveal two moon-gold coins. "I've inscribed a message for AmaSikhozi in each of them," the princeling continues. "If she won't help them herself, she can have them escorted to Khaya-Siningwe. My aba will not turn them away."

He's probably insane. I am not my emotions. "How much did all this cost, Musalodi?"

"In total? About twenty mountains."

I am not my emotions. I am not my emotions. "Twenty mountains. Do you have *any* idea how much that is? Do you even know how much you're holding in your hands right now?"

"These coins are meaningless to me, Ilapara. I feel nothing giving them away. But it makes all the difference in the world to these poor people. It's the right thing to do."

"There'll be more Faraswa here tomorrow when the next caravan comes in. What then? Are you going to buy them all too?"

"I don't intend to be here tomorrow," Salo says. "I'm here *today*, so I can help these people *today*. All for twenty measly coins."

"Measly, he says." Ilapara shakes her head, at a loss. "You've never had to work for a living, have you. Never mind that: What about the fact that you're supporting the trade? Your money will only encourage these slavers to keep doing what they're doing."

"Maybe, but there'll always be a buyer, and whether that buyer is me or someone else is of no consequence to these men. What's better for the victims at the end of the day?"

Ilapara holds his gaze, trying to think of a way to dissuade him from this madness. But this is such a gutsy thing to do she can't help but approve a little. By Ama, he makes her miss home so much it's nauseating.

She takes another look at the men around him. A short light-skinned man stares back at her with curious blue eyes and a slight smile, the kind that's probably a permanent facial feature, as if he finds the fabric of existence amusing. He's a little too handsome to be trustworthy. She decides she doesn't like him. "And who's this? Another slaver, I presume?"

Salo shakes his head. "Not at all. This is Tuksaad; he's coming with me to Yonte Saire."

"Uh-huh." At this point she's just going along with whatever he says. "And you?" She turns her scrutiny on the skinny, ragged boy next to Salo, whose ruby eyes quickly fall to the ground when they meet hers. An old woolen hat is drawn over his head, covering what must be tensor appendages. She tilts her head and addresses him in Izumadi. "Wait a second—haven't I seen you around before?"

"He's a friend," Salo answers for him. "He'll be driving one of the wagons to the Plains."

All right. Time to leave this craziness. "Musalodi—Salo, look. It's possible a hostile warlord is making a move on the town, so there might not be a caravan leaving tonight. You should find lodging as soon as possible and stay indoors until the storm passes. Even now you're putting yourself at risk by being here."

"She doesn't know," remarks the pale-skinned one, and Ilapara almost does a double take because he's just spoken in Sirezi, and his eyes are a bright shade of green, when they were blue not a moment ago.

She almost shows alarm, but Ilapara is good at controlling herself. "Know what?" she says, and Salo stares blankly at her with those reflective lenses of his like he's trying to figure out how much to tell her.

"Let's see these wagons off, and I'll explain everything," he says at length. "Can you wait that long?"

The wise thing to do would be to leave, but she can't bring herself to do it. If anything happened to him afterward, she'd never forgive herself. "All right," she says with a sigh of resignation. "I'll wait."

It'll be a slow trek southeast for the wagons along the narrow, bumpy road to Khaya-Sikhozi. Ilapara hasn't made the trip in three years, but she remembers erratic skies and endless stretches of flat savanna bristling with wildlife.

She watches with mild envy as Salo sees off the Faraswa boy and the Dulama mercenary, handing each of them a moongold coin. The boy seems to struggle with the reins at first, but he gets it right fairly quickly. As he rolls away, following the mercenary's wagon, Ilapara glimpses a familiar crimson-eyed face inside the cage behind him. Those eyes are still dead to the world, but seeing them now floods her with a fragile hope that maybe the world isn't as bleak as she thought it was. Maybe.

Once the wagons have set off, she leads both Salo and Tuksaad to a relatively sheltered blind alley not too far away and folds her arms.

"Well?" she says to the two young men. "What don't I know?"

A heap of rubbish is festering in one corner. Salo stares at it for a moment before letting out a long sigh; then he extends his free arm and lights it up with incandescent reddish markings that weren't there before. The thickest one is a single ring encircling his forearm. "I'm a mystic, Ilapara. I didn't want to, but I had to reveal myself a short while ago. I had no choice. It's why this place is so empty."

She eyes the shards expressionlessly—shards, because that's exactly what these markings are, and they're the last thing anyone wants to see in this town or in any other stopover town in Umadiland.

The revelation is like a needle knitting together every odd detail she's noticed about him, and suddenly he makes a whole lot more sense—the staff, the lack of red steel, the coins he said contained messages, the unsettling aura about him. She has questions, all right—*many* questions—but at least now she knows where to place him.

And that means she knows how to read him. "Siningwe, right? Your clan hasn't produced a mystic in years, has it?"

He stiffens, dims his shards, and drops his hand. He gives a non-committal shrug.

Interesting. "Were they really so desperate that they'd ask a man to awaken?"

"You tell me," he says a bit curtly. "An Umadi witch attacked my kraal with tikoloshe and sacrificed dozens of my clanspeople to her lord, the same lord who apparently owns this wretched excuse for a town. Is that desperate enough for you?"

Tuk's expression falls, and his eyes darken to brown, but he says nothing. Sounds impossible to Ilapara's ears, yet she can't doubt the pain in Salo's words. He watched his people die, and that is what has driven him here.

A surge of anger grips her on his behalf, surprising in its intensity because she thought she'd abandoned her people. She wants to ask, to learn more about what happened, but sensing this isn't something he wants to talk about, she lets it go. "I'm sorry. I didn't know."

The defensiveness seems to bleed out of his shoulders. "It's all right. You couldn't have." He watches her quietly for a while. "You're taking this surprisingly well, all things considered."

She raises an eyebrow. "What did you expect?"

"I . . . nothing. Actually, your reaction is encouraging."

"Is it?"

"Yes. See"—he fiddles with his spectacles rather unnecessarily—"I was . . . hoping to convince you to come with me. Your cousin told me why you left the Plains, and I thought . . . well . . ." He leaves his sentence hanging.

"I see. I'm a girl who wants to be a ranger, and you're a boy who wants to be a clan mystic, so let's be friends."

Salo gives her a lopsided smile. "That's not it at all, though I can't blame you for seeing things that way."

"How else should I see them, then?"

"For starters, it'd be nice to have someone from home with me. It'd be even nicer if said someone could wield something like that." He juts a finger at her spear. "I've been told the Yontai is quite dangerous these days."

Ilapara smiles without humor. "And what tells you I'm any good at wielding it? Maybe I'm just carrying it around for the look of it."

"Hardly. I heard you were a menace to the Sikhozi boys, that they stopped training with you because you embarrassed them too much."

"Birosei exaggerated my abilities," she lies. "I was just as good as any of them, not any worse, not any better. That's what bothered them the most."

"Well, it doesn't bother me," Salo says, and he means well, but a flash of annoyance heats up her chest.

"It shouldn't. The Yerezi idea that women should be confined to books and magic is a thousand shades of silly. I could have done the bull pen in my sleep."

Salo beams like she has proven his point. "I completely agree, which is why you'd be perfect for this. So what do you say?"

Next to them, Tuksaad clears his throat. Those strange changeable eyes of his are murky now. "Forgive my intrusion, but we can't stay here," he says. "We really need to leave."

How odd to see someone so obviously foreign speak Sirezi so fluently. It isn't a Great Tribe language like KiYonte, Dulamiya, or Izumadi, so there's not much incentive for foreigners to learn it.

"You realize that going up the World's Artery is out of the question now," she says to both of them. "If you're the one who emptied these streets, one of the Dark Sun's disciples will come after you. In fact, he's probably on his way here as we speak. I'd say your best chance of staying alive is to follow those wagons back to the Plains."

"Not an option," Salo says. "The queen has sent me on a pilgrimage to the Red Temple. I intend to see it through."

"You're not listening. Continuing with this journey of yours will only get you killed."

"Tuk says he can take me there safely. He says he knows another way. I believe him."

"There is no other way. Not unless you plan on risking the open wilds on your own." Upon Salo's wooden expression, Ilapara feels the blood leach away from her face. "That's your plan? By Ama, do you know how stupid that is? Are you trying to get eaten by kerits and dingoneks? Because that's exactly what will happen."

"I'm no stranger to the open wilds, Ilapara," Salo says. Then he adds with a knowing smile, "Besides, I don't think I have to worry too much about predators."

"Then what are we waiting for?" Tuksaad says.

Salo looks at Ilapara with a forlorn expression, and despite herself, it gets to her.

"By Ama." She rolls her eyes up to the sky and shakes her head. "Why has this boy come to try my patience so?" She sighs with exasperation. "We need to get you out of town."

Salo obviously tries not to look too hopeful when he says, "So you're coming?"

"Only until I know you're safe," she warns him. "Then I'll decide what to do. Come on. My kudu is at the livery across the road."

"How fortuitous," Tuksaad says as he falls into step behind her. "We were actually headed the same way. Do you think I could get a good mount for a couple of silver rocks?"

She doesn't trust him at all, but it's hard to keep frowning at him when he smiles like that. "With the town spooked, you'll need a heck of a lot more than a couple of rocks to get them to do business with you."

"I'm . . . on a tight budget," he admits with a wince.

Next to her Salo fishes out yet another pair of moongold coins from his purse. "Then it's a good thing I have these left."

While Ilapara tries not to clench her jaw too hard, the joy on Tuksaad's face couldn't be easier to read if he spelled it out on his forehead. "You don't mind? I'd pay you back, of course."

"No worries," Salo says with a shrug, then quirks an eyebrow at Ilapara. "Will this be enough, though?"

That's more than double a peasant's yearly wage in the palm of his hand, and he doesn't even know it. Ilapara has to fight off a groan. "We'll see what we can do."

The livery yard sits on a wide crescent street branching west off the Artery, with a perimeter walled in by wooden paling.

As one of the most profitable businesses in town, it is Seresa's best equipped, with facilities designed to cater to every manner of riding beast, from docile mules to predatory cats. The charms of hypnotic Blood craft built into the stables lull the animals into calm and manageable states, each fed a diet appropriate to its species.

Such attention to detail is why Ilapara hasn't minded paying the exorbitant daily fees to keep her red kudu housed there. She remembers being apprehensive about his willful temperament when she first stole him in Kageru, but now she doesn't think she could buy a better mount even if she had the money. He is quite simply perfect for her.

She named him Ingacha, the lone warrior, which seemed appropriate after their narrow escape from the retribution of a warlord. *And here I am, flirting with the same kind of danger by associating with a marked target.*

Salo gazes at the buck with open wonder as the liveryman drags him out the wooden gates by his reins. He adjusts his spectacles and leans forward as if to take a closer look. "That's a red kudu, isn't it? I've heard they can take on a whole pack of hyenas by themselves."

"And I've heard," Tuk adds, "that they can't be completely tamed, not even by sorcery." She's learning that his eyes gain a green cast whenever he's amused by something. "They say only a certain kind of person can handle one. A kindred spirit, so to speak."

Sounds to Ilapara like he's saying something about her in an underhanded way, but before she can verbalize her pique, Kudi the liveryman arrives with Ingacha.

"You owe me big, Ilira," he says, flinging the reins at her like they itch. "I could get in trouble for this. You know I'm supposed to lock everything down when a hostile magic man comes to town."

"I know, Kudi, and I'll make it worth your while." She strokes Ingacha's glossy neck to calm him down. The buck grunts indignantly and flicks his massive ears; she suspects he doesn't care for the beast-taming magic they use here. "My friend needs a mount," she tells Kudi. "What do you have?"

Kudi shakes his narrow head. "Not today. I'm risking a lot as it is."

"Would a mountain change your mind?"

"Ha! For a mountain I'd hunt you a grootslang and saddle it myself."

With a look she tells Salo that it's up to him what happens next. He doesn't waste time showing Kudi one of his last moongold coins. "We don't need a grootslang, Red-kin. Just the healthiest, fastest mount you have."

Kudi is wise, and the wise of Seresa never forget why they are here. He keeps his face neutral as he accepts the coin and holds it to the suns; moongold gains a unique iridescent sheen in sunlight, like it has cold flames trapped inside. "Equine or bovine?" he says when the sheen appears on the coin. For a man holding more than a year's wages in his hand, he contains his excitement rather well.

"Equine, preferably," Tuksaad says.

"I have just the thing," Kudi says, pocketing the coin with a huge grin. "Come with me, and I'll show you."

Tuksaad follows him, and they disappear behind the gates.

Salo proceeds to question Ilapara about her time in Seresa, why she chose the town, how much she earns at the general dealer's. She tries to answer him politely—his curiosity is innocent, after all—but she can't take her mind off the elapsing minutes. Salo should be out of Seresa by now.

"A good name, Ingacha," he says, inspecting the buck's straps and fittings with the easy manner of someone who grew up tending livestock. "He does look a bit like a warrior, doesn't he? Fierce, brave. All he needs is the touch of a mystic, and he'll be as tough as any moon-blessed quagga out there."

Ilapara gives a snort. "There's no chance of that happening."

"No?" Salo peers at her over the kudu. "I beg to differ. I think there's a good chance that it might. If you want it to, that is."

Ilapara looks the boy squarely in the face. "What are you saying, Musalodi?"

"I think you know," he says, and she keeps frowning at him, but then she sees her own uncertainty reflected in those lenses of his, so she turns her face away to glower down the deserted street.

"Come with me," he says. "Come with me, and I'll bless you with my power. You and your buck. You can be the Ajaha we both know you are."

"You know nothing about me."

"Fair enough, but I know this town. I've seen what it's about, and I just can't believe you like being here. This is a horrible place, Ilapara. And look at how much you're paid: a pittance."

This time she manages to hold the glare. "This is the real world, not some sheltered paradise where everything is sanitary and wrapped in neat little roles for boys and girls to play. Out here I can hold my spear without anyone frowning at me. Men cast spells every day, and no one loses their minds over it. You only need to spend a day out of the Plains to see just how stupid and senseless our traditions are."

The look on his face is hurt at first, but then it hardens. "Maybe our people aren't perfect, but I'd rather live among them than out here, where human beings get sold in markets like livestock."

"Well, I'd rather be free than live in a pretty prison all my life."

"Is that how you felt? Imprisoned?"

"I'd have expected you of all people to understand," she says with heat in her voice. "I don't know how you're a mystic, but I seriously doubt your clanspeople welcomed your study of magic."

He is quiet for a time. "Maybe they didn't," he finally says, "but at least I didn't abandon them. I stayed and tried to make a difference."

"Yeah? And how's that working for you?"

He turns his face away. This time he stays silent.

Above them a flock of noisy carrion birds spirals with the updraft. Salo seems thoughtful as he stares up at it. Then he says, "I could pay you. It could be a job. You watch my back for the duration of my pilgrimage, and I'll pay you what you're actually worth, not these peanuts you get here. After that? You can come back here if that's what you want."

She's tempted. She really is, but he's so trustful and presumptuous it vexes her. How could he just place his life in the hands of strangers? He doesn't even know her—even worse, he doesn't know Tuksaad, and he's getting ready to run off with him to Ama knows where.

But he has money, a corner of her mind says. *Money you desperately need. And it's not like there's a line of people waiting to hire you, is it? So why not?*

She casts an impatient scowl toward the gates. "What's taking them so long?"

Salo follows her gaze. "I'm sure they'll be out in a few. Saddling a mount takes time."

Her skin tingles with awareness; her forehead crinkles up with worry. For some reason she feels hunted, like someone has drawn a bow in her direction and is about to let loose.

She looks around; a rustling breeze stirs her head scarf. The carrion birds are still circling above them, still crowing loudly. But the streets are quiet, perhaps *too* quiet.

Something is off.

An old beer hall sits farther up and across the street, a place Ilapara knows well. Music and drunken voices should be coming out of that place, even with a hostile mystic in town, if only because alcohol has the tendency to dilute fears.

Today it's dead silent.

Gripping her spear with both hands, she steps over a murky rivulet and onto the street, straining her ears. But all she detects is the sigh of her own breath and the crowing from above.

"Is something wrong, Ilapara?" Salo says.

She turns around. He looks so unsuspecting, this boy, this naive creature of the Plains, with his straw hat and loincloth and staff and spectacles. He shouldn't be here.

Ingacha raises his head, flaring his ears. She walks to him and checks the cinch of his saddle. "Where did you leave your mount?"

"Outside town," Salo says. "I didn't want to bring him in. Why?"

"We'll ride Ingacha to wherever you left your mount; then you'll go as far away from here as you can. Understand?"

He stares at her. "You're not making any sense, Ilapara."

"There's no time to explain. You need—"

A sudden ruckus comes from within the walls of the livery yard. Then she spots something gray and shimmery slipping out the gates: it's coming up behind Salo and it's long and meandering and fiendishly fast and it's rearing its head and it's about to strike and its fangs are a foot long, so she pushes Salo out of the way—

No, she *shoves* him with her free hand so forcefully he tips over with a yelp, but her attention is solely on this thing that's coming, because its jaws are yawning open and its fangs are dripping with venom, so there's no time to think, no time for anything at all but movement, movement or death.

So she moves. She strikes with her spear, whipping its point down and thrusting forward into the advancing maw, and by the time her mind has caught up to her body, an upper jaw is impaled upon the sleekness of her aerosteel weapon.

A human upper jaw, attached to the body of a giant serpent.

She recoils in horror, pulling her spear out. As the creature falls to the ground, she sees that no, actually, this is really just a horrifically huge cobra with no resemblance to a human at all. Then it writhes on the ground, and the maze of markings on its serpentine head comes back into view. She almost screams because her sight is proven false again, and dear Ama, that *actually is* a human head on the serpent, complete with a beard and bright reptilian eyes. Familiar eyes.

Terror strikes her as she finally understands what she has killed. This creature could be nothing but an ilomba, a serpent of Blood craft sent by a mystic to kill her. Its master carved his Seal onto its hood so she would see his face when she saw the markings. Now it is writhing and tossing mindlessly on the ground, and he saw through its eyes that *she* killed it.

Off to her side, Salo is fumbling about for his spectacles on the ground, which were dislodged from his face when he fell. The animals in the livery behind them are still in uproar. Ingacha's huffing and brandishing his horns angrily, scratching the earth with a foreleg like he wants to charge. A second sinuous horror has slithered out of the beer hall through a first floor window, advancing with its head reared high, its hood spread out, threatening.

Ilapara charges toward this second monster, careful not to look at it directly, and this might be the most terrifying thing she's ever done, but her heart's beating steadily, and she's in total control of her body. The magic of the Seal on the serpent's head gives it a constant and dizzying shift in appearance; one second she sees a horrible snake with foot-long fangs, the next a human face with reptile eyes. Worse, the two looks seem to merge, and the face unlocks its jaws unnaturally, like it could swallow her whole.

They meet in the middle of the street, and it lunges for her with its jaws wide open, its face rapidly shifting between cobra and man and a horrid hybrid of both. She rolls to her right just in time to avoid its lethal fangs, and quickly she whips her spear outward, gritting her teeth when she feels its cutting edge biting into the ilomba's side. It hisses in anger and flings its tail toward her, but she's already ducking and pivoting on her feet to bring her spear around for another blow. She feels the slightest resistance before her weapon pulses with Storm craft from its enchanted witchwood core, and then a chunk of the serpent's head is parted from its body in a spray of blood—only for the rest of it to twist around so fast she doesn't notice its long tail lashing through the air until it has smashed her across her chest, knocking her back.

She flies and then hits the ground with the grace of a flung doll. She gasps for breath. Wet mud clings to her head scarf as she forces herself to keep moving, stumbling up to her feet while using the blunt end of her weapon for balance.

"Ilapara! Watch out!" Salo cries.

She looks, and along the crescent street of beer halls, shacks, and the livery's wooden paling, the largest ilomba yet is closing in from the west.

Her heart sinks into the pit of her stomach, and her knees almost fail her, but not because of the snake; she has killed two of these things already, and she would face another without fear. But another monster has drawn her gaze westward along the same road, a galloping blue-eyed abomination of a cat with a mane of metal spines flared out in anger, and this she knows she cannot oppose.

"Get out of the way, Ilapara!"

Somehow her feet move just as the cat leaps into the air. She raises an arm, bracing for death, but death does not come. Instead, the giant cat has pounced upon the ilomba, not her. Then she notices the saddlery attached to the cat and understands.

By Ama, that's the Siningwe totem in the flesh. Salo really is a mystic.

The fight between totem and serpent is brief. The ilomba attempts to coil itself around the cat, but the cat bats it away with its metal paws—and gets punished for it with several quick bites laced with deadly venom, all of them to the neck. But they only seem to anger the cat further, for it snaps its jaws into the serpent and twists, severing the spine. The ilomba goes limp in the cat's maw and is promptly tossed to the ground.

When something bursts out of the gates to the livery right then, Ilapara whirls round with her spear, ready for anything.

Then she lets herself breathe a sigh of relief. "A rather convenient time to show up, Tuksaad." She begins to stride toward Ingacha, who didn't run away even when he should have. "Where's your mount? We need to leave—*now*. There could be more of these things."

Tuksaad's eyes are black as ink and cold as steel. Pearls of blood spatter his face. He's wearing that little smile of his, but it's dispassionate, coolly calculating. Ilapara's sure he went in unarmed, but he's carrying a long blade in one hand, slim and slightly curved, with a golden gleam. Might be her eyes are playing tricks on her, but it looks somewhat translucent.

Ilapara braces her foot on one of Ingacha's stirrups to mount him. "The disciple who rules this town controls these things remotely. That means he's nearby. We don't want him finding us."

"I sensed them." Salo's straw hat is askew on his head. His eyebrows are arched high with panic, and dust now covers half his body. "I sensed them, but I wasn't paying attention. I thought they were people or . . . something else, something harmless. I didn't think—oh, dear Ama, there were two in the yard, weren't there." He looks to Tuksaad. "Are they dead? Where's the liveryman?"

"Don't worry," Tuksaad says. "I took care of them."

"Then we must leave." Salo visibly gathers himself. "If you don't have a mount, Tuk, you may ride with me."

But Tuksaad grins and turns his head toward the gates. "You can bring her out, friend," he shouts. "I need to get going."

A visibly shaken Kudi comes out of the gates, pulling tensely at the reins of a muscular zebroid warmount with a jet-black coat and metallic stripes. By its size and the two great horns that curve like sickles from its head, the creature must be an abada. Its lower legs are all exposed metal musculature, with hooves so bulky they could probably pulverize bone. Looking at the warmount, Ilapara figures it is probably worth the whole moongold coin.

Kudi's jaw drops when he sees the giant cat, even more when he sees Salo approaching and then mounting it. He shakes his head in horrified disbelief. "What the devil is going on, Ilira? What did you do—did you give me stolen money?"

What Ilapara has done is defy the will of a warlord's disciple, and in Umadiland, there is only one way that can end. But now's not the time for regrets.

"Go home, Kudi," she tells him. "The money's clean. Go home and stay there until this is over."

He doesn't need to be told twice. "I want no part in whatever this is." He quickly hands Tuksaad the abada's reins and makes himself scarce.

"Follow me and stay close," Ilapara tells Salo and Tuksaad, then spurs Ingacha down the crescent road and leads them west toward the boneyards.

The implications of what she's done don't hit her until moments later, when she has to weather a powerful surge of sorrow that wells up inside her without warning, the deeply discomforting realization that this will be her last time in this town, for there is no way she could ever return.

The boneyards rest upon a mountain sited in the west such that its shadow creeps over the town like a pall every dusk as the suns sink behind it. To the wise of Seresa, this deathly shadow is always a reminder of what can happen to those who forget their place, those fools who think they can get away with breaking the rules.

Ilapara once vowed that she'd never be counted with such ill-advised company, and yet in the end, all it took for her to break that vow was a desperate Yerezi boy.

And it just had to be a Yerezi tribesman, didn't it. So much for leaving the past behind and forging a new future for herself.

A rocky path skirts the boneyards on their northern boundary. Ilapara has never used it before, but she's heard the route's the best way to get over and behind the mountain and hence the quickest way to disappear from town.

So she leads Salo and Tuksaad due west of Seresa, first at a canter through the poorest, most desperate part of town, where the shacks are cramped together and the streets are winding. Then they fall into a gallop when the town ends abruptly, giving way to massive rubbish heaps.

The incumbent authorities never care enough to dig pits for the proper disposal and recycling of rubbish, so it all ends up piling up at the edge of town to putrefy or get scavenged by rats and the utterly destitute, a vile sea of refuse sloping westward, a pervasive shroud of noxious stench, and the mountain is like an island rising out of it.

They ride in silence. To keep her thoughts from spiraling into depressing territory, Ilapara focuses on moving her weight in tandem with Ingacha's fast lope, on the clatter of his hooves as they race away from the life she worked so hard to build. Even when the ascent grows steeper and they slow down to a trot, the town quickly falling away beneath them, no one speaks, and Ilapara is grateful for the silence.

They almost crest the mountain in this manner, and Ilapara's certain she's seen the last of the town, and a part of her wants to break into a gallop again just to get it over with, but then Salo gasps loudly behind her and says, "The coins."

A fork in the rocky path just ahead, right next to a gnarled acacia tree. The path branching right and upward must lead to the boneyards, so the one going left and downward must be the one they need to take. Ilapara doesn't stop.

"The coins! One of them is back! I can feel it."

Ilapara stops, takes a moment before she looks back, takes another moment to realize that she's furious—*furious* with Salo, this boy who's taken everything from her with his recklessness. She breathes in deeply, breathes out.

I am not my emotions.

She looks back.

Salo has come to a complete stop. His expression is pure distress. "Why is it back?"

Behind Salo, Tuksaad reins in his abada. Concern puts wrinkles on his forehead; his strange eyes are tinged rich brown like a dusky sky. "What about the other one? Can you tell where it is?"

"Still on its way to the Plains," Salo tells him. "But the other one . . . oh no."

Salo's leopard bounds up the path unexpectedly, and Ingacha almost bolts away with Ilapara, but she manages to rein him in. She strokes his neck and coos into his ear, glaring at Salo's retreating back.

"Where are you going?" Tuksaad says, spurring his abada to follow. "We can't afford to stop."

At the fork Salo branches up toward the boneyards, heedless of what lies ahead. Tuksaad follows him, and reluctantly, Ilapara coaxes Ingacha into motion and follows them, too, because she's with them now; this is the choice she's made.

Lining the winding path up to the boneyards on either side are the severed heads of those who most recently angered the rulers of Seresa for one reason or another. They're all affixed to pikes so that they stand at eye level and face anyone walking up the path, like a horrid caricature of a welcoming party.

The stench is devilish. It worsens at the summit, where the path flares into an open space overlooking the town of Seresa—open save for the fetid, headless corpses littering the place among black clouds of buzzing flies. A feral cur with a mangy coat growls as it retreats behind a bush at the edge of the clearing, a partially masticated arm caught between its jaws.

Ilapara grimaces. She's no stranger to death, so the horror doesn't quite pierce through the mental barriers she's learned to erect around herself, but when she sees the maggot-infested head of a young Faraswa woman grinning at her from across the open space, it's a little too much.

She covers her face with her head scarf, leaving only her eyes open to the world because she doesn't trust what her face will reveal.

Salo and Tuksaad have stopped by the east-facing ledge of the bone-yards, where the mountain falls away and spreads into the town below. She brings her nervous buck to a halt next to them, thankful to turn away from the sights around her, though she thinks she can feel the gazes of the dead crawling up her back.

In the distance, the World's Artery is a wide gravel snake cutting the shantytown in half, stretching from south to north for as far as the eye can see. An ugly thing, this place. She's always known this to some extent, and maybe she's deliberately ignored it, but seeing the view from up here, the ugliness is hard to escape. It's alive. A real, tangible thing she can reach out and touch. Something she can smell.

As she tracks the column of smoke rising from the center of town, she begins to realize why Salo and Tuksaad are both still as death next to her. She can just about see it; there, on the World's Artery, just a stone's throw from the general dealer's, a wagon stands caught in a storm of raging moonfire. Among the figures standing around the wagon is a man in a horned helmet.

I know you are watching, interloper.

Magic rattles her inner ear and slices into her soul, carrying with it a disembodied, sibilant voice that makes her think of giant serpents or mountains of ice grinding against each other.

Your business here was profitable for us, so I'll let you escape. But you broke our laws, and a price must be paid. I have claimed half of your purchase and sacrificed it in my lord's name. Consider it . . . compensation for the trouble you caused. Now be gone, and never show your face here again.

"But why would he do such a thing?" Ilapara hears herself say. "It's bad for business." And her words sound so foolish and inadequate, even to her own ears.

"I killed them," Salo says. "*I* did this. Everything I touch turns to dust. And I thought I was being *so* good." Tears glitter on his cheeks, something torn and jagged in his voice. "I'm a blithering fool."

She was angry with him, furious that he could come here and ruin the life she was trying to build for herself with his well-intentioned naivety . . . and yet now, listening to the sorrow in his voice, she can't help but hate herself for ever becoming so comfortable with evil that she could live in its shadow and not do a thing about it.

That she would be angry with someone who did in a day what she never found the guts to do in three years.

"We must go," she says. "We must leave this place and never come back."

25: The Maidservant

Southern Umadiland

The shadow of dusk is thickening over the savannas of Umadiland when the Maidservant emerges from the Void just outside the gates to her warlord's umusha. Riding the currents of her metadimensional sorcery, River emerges, too, spear in hand, and for the first few seconds they both stare mutely at the gleaming mystic Seal hanging weightlessly above the umusha, an impossibly black sphere spinning in place as it spills out a sea of colors from its brilliant halo.

River is tense as he stares up at the Seal. "Do you feel it?"

She knows exactly what he's asking. The power rooted to this land has always been dazzling in its strength to any mystic attuned to the earth; today it is so overwhelming she can almost feel her tattoos vibrating. A shiver of worry makes them throb with pain. "I feel it," she says, and River sniffs.

"His power has grown since we were last here."

"He must have taken another important town," she posits.

River briefly glances at her before looking back up at the Seal with a sneer on his face. "I doubt he lifted a finger. We're the ones who do all the work while he sits comfortably in there. Must be real nice for him."

"Our lord rules over more territory than many kings of the Redlands," the Maidservant says and then looks River in the eye. "Do not make the mistake of underestimating how powerful that makes him." *Assume you are being watched.*

From the way his sneer loses its edge, he must note the true warning in her words. He clears his throat and motions for her to lead the way. "We should go in."

She looks at the wooden gates, feeling another discomfiting tremor. "Yes. I suppose we should."

Designed along southern Umadi traditions, the Dark Sun's umusha is a stockaded village of rounded huts built entirely of straw, with arched portals so low people have to bend down to go through them. Ribbons of smoke spiral upward all across the umusha from outdoor cooking fires.

As the Dark Sun's place of birth, the village was where he first laid his arcane roots, becoming the seat of his power—his umusha—upon his ascension to the rank of warlord. No other mystic draws strength from the land beneath it.

River and the Maidservant quietly make their way through dusty compounds toward the throne hall. This isn't any ordinary village; anywhere else the residents would flee at the mere sight of them, but the people here—though they do give them a wide berth—are far more curious than afraid.

Children in hide loincloths follow them from a short distance away. Men and women come out of their huts to watch and gossip.

Like they believe themselves safe, like they know neither disciple would dare risk their lord's ire by needlessly harming the residents of his umusha beneath the light of his Seal.

She isn't proud of it, but the Maidservant finds their lack of fear rather vexing.

An old, spiteful voice rises at the back of her mind with an accusation: *You think yourself above such petty desires, but you are not. You are the very thing you hate. You will lose yourself to it.*

She clears her thoughts by focusing on the pain of her tattoos and thinks of nothing else until they arrive at the steps to the throne hall, a thatched structure whose convex roof curves into the ground on either of its longest sides. A pair of spearmen in darkly colored kikois stands guard by the hall's entrance; they open the large wooden doors as soon as they spot the Maidservant approaching with River.

Past the threshold, River frowns. "I sense we're the last of the summoned to arrive," he says. "The big man isn't here, though, so at least we're not late."

If River weren't such an idiot, he'd know that his Axiom, inelegant though it is, has just enough affinity with the temporal aspect of the Void to give him a mild approximation of clairvoyance. But like almost every male mystic of Umadi stock, River used a cheap trick to build his Axiom. He wouldn't understand its intricacies if they were laid out before him in clear ciphers.

Just as he predicted, the Dark Sun's four other lieutenants have already arrived and are standing before the high wooden throne at the front of the smoky, torchlit hall, waiting for their warlord.

The Dark Sun holds sway over more than a hundred mystics scattered across his territory, men and women who draw from the land by his grace, but these four mystics, six including Black River and the Maidservant, are his lieutenants, his most trusted disciples, who command other mystics and their militias on his behalf. Each has roots spread across large tracts of his land—rewards for acts of outstanding loyalty.

The first of the four to notice the Maidservant approaching with River is the only other woman in the group, a crone in a gray caftan and a lofty headdress, leaning on a curved walking stick of knotted witchwood. Her face is painted ash white, crinkling as she gives the Maidservant a ghoulish smile. "Ah. What is that smell you two bring? It tickles my nose."

"The smell of your own breath," River says with a smirk.

"No, I think not. I think 'tis the smell of death." She leans closer as the Maidservant and River join the group, watching them with manic eyes. "Much blood has been shed by your hands very recently, has it not? Yes, I can almost taste it."

River folds his arms across his broad chest, his smirk turning to a scowl. "We were dealing with a free agent."

"Oh, but I do not criticize you," the old woman says. "Shedding blood is the right of any disciple. I only wish to know if you shed it well."

At this River seems to relax. "Nice to see you, too, you old bat."

She was named Seafarer after sailing the waters of the Dapiaro for many years on her own. The Maidservant doesn't think the woman is quite sane—whatever counts as sane for a warlord's disciple, in any case.

The other three lieutenants watch the exchange with quiet interest.

"Gentlemen," the Maidservant says to them in greeting. "Seafarer. It's been a while."

They all nod back, and the one known as Sand Devil gives a sly, black-toothed grin. "Indeed it has. I'm surprised you even found the time to show up. What with how busy you've been lately."

Sand Devil is a balding man two heads shorter than the other male disciples in the room, though what he lacks in height he more than makes up for in his capacity to annoy. Hailing from the same region as River, he wears only a nut-brown kikoi and holds an enchanted spear of tronic bone and witchwood in one hand.

He tilts his head now and squints at the Maidservant. "But I wonder: Is it still you in there? You seem . . . less of yourself somehow."

Noting the silent chuckles from the other two men next to him, she bites off an emotional reaction. "I don't know what you mean."

"I'm just saying. Playing with that kind of magic has a price, doesn't it?" Sand Devil rakes her naked body with his eyes, and his grin widens. "Sooner or later the spirits will come calling."

"Watch it," River says, stepping forward dangerously. The Maidservant stops him with a gesture.

"I appreciate your concern, Sand Devil, but I feel just fine."

"We know what you did in the Plains," says Hunter, a proud man whose thick gray beard is an art form unto itself. An intricate network of scarification and red tattoos shows beneath his sleeveless crimson robe. He wears a wooden helmet crowned with the prominent sickle-like horns of an abada and holds a knotted staff with the tail of a tronic wildebok affixed to one end.

But it's his eyes that are most striking, a reptilian medley of bright yellows, greens, and reds.

"Can you tell us what in the Blood Woman's name you were thinking, provoking the ire of the Yerezi queen?" he says.

"Leave her alone." Seafarer wags a moody finger. "What she gets up to is no one's business but hers and the Dark Sun's."

Hunter glares at her. "Not if it will drag us all into a war we can't afford to fight."

"What's the matter?" River says with an acid sneer. "Is the great Hunter afraid of war? Are you the coward I've always known you to be after all?"

Fury sparks in Hunter's brilliant eyes, but before he can close the distance and attack, Northstar, the stolid, ax-wielding brute of a man next to him—wearing a grass skirt and armor pieces of tronic bone—puts a meaty hand on his shoulder and squeezes. "Behave. Our lord is near."

Hunter shrugs off Northstar's hand and glares at River. The Maidservant suffers a wave of hatred for having to tolerate any of them.

"I'd forgotten how much I love these meetings," Sand Devil says with evident glee. "Like a big, happy, dysfunctional family reunion."

"My trusted lieutenants. Welcome." With the sound of that resonant voice comes a cold shadow that falls upon the throne hall, signifying the arrival of the man himself, the one to whom they all owe fealty.

The shadow is quite literal, as the Dark Sun uses sorcery to bend light around himself so that his face is always veiled in darkness. All anyone ever sees of his features are a square-jawed outline and the unnatural red gleam of his tronic left eye, which is said to have come from a dingonek.

A patterned robe of crimson and gold hangs on his lean frame in loose folds. He is easily the tallest person the Maidservant has ever seen, a giant even next to Northstar. As he saunters barefoot from a side door to his throne, hands clasped behind him, Hunter bows, and the others follow his example. "Great Muchinda."

"We are honored to be in your presence, Muchinda," Sand Devil says.

The warlord's tronic eye seems to flicker in what the Maidservant would guess is amusement. "Yes, I'm sure you are," he says, and then he continues to his throne.

The Maidservant shudders with rage she can't express. Her hatred of this man burns with the fires of a thousand suns, and yet it is imprisoned in her body, locked behind a curse that warps her will and binds it to his. She would sooner slit her own throat than see him come to harm.

But soon I will be free, she tells herself, *and then I will laugh over your corpse.*

The Dark Sun relaxes into his throne and brings his fingers together, his tronic eye glaring in the shadows that enshroud his face. When he speaks, his sonorous voice fills the hall like something that belongs in a deep subterranean cavern.

"The world," he says, "the natural order of things, stands on a precipice of calamity, and a guiding hand moving in the shadows keeps pushing us closer to the edge. Why? I cannot say. Its intentions continue to elude me, but its workings are impossible to miss."

The glare of his eye winks out, and he falls into a spell of introspective silence, as though he has forgotten he has an audience. The Maidservant briefly scans the other lieutenants and sees the same worry she feels on their faces. The Dark Sun is at his most ruthless when he's in a thoughtful mood.

Abruptly the red eye pierces the veil of shadows, and the warlord returns to his speech. "By now I'm certain you've all heard of the massacre that recently struck King Mweneugo Saire from the face of the earth. He and his entire family were slaughtered. By his own men, if the rumors are to be believed." His head lists to one side, and his red eye locks onto one of his lieutenants. "I see the news pleases you, Sand Devil. Tell me why."

Sand Devil shows his blackened teeth, not bothering to hide his glee. "I say good riddance, Muchinda. Mweneugo was a menace to our people. His legions pressed well south of the Yontai, usurping land that belongs to the Umadi. May he forever rot in the underworld."

"Good riddance indeed," Seafarer crows.

Next to her, Hunter rolls his reptilian eyes. "Why do you care about land that isn't ours? He took it from our northern enemies, and it only made them weaker."

Sand Devil frowns. "I care because less land for them means less land for us when we begin our northward expansion. With Mweneugo's removal, we'll be in prime position to take our tribelands back from the Yontai."

Huffing a mirthless laugh, Hunter says, "Your shortsightedness can be astounding at times."

The Dark Sun raises a hand to intervene. "King Mweneugo was a menace to the northern warlords, true, but he was also conservative in his ways. He saw no need to expand his lands beyond the establishment of a buffer zone, even though he certainly had the means to do so. What he lacked was the will, and that made him tolerable at the least, perhaps even preferable to an alternative."

The Dark Sun drops his hand and settles it onto his throne's armrest. "But the so-called high mystics are now set to replace him with a new king, one who, according to the whispers, harbors great ambitions of empire. His wish is to bring all the Redlands under his dominion within his lifetime. Do you know what that means, Northstar?"

The big warrior mystic grunts. "It means he poses a direct threat to us, Muchinda."

"A grave threat," the warlord agrees. "Umadiland might belong to the Umadi, but we are not one people. We are a fluid collection of fiefdoms divided against ourselves. We stand no chance faced with the organized legions of the Yontai, especially not if the high mystics and their covens stand with them. Which leaves us with two choices." The warlord ticks off one finger. "Sit and wait for the new king to gather his legions and pick us off one by one." He ticks off another. "Or change the way we do things so that he finds that we are ready for him."

"We must prepare ourselves, Muchinda," Seafarer says, the heavy jowls on her face shaking in her vehemence. "I will die before I bow to foreign masters."

"My sentiments exactly," the Dark Sun says. "But how would we do this?" The warlord's red gaze lands somewhere next to the Maidservant. "Black River?"

River almost scratches his head before he catches himself and lets his hand fall. He grimaces. "Er . . . perhaps we should . . . send assassins to deal with this new king, Muchinda."

The Maidservant almost shakes her head. *Idiot.*

"Absurd," Hunter scoffs. "Even if the assassins got to him, which is unlikely, the high mystics would trace them back to us, and then we'd have every legion and Jasiri guardian riding down the Artery—exactly what we're trying to avoid." He addresses the warlord. "Muchinda, I propose that we begin building alliances with the other fiefdoms. We must present a united front, or the legions will find us easy prey."

Sand Devil snorts. "A sound plan in theory, but alliances would never work. Warlords have warred over Umadiland for centuries. Good luck undoing that kind of ingrained thinking overnight."

Northstar gives a nod of his head. "War is indeed the Umadi way. It is written in our blood, the essence of our ancestral gift. Any alliance would break almost as soon as it was formed."

"I am inclined to agree," the Dark Sun says, and then he finally looks at the Maidservant. "What about you, my dear Maidservant? How would you solve this problem?"

She wants to roar and attack, but the curse holds fast, and the pain searing her skin is what keeps her from ripping her hair out in frustration. "Great Muchinda, I believe there is only one solution," she says. "If you cannot ally yourself with your peers, then you must conquer them. Bring all of Umadiland under your Seal, and you will be powerful enough to repel any KiYonte invasion."

A chilly silence engulfs the hall as everyone takes a second to envision what such a thing would look like. How powerful would a warlord be if his shards drank from all corners of Umadiland? Would he even be human?

Sand Devil breaks the silence, releasing a heavy breath as he shakes his head. "Impossible. That's why no one's done it before."

"But if there's someone who can," the Maidservant says, "it is you, Muchinda."

The worst thing is that she actually believes these words, because unlike most warlords, the Dark Sun is no simpleminded brute. He shows order and restraint in the way he deals death. He has a vision, plans that go beyond the mere holding of territory.

While most other warlords punish their disciples for breathing without their permission, the Dark Sun built a hierarchy that rewards disciples who show ambition and initiative, giving them a fair degree of autonomy to expand his territory on his behalf. Other warlords will attack and invade a weak enemy the first chance they get, but the Dark Sun will wait until he knows he can hold a territory before he moves to conquer. He expects the same of his disciples.

She despises him, but even she must acknowledge that he is a worthy foe.

"I want you all to think heavily on this matter," the Dark Sun says at last. "We will convene in a week to discuss it at greater length. Come with ideas. We *will* avert this disaster before it comes, by all means necessary, even if it means taking all of Umadiland for ourselves."

"We are your humble servants, Muchinda," Sand Devil says with a bow, but he is wasting his breath. Flowery expressions of praise and adulation can never win the warlord over. That doesn't stop Sand Devil from trying, though, much to his constant disappointment.

"I have one other matter I wished to discuss with you," the warlord says. "Before you arrived, Hunter informed me of something interesting. Apparently a young mystic on his way to Yonte Saire saved a thief from execution in Seresa and escaped before either of them could be apprehended."

"He did not escape, Muchinda," Hunter says with an indignant timbre in his voice. "I let him go after exacting a heavy price for the trouble he caused. I did not see the need to take things further."

"Either way, the result is functionally the same," the Dark Sun says. "In any case, I am not interested in whatever laws he supposedly broke. What interests me is that this mystic is reportedly Yerezi, which is curious, considering the Yerezi do not allow their men to wield sorcery. Not as far as I know." He lets this marinate. "It raises questions, does it not? Why now? And is it a coincidence that he is journeying thousands of miles to Yonte Saire so soon after Mweneugo's death? I'd find that hard to believe."

Hunter clears his throat. "Muchinda, they did just suffer an unprecedented and unprovoked attack on one of their kraals." He glances at the Maidservant. "From one of our own, for that matter. This mystic might be an emissary under the guise of a Bloodway pilgrim, sent to broker an alliance with the new king." Belatedly, Hunter adds, "An alliance against us, that is."

The Dark Sun appears to consider this. "I sense we're missing a vital piece of the puzzle," he says at length. "Whatever the case, such an alliance must never come to pass. The Yerezi tribe may be small, but their sorcerers are very cunning and their cavalry exceedingly effective. If they allied with an expansionist KiYonte king, we would face pressure on two fronts. Divided as we are, this would be catastrophic. We cannot allow it."

He falls into another thoughtful episode while his lieutenants wait in silence. The Maidservant feels River watching her, but she doesn't look to him.

"Yes, I have many questions for this Yerezi mystic," the warlord says, returning to the present as if he never left. "Send whoever you can spare after him, or go after him yourselves if you can. I want him brought to me alive if possible, and if not, my necromancer will extract whatever information she can from his corpse. You are dismissed. Except for you, Maidservant. And you as well, Black River. Stay. I wish to have a word with you."

If he somehow divines the worried spasm that takes hold of the Maidservant, he makes no show of it.

She bows. "As you wish, Muchinda."

Next to her River maintains a stiff posture while the others share meaningful looks before bowing and quietly retiring from the hall, though Hunter doesn't miss the opportunity to toss a smirk at the Maidservant on his way out.

Upon their exit the Maidservant and River move to stand in a central position before the throne and wait for their warlord to address them.

"So," he says. "Tell me. How did you do it?"

By the focused intensity of his tronic eye, the Maidservant knows he's talking to her. "How did I do what, Muchinda?" she says as evenly as her voice will allow.

"Those sacrifices you performed in the Plains," he says. "The rush of power was . . . intoxicating. I didn't think it was possible for someone so sullied by blood as you are to perform sacrifices so potent. Each of them felt like . . . a mother offering up her beloved child to me. Are the Yerezi like the Faraswa, perchance? Is there some hidden power in their blood that makes it especially potent?"

"Not at all, Muchinda." The Maidservant knew he would ask her this, so she has an answer prepared, with just enough truth to satisfy the question and no more. "It is simply an old ritual I pieced together after extensive reading. At the zenith of a waxing half moon, shed the blood of the innocent in an unconquered stronghold beneath the light of a Seal, and it will drink the power of the fallen."

He probably knows that, like most other sacrificial sacraments, the one who benefits from it cannot be the one to perform it. What she doesn't tell him, however, is that this particular ritual is Black magic.

The Dark Sun leans forward in his throne, his interest palpable. "And you did this merely as a gesture of your loyalty to me."

I did it to secure my freedom to burn you and everything you stand for to the ground. Blanking her mind with pain to mask deceit as best as she can, she says, "I also wished to test the ritual, Muchinda, as well as probe the Yerezi defenses." She quickly adds, "In case you ever decide to make a move in that direction."

The warlord is silent for a time, thoughtful, and the Maidservant realizes her mistake. *I wasn't convincing enough. He knows I'm hiding something. He'll compel me to tell him the truth.*

He relaxes into his throne as if he has dismissed whatever was troubling him. "I see. In any event, whatever your reasons, I always reward loyalty and initiative, and you have proven, once again, that you are not lacking in either."

She should have been more careful, more resolute in her story. Worry clouds her thoughts like a dense fog, but she maintains an appearance of calm. "I live to serve, Great Muchinda."

The red eye swivels away from her. "What about you, Black River? Are you loyal to me?"

"Of course, Muchinda. I also live to serve."

"So you would do anything I asked of you."

A trap.

River hesitates before giving his answer. "Within reason, Muchinda."

Amusement comes thickly in the warlord's voice. "Within. Reason. Explain."

River winces. "Say, if you asked me to slit my own throat, for example, I would find it difficult to obey, seeing as I enjoy being alive. But that is not to say I am not loyal to you, Muchinda."

"Mm. And what if I asked you to slit someone else's throat instead? Would that be within reason?"

A subtle air of danger has pervaded the hall now, an undertow passing between the Dark Sun and the Maidservant beneath their spoken words.

"I would do it without hesitation," River says, oblivious to the deadly spear aimed at his chest, the sheer drop he's slowly being nudged toward.

"Are you certain?" the warlord says, and River stands straighter in an attempt to exude confidence.

"Yes, Muchinda."

"Then prove it." The Dark Sun lifts a finger and points at the Maidservant. "Slit her throat."

She remains still. Inside her mind, a rattling door begins to shake like it will explode from its hinges. She pushes back against it with everything she has. *Not yet. Not when I'm so close to freedom.*

Next to her, River gapes at the warlord, then at her, then back. His lips move in several false starts before he finally manages something coherent. "I beg your pardon?"

"Kill the Maidservant," the warlord repeats, slow and with authority. "Or was I not clear?"

"Muchinda, I—"

"I have ordered you to slit someone's throat, which you said you'd do without hesitation if I asked it of you, and yet here you are, hesitating. Are you a liar, Black River?"

River licks his lips nervously. "No, Muchinda. I hesitate only because . . . because the Maidservant is your trusted lieutenant, and I don't believe you'd want her—" He stops when the shadows in the hall grow noticeably darker.

"Are you questioning my sanity?" The warlord's voice is barely above a whisper.

"No, Muchinda."

"Then why would I ask you to do something I don't want you to do?"

Letting his shoulders sag, River hangs his head. "Muchinda, I . . . cannot."

"I see."

"Anyone else, and I'd do it, but . . ."

"But you are smitten," the warlord says. "A pity your object of affection doesn't feel the same for you. In fact, I sense she is quite incapable of any sort of sentiment." The red eye turns to the Maidservant, and she almost feels its heat. "Isn't that right, my loyal lieutenant?"

The door in her mind shakes so violently it almost drowns out the world, and for a brief second she's tempted to yield. But that second passes, and her hatred holds, giving her a reason to stay rooted in this world. "You are right, Muchinda. I am incapable of sentiment."

In the corner of her eye she catches River's hurt look, but River isn't why she is here, why she endures pain and battles the underworld's call every second of her life. Why she tolerates the chains that bind her. River is nothing.

The warlord leans forward. "Are you loyal to me, Maidservant?"

"Absolutely."

"Is there anything you wouldn't do if I asked it of you?"

"You could compel me to do anything, Muchinda," the Maidservant says. He could always strip her of her will and force her into obedience, but he derives his pleasure from getting her to do his bidding willingly. He knows she would sooner obey him than be stripped of her will. That is his victory.

The gleam of teeth shows briefly through the warlord's veil of shadows. "Then you know what to do."

She does, and River doesn't even fight her. He stands still and watches her with those stupid, trusting eyes of his even as she brings a crackle to the hall by drawing power into her shards. He watches her even as she shapes the Void into a gleaming spear, even as she hurls it toward his chest so that it impales him, bringing him down to his knees as he gurgles blood. He watches her even as he falls to his side and dies.

River is nothing.

You will lose yourself to it.

The Dark Sun rises and begins to descend the steps to his throne. "As much as I enjoyed your sacrificial offerings, whatever agenda led you down this path may have created an enemy we cannot afford." He stops next to River's body, but his red eye never leaves the Maidservant. "Your attack put the Yerezi on alert, made them aware of their vulnerabilities, and possibly convinced them we're a problem in need of solving. Because that is what will happen should the Yerezi queen ever join forces with an ambitious KiYonte king; we will be solved. It would be over for us long before we'd marshaled any sort of credible defense. Do you see now why I am not entirely pleased by your actions?"

River is nothing.

The Maidservant bows, though her chest is a seething cauldron. "Forgive me, Muchinda. I will be more thoughtful from now on."

"I know you will." Only now does the warlord spare a moment to take in River's bleeding corpse, but it is only a moment. He turns his back and begins to make his way toward the exit, stopping after a few steps. "And next time, my dear Maidservant . . ." Shadows thicken all around her like a shroud. "When I ask you why you did something, don't lie to me. Understood?"

River is nothing.

"Yes, Muchinda."

The shadows relent. "As a reward for your loyalty, you may extend your roots to the Valau borderlands. The least I can do, everything considered."

That is enough land to add a sixth ring to her shards, but it is all she can do not to scream. "You are most generous, Great Muchinda." *One day I will cut your head off with a blunt knife.*

The warlord nods in acknowledgment and departs, leaving the Maidservant alone in the empty hall with River.

River, who is nothing.

River, who is nothing now but wasn't nothing before.

The Maidservant discorporates and billows away as fast as the wind will carry her.

PART 5

MUSALODI
*
THE MAIDSERVANT
*
ILAPARA
*
ISA

Fire craft—magic of flame

Controlled combustion of the moon's essence into extremely destructive fire. Decidedly the most commonly practiced craft.

—excerpt from Kelafelo's notes

"Why the long face? Did you not get your share of pumpkin porridge?"

"I hate my stupid eyes and these stupid glasses. I hate that I have to wear them all the time. It's not fair."

"No, it's not, but our scars tell the stories of who we are and what we've survived, and you, my dear child, have survived things that would have broken grown men. Wear your scars proudly; they do not define your failures but your victories over life."

26: Musalodi

The Open Wilds of Umadiland

When Salo turned seven, his mother made him honeyed millet bread and took him down to the lake to throw rocks and make them skip over the water. They danced in the shallows and splashed each other silly, the droplets glistening in the sunlight like crystals, their giggles floating like a breeze. And when they returned home, they painted each other's faces and laughed some more, until their stomachs hurt and they were so tired they fell asleep entangled in each other. It is Salo's fondest memory.

Now, as he gallops across the open wilds of Umadiland on a giant totem of the Yerezi Plains, he takes refuge in that memory, trying to recover even a speck of the peace of mind he felt that day, the sense that even if he never had anything else, he would be just fine. His surroundings grow dim, and for a moment he imagines he's not part of the world, like a wandering ghost whose time has long since passed, who can be neither touched nor hurt by the happenings of the universe.

A cowardly thing to do, perhaps, but the alternative is to hurl himself to the ground and weep until he has purged himself of lungs.

Tuk leads the way at a fast trot, but it's too slow for Salo. He wants to push Mukuni as fast as he knows the cat can go, so fast that his paws barely scrape the ground. Ingacha and the abada are creatures of flesh and blood, though, so there's no choice but to let them set the pace.

Acacia trees and granite outcrops pass them by like slumbering beasts. Herds of wildebok and para-para stampede away from them on sight. The suns bid the world goodbye in a fiery blaze of color, giving way to a star-speckled sky whose light is enough to see by. No one speaks the entire time.

By tacit agreement, they stop and set up camp next to a creek several hours after nightfall. While the others unsaddle and water their mounts, Salo forages for dry brushwood to make a fire, then divvies up the musuku wine, mealie bread, and dried meats he brought from home—the last of his supplies, so he'll have to hunt from now on.

They eat quietly. Words feel too much like cheating to Salo. He can still speak and breathe and smoke and eat, but what about the Faraswa people who died because he was too damned self-righteous to let things be? By Ama, was Mhaddisu one of them?

How many people will I kill with my weakness?

When they are done eating, Salo drapes himself with his crimson blanket cloak and lights his pipe. No need to worry about predators with Mukuni around, but distant growls and cackles drift to their camp occasionally, reminding them each time that they are trespassing.

The abada and Ilapara's buck lie on the grass nearby, watching Mukuni very carefully; the two animals seem to have formed a tentative alliance based on their mutual fear of the cat. *I'll have to do something about that.*

Salo stews in his own thoughts for so long he's almost startled when Tuk addresses him from across the campfire. "Just so you know, my planned route will take us past one of the Primeval Spirits."

Salo lacks the energy to respond, so he stares morosely at the crackling fire and keeps puffing on his pipe.

Ilapara's interest, however, has been piqued. She loosens the scarf wrapped around her head, peeling it off a little to reveal a curious frown. "Which one?"

"The Lightning Bird of Lake Zivatuanu," Tuk replies. "Also known as the Great Impundulu. I intend for us to charter a Tuanu waterbird and sail up the lake. The World's Vein isn't far from its northernmost shores—probably a two days' ride at most. And once we reach the Vein, it'll be a straightforward journey east to Yonte Saire."

Salo knows little about the ancient manifestations of Red magic commonly referred to as the Primeval Spirits, as there aren't any in the Plains. They supposedly have deep and esoteric connections to the lands they roam and are capable of bestowing rare knowledge and spells onto worthy mystics—probably why it is customary for pilgrims of the Bloodway to visit and commune with one or more of them.

Salo might have considered doing so had it not required that he veer far from his planned route to Yonte Saire. But that has happened anyway, so maybe he'll get to visit one after all. He just can't be bothered to care.

Ilapara's frown deepens. "Aren't the Tuanu highly intolerant of foreigners in their lands?"

"They are," Tuk says, "but the Tuanu will make an exception for a sorcerer who wishes to commune with the Lightning Bird—if they can pay with something valuable, that is."

"Something like what?"

Tuk smiles, but it doesn't lighten his eyes. "Let me worry about that."

"I don't like being left in the dark," Ilapara says. "If I'm following you somewhere, I'd like to know what I'm getting myself into."

"Fair enough, but I have a good reason for being reticent. I know I haven't done anything to earn your trust, but I swear I'm only doing what I think is best for all of us."

Ilapara looks like she wants to argue, but then she purses her lips and crosses her booted feet in front of her. "All right. If you want to earn my trust, how about we start with who the devil you are and where you're from."

Tuk smiles into the fire and seems to consider his answer. Eventually he says, "I guess there's no point in lying, is there. And why should I? I'm not ashamed of who I am or how I came to be." His lips say one thing, but he starts rubbing his hands together like he's about to meet the malaika of death. "I came from the Enclave beyond the Jalama Desert, though I'm originally from the Empire of the West, far across the waters you call the Dapiaro."

That confession immediately draws Salo out of his silent brooding. "You're from the Empire of Light?"

"The very same," Tuk replies, and then he seems to struggle with his next words: "I was . . . made there."

"Made," Ilapara repeats. "What do you mean, you were *made*?"

Tuk chews on his lower lip for a long moment. "I'm what they call an atmech, Ilapara, the creation of a heretic necromancer—and by the way, that's what the Empire calls anyone who chooses the moon over the suns. *Heretic*. They don't like lunar magic very much. They like you Red folk even less."

Salo isn't distracted by the attempt to obscure the atmech revelation, because now that he knows, Tuksaad makes a lot more sense to him. "You're a machine, aren't you? A vessel powered by a mind stone."

Tuk's jaw clenches just the slightest bit. "No," he says, "I am an atmech. A machine can't ever be alive, and I am alive."

This is obviously a sensitive subject, but Salo ignores the cues. "Your bones are metal."

"My bones *contain* metal, and even so, the rest of me is flesh and blood. Cut me and I feel pain just like everyone else. I can feel joy; I can fall in love. I have a heart. Does that not make me alive?"

Tuk stares back like he wants an answer to his question, but Salo doesn't know what to say. What is there to say? It hurts no one to commandeer animal spirits for machines, but dealing with human spirits? Now that's necromancy: otherwise known as that dirty art forbidden to all Yerezi mystics. How would one even trap a human spirit in a mind stone?

"And what about you?" Tuk says indignantly, clearly upset now.

Salo lifts an eyebrow. "Me?"

"Yes, you. You question my humanity because of what I'm made of when your own eyes are synthetic. Do they make you less human?"

At the mention of his eyes, Salo grits his teeth. "What are you on about?"

"You keep them hidden, but those eyes of yours were made for an atmech, albeit an old-fashioned one." Tuk tilts his head to one side. "Why do you think I first noticed you? I felt the resonance and recognized it for what it was. I can still feel it. Imagine my surprise."

Ilapara stares at Salo, and her probing gaze heats up the side of his face almost as intensely as the fire. He doesn't look at her.

He's never known where his eyes came from, and he's never wanted to know. He'd rather forget the whole issue and never have it mentioned again. But to find out that someone else—or some*thing* else—might have worn them before him?

A knot of black emotions twists his soul. One of his fists clenches around the folds of his cloak.

Tuk's anger melts from his expression, and his voice softens. "They're faulty, aren't they? There's something off with the resonance. That's why you need charmed glasses to see." When Salo fails to respond, Tuk looks down at his feet and sighs. "Look, I'm sorry for attacking you like that, all right? I guess I'm not . . . as over . . . my past as I thought. I clearly have insecurities I need to work on, but I want you—no, I *need* you to feel free to ask questions about me. I have to learn to talk about who I am without getting upset."

Tension hangs over the campfire as thickly as smoke.

"So a heretic mystic made you in the Empire," Ilapara says. "Why?"

Despite his professed desire not to get upset, Tuk's eyes gleam darkly. "Heretic creations are technically illegal in the Empire, but the elites there like to keep my kind for all sorts of purposes. Servants mostly. Expensive pets sometimes. Toys."

"Are there many heretics in the Empire?" Ilapara asks.

Shaking his head, Salo blows out a cloud of smoke. "I don't like that word."

"Me neither," Tuk says. "Do you know what they call the moon?"

"What?"

"It translates to 'the Vice.' They call their suns 'Valor' and 'Verity'— pretty much what you call them—but Ama Vaziishe isn't 'Mother of Sovereigns'; she's 'the Vice.' That alone should give you an idea of what they think of Red magic and those who practice it."

By the scornful look in his eye, he clearly finds the name ridiculous. "To answer your question, Ilapara, worship of the moon—and Red magic in general—isn't popular in the Empire. You could even say it is proscribed. You'll only ever find Red magic in underground cults or highly guarded temples and academies, the latter so it doesn't corrupt the rest of society." Tuk curls his lips almost unnoticeably. "Hypocrites. Imperial elites will openly shun Red magic, but the bulk of them certainly don't mind indulging in its creations. I know this from personal experience."

By now Salo's earlier discomfort has ebbed away into curiosity. "Why do they fear us so?" he asks.

Tuk seems to think about it, then exhales deeply, like the day's journey is finally catching up to him. "Take your pick: ignorance, misinformation, religious propaganda. But I'd be lying if I said the fear isn't a little well founded. Red magic is notoriously difficult to wield, but those of you smart enough to figure it out can do some pretty horrific things."

Salo's thoughts drift back to Seresa, to the terrible serpents, the burning wagon, the stench of rotting flesh swirling around him. Did he hear cries? Maybe he didn't, but he can certainly imagine them.

"And then, of course, there were the Hegemons," Tuk says. "Ever heard of them?"

Both Salo and Ilapara shake their heads, which makes Tuk smile for some reason. "Only in the Redlands," he says. "Anyway, the Hegemons were a succession of horrendously powerful lunar mystics who ruled over an empire they called the Ascendancy. At its height it nearly spanned the entire world beyond the Redlands. That's six continents, if you'll believe it."

"*Six* continents?" Salo finds the scale astonishing. What are the Yerezi Plains compared to such a monster?

Tuk nods with a solemn look. "Unfortunately, as is often the case with people of unequaled power, these Hegemons were extremely destructive people. They had a penchant for bloody conquest and liked to enslave entire populations. It took a united front of solar magic and centuries of war to finally bring them down, and when the last Hegemon fell, what remained of the Ascendancy became the fragmented world powers that exist today. The biggest one, the newly formed Empire of Light, vowed that the world would never see another Hegemon, and so far they've managed to keep their promise."

An entire history Salo has never heard of, a shock because he's never given much thought to what happens beyond the Redlands. He certainly didn't think the history could be so momentous. "How did you end up in the Enclave, then?" he says. "What *is* the Enclave, anyway? I know it as that strange place beyond the northern desert with strange people we don't talk to."

Ilapara snorts. "That's as much as I know myself."

"You shouldn't feel too bad about it," Tuk says, clearly amused. "The people there are as ignorant of the Redlands as you are of them." His smile weakens as he prods an ember in the fire. "I ended up there after my maker learned of my . . . living circumstances back in the Empire. She arranged for my escape and put me on a windcraft to the Enclave's capital."

"A windcraft?" Salo and Ilapara say at the same time.

355

"A ship that flies on magically generated currents of wind." Tuk's eyes twinkle at their amazed expressions. "Windcrafts are how most people cross the oceans, though you folk don't know of them, given how they all circumvent the Redlands—deliberately so, I should add."

Salo and Ilapara glance at each other, and he sees his worry in her eyes; if the people beyond the Redlands can fly across oceans, then they must be mighty indeed.

"As for what the Enclave is," Tuk goes on, "when the Ascendancy fell, many moon worshippers fled to this continent in fear of persecution, but they didn't really fancy entangling themselves with the indigenous peoples—you folk, in other words. So they stayed in the unsettled regions north of the desert and established the Enclave."

"That's why we keep away from them, though, isn't it?" Salo says. "They are of the moon, but they are not like us. They are not quite Red. They accept the foreign customs of the Empire and shun our ways, so we shun them too."

"In their defense," Tuk says, "they shun you mostly because they can't afford to be seen associating with you. A survival strategy."

"How so?" Ilapara says, and Tuk leans forward.

"The thing about the Ascendancy is that they revered this place. That's why they never invaded. On top of that, their brand of magic was not too different from yours. Tamer and more technological, perhaps, but they used axiomatic ciphers just as you do." Tuk spreads his hands. "Can you see why the Enclave had no choice but to distance themselves from you?"

Salo ponders the question for a moment. "I guess they didn't want the world to think they were a new incarnation of the Ascendancy."

"They *had* to become less Red, so to speak, or risk being exterminated in retribution," Tuk says. "But they took things a little too far, if you ask me. They changed their magic so much it needed a new name; they call it Higher Red and yours Lower Red. And no one campaigns harder to keep this place quarantined. They don't want you folk having contact with the outside world until you're more civilized."

Ilapara gives Tuk a sharp look. "You don't think us civilized?"

"That's not my opinion," he says, palms raised and eyes flashing green with humor. "I'm simply telling you what the Enclave believes."

"Then what *is* your opinion?" Ilapara says.

"I've seen people in glistening cities do the most savage of things, and people in the heart of the hinterlands do the noblest. I don't think civilization is a place or a culture or a level of technological development. I think it's simply the recognition that all life is valuable and must be treated as such. Everything else follows from there."

Salo digests that in silence as he pokes the fire. "What do you mean by hinterlands?"

"These are the hinterlands," Tuk says as he takes in his surroundings with his arms. "Or the Lost Lands of Sylia, or simply the Red Wilds. That's what they call this place, why I crossed the Jalama Desert to come here. I wanted to see it with my own eyes. You're all quite mysterious to the rest of the world, you know."

"You must hate it, then," Salo says. "How can you not after what you've seen?"

"Hate it? I've never felt more alive!" When Salo and Ilapara give him mistrustful looks, he grins. "The honest truth. The whole continent of Sylia has a deep connection to Ama Vaziishe—that's why the Enclave was established here. But there's no doubt that this connection is strongest in the Red Wilds, the land of Primeval Spirits and tronic beasts. Here it feels more . . . visceral. My blood feels thicker in my veins, and my heart beats louder. Here I am at home."

Everything Tuk says stays with Salo late into the night, joining the cacophony of thoughts swirling restlessly inside his mind. He rests facing the milky spirals of the Devil's Eye, that conspicuous constellation whose bright core marks the world's celestial south pole, and he spends a long time staring at it in thought. His aago always said that the Eye was getting bigger and that the devil rules over a realm of ice beneath it that will one day engulf the rest of the world. He used to have nightmares about that story as a child, but now, after seeing the things he's seen today, gruesome things that plague his vision whenever he closes his eyes, now he thinks that maybe the story being true wouldn't be such a bad thing. Why, it would be exactly what the world deserves.

Just before sleep claims him, the night lights up briefly as a ball of fire streaks across the sky and then upward, accompanied by a deep rumbling, like thunder from a distant lightning flash.

27: The Maidservant

Southern Umadiland

At dawn she retreats above the tree line, on a mountain in the high-velds of the south, where nothing but the hardiest shrubs can thrive. There she draws essence into her cosmic shards, sinking it into the earth beneath her feet when they become saturated. The essence spreads down the mountain at the speed of an echo, like roots seeking nourishment from the soil, and she feels a rush as her ancestral talent begins to work, expanding her pool of power.

Slow as the rising of the suns, the same wave of euphoria she felt at her awakening overtakes her now, so intense she falls to her knees, gasping for breath. Ahead of her a vast woodland spreads southward from the base of the mountain and into the Great Tribe kingdom of Valau, its trees brimming with leaves in every shade of red, from rust to vermilion. In her euphoria the colors are unnaturally vivid, dancing and bleeding into each other, and for an instant she feels one with them.

And then the feeling abates, and when she looks at her forearms, she sees that a sixth set of rings has appeared on her shards. They now draw from a greater swath of her lord's territory, including the mountain beneath her. Others drink from it, too, besides her master. Seafarer. Hunter.

There used to be another, conspicuous now only because of his absence.

A pang of sorrow stabs her chest, and she has to find relief in the burning pain of her cursed skin. She remains on her knees on the mountaintop for a long time, trying to scour her mind clean with pure-white agony.

Her focus is imperfect, though, and she can't stop seeing a pair of trusting eyes watching her, forgiving her even as she dimmed the light of life they held.

Weariness envelops her like a hateful embrace, so heavy she feels it might pull her down into the ground and keep pulling until she reaches the furnaces at the center of the world. She wonders what it would feel like to burn there until she was nothing, until her atoms were separated and reassembled into something else, perhaps something better.

I want this to end.

I'm tired.

I want to remember the taste of peace.

But no. She has gone too far along this path, shed too much blood and caused too much sorrow. Something must justify what she has become.

Nothing can justify your existence, says the bitter voice in her mind. *You seek to rationalize your crimes, but they will stain you till the end of time. You have already lost yourself to the underworld; all that is left is for it to take you.*

She summons her tronic mind stone and returns to the business of breaking its protective charms with her Yerezi talisman. She sits in a posture of meditation, the talisman's illusions floating in front of her, and for a time she loses herself to the indifferent world of cold logic and cipher prose.

Then a strange presence reaches out from hundreds of miles away to entangle itself with the talisman, taking her mind away from her work and into a false plane that knits itself together around her like a waking dream.

In this plane she takes shape on a marble platform floating somewhere in the middle of an ocean, though somehow she remains aware that she isn't really here but is on a mountaintop in the Umadi highvelds. The skies above this false world are bright with stars, and calm waters stretch away from the platform in every direction, no land in sight.

She is not alone. On the platform just a few yards away is a metallic statue of a woman—rather, a statue of a creature with the body of a woman and the head of a tronic hyena.

As she watches, the creature moves, as fluid as if its limbs were real flesh and not metal. The Maidservant instantly knows exactly who that thing is supposed to be.

"You." Her words come out strange, like she has spoken a language she shouldn't know. "What have you done? What is this?"

"Relax." The Yerezi witch takes a few steps closer. When she speaks, her snout remains shut, not moving to form words. "I bound your talisman to mine so I could reach you if I needed you again."

"My business with you was concluded."

"Your business with me did not produce the desired result. There was . . . an unforeseen obstacle. I need your help removing it."

"That's hardly my problem."

"Ah, but if you do nothing, sooner or later it *will* be your problem, and then you'll wish you'd acted while you still had the chance."

The Maidservant fails to detect deception from the woman, so she humors her. "Explain yourself."

"A boy from the clan you attacked faced a redhawk about a week later. The queen should have never allowed such sacrilege, but somehow the boy had discovered a dangerously powerful aspect of Red magic— a power she now wants for herself. I don't know her exact plans, but I believe she's in league with a certain KiYonte high mystic, an old acquaintance of hers, and I believe that if they succeed in whatever they've planned, they will become grave dangers to both your tribe and mine. The queen sent the boy on the Bloodway; he is on course to Yonte Saire as we speak. You must stop him before he gets anywhere near the city."

This has to be the same mystic the Dark Sun spoke of, in which case there are already people going after him. But the Maidservant doesn't disclose this to the woman. She wants to hear more about this aspect she spoke of. "Why can't you stop him yourself?"

The hyena shrugs. "My hands are tied. I cannot leave my clan without rousing suspicion, and the queen has eyes on him. It would be too risky for me, but if you sought out the boy, no one would ask too many questions."

"I still don't see why this is my problem."

The woman's tone grows more biting. "Irediti has always despised your tribe, my Umadi friend. If she and her KiYonte ally acquire what the boy will extract from the Red Temple, I can promise you she will use it to wage war against your tribe and raze every last inch of your savannas to ash. She must be stopped. The boy must be stopped."

The Maidservant carefully watches the hyena witch. She might be a monstrosity in her current form, but her worry is an almost tangible wave pushing outward away from her. She is afraid of this boy and the aspect he wields, whatever it is, and she is clearly threatened by the idea of her queen getting her hands on it.

Why, though? Would it really make her that powerful? "What is this aspect you mentioned?"

The woman shakes her doglike head. "I cannot reveal specifics, but rest assured it is dangerous."

"Then you can forget about getting any help from me."

"You don't understand. I cannot—" The woman stops talking, perhaps realizing she'll get nowhere unless she is more forthcoming. She sighs. "Very well. But I need your word that you'll stop him if I reveal the aspect's secret."

The Maidservant's interest has grown from a mere spark to an inferno. If this power is real, it might be a faster solution to her problems. "You have my word."

"They call it the Elusive Cube. An All Axiom that bends to the six crafts of Red magic. But that's not what makes it so dangerous—not even close. You see, an All Axiom is an automatic key to an ancient power in the temple of Yonte Saire."

The Maidservant listens closely. "And what power is this?"

The hyena witch takes a moment, perhaps trying to compose a response that won't reveal too much. In the end, however, she reveals everything.

"The ultimate ancestral talent."

28: Ilapara

The Open Wilds of Umadiland

As the suns rise on her first morning with Salo and Tuk somewhere in the savannas of Umadiland, Ilapara awakens next to a dead campfire to find a charcoal-colored fleece blanket draped over her. She sits up, looking around the camp, and sees Salo still sleeping beneath his crimson cloak on the other side of the fire. Tuk is already up, though, and for whatever reason, he's hugging himself and staring intently at something in the southeast.

She gets up, grimacing at the stiffness in her shoulders from sleeping in her breastplate. Dear Ama, what she would do for a bath and a change of clothes. Tuk doesn't look her way as she walks toward him, clutching the blanket in one hand.

She has yet to fully process the wild things he told them last night about who or even *what* he is. She's not sure if she believes any of it. "This yours?" she says as she stops next to him, holding out the blanket.

A pale-blue cast dances in his eyes this morning. He doesn't look away from the flat horizon. "You can keep it," he says. "I have a cloak, so I don't really need extra covers."

Her automatic instinct is to reject the offer of charity, but last night was chilly, and the only reason she slept at all was probably because of the blanket. "Thanks," she says, with sincerity.

"What are friends for?" A crooked smile grows on his face, like he's challenging her to dispute the claim that they are friends.

She smiles, too, not taking the bait, and for the first time she notices the little pendant dangling on a thin chain around his neck, a stylized eye of blue metal that had previously been hidden beneath his black sleeveless dashiki. She also notices he's wearing an ornate golden ring on each middle finger. *How wealthy is he, I wonder?*

"What are you doing here?" she says. "Is staring blankly at the horizon an outworld ritual?"

"I get this itch sometimes," he says.

"Okay. Forget I asked."

He gets a dimple on his cheek, his eyes flicking to green. "I'm being serious. I can't explain it. I think I feel it when . . . something interesting is happening. I felt it right before Salo ran past me yesterday."

Ilapara eyes him doubtfully. "Really?"

"That's why I was paying attention."

"And you feel it now?"

Tuk nods, pointing ahead. "Whatever it is, it's that way."

She looks, too, seeing nothing. "That's where we came from."

"Yep."

A tingle of worry makes her frown. Following her instincts, she reaches into a pouch on her leather shoulder belt and fishes out the only soul charm in her possession. Tuk watches with blue-eyed interest while she palms the charm and possesses herself with the jackal spirit it contains.

She closes her eyes to receive the spirit, weathering a rush of dizzying flashes from a life spent hunting across the savannas and scavenging for carrion, relying on superior auditory senses to detect prey and avoid larger predators. Then the rush subsides and the merge completes, and when she reopens her eyes, her vision has an overlay painted in brushstrokes of vibrations and sound.

On that overlay, a radiant glow hangs over the southeastern horizon, getting brighter by the second. Ilapara narrows her eyes, willing the jackal spirit to give her a clearer image. It expends all of its power to comply, but for the briefest second the glow becomes discernible to her as a brilliant cloud of individually distinct, regular vibrations.

"Shit."

"What is it?" Tuk says, his irises darkening into pools of blackness.

"We need to leave. Now." Ilapara looks about and finds Ingacha grazing on a knotted bush just west of the camp. She moves to pick up his saddle. "Salo! Wake up. We need to get moving."

He stirs, then sits up, putting on his spectacles. His gaze tracks her as she makes her way to her buck. "Are we in danger?"

"I think so."

Mercifully, the boys don't ask any more questions. They quietly follow her example and resaddle their animals and are ready to go within minutes. But Ingacha seems more excitable than usual today, and when she mounts him, he rears up, grunting loudly and almost pitching her off the saddle. "Whoa! Easy there."

She needs several long seconds to get him back under control, and when she looks, she sees that Tuk is also struggling to stay mounted on his horned abada. It's bucking and tossing its head, making him rock back and forth in his saddle. He seems to take things in stride, though, and when it finally settles down, his eyes sparkle with delight.

"A good morning to you too," he says, patting the mare's neck. "Someone's excited today."

"What the actual devil was that?" Ilapara wonders aloud. Then her gaze falls on Salo, standing next to his leopard, and she immediately knows he's involved somehow. He has the most obvious guilty look she has ever seen. "Salo? What just happened?"

He shifts on his feet, looking everywhere but at her. "I . . . may have blessed your animals last night while you were sleeping? Made them jumpy, I guess."

"You *what?*"

"We need to go faster," he says with a defensive shrug. "Ingacha and the abada—"

"Wakii," Tuk says. "I've named her Wakii. It means 'scales of justice' in a northern dialect." He looks down at his mare and grins widely. "My goodness, but did you really bless her?"

"She couldn't keep up with Mukuni and was skittish around him," Salo explains. "Ingacha too. I had to do something."

Ilapara closes her eyes and takes a deep breath—*I am not my emotions*—and then lets it out. "We'll discuss your *complete* lack of personal boundaries later. Right now we need to go."

Salo nods quietly and ties his staff to the harness on his saddle before mounting his clan's totem, and then they set off into the northwest, the kudu and the mare taking to their newfound power like they were born to it.

◆ ◆ ◆

The ravens appear half an hour later.

They streak by overhead, cutting across the sky in a black chevron and then arcing back to make another pass over Ilapara and the other two riders. Her blood cools at this rather unnatural behavior, and she tracks the birds as they fly over her, only for her eyes to settle on the many bright points of scarlet light moving in the grasses not far behind, closing the distance alarmingly fast.

She chokes on her breath, disbelieving her eyes. It is said that dingoneks were the creations of a warlord who used them as foot soldiers during her terrible reign and that upon her death the magic brimming inside the creatures grew wild and volatile. Ilapara has never seen one before, but she's heard enough horror stories about them to recognize those lights for what they are.

"We're under attack!"

Just ahead of her, Tuk and Salo look over their shoulders, and she watches them utter curses that don't quite reach her ears.

"Tell me those are not what I think they are," Tuk shouts, his eyes wide and blue with ghoulish excitement. He glances over his shoulder again and lets out a loud, incredulous laugh. "My goodness, they are!"

For some reason Salo looks up fearfully at the skies toward their far right. Ilapara spurs Ingacha a little faster to catch up with him on his left flank. "What is it?"

With one hand, he draws his staff from its harness. "We're not alone," he shouts.

Behind them a pride of heavily built feline-reptile hybrids finally comes into view, and they begin to fan out as they draw nearer, an obvious tactic to cut off possible routes of escape. Their eyes are like brilliant coals of moonfire. They have scales in place of fur, with spots that burn like molten rock. Ilapara shudders when she sees how they each leave behind trails of blackened grass that smolders without bursting into flames.

She looks ahead and is met with an endless stretch of grassland dotted by acacia trees, no sign of shelter or refuge in sight. A growl of frustration rises up her throat. "We can't outrun them! They're too fast!"

"Someone's controlling them," Salo shouts back. "I think it's the same mystic from the town. There!"

He points, and when she looks in the skies to their far right, her heart momentarily stops beating. *Dear Ama, not him.*

The kongamato is a deltoid shape in the skies, sleek and silver, with a helmeted man bestriding its neck. It swerves toward them just as the first of the dingoneks breaks away from its pride in a menacing charge.

Ilapara lets her mind sink into her spear hand, preparing to fall back and deal with the animal, but she hesitates when she sees Tuk raising his gauntleted hand and balling it into a fist. To her surprise the armor piece expands on his arm, silver panes sliding over each other to reveal a barrel shrouded in a red halo—which he points at the charging beast.

Crack!

His arm recoils slightly as a blast of moonfire erupts from the barrel and punches a hole straight through the dingonek. The beast goes down as if a crushing weight has slammed it from above, but the rest of the pride simply sidesteps its tumbling form and keeps pace with their high-speed gallop.

Tuk releases several more blasts from his strange weapon, taking out a second reptile-cat and cowing a third into slowing down, but that still leaves more than Ilapara can count in one glance.

"He's casting a spell!" Salo shouts, and sure enough, the rider on the kongamato has started gathering fire around his staff.

Worse, a pair of dingoneks has drawn level with Salo on his right flank, making ready to pounce. Ingacha grunts beneath Ilapara as she steers him with her hips to intercept, putting herself between Salo and the attacking creatures. They close in on her buck, and there's a terrifying instant during which the closest one leaps forward and she sees into the red-hot interior of its jaws.

But she feeds that terror into her arm and thrusts her spear before the dingonek can bite. She feels a ripple in the aerosteel as a bolt of red lightning arcs from the tip and into the creature.

The beast probably doesn't die, but it emits a piercing caterwaul as it topples over. The other dingonek tosses it only a passing glance before bounding onward in pursuit, threads of drool dangling from its canines, eyes scarlet with untamed magic. This time Ilapara raises her weapon and swings it in a wide arc so that the ensuing bolt lashes outward and behind her. The dingonek doesn't change course in time to evade the bolt and is left tumbling in the dust.

Above and still to Ilapara's right, the rider on the kongamato now has a sphere of red fire hovering above one palm. She glances at Tuk, who's staring at the fireball with a worried look in his eye. "Try aiming up!" she shouts.

He checks his gauntlet and shakes his head. "Still charging!"

With an anxious shiver she takes a peek over her shoulder and sees that he's more than halved the dingoneks chasing them. They also seem to be hanging back a little now, almost like they know what's about to ensue. She looks back up in time to see the rider on the kongamato releasing his spell and is not in the least surprised by how slowly the fireball floats down toward them.

"If you have magic that can save us," she shouts at Salo, "now's the time to use it!"

Riding on his clan totem, Salo bites his lip in thought while he stares up at the approaching spell. A moment later he comes to some decision, setting his shards aglow and adjusting his grip on his staff. "Ride closer!" he shouts.

Tuk and Ilapara immediately obey, steering their mounts closer to Salo so that they flank him in a tight formation.

"How long till you can blast that thing again?" he shouts at Tuk.

"Not sure," Tuk shouts back. "Maybe a minute."

"Then I'll buy you a minute!"

Magic is now swirling around Salo's arms. Ilapara's ears pop from a change in pressure, and she feels the air around her thickening. The ball of heat flattens and stretches until it is a bar of red flames—a bar that then folds on itself to become the flapping wings of yet another kongamato, this one a spirit of pure moonfire. A massive triangular head appears between the wings, and fire comes out when it opens its long bill and dives down toward them.

"Salo!"

He fails to respond.

She braces for the worst.

But suddenly a cocoon of fast-moving wind rises all around them, encasing them in a dome of rapidly swirling grass and dust that matches their speed so that they are always at the center. The winds are so thick she can't see much beyond the dome, and when the flaming spirit finally slams into it, the entire world becomes red fire.

Ilapara gasps. The flash of heat is barely tolerable, but the moonfire gets sucked into the dome's currents and slingshots around them like honey poured onto an upturned, rotating bowl.

Salo raises his staff and screams in effort. "Tuk!"

A visibly fretful Tuk checks his gauntlet again, only to shake his head. "Not yet!"

Outside the dome, a portion of the red flames coalesces into the spirit's hammer-like head. Ilapara watches as it rears back and smashes into the dome with so much force part of its fiery bill makes it through the barrier, though not far enough to do them any harm.

Salo cries out again, his staff trembling in his hand. It strikes Ilapara that he is recently awoken; his power can't be much compared to a high-ranking Umadi disciple, let alone a lieutenant of the Dark Sun. In fact, that they aren't already dead is no small wonder.

"Tuk!"

"Hold on, Salo! Almost there!"

The magic pulsing from his shards becomes too bright to look at. Ilapara once heard that magic has a certain peculiar taste when it is cast in great concentration, something akin to the tingle of lightning on one's tongue. She begins to feel such a tingle, except throughout her entire body, as though the fabric of space were being stretched and warped around her.

"On my mark," Tuk finally shouts, and he waits three infinitely long seconds before his eyes go wide. "Now!"

Mukuni emits a roar Ilapara feels in her bones as Salo raises his staff—and with it the entire vault of fire. The dome curves outward and upward first, becoming a bowl of fire, and then inward at the top into a sphere that completely envelops the spirit. It thrashes violently inside its new prison, and from the way Salo shouts, she can tell he won't be able to keep it imprisoned for long.

Tuk has already fallen behind on his abada and takes aim with his gauntlet. The ensuing discharge of moonfire is so fast Ilapara almost doesn't see it tearing into the skies. But she sees the chunk of underbelly that subsequently rips away from the disciple's kongamato and hears its screech, so terrible it hurts her ears. The creature flaps uselessly for a moment, stalling in the air, and then plummets down with its flailing rider. They hit the ground seconds later with a great booming thud.

An explosion above makes her shield her face with a hand, the winged spirit finally roaring out of its prison. But it has expended itself considerably, so Salo manages to guide it away and over them in a radial starburst. It gradually loses its form and fizzles out into floating embers.

She doesn't waste time. Her instincts take over, and she directs Ingacha to gallop toward the fallen beast, ignoring the pounding inside her chest. The beast is still stirring when she arrives, and its rider is a motionless lump next to it, tangled unnaturally in the harnesses. She is off her kudu in an instant, bringing her spear with her. The rider senses her approach and blinks his reptilian eyes open, but given the state of his mangled limbs, it is probably all he can do.

Apart from speaking, it seems. "You," he rasps, his unsettling eyes fixing on her. "I know you."

Ilapara doesn't give him a chance to say another word. She thrusts into his chest, and as his life leaches into her weapon and their gazes connect, she sees fear in his eyes, the fear of a predator suddenly forced to confront his own mortality.

The world may be a dark place, but it seems that even the darkness can be made to be afraid.

She used to hold the rules of surviving in Umadiland sacred, but now, having broken the most sacrosanct, she feels like a part of her soul has been liberated.

Next to her the kongamato snaps its long, toothed beak. She proceeds to finish it off with a single deep thrust, grimacing at the reek effusing from its torn bowels.

Salo and Tuk join her as she remounts her buck. They stare grimly at the dead creature and its rider. Neither of them comments on what she has done.

She notices that Salo is breathing heavily and that his shards are still pulsing furiously with lights.

"Everything all right?" she asks him, getting worried.

He nods, though he looks like he's just run a hundred miles. "I . . . borrowed a lot from the future. My shards are making up for it."

That makes no sense to her, but she's relieved their hearts are still beating. "To make things perfectly clear," she says, "I expect to be paid for this. Handsomely."

Both boys chuckle despite the circumstances. "Keep me alive, and I'll break into the queen's personal vault if I have to," Salo says.

"Good." Ilapara goes on to scan the horizon and sees that the dingoneks are nowhere in sight. They've probably fled now that their master is dead, but they might return. "We should keep moving," she says, and no one objects.

She falls back a bit, however, when she spots a flock of ravens soaring on the winds in the east. She squints in thought for a moment, but the flock retreats before she can make her mind up about it.

29: Isa

The simple pleasures a king can enjoy while confined to the Red Temple: taking long walks along vaulted walkways and beautifully landscaped gardens, awaking to the uplifting sounds of choral music and drums, and braiding a friend's hair beneath a tree by a pond.

Except that Ayani isn't really her friend, nor are Nadi and Lisha, the other two girls braiding Ayani's hair. They are Saire servant girls who lived in the palace before what has come to be called the Royal Massacre.

They were understandably awkward with her at first, when she came upon them during a solitary walk along the temple's cloisters, but she settled smoothly into their conversation and proved that her fingers were up to the task, if a little slow. They all lost loved ones to the attack, and the pain is still raw for each of them, but they reminisce fondly about their old lives in the palace.

Ayani speaks at length about how much she misses the palace kitchens, but Nadi whispers to Isa in an aside that *kitchens* in this context is actually code for "head chef"; Ayani just won't admit it because the man was married and old enough to be her father. Lisha lost a sister during the attack and at one point has to stop braiding Ayani's hair to wipe her eyes and recover her composure. Nadi keeps the conversation lighthearted with her perkiness and natural talent for amusing prattle, and she looks and talks so much like Cousin Zenia that Isa's eyes keep prickling with tears.

Still, the easy chatter reminds her she's human, and not the only human in the world, for that matter.

A distinctive voice makes them all freeze. "Your Majesty. I'm sorry to interrupt."

The four of them quickly rise to their feet and give womanly bows, though Isa's bow doesn't have to go as low as the others. "No apologies necessary, Your Worship."

She bids her new friends goodbye and joins Itani Faro of the Arc along the meandering garden paths. The old high priest walks with his hands clasped behind him, his red grand boubou falling to almost sweep the ground.

"It is nice to see you smiling again," he says. "Truly smile. Given your circumstances, it would be quite easy for you to lapse into gloom and forget what you're living for. You mustn't ever let yourself forget."

Forget? But how can she forget when blood is all she sees every time she closes her eyes? "I'm not sure I know what I'm living for, to be honest." Itani Faro is one of the few people in the temple around whom she can be her miserable, grief-stricken self.

"You are living for those girls back there," he says, "and many others like them. You are living to protect them from those who would murder them for no crimes of their own. You are living for your father's legacy, for the kingdom, for yourself, Your Majesty."

He gives her a meaningful look as they come to a stop. "You deserve to live a life full of happiness too."

Suye will never follow me around like a cheerful little gadfly again. I will never argue with Ayo or gossip with Zenia or hide from my mother.

Isa's eyes fill with angry tears. "I cannot be happy until the day Kola Saai faces justice for what he did to my family."

"That day could not come too soon, Your Majesty." The Arc surprises her when he brings one hand out from behind his back and extends two scarlet flowers. "These bloomed on the night of the attack. I was going to gift them to the House of Forms, but I've decided to give them to you instead. You may do with them as you wish."

The flowers are bloodroses, symmetrical and concentric in form, with wispy petals as thin as razors and just as sharp. They are unequivocally the loveliest things she has ever seen.

Her hands tremble as she reaches to accept them. "Your Worship . . . I have no words."

The Arc gives her the hint of a smile. "Be careful not to cut your fingers on the petals."

Isa gazes at the flowers with wonder. She has never held fresh bloodroses before—not many mere mortals are ever so lucky. Their delicate scent is strangely evocative; they smell like desire and everything her heart yearns for. "Do they really grant wishes, as they say?"

"The sorcery behind them isn't something we understand, despite our best efforts. I cannot give a definite answer to your question. Let me say: perhaps, if the wish is reasonable enough."

Isa already knows her first wish: the Crocodile's head on a pike. She hides this from her face as they start walking along the stone path again. "Have you learned who helped Kola Saai bewitch the Royal Guard?" she says. "There was magic involved, which can only mean he worked with a mystic."

The Arc clasps his hands behind him. "My investigations have not been fruitful in that regard, but I can tell you that it wasn't one of ours."

Isa knows there are two groups of mystics in the kingdom, the bulk of them clustered in this city: those who receive their educations at the House of Forms and pledge themselves to the covens of the Shirika, as their ancestral talent would dictate, and those who shun the covens, preferring to practice their sorcery in dingy Northtown hovels and unregistered undercity sanctuaries. If Kola Saai's hired sorcerer wasn't the former, then they were the latter. "So we're talking about an independent," she says.

"Not impossible, but unlikely." When Isa's brow creases in confusion, he adds, "The sorcery that afflicted the Royal Guard was delivered through an elixir, slipped into their food somehow, but it is inconceivable that they were the only ones exposed to its power. That the elixir acted on them alone, leaving barely a trace of itself in their bodies, suggests a level of finesse that would be highly uncommon for an independent alchemist."

Isa frowns at the bloodroses in her hands, her thoughts racing to make sense of what she's hearing. "Then we're talking about someone foreign."

"It would seem so, Your Majesty."

A headman consorting with a foreign mystic to take the throne. Isa would have thought such a thing impossible only weeks ago.

She finds herself feeling weak and adrift, trapped in the depths of an endless nightmare. She stops to face the old sorcerer, and he turns to her as well. "Forgive me, Your Worship, but I still don't understand why the Shirika are letting him get away with this. I thought there was a covenant that bound them—that bound *you* in service to the Saire king. Isn't that why our clan agreed not to have a standing legion? To appease the other clans because we had the gods forever on our side?"

The Arc answers with characteristic bluntness; he is not a man for coating his words in honey. "It is not common knowledge, but our adherence to the covenant was entirely voluntary, and subject to change should the rule of a Saire king ever become inconvenient to us. As it happens, my colleagues grew impatient with your father's lack of ambition."

Isa blinks at the man. She's never heard anyone accuse King Mweneugo of lacking such a trait. "Please explain this to me so that it makes sense, Your Worship. I've always thought my father was a strong king."

"His strength was beyond question. Mweneugo had firm convictions and a clear vision. He knew what he wanted to accomplish and how to go about it. But he was too comfortable with the way of things, reluctant to project his considerable power beyond the bounds of the Yontai. With all ten legions and the Shirika behind him, he could have extended the Yontai's reach across the rest of the Redlands, incorporating every tribe into an empire that stretches all the way from the southern cape to the northern desert. This has always been in the Shirika's sights, but the logistics didn't become favorable until shortly after your father's ascension to the throne. Mweneugo, however, was completely unreceptive to the idea of empire."

Isa remembers the conversation in the king's study when Ayo argued in favor of KiYonte expansion. She thought him foolish and arrogant at the time, but now it seems he was the only one attuned to the Shirika's mood.

Dear Mother, was that only weeks ago?

Something distant flickers in the Arc's gaze. "My colleagues respected him, as they respected his father before him, but he was too much a guardian of the status quo when they wanted a conqueror. The Crocodile, however"—the Arc bares his teeth—"reptile that he is, sensed opportunity in the air and hatched a scheme to lure the Shirika away from Mweneugo by convincing them that *he* was the conqueror king they sought. Of course, I shunned him right away, but my colleagues . . ." Disgust contorts the old mystic's lips. "I did not know they would be so fickle."

A member of the Shirika speaking ill of his colleagues? Isa breathes deeply to stop her world from spinning. "Then how can you be sure that it wasn't one of them who helped him with the massacre?"

"They would not have involved themselves directly," the Arc says. "It would have been reckless and illogical. I suspect they promised the Crocodile that they'd look the other way should he move to take the throne—provided, of course, that any associated violence couldn't be linked back to him."

"Hence the use of a foreign alchemist," Isa concludes.

"Indeed."

Whoever they are, they're probably thousands of miles away by now. It suddenly occurs to Isa that without a legion of their own, all the Saires had standing between their total oblivion and continued predominance over the other clans was the Shirika. Great mountains, to be sure, so great they were all too easy to take for granted, but somehow, Kola Saai managed to convince them to move.

And yet . . . Isa dares to meet the Arc's gaze, this god in flesh. "Why are you helping me? Why have you gone against your brothers and sisters?"

"I disagree with their methods," he says. "I'd like to see a KiYonte empire in my lifetime, but this is not the way." He gazes thoughtfully down the stone path. "You will find this upsetting, Your Majesty, but your father is the unwitting architect of your clan's predicament. I recall having a long discussion with him during which I warned him of what could transpire, but he chose to disregard my advice. He was too lenient with the headmen, made too many concessions in the name of peace when he ought to have tightened the reins. He was the first king with the power to give the Yontai what it really needs—not empire but unity—and he squandered the chance."

A mix of confusing emotions rocks Isa's already unstable world. "Unity, Your Worship?"

"The end of all clan divisions," he says. "Every headman ousted and all the legions united under the mask-crown. Our divisions serve no purpose but to give grasping men like Kola Saai the weapons they need to control and weaken us."

He says us *like he sees himself as KiYonte, as one of us, not apart from us as he truly is.*

Isa brings one hand to caress the marks on her neck, the snaking lines of the four-tusked elephant. She was born with them by virtue of being a Saire, a brand that will now be the death of her people. "I thought the clans were sealed in blood a long time ago. Are they not inescapable?"

The Arc seems pensive. "I suppose they are. Getting rid of them would be next to impossible. But that wasn't what I had in mind when I spoke to your father. I had a more . . . brute-force solution to the problem. I even offered him the services of my guardians. He could have secured his hold on the entire kingdom in one night had he agreed."

Isa is shocked to hear him speak so freely of assassination, and by divine Jasiri for that matter, but something he said grows at the back of her mind like a seed scattered accidentally by the wayside. She considers him carefully. "You said next to impossible."

Genuine confusion spreads across the Arc's face. "I beg your pardon?"

"You said getting rid of the clan marks would be next to impossible," Isa repeats. "That is not the same as saying it is impossible. If it can be done, if there is a chance these marks can be erased—"

"Part with the thought, Your Majesty." The Arc's voice carries no threat but a dire warning. "You do not know what you speak of."

"It would save so many lives," Isa says like she hasn't heard him. "The sudden removal of these marks would sap interclan hatreds and stop the violence before it even started. And even if violence broke, my people wouldn't be easily identified."

For a heartbeat the Faro gazes longingly at her, like he wants to tell her whatever it is he knows, but then he shakes his head. "Forgive me for bringing it up. These are merely the musings of a disheartened old man. Your father was like a son to me. He could have done so much. So, so much. Those who killed him took a bright star out of my sky, and I wish them nothing but evil." He bows to Isa. "Good day to you, Your Majesty."

And then he leaves her standing there with two bloodroses, unaware that he has ignited a flame in the pit of her stomach, that he has thrown her a sliver of hope, one she has latched on to like a drowning woman to a lifeline.

◆ ◆ ◆

Later, she visits Jomo in the citadel's administrative wing, where he has commandeered office space for himself among the clerks who serve under the high priest.

She finds him seated behind a desk cluttered with paper, sorting joylessly through a stack of mirrorgrams with puffy, unfocused eyes. The top buttons of his embroidered indigo shirt are undone, the matching kufi hat is awry on his head, and the fuzz on his cheeks is beginning to move away from stubble territory and into a full beard. Isa has never seen him look so disheveled.

In the corner, a young male votary in a crimson tunic and white face paint types away at the brass keys of a mirrorgraph, concentrating on the string of illusory ciphers flashing above the machine's central crystal as he translates them into demotic script—incoming messages sent from distant mirrorgraphs.

Upon Isa's appearance, both men snap their heads to the doorway. The votary is the first to rise from his chair and bow. "Your Majesty."

Jomo's face brightens a little, and he starts to look around for his cane, but Isa quickly motions for him to remain seated.

"Please, don't. I can come back later if you're busy."

Behind his desk, Jomo snorts. "Attending to you is literally part of my job description. I'd be a terrible herald if I sent you away because I'm too busy." He gestures at the chair in front of his desk. "Please, Your Majesty, sit."

The votary politely excuses himself while Isa settles down. Her lips quirk involuntarily when she notices the half-empty bottle of Valausi rum on the table. Some indulgences are difficult to give up even in the worst of times, it seems.

"You haven't slept at all since we last spoke, have you?" she says, eyeing him. "At this rate I might have to order you to get some rest."

Jomo blinks at her several times, then sits back in his chair with a heavy sigh, scratching his beard. "I look terrible, don't I."

Isa nods, her smile widening slightly. "Nothing a bath and a few hours in bed won't fix."

"Honestly, Isa, if I knew being herald would be such a drain on my soul, I'd have run off the moment you asked me."

"See, that's why you should have taken the throne," Isa says, feeling her eyes gleam with humor. "Everyone knows it's the herald who does all the work."

Jomo smiles. "Maybe, but I'd look like a proper elephant in the mask-crown, so I saved everyone a world of horror."

"I think you'd look majestic in the mask-crown."

"You're being kind, but thank you."

Isa nods at the pile of missives on the table, thick white papers covered in the uniform, monochromatic red print produced by a mirrorgraph. "Anything interesting?"

He grimaces. "Love letters from my admirers. Let's see." He leans forward and starts flipping through the papers, then pulls one out with a look of grim amusement. "This one is from a proud Dulama pilgrim demanding immediate entry into the citadel, like I'm the one who put up the motherdamned barrier around it. By his tone he'll probably expect me to prostrate myself in apology."

Jomo shakes his head and pulls out another missive. "This one is from a Saire textile maker demanding that I, and I quote, 'take the Shirika to task' for giving his competition some sort of unfair technological advantage. Interesting and quite frankly alarming, because this isn't the first complaint of its kind to reach my desk, but what's even more interesting and alarming is that these people seem to think I have any sort of hold over the Shirika. Take them to task? More like hand them my nut sack on a platter."

"What of the Mkutano?" Isa says, getting to the point of her visit. "It's in two nights, and I still don't know what Kola Saai has planned. I'm getting nervous."

Jomo's wry little smile dims, and he starts searching through the missives again. "I was going to tell you over dinner tonight, but since you've asked . . ." He pulls out a paper bearing the bright-red seal that marks it as an official mirrorgram from the kingdom's highest court. "Apparently, and this came in literally an hour ago, the House of Law has determined 'that it is within the assembly's purview to decide the matter of the Sentinels by vote.' Never mind that this has never been the case in centuries of continued Sentinel existence." Jomo tosses the paper on top of the others and regards Isa like he's defeated and tired of life. "In other words, you were right. Kola Saai is going for the last bit of power we have, and the Shirika have endorsed it."

Jomo's office looks toward the main temple structure at the center of the citadel, where the spires of the Shrouded Pylon rise from an inner courtyard and disappear into the skies. Somewhere out of sight, high above the temple complex, the Ruby Paragon will be spinning between the spires, visible to everyone down in the city.

Isa leans back in her chair and stares out the windows, feeling weary to the bone. She knew the Crocodile would come for the Sentinels eventually, but she didn't think he'd do it so quickly. *The Shirika really are in bed with him. But how did he buy them off? Was it really just because they wanted an empire and Father wouldn't give it to them? Why do I find that hard to believe?*

She knows it's no coincidence that the court should decide this now. As the highest court in the kingdom and one of seven supposedly apolitical institutions headed by a member of the Shirika, the House of Law is just another extension of the Shirika's will.

"And that's not even the worst of it. Here, take a look." Jomo slides a leaflet across the table, and Isa feels a chill as she picks it up. Splashed across the page is the image of a grotesque elephant-cockroach hybrid trampling all over a map of the kingdom. *The Pestilence Must Go* is written beneath.

"That lovely little piece of propaganda is from a new group of rabble-rousers calling themselves the Wavunaji," Jomo says. "Reapers of vengeance. They've posted flyers like that all over the city, and the way they preach about the Saires, Isa, you'd think we were vermin shat out straight from the devil's asshole."

Isa shakes her head, the flyer trembling in her hands. "I think that sentiment comes through quite clearly right here. Dear Mother, is this how they see us?"

"There are mobs of them roaming the streets with machetes—I've seen them—and the only reason they haven't started killing us on sight is the Sentinels I've deployed to patrol the city, much to the City Guard's displeasure, I should add. I've even sent detachments to other towns and villages in the province, and more to escort Saire convoys evacuating from other provinces. What do you think is going to happen once we lose them?"

Isa drops the hateful flyer onto the table with a shudder. "I'd have to abdicate before it came to that. No crown is worth that much blood."

"It wouldn't guarantee our safety, though, would it?" Jomo nods cynically at the flyer. "That kind of hate wouldn't just die because you're not king anymore."

"But it'd be worse if I still am," Isa argues. "The Sentinels are the only reason it makes sense to hold on to the crown. But if we're going to lose them anyway, why not use the crown to bargain for our people's lives while they still have them?"

Jomo blinks tiredly, then covers his face with his big hands, shaking his head. "We need more time, Isa. I'm telling you, if in two days the Sentinels no longer exist, there will be blood, whether you're still king or not. We need to at least delay this vote; then maybe afterward we can negotiate something that will guarantee our continued safety."

Her eyes briefly fall onto the flyer, and she shivers again. "Have you heard anything from the headmen?"

"I've sent missives to the friendly ones, but they haven't replied. I think they're all spooked and would rather wait and see which way the wind blows. Can't say I blame them, though. Life's a lot riskier with an unpredictable Shirika."

Isa's gaze follows the line of maps displayed along the walls of Jomo's office, each one outlining a different province. She is supposed to be king of all those provinces and their peoples, and with the Shirika on her side she would be. Without them, however, she is weaker than the headmen and an ineffectual representative of her clan.

What power do I have that the headmen don't?

"You know," she says, a half-formed idea taking shape in her mind, "if delaying the vote is all we need to do for now . . ."

Jomo stares at her, waiting, and then his lips stretch in a sardonic smile. "You're welcome not to leave me in suspense, Your Majesty."

"The orators who stand in the streets and market squares," Isa tries to explain, "spouting whatever opinions they are paid to spout. Do you know why no one ever argues with them?"

"Ha! Because they never give you a chance to speak . . . oh." He tilts his head in thought, a slow smile spreading across his face until he's beaming from ear to ear. "My dear cousin, that's brilliant!"

She sits back into her chair, the walls of reality closing back in around her. "But it'd be temporary. Delaying the inevitable, if anything."

"But Your Majesty." Still grinning like a fool, Jomo reaches down, unearths two clean glasses from somewhere behind the desk, and places them on the table. He proceeds to fill both halfway with golden Valausi rum. Isa doesn't refuse hers when he hands it to her. "Every minute we buy is one more minute we can use to buy another. And so long as I have you, I'll keep buying minutes until the Mother has no choice but to give me all the time I damn well need."

His enthusiasm is deeply encouraging, and as they sip on their rum together, another plan forms in a corner of Isa's mind. The Arc dangled something in front of her today, unwittingly perhaps, but it could be the key to solving the woes facing her clan.

Central to acquiring this key, however, and perhaps to understanding how Kola Saai managed to bend gods to his will, is the answer to a question she suddenly can't get out of her head: *What do gods want? What could a mere mortal offer a god to gain favor?*

30: Musalodi

Approaching the Southern Tuanu Borderlands

They flee across the savannas at a moon-powered gallop, each pace featherlight on the muscles and easy as breath. Broad-leaved woodlands crop up around them the farther north they travel, which slows their pace a little, but they still cover great distances each day.

He keeps his senses cast outward for much of the time, unable to move past the suspicion that there are multiple pursuers converging on their position from many directions. He has no spells of any craft to augment his powers of observation, yet his shards keep thrumming with faint ripples of distant magic that keep pace with them as they race toward the Tuanu borderlands.

Surviving the encounter with the dingoneks and their master has given him some measure of confidence in his abilities and those of his companions, but beneath that fragile confidence is a current of terror that won't subside. Tuk insists they'll be safe once they cross into the woodlands bordering the Tuanu lake, claiming that they are heavily patrolled and that whoever is chasing them likely won't continue their pursuit past that threshold. But when Salo asks why crossing the borderlands would be safe for them and not for their pursuers, Tuk smiles and hedges at the question, begging that they trust him.

Reluctantly, they do.

When they stop to rest on the third evening of their journey together, Salo takes his bow and goes hunting while the others tend to their beasts. He returns with two bush fowl, which he skins and guts with his steel knife before rubbing them with spice and setting them to roast on spits. Tuk eats heartily, then calls it a night after a few hours of lighthearted conversation, leaving Salo and Ilapara to exchange stories about their overnight hunting trips in the Plains.

"They call her the Maidservant," she says after a lull in the conversation. Salo can't read her face from across the campfire, but her nose ring shimmers in the wavering light. "The witch I'm pretty sure attacked your kraal? Yeah, she's one of the Dark Sun's favorite disciples, helped him expand his territory quite a bit these last few years. No one knows where she came from, but people are *terrified* of her."

Salo tastes bile on his tongue, the bush fowl beginning to sit heavily in his stomach. "What do you know about her?"

"Only what they whisper in beer halls, and none of it's good." Ilapara picks her teeth with a splinter of wood, a distant glimmer in her eyes. Her voice holds a note of hesitance when she speaks next. "Did you . . . lose anyone in the attack? It's fine if you don't want to talk about it. It's just hard for me to accept, you know? In my mind the Plains are impenetrable."

He considers brushing her off or changing the subject but then remembers Monti's ama and the promise he made. He has no right to shy away from this. "I know what you mean," he says. "And yes, I lost a friend." Salo takes a heavy breath to compose himself. "His name was Montari, a charming kid, always moving, small for his age, intelligent. He pestered me into teaching him matje until I had to sweat to beat him. I'm sure he'd have grown into a master given time." Salo smiles at the memory. "Monti was a lot smarter than I was at his age."

Pensive silence drifts and settles around the campfire. Salo twists Monti's wristband, lost in thought, and he can almost hear Monti's bright laugh, see his impish grin.

Then the memories turn to ash, leaving Salo trembling with anger. "He was a good kid. Far too young to die. And to a tikoloshe, no less."

Ilapara's eyes glimmer in the darkness, and she seems to mull over her words. "I'm sorry for your loss. Forgive me for bringing it up."

"No." Salo takes his spectacles off to wipe his eyes. "I want to talk about him. It's the least I can do."

They let the rest of the night pass in silence. Before they set off the next morning, Tuk sits on a fallen tree trunk, pulls out a map from his knapsack, and studies it. "I can't believe how fast we've traveled," he says at length. "If we keep up our speed, we'll reach the borderlands by afternoon today. Although"—he tilts his head, a blue light flickering in his eyes as he roams the map—"if you want, Salo, the sixth waterfall along the River Fulamungu is maybe a day away from here. We could take a detour so you can commune with the Grootslang spirit that resides there."

Salo drifts closer to take a look at the map because it's not like any map he's ever seen. Rivers, lakes, and mountains of the Redlands are inked onto the glossy paper in brilliant colors that seem to shift with the light. Names are written in artistic script, cities marked with stars and the Primeval Spirits with stylized glyphs. Tribal borderlands have been left deliberately fuzzy, however, to show how they shift and change like the sands of a beach.

A charm was woven onto the paper, and it marks the map's location with a throbbing red light. Right now the light is somewhere south of a large body of water a great deal longer than it is wide. The lake's southernmost tip lies in the interior of Umadiland, and it stretches northward for almost a thousand miles—well into the jungles of the Yontai—terminating just south of the continent's second major roadway: the World's Vein. It's a blue snake on the map, cutting the Redlands in half in a general east-west direction and intersecting the red Artery in Yonte Saire, the heart of the continent.

"What do you think?" Tuk says, snatching Salo's attention from the map. "Do we detour and visit the Grootslang of Fulamungu, or do we continue? Your choice."

Salo is practically looking over Tuk's shoulder, standing close enough to catch the whiff of his sandalwood musk. A mystery how the guy can still smell this good after all the traveling they've been doing.

"That's one incredible map, Tuksaad," Salo says. "But I think we should keep going. No detours." And if he's going to commune with a spirit at all, it certainly won't be the Grootslang. He shudders at the idea.

"Just so I can prepare myself," Ilapara says. She has just finished saddling her kudu; now she's standing next to it with her hands on her waist. Salo has yet to see her without that head scarf of hers. "So you *are* planning on communing with the Lightning Bird of Zivatuanu when we sail up the lake?" She gives Tuk a pointed look. "If we even sail up the lake?"

Tuk smiles confidently and starts folding his map. "We will."

Salo spies a flight of ravens in the east right then. Ilapara notices, following the line of his gaze.

"What is it?" she says.

He watches the birds until they disappear into the horizon. Perhaps it's time he had a conversation with the queen.

"Give me a minute," he says and walks away from the camp for some privacy.

Leaning against a tree just out of earshot of the others, he extracts the queen's medallion from a pouch on his waist. The Seal carved onto its faces strobes at him unpleasantly, two colorful suns setting over a flat horizon.

Am I really doing this? But what choice do I have?

Now that he has awoken, his connection to his talisman feels stronger and more intuitive. Some of the inner workings that were once a mystery to him are now open secrets; for example, he now knows that he can use the talisman to aid and modify spell casting on the fly. He also knows how to entangle it with another talisman using a mystic Seal.

And that's what he does. With a thought he rouses the red steel serpent on his left wrist and commands it to seek out the one who cast the Seal on the medallion. The serpent obeys, and lights flash from its crystal eyes as its core transcends distance and forms a link with another talisman far away—

Reality shifts around Salo, an endless plain of golden grass taking shape around him, spreading out for as far as the eye can see. Two prismatic suns can be seen sinking into the horizon, bathing the grasses in varicolored twilight, while across the plain, the moon is rising full and red in all her glory.

Salo knows instinctively that this plain isn't real; it is merely the false mental construct AmaYerezi created for her talisman—her construct and not his because he hasn't yet created one for himself. A part of him remains aware of his *real* surroundings: the woods not far from the Tuanu borderlands, an hour just after daybreak. But the detail woven into this false world is so true to life he doubts his senses.

In front of him the queen appears as the shapely outline of a woman made of golden-red light, a dazzling silhouette almost too bright to gaze upon. He executes a bow, and when he speaks, his words come out differently, though in a strangely familiar way. "Your Majesty."

She watches him for the longest time, and the weight of her faceless gaze is almost too much to bear. "Hello, Musalodi. It is good to finally hear from you, though I'm surprised it has taken you so long to contact me."

Salo struggles to find a worthy reply. "I wasn't sure what I'd say, Your Majesty. The emissary's commands were clear."

"I take it you have something to say to me now."

He swallows nervously as he thinks of how best to couch his current circumstances. "I have encountered trouble, Your Majesty. When I passed through a town along the World's Artery, I . . . provoked the ire of a local mystic. He pursued me and the pair of warriors I've enlisted to accompany me, and while we managed to deal with him, I fear I'm still being pursued by other parties. I've had to take an alternate route; I'll be traveling north to the World's Vein and then east to the city."

Salo suspects she already knows all of this. If she does, however, she gives nothing away, though the amusement in her voice is hard to miss. "I wonder: Does your predicament have anything to do with the wagonload of Faraswa refugees that entered our borders recently?"

"They arrived safely?"

"I hear your father has agreed to take them in, though it was quite presumptuous of you to send them here without consulting me first."

Salo closes his eyes, overcome with emotion. He doesn't think he's ever loved his father more than he loves him now. "I apologize, Your Majesty. I didn't know what else to do."

"No more unnecessary risks. I need you alive and well in Yonte Saire. And be swift; the longer you dally, the fewer avenues we will have to take action against whatever threat is mounting there."

Salo feels his heart begin to gallop. "Action, Your Majesty? What sort of action do you mean?"

"That's what I'm sending you to find out. A great tempest is brewing on the horizon, with Yonte Saire at the epicenter. We need to find out what's going on there and prepare ourselves, or it will be our undoing."

This does nothing to help Salo's nerves, so he broaches the subject he's wanted to discuss from the beginning. "Your Majesty, I have to ask, did you send someone to watch me?"

The faceless silhouette smiles. Salo doesn't see it, but he feels it in the air between them. "Your mother and I grew up together in the Queen's Kraal. Did you know that?"

Are you trying to distract me from the fact that you have a spy tailing me? "I did, Your Majesty." The two of them were once more than good friends, according to some whispers.

"We had much in common, Asanda and I. But what really drew us to each other as we grew into young women was our shared resentment for the Asazi old guard and their mystics. We found their ways suffocating. Too conservative. We looked to the mystics of our sister tribes and envied them their freedom to explore, to just . . . immerse themselves in the arcane without rules or restrictions. We saw the incredible things they did and wondered why we couldn't do the same. But then I grew up, and she did not. And when the council of chiefs chose me as their queen, it was the end of our friendship. She couldn't forgive me for it—I doubt she ever did."

The queen gazes at the eternal sunset in the distance, lost in the past. "Asanda was too ambitious for her own good. I tried to rein in her forays into the darker side of magic, to reason with her, but the wedge between us only grew larger with time, and her thirst for power was insatiable."

Why are you telling me this? Salo wonders, waiting for the queen to make her point.

"I don't know where she found the framework for that Axiom of yours, but I know she consorted with a certain cult of apostates in Yonte Saire during her pilgrimage, and I know that upon her return she summoned an ancient spirit of immense darkness, by way of a blood sacrifice on the eve of a New Year. The spirit changed her, inflamed her desires, made her obsessed." The queen turns her faceless gaze on Salo, and there is boiling acid in her next words. "Then she seduced a young warrior from a powerful line of chiefs and bore him a son. I knew she was up to something, but she was smart; she knew how to insulate herself from the consequences of her sacrilege."

It is never easy for Salo to reconcile the power-hungry megalomaniac everyone else remembers and the woman he knew—save for those last few months before her death. Maybe he never knew her at all.

"Let your mother's demise be an example to you of what can happen to the overly ambitious. Shortcuts to power will always take you through the mire, and sometimes, you never come out."

Salo suspects there's a second, deeper warning somewhere in these words, though he fails to parse its exact nature. He suddenly regrets this conversation altogether. "I understand, Your Majesty."

"Travel well, Musalodi. I expect to hear from you once you reach Yonte Saire." Then the queen disappears into the prismatic sunset, leaving Salo to emerge from the talisman feeling like he has a solid weight sitting somewhere deep inside his chest.

Strictly speaking, when he touched Ingacha and Wakii, blessing them with portions of his arcane power, he weakened himself by reducing the flow of essence he can draw into his shards. In practical terms, however, all the two animals needed to become as mighty as any moon-blessed quagga of the Ajaha cavalries were the tiniest slivers of his power, so tiny he can barely perceive their absence.

If he concentrates, though, he can sense two other tethers besides Mukuni's pulling at his mind now, both in their own unique way. Ingacha is a proud, defiant presence, while Wakii is an excitable thrum. Both are weaker than Mukuni's tether, but if he wants to, he can project his will across them, communicate with the minds on the other side, or even feed them more of his power.

Now he understands why his tribe's ancestral talent is so potent. He could bless an entire regiment and their warmounts before he started to feel the drain on his power.

Hours after his conversation with the queen, as they trot through a light drizzle, a strong sense of unease besets him across all three tethers. Mukuni starts growling at the surrounding woodlands. Ahead of him, Wakii slows down, neighing and tossing her head nervously.

Tuksaad brings her to a complete stop and looks back at Salo and Ilapara, biting his lips like he's fishing for the right words. "Listen," he says, "I'm pretty sure we're about to get ambushed, but everything will be all right if you don't panic. Just let me take the lead, understood?"

Behind Mukuni, Ilapara reins in her buck and draws her spear from its harness by Ingacha's side. She scowls at the woods first, then at Tuk. "What the devil are you talking about? What ambush?"

"I need you to put that away, Ilapara," Tuk says, eyeing her weapon. "We need to be as nonthreatening as possible. That's the only way we'll get out of these woods in one piece."

Salo quickly scans their immediate surroundings with his shards. The woods aren't thick enough to form a canopy, but anything more than several hundred yards away might as well be invisible. He comes up with nothing save the vague sense that they are surrounded. "Did you know this was going to happen?" he says to Tuk, failing to keep the panic out of his voice.

"Not so soon."

"So you knew! Why the devil didn't you warn us?"

"I didn't want to cause you needless worry."

"Needless? We're about to get ambushed, Tuksaad!"

Tuk's expression remains serious, but his eyes turn a traitorous green. "Let me handle it, and we'll be fine."

"I don't see what's funny about this," Salo says.

"I'm not laughing, am I?"

"Your eyes!"

"I can't help that," Tuk says, and this time a dimple materializes on his face. "Look, just follow my lead, all right? No spells." He looks at Ilapara. "And put that blade away, for Ama's sake."

Ilapara clenches her weapon stubbornly. "I won't be killed without a fight."

"No one will be killed if you just hang back and let me do the talking."

She glares at him for a long moment but then purses her lips and returns her weapon to its harness.

"Salo," Tuk says, "keep your cat friend in line."

Salo is too fixated on the surrounding woods to respond. They seem particularly ominous now.

With Tuk in the lead, they set off at a slower, more cautious pace. Mukuni and the other animals remain agitated, and for good reason: barely five minutes pass before frenzied howls erupt in the woods around them, followed by the emergence of husky figures in skimpy loincloths, white body paint, and layered necklaces of beads and copper. They move so quickly it's only a matter of seconds before Salo and the others find themselves trapped inside a thicket of spears and ornate bow-like weapons with arrows that seem to be made entirely of red light.

Their assailants are not alone. They've come with frightful horned jackals on leashes, and the blasted things won't stop snapping their teeth. Salo barely musters the clarity of mind to keep Mukuni from attacking.

Ilapara is a stiff presence behind him. He can tell it's taking all her self-control not to draw her weapon. A part of him would feel better if she did.

One of their attackers—perhaps the group's captain, since he appears to be wearing the most intricate necklace of them all—comes forward and demands something in a language Salo can't understand.

He shares a worried glance with Ilapara, but Tuksaad surprises him yet again by replying to the demand in the captain's language, speaking with his hands raised in a show of peace.

The captain glowers up at him and says something else. Tuk replies confidently, pointing at his gauntlet. He seems to ask for permission from the captain, which the captain grants with a nod.

All eyes watch as Tuk raises his left arm, pointing his clenched fist toward the branches up and off to the side. A hiss as a silver barrel telescopes out of the gauntlet, rapidly gathering a nimbus of moonfire.

Then the branches explode with a loud crack, sending the Tuanu jackals into a snarling frenzy.

Tuk ignores them, releasing five more blasts in rapid succession. Mukuni growls, and Salo holds his breath, expecting to be attacked. But the captain and his men behold Tuk's gauntlet with pure wonder, like they've come upon a yet-undiscovered vein of moongold.

A big smile breaks on the captain's face, and he nods at Tuk. He shouts a command at his men, and the thicket of spears draws back, the bows going slack, their glowing arrows disappearing into thin air.

"We have to follow them," Tuk says. "It'll be a two-hour walk to the lake from here."

Without protest, Salo and Ilapara prod their mounts into motion and follow, flanked by potentially hostile armed men and their snarling jackals.

"What on Meza just happened, Tuk?" Salo asks and flinches when one of the spearmen glares up at him.

"I have bought us passage up the lake," Tuk says.

"How?"

"I offered them my gauntlet in exchange."

"*What?* But you can't! This is *my* pilgrimage, Tuksaad. *I* should bear any costs that need paying. And that's a *really* valuable and powerful weapon!"

On his abada, Tuk sighs. "Now you know why I didn't tell you. I had a feeling you'd react like this. Look, it's done now, and it's best if we limit our talking. We don't want to make them suspicious."

Salo cranes his neck to look behind him at Ilapara. They both shake their heads when their eyes meet.

31: The Maidservant

The Tuanu Borderlands

The Maidservant shadows her quarry from the infinite depths of the Void, spreading her flies and thus her consciousness across miles of woodland so as to evade detection.

Earlier she witnessed a most astonishing sight: the great Hunter, lieutenant of the Dark Sun himself, flung down from the skies by three youths. She felt his power extinguished from the land they both drew from like a whooshing wind, felt it become a roaring absence the Dark Sun surely sensed as it tore open. How she would have loved to watch her hated lord's reaction.

The Yerezi mystic has become very interesting indeed.

She would have attacked him already, wrung out the secrets from his mind and destroyed his body so the Dark Sun would learn nothing from him, but there is another presence shadowing him through the Void.

So far she has kept herself concealed from the presence, drawing the thinnest stream of energy from the profane door in her mind, which she learned can shroud her footprint in the Void and make her much harder to detect. Occasionally she sends ripples through the Void like a bat using echolocation to discern the nature of its surroundings, but the presence must have superior protections since it successfully deflects her scrutiny, keeping its nature hidden.

She'll just have to bide her time and let the presence reveal itself.

They follow the mystic and his companions northwest into the Tuanu borderlands. They watch from a distance as he is accosted by a patrol of Tuanu warriors, and though at first it seems he will have to fight his way through, for some reason the warriors lower their weapons and start *guiding* him deeper into their territory.

This puzzles the Maidservant since she knows the Tuanu to be generally hostile to foreigners. She wants to venture closer and perhaps listen in, but she senses the other presence slowing down and banking southwest.

One of the other parties hunting the mystic must have gotten too close.

The two of them are not the only ones on the mystic's trail. The Maidservant can sense at least five other groups in pursuit, all of them making good time despite having to move stealthily across lands ruled by hostile warlords. But only two groups are close enough to cause trouble should they be allowed to continue.

The first is a death squad Sand Devil dispatched from a distant village in the east—over a dozen men with red skulls for masks, led by a disciple and drunk on tonics that make their blood boil with rage. They are approaching on mutant kerit bears, meaty creatures with spikes on their shoulders, erect manes, and no lips to cover their ghastly teeth; they're still some distance away, but the mystic has slowed down considerably. Should they keep going past the borderlands, they will catch up to him sooner or later.

The other group of concern is a detachment of militiamen loyal to Northstar, machete-wielding warriors in grass skirts coming from the southwest on giant, swift-running sable antelope. Given the mystic's current speed, they will intercept him within the hour if they maintain their pace.

It is this latter group that the other presence in the Void veers off to confront, and the Maidservant follows, keeping far enough away to remain cloaked in Black magic, yet close enough to see what the presence does with her own eyes.

The suns are behind her, and the flat woodlands spread out into the distant horizon, where a great mountain range can be seen shrouded in a haze. Movement in the trees below catches her attention, about a mile ahead of her; then a dozen figures come into view, bulky men riding even bulkier antelope with massive arching horns.

Their spear-wielding leader wears a wooden mask with no eye slits. His naked chest is an intricate network of scarification and tattoos. Judging by the red fires throbbing around his charmed spear of witchwood and tronic bone, the Maidservant guesses his strength lies in Fire craft.

How typical, she thinks. Rare to find a male mystic of Umadi stock who isn't seduced by the destructive potential of moonfire. Rarer still to find one whose Axiom can actually put the craft to effective use.

He must sense something in the air, given how he slows down and calls a halt, searching the skies through his eyeless mask. His men wait patiently behind him, secure in his power and in the power of the lord they all serve.

They don't realize that they are already dead.

The Maidservant ghosts just a little closer as she waits with bated breath for what she knows is coming, and when ravens *explode* out of the skies and swoop down onto the men, she is not disappointed.

Antelope bleat and rear up in alarm. The female silhouette she can just about glimpse at the center of the flock is a knife-wielding blink of motion whose blades are pure Void craft. They dart from one mount to another, tearing bloody smiles open and leaving the men clutching at their slashed throats.

In his desperation, the disciple detonates a spherical ward of moonfire that incinerates everything in its path as it rapidly expands away from him—everything including his dying men and their beasts. The ensuing shock wave is powerful enough to level some of the surrounding trees, but his attacker releases a counterward of Void craft that bends space around her to slow the fire's approach. She storms upward and out of the sphere's radius, escaping to a safe height before her ward breaks down and the fires dissipate.

But the attacker must know, as the Maidservant knows, that most Umadi mystics, especially those of the male variety, are rarely capable of sustained sorcerous battles. That spell was in all likelihood sitting at the back of his mind, waiting for him to unleash it at a moment's notice. It will be seconds before his Axiom can provide enough Fire craft for him to perform another spell.

Sure enough, the attacker hurtles back down even before the disciple has reoriented his antelope to face her.

A brief struggle, a flutter of dark wings, the flash of a knife pulsing with shadows, and then the flock retreats back upward while the disciple falls boneless off his saddle. His beast vaults away without him.

Her curiosity sated, the Maidservant withdraws from the scene before she is detected. Now she knows why the attacker's presence was so odd to her: deadly though she may be, the attacker is no mystic. She is a manifestation of the Yerezi ancestral talent, given the power of magic by a mystic of her tribe.

This must be what the Yerezi witch meant when she said her queen had eyes on the boy.

Mystic or not, the Maidservant decides that she might need help taking the boy and acquiring his secrets. She is confident in her own abilities, but she will not make the mistake of underestimating him. Not when she saw what happened to Hunter. The stakes—her peace of mind and the freedom to end her torment and finally fulfill her vow—are much too high.

32: Ilapara

Lake Zivatuanu

When a sprawling village reveals itself past a dense thicket of bush after two hours of silent trekking, Ilapara has to grit her jaw just to keep it from dropping to her chest.

Lying beyond the village is a body of water so vast it seems to her like the frontier of the world. The water goes on and on forever until it melts away into the sky in a shimmery blur, promising abysmal depths she shudders to think of.

"And here it is," Tuk says from astride Wakii, wonder brightening his voice. "Lake Zivatuanu, the longest freshwater lake in the world."

Salo whistles and slowly shakes his head. "I thought our lake was big. And look at those ships!"

Ilapara is just as awestruck. All the lakes she's ever seen were puddles in comparison to this landlocked sea. And gliding over the water in the distance are vessels so majestic and fanciful they seem like giant birds. They even have ribbed winglike structures jutting up from the hulls, outstretched as if to take off in flight.

"Will we be sailing on one of those?" she asks, hating the anxiety she hears in her own voice.

"That's the plan," Tuk says. "We should count ourselves lucky, you know. The Tuanu don't let many foreigners sail on their waterbirds or even come close enough to see them."

"Waterbirds," Salo echoes, looking out at the ships in the distance. "Now I understand the name."

They are led down gravel streets lined with graceful triangular stone huts featuring wide decks. Unfriendly eyes peer at them through mazes of body paint. A fishy smell suffuses the air, but the streets are clean and cared for. Nothing at all like a stopover town, and Ilapara finds that she is grateful for it.

"Those are no ordinary sailing ships," Salo says ahead of her. "If I had to guess, I'd say they're a secret these people guard as jealously as we guard our red steel and talismans."

"Over a hundred villages surround this lake," Tuk replies. "The waterbirds are the heart of Tuanu culture and the lifeblood of their economy. Makes sense that they'd want to keep the secret of what they are."

By the time they reach one corner of the village center—a square of dry earth surrounded by the largest huts they've yet come across—there's a small crowd trailing behind them.

"How is it you know so much about this place, Tuk?" Ilapara says as they come to a stop.

Tuk smiles, watching the Tuanu captain approach him. "Later," he says.

He goes on to exchange a few words with the captain, after which he dismounts and hands Ilapara the reins of his abada, smiling reassuringly. Even so, a feeling of wrongness runs through her as she watches him follow the captain up the stairs to the largest hut in the square and then disappear beyond the arched wooden door.

Salo stares at the door as well, the line of his jaw visibly tense. "What now?"

"I guess we wait," she says, because it's not like they have any other choice.

More villagers trickle into the square. Children chase each other across the open space while their parents point at Mukuni and murmur to each other, occasionally throwing Salo glances that raise the hairs on Ilapara's skin and make her itch for her weapon. The Tuanu warriors remain on guard nearby with their bows, spears, and leashed jackals, ready to spring at the slightest provocation. Obviously they think Salo is the bigger threat.

"A friendly lot, aren't they?" he says, clearly nervous.

"They know what you are," Ilapara says. "And I've heard they don't like mystics very much. Just don't give them a reason to want you dead."

"I feel much calmer now, Ilapara. Thank you."

She smirks, saying nothing.

At last the captain emerges from the hut with Tuksaad, the former looking mightily pleased and the latter with a subdued, slightly smug grin. Stepping forward with his hands on his waist, the captain bellows something that might as well be a proclamation of victory given how his men raise their weapons and cheer.

Salo watches them anxiously. "What's happening?"

"I think Tuk just sold his gauntlet," Ilapara says, looking up at the strange young man. "He's not wearing it anymore."

"I get that it's a powerful weapon, but isn't their reaction a bit much?"

"I bet Tuk will know the answer to that question."

In front of the big hut, Tuk bids the captain farewell, getting a vigorous handshake before he is allowed to leave, and as he walks over, the grin he was smothering spreads to the rest of his face.

"Success, I presume," Salo says to him.

His eyes are as bright blue as the New Year's Comet. "Indeed. There's a ship about to set sail, in fact. It awaits us by the docks."

Ilapara gives the cheering men one last glance. "You'll have to explain this to us at some point."

"I will, but on the ship." Tuk starts prodding Wakii toward the young warrior waiting for them on the other side of the square. "Come on. This way."

◆ ◆ ◆

A full-bosomed Tuanu woman in a long green khanga is waiting for them at the docks with her three sons, and by the heavy set of her brow, she's clearly not pleased that her waterbird has been chosen to transport the foreigners. While her sons load crates of mouthwatering fruits onto the ship, she gives Tuk a long, winding speech involving furious gestures, like he's the cause of her every woe on the planet.

Tuk nods apologetically the whole time, but the smile he wears when she finally allows them to board mirrors the one on Salo's face.

Ilapara tries not to hate them for it.

Up close, the vessel is even larger than it appeared from afar, a looming presence of exquisite carpentry. The sight of it makes her stomach feel unsettled. *Am I really doing this?*

"The ferrywoman and her sons are going up north to trade for livestock," Tuk says as they lead their animals along the landing stage. "There'll be room for our mounts belowdecks, but I've been warned it reeks down there, so we might want to stay up on the main deck."

"I don't mind," Salo says. "I want to see everything."

"You and me both, my friend," Tuk says, and Ilapara makes a face behind them.

By the gangplank she plants her feet on the landing stage and traces the glossy vessel with her eyes, from the swan figurehead at the prow to the slightly upturned and tapering stern, lingering on the reddish, diaphanous winglike structures currently tucked into the broadsides. When Salo notices the look on her face, he throws her a smirk.

"Is something the matter, Ilapara?"

She cuts him a warning glare with her eyes. "Why would you say that?"

Not heeding the warning at all, he says, "Khaya-Sikhozi is pretty dry, isn't it? No lakes, no rivers?"

"We have rivers. What's your point?"

His grin widens. "Don't worry. I'm a good swimmer. If we should sink, I'll be sure to save you."

That will not do. Not even a little.

Smiling dangerously, Ilapara grabs Ingacha's reins and braves the wide gangplank, outwardly calm and composed. Just to make her point, she stops halfway up to look back. "For your information, Musalodi, I happen to be a *superb* swimmer, so if anyone's going to be saving anyone, it'll be me." She flicks her head away, then walks up onto the deck. Salo chuckles as he follows her.

Her confidence wavers, however, as soon as her boots hit the main deck. She can swim just fine, but she's always been a child of the fields and the open plains, where she has a strong measure of control over her own destiny. To step onto this ship now is to give up this control and put herself at the mercy of the winds and the waters, whose capricious temperaments she can never predict.

Dear Ama, let this trip be mercifully short.

Salo helps lead Ingacha and Wakii down a steep ramp to the animal stalls in a lower deck, using his blessing to lull both animals into relaxed states. His totem remains wide eyed and alert where he has curled up by the starboard bulwarks.

With the animals settled, they take the time to explore the vessel. Its sleek, fluid lines, flowing from bow to stern, lend the ship a distinctly avian feel. A complex system of ropes, pulleys, and netting weaves over the decks like a canopy. Its lovingly polished surfaces don't quite gleam with newness; indeed, the whole vessel bears the aura of many storms weathered, but only in that graceful way of things that grow better with age, like a fine wood or high-quality wine.

Ilapara feels the dread in her stomach unknotting itself. *This isn't so bad.*

"Curious," Salo mutters to the side. When she looks, she finds him with his shards softly aglow, searching the air with empty fingers.

"What is it?" she says.

"This vessel has been recently possessed by a spirit . . ." He tilts his head up. "But where's the mind stone?"

He dims his shards when the youngest of the ferrywoman's sons—a boy who's seen perhaps fifteen comets—begins to arrange a set of musical instruments on the benches bolted down toward the bow of the ship. If Ilapara didn't know better, she'd say he was setting up for an ensemble's performance.

"The Tuanu have an ancestral talent that makes mystics practically redundant," Tuk says while he watches the boy. "That's why they kill anyone caught trying to awaken."

Salo's face contorts with a grimace. "And I was beginning to like this place."

"Come now, Salo," Ilapara says. "It's not like the presence of mystics is always a good thing. Sometimes people are better off without them."

"That's certainly true for these people," Tuk says. "They were slaves to their mystics until they realized they didn't really need them. Their talent allows trained individuals to replicate any charms of Red magic, no matter how powerful or complex. All without casting a single spell."

By the worried look that visits Salo's face, he must be thinking what Ilapara is thinking. "That answers why they were so excited about the gauntlet," he says. "They'll be able to make more weapons just like it."

"I'm counting on it," Tuk says, evidently oblivious to their concern.

Ilapara scowls at him. "But why would you do such a thing, Tuk? Can you imagine the threat they could pose if all their warriors got their hands on one?"

Tuk huffs like that's a ridiculous idea. "They won't pose a threat to anyone who doesn't threaten them. All they want is to live their lives without anyone coming here to bother them."

"But what if they decide to go beyond that? With that kind of weapon, why wouldn't they?"

"Sorry, Tuk," Salo says, "but I'm going to have to agree with Ilapara. The weapon you've given these people could cause much suffering. They don't call these the Redlands for nothing. An imbalance of power often leads to bloodshed."

"I'm an outsider, I know," Tuk says. "But hear me out, all right? What if I told you that the only reason these people continue to exist as they are is that they've always paid tribute to the KiYonte kings for protection? And yet they still lose people regularly to Umadi raids. This village is especially vulnerable since it's practically in Umadiland. But that won't have to be the case anymore. With what I've given them, they can fight back."

Ilapara softens her expression, moved by his sincerity, but she still shakes her head. "Let's hope it stays at self-defense. I shudder to think what would happen otherwise."

"Ama forbid the warlords ever learn to make gauntlets of their own," Salo adds.

"It won't come to that," Tuk says. "You'd need some extremely sophisticated machines to cast the type of charms we're talking about, and you won't find them in the Redlands. Also, the Tuanu don't sell their charmed artifacts to outsiders. I wouldn't have bartered my gauntlet otherwise."

The ferrywoman comes up to the main deck with her other two sons, but instead of pulling some ropes or hoisting the wing structures like Ilapara expects them to, they all sit on the benches behind the arrayed musical instruments. The ferrywoman picks up the mbira, the oldest of her sons sits behind the drum set, and the other two pick up lyres of different sizes.

Ilapara trades baffled glances with Salo, Tuksaad just grins like he knows what's coming, and at the bow, the Tuanu sailors begin to play.

First, the ferrywoman delivers a dramatic opener with her mbira; then her sons join in with percussion and strings. Instantly the most rousing music Ilapara has ever heard, and when the ferrywoman graces it with her powerful voice, she can't help but laugh in delight at the sheer brilliance of it all. The music enraptures her so thoroughly she almost misses the moment everything starts coming to life around them.

The mysterious machines belowdecks begin to rumble. The ribbed winglike structures unfurl, stretching outward and upward as if to meet the suns. Ilapara realizes that a spirit must have impregnated the vessel, though she can't tell where it could have come from.

Then the vessel steals into motion so gracefully there's not even a tremor on the deck. The diaphanous wings flutter slightly with signs of life. Thin wisps of white-red light droop from the wing tips like delicate threads, swaying in the wind as the waterbird begins to sail away from the shore. Ilapara gapes, astonished, because she has never seen a spirit manifest in such a manner.

"I bet the view's splendid from back there," Tuk says, pointing astern, so the three of them venture there to watch the village's triangular huts drift off into the distance. The skies are stained gold as the suns dip behind the woodlands in the west. A small crowd of Tuanu is standing by the docks to see them off; Salo waves at them and is visibly pleased when many wave back.

"It's like we're flying," Ilapara says, failing to decide whether she should be elated or terrified. "By Ama, how fast can this thing go?"

"Probably half as fast as a moon-blessed warmount at a gallop," Tuk says. "Except it never has to stop. We should reach the northernmost shores in less than two days."

"But *how* is this happening?" Salo says, looking utterly perplexed. "Spirits expend themselves quickly unless hosted in a mind stone with a plentiful reserve of power to keep them going. I can feel the spirit moving the ship, but where's the power coming from?"

"It might have something to do with the music," Tuk suggests. "Maybe it conjures the spirit?"

Salo looks back at the ferrywoman and her sons. "The music is definitely how they're controlling the spirit. I'm just not sure why it doesn't expend itself with no obvious power source."

"My knowledge of spirits is rather limited," Tuk admits, "but speaking of which, I was told the Lightning Bird will make an appearance at some point during the journey. If you don't want to commune with it, they said you can just ignore it . . . although that would be quite the wasted opportunity, wouldn't it?"

"We'll see," Salo says with a distant look.

Ilapara is getting the hang of reading Tuk's eyes; the guy is trying not to push, but he *really* wants Salo to commune with the spirit.

"Tuksaad," she says to him, leaning against the gunwale and turning to face him. "Maybe you can answer my question now?"

"What question?"

"About how you know so much about this place."

Looking out at the receding village, Tuk smiles. "Diligent study, I guess. Before I crossed the Jalama, I read every book I could find on the so-called Red Wilds. There aren't many, but I was lucky to come across a few well-informed journals written by previous explorers."

"And the languages?" Ilapara asks. "Did you learn those from journals too?"

"Hardly. I bought a language skill nexus in Ima Jalama and spent a few days staring at it. You could say I got the languages hypnotized into me. Painstakingly so."

"A skill nexus?" Salo says, echoing her thoughts.

"An artifact of hypnotic Blood craft," Tuk explains. "It can teach you certain skills, provided you're smart enough to avoid getting trapped by its magic. Well, at least that's what the Dulama merchant told me when I bought it from him. A part of me thought it was a hoax, but I was desperate." Tuk shrugs, smiling. "Turns out he was right. Now I speak most of the continent's languages."

"So *that's* what it's called?" Salo says. "A skill nexus."

"You've used one before?" Tuk asks, his forehead crinkled.

"Actually, I *have* one. It's how I learned ciphers. A carving of a grove."

"Mine was a tapestry," Tuk says, which makes Ilapara's ears prick.

Her maternal uncle, who trained her in the art of combat, used to tell her he acquired his skills from a magical cloth. Could this be what he meant? A skill nexus?

"You won't find that kind of thing in the Enclave, you know," Tuk says. "They can't make them. They've gone so high level with their magic they've forgotten the first principles that make it possible. Educated fools, if you ask me."

"That gauntlet didn't look foolish to me," Ilapara observes, then gives Tuk a pointed stare. "And neither do you, as a matter of fact."

His mouth curves into a humorless smile, and his eyes briefly fall to the deck. "Fair enough. I guess it's true that Higher technology is second to none. But if you asked mystics of the Enclave to conjure fire, command beasts, or do any of the other types of magic that come so easily to you folk, they'd look at you like you'd lost your mind."

Salo frowns. "Is that really true?"

"Oh yes." Tuk leans against the bulwarks and watches the ship's slip-stream with a faraway look in his eyes. "The Redlands are the only place in the world where magic is still practiced in its pure form. The rest of the world runs on technomagical charms, but casting spells like what you did with the winds, Salo"—Tuk shakes his head with awe in his eyes—"that's an art they lost long ago. One of the reasons they fear this place, in fact."

Behind them the music winds down now that the waterbird has reached cruising speed. Only the bright and lively trill of a lyre remains, powering the vessel ever forward.

"You know what, Tuk?" Salo says, tilting his head with a thoughtful look. "Meeting you has made me realize just how insular I've been. You came from another continent, yet you know far more about my fellow Red people than I do. Clearly I need to do better."

"So do I," Ilapara says. "But curiosity about other places is often a luxury for those who can travel, isn't it? And you know how our people feel about leaving the Plains or even interacting with outsiders."

"I can't say I blame them after some of the things I've seen," Salo says, looking out at the horizon. "But maybe we lose a lot more than we gain by being so isolated."

"You shouldn't beat yourself up about it too much," Tuk says. "Many people of the outside world are just as insular and disinterested in other cultures."

"Why are you so different, then?" Ilapara asks him.

He thinks for a heartbeat, his eyes shifting into a duskier green. "You could say I'm on a journey of self-improvement. I want to be the best possible version of myself."

Salo considers him. "Is that why you want my blessing?"

"It will certainly help me reach that goal."

"But is that the *only* reason?" Ilapara asks, finally, because she's been wondering about his real intentions for a while now. What does he really want with Salo?

He seems to catch on to the question behind the question. "I've told you the truth since we met. So if you're asking if my motives are purely altruistic, then the answer is no. But if you're asking if my motives are unworthy"—he flashes his dimples in a rather handsome grin—"then the answer is still no, though you'd be wise not to take my word for it."

Salo smiles, and Ilapara fails to restrain a laugh. "At least he's straightforward."

Tuk's eyes flash a brighter green. "I am rarely anything but, my dear Ilapara."

Maybe he's not so bad, she decides. She's still not sure about him, and she'll be watching him closely, but maybe he really is what he seems.

In the distance, the Tuanu village has become a blink of light. They all watch the tiny glow until it fades into the twilight.

33: Isa

A strange dream troubles a king of late.

She is the lowest of the low among man- and womankind until one day she plucks a red petal from a bloodrose and makes a wish. Then she is transformed and becomes the most beautiful, most powerful, most intelligent person in the world. She proceeds to live a life of bliss, envied and admired by all and assured that she is meaningful now, that her power and virtue somehow make her life objectively significant, absolute.

But then she casts her gaze upward and finds that she can now see a pantheon of beings who dwell in the skies, who she could not see before because her eyes were closed in her wretchedness. They are perfect in mind and body, more perfect than she is even in her newly exalted state, and though she tries to be content with what she has, their presence in the skies shows her an inescapable truth: She is but a travesty of true beauty and intelligence. A fiction.

The truth torments her, and eventually she gives in and plucks a second petal from the bloodrose, making another wish. And a great wind rises to snatch her from the world, elevating her into the sky pantheon, where she becomes a god. The mountains roll away in fear of her awesome power and beauty. Mortals fall to their knees in worship and build temples in her honor. She rules over them from her celestial throne, secure in her power and objective significance.

At least for a time.

One day, however, she spots the foot of a staircase leading up into the stellar vault, and with her godly eyes she traces it all the way up to its highest extremity. There she sees, much to her dismay, yet *another* pantheon of gods. *Greater* gods. Gods as great to her as she has become to the mortal shell she left behind.

In a panicked rush she dislodges yet another petal from the bloodrose. Its razor-sharp edges cut into her fingers, but she pays no heed to the pain as she makes her wish. To her relief she ascends into this newer and greater pantheon, where her mind expands into the cosmos as she becomes aware of the stars themselves spinning about their axes.

But alas, soon she finds that there are *cosmic* gods, and that there are gods above these gods, and yet more gods above those. She keeps plucking petals from the bloodrose, on and on until her blood-soaked fingers are shredded to the bone, ascending through rank after rank of godhood, each one more magnificent than the last, but no matter how high up she goes, she always finds that there are yet more gods above her, gods more awesome and more powerful.

Perched on the only chair in the citadel's makeshift throne room, Isa gently traces the moongold mask-crown in her hands with her fingers and feels a shiver at the memory of the dream. She has no ambitions of godhood, but the dream that haunts her contains a truth she cannot ignore: the idea that she is powerful is nothing but a fiction so long as there are those above her who can change her destiny with the flick of a finger.

Can a piece on a game board ever claim to be powerful when it is a slave to the hand that moves it?

"It is time, Your Majesty." The Arc's scarified face stares grimly at her. "Remember, you are in total command of the mask. Simply order it to take you to the Meeting Place by the Sea, and it will be so. I should warn you, however: you may feel disoriented upon arriving. If you do, relax, and let your mind adjust itself."

Glowing rubies in small openwork frames float magically in the air above the throne room, casting a warm light on the bamboo struts and arches of the ceiling and on the red tapestries lining the walls. Isa keeps caressing the mask, and her varnished nails glitter up at her like cut amethysts, complementing the silken length of violet cloth wrapped around her body. The garment leaves her back, navel, and shoulders bare, exposing the golden filigree painted onto her bronze skin. It hugs her hips and legs until it flows into a long train that will sweep the floor behind her as she walks. A disk of golden beads sits around her neck in a near-vertical position so that it almost frames her face. Ornate golden bands coil up her forearms. Her hair has been braided halfway and left to flare into a crown of tight curls at the back. She is no princess tonight, no simpering woman, but a king.

"If the likes of Kola Saai can handle the Meeting Place," she says, "then so can I, Your Worship."

The Arc nods with approval. "Good. The stronger your resolve, the easier it will be for you." He glances at the young men standing in the throne room with them—Jomo in his blue robes, looking freshly washed and shaved, and a contingent of Sentinels in smart green tunics and aerosteel armor—all of them watching carefully. "As I'm sure you know," the Arc says to Isa, "you are allowed to take two others with you to the Meeting Place by the Sea. They will be unarmed, however, since weapons do not carry into the Meeting Place, only minds."

Jomo steps forward with his gilded cane, his leg brace squeaking as he does so. "I am the herald. I should go with you. My mother always accompanied your father to the Mkutano in the Meeting Place by the Sea."

Obe Saai follows him, hands clasped respectfully before him. "As your honor guard, I should come with you, Your Majesty."

"You stay away from my cousin!" Jomo says, wheeling around to face him with blazing eyes. "Your kind should not be welcome here after what your uncle did."

"With all due respect," Obe says, meeting the herald glare for glare, "I am not my uncle."

"A crocodile is a crocodile."

Isa has to physically hold in a sigh. She suspected this would happen. "Neither of you shall be coming with me."

Both young men look at her with hurt in their eyes. "Oh, come on, Your Majesty," Jomo says. "Leaving me makes no sense!"

"You may accompany me next time," she clarifies. "Tonight I will take Sentinels Dino Sato and Ijiro Katumbili."

At this, both Jomo and Obe go from hurt to indignant. Dino Sato is Isa's other honor guard, and Ijiro Katumbili is probably the youngest warrior in the room, a strapping, bright-eyed fellow with the look of innocence about him. Isa doubts he has yet seen his seventeenth comet.

Both warriors step forward, failing to hide their surprise.

"I need their experience," Isa says to the indignant pair. "Dino and Ijiro are princes who have traveled to the Meeting Place by the Sea with their fathers before. This won't be their first time there. I can't say the same for you two, can I?"

This reason is partly true. The real reason she wants to leave Jomo and Obe, though, is that she doesn't want their strong emotions clouding her judgment.

"You will respect Her Majesty's wishes," says the Arc, ending all discussion on the matter.

He retrieves a moongold timepiece from the folds of his crimson boubou and gives its ticking face a glance. "Are you ready, Your Majesty?"

Smothering a tremble with a heavy breath, Isa dons the mask-crown. As it unfolds itself to cover her face, she feels it working its sorcery to give her the visage of a metallic four-tusked elephant wearing a crown of spikes, with eyes that glow like burning charcoal. Controlling its expressions is instinctual; the mask-crown will reveal only that which she wishes it to.

She senses an immediate change in how the warriors look at her, sees it in their awed expressions. With the mask-crown glinting on her face, they now see the imposing man who wore it not a month ago, not the frightened young woman wearing it now. *Good.*

She rises to her feet and walks down the dais with the poise of a princess who is now king, holding out her arms for her chosen warriors. With all eyes watching, Dino Sato and Ijiro Katumbili step forward to meet her, each one taking an arm in his.

"Do not forget that the Meeting Place is a construct," the Arc says to her. "It won't feel like it, but nothing there is real, and no one can harm you. Your minds will be entangled in the Void, but your bodies will still be here. Should you wish to return, simply will the mask to bring you back, and it will obey."

Isa takes another breath to put steel in her veins. "Understood, Your Worship."

He bows his head. "Good luck, Your Majesty."

While the Arc steps back, Ijiro leans in, looking rather nervous and a little guilty. "I've never been to a Mkutano before, Your Majesty," he whispers. "I have five older brothers, so I never got the chance."

She tries to look reassuring—as reassuring as a metallic four-tusked elephant can look. "It'll be my first time, too, so perhaps we can take strength from each other."

Relief loosens the tension in his shoulders. "Yes, Your Majesty."

Next to them, Dino smirks. "Relax. Don't worry. Just don't think too much, and you'll be fine."

Dino Sato is light skinned where Obe is swarthy, with fine-boned, sharply defined features. Where Obe hides his sensuality beneath a rigid guise, Dino wears his on his sleeve. Where Obe's good looks lie in his secret smiles and intense gaze, Dino will capture the room's attention the instant he walks in. He is charming and knows it.

Of late he's been distant with her. Sometimes she worries she's losing his friendship, not only because she enjoys his company but also because it would be a politically catastrophic loss to her right now. He's a direct line of communication to his father, the headman of the Sato clan and wearer of the Impala mask. He might be key to securing the headman's support.

Ijiro's father, on the other hand, is the Bonobo, one of the Crocodile's closest allies. The conniving part of Isa is taking him along as her escort mostly for the shock effect. Let them see that she isn't completely powerless, that she holds their sons by the leash.

"Are you ready?" she asks them both, and they nod.

"Remember, no thinking," Dino says.

"Will yourself away, Your Majesty," the Arc says. "Command the mask to take you where you need to be."

But his voice is fading away because Isa has already commanded the mask, and now she feels it yank her mind out of the fabric of existence and into—

Oblivion. There is nothing here, and yet there is everything. It is a lonely, transient moment of painful immortality, a cold, deathless hell where she has no form, no words to speak, no eyes to see, and no ears to hear herself scream—

She is suddenly whole again. The temple's bamboo arches and cloisters have vanished. She now stands at the shores of an endless expanse of water that glistens in the starlight. The beach stretches out before her until it curves away, bounded on one side by the seas and on the other by dense jungle.

By her side, Ijiro's breath comes out in rapid gasps. She squeezes his arm gently. "Are you all right?"

"Shouldn't we be asking you that, Your Majesty?" Dino says, then shakes his head and sighs at Ijiro. "He's thinking. I told him not to do that."

She pulls away from Dino to better attend to the younger Sentinel. "Come on, Ijiro. Breathe. It's all right. You're here now. We're all here. We're safe."

She needs to hear those words too. Crossing through *that place* took a piece of her soul from her, made her feel like she was nothing, or like she was the only person alive in the universe. How anyone can stand repeatedly crossing through such a place is beyond her.

Ijiro fights to bring himself under control. His broad shoulders heave, fists clenched by his sides. "I'm sorry, Your Majesty. I'm all right now."

"Yes, you are. And you have nothing to be sorry for."

Ijiro nods, wiping his eyes. "Thank you, Your Majesty."

"Very touching," Dino says, "but it looks like the Mkutano is about to begin. Perhaps we should walk a little closer so we can actually, you know, attend."

Isa casts a glance at the waves breaking on the shore, then up at the starry skies glittering on the waters. She suffers a shiver of dread when she realizes she doesn't recognize any of the stars up there. The Devil's Eye, whose milky upper spirals are always at the southernmost edge of the horizon, is nowhere in sight. Wherever she is now, she is no longer near the world's equator.

And these waters . . . is this the Dapiaro of the West or the eastern Inoetera? What exotic lands wait on the other side? *Is this truly not real?*

"Your Majesty." Worry has slipped into Dino's voice. "We must join the Mkutano before it begins. Are you sure you're all right?"

She looks away from the ocean. "Yes, Dino. Let's go."

Yards away along the beach, eleven stone pillars jut up from the sands around a depression so that they form a circle, each pillar reaching fifteen feet into the air. As they walk closer, Isa realizes that the pillars aren't pillars at all but massive thrones with elongated backrests, complete with steps leading up to the seats.

The ten headmen are already there, each one sitting on his throne, flanked by his two escorts. Their enchanted masks gleam in the starlight, their eyes glowing with magic. A fire burns in the depression at the circle's center, which is deep enough for the headmen to see each other over the towering flames.

The Bonobo is in the middle of a speech when Isa arrives—she knows that he is this month's Speaker, the headman elected to preside over the Mkutano. He stops speaking when he notices that everyone's looking not at him now but at her.

"All hail Isa Saire!" Dino announces. "King of Chains, Great Elephant of the Yontai, she who straddles the center of the world and rules its beating heart!"

It might not be deliberate on their parts, but what happens next tells Isa exactly who among them is her enemy, who is ambivalent, and who she might consider a friend: the Kestrel and the Lion both rise to their feet and bow; the Impala inclines his head respectfully where he sits; the Buffalo and the Caracal watch the others carefully; the Jackal, the Hare, and the Rhino relax into their seats; the Crocodile bares his teeth in a smile, and the Bonobo steeples his hands, looking down at her from his throne like she's a bug crawling on his expensive carpet.

"Your Majesty," he says in a voice dripping with hardly concealed distaste. "We were not expecting you."

Isa takes her time as she sweeps her gaze around the Meeting Place and the men sitting on their thrones.

Like their predecessors—and their sons and nephews today—all of them served in the King's Sentinels for six comets, went on to command their clan legions upon graduating, and then rose to their current stations when their fathers passed on. And while some of them have let themselves grow plump and soft with the years—like the Impala and the Rhino—it is clear to Isa that each was not only born to power like she was but groomed for it.

These men all know the stench of weakness when they smell it, and if she falters even for a second, she knows she will never have their respect.

Brocades and silks hang in drapes over their bodies. Gold shimmers on their fingers and dangles around their necks. The Buffalo wears the fattest diamond pendant because his clanlands are rich with diamond mines. The Hare has emerald rings on every finger for a similar reason.

If Isa is ever going to bend these men to her will, she knows she will have to stand her ground, starting right now.

"This is my first Mkutano since I was crowned," she says to the Bonobo. "I wonder why you thought I'd miss it. Could it be because you've elected a regent while a king yet lives?"

The Bonobo smiles down at her, steepled fingers tapping against each other. He's a powerfully built man with a booming voice and muscles that bulge out of his golden robe. When he glares down at Ijiro, Isa feels the boy stiffen and breathe in sharply.

He fears his father. Isa can't say she blames him, though. Not when she can feel her heart threatening to rise up her throat.

"You left us no choice, Your Majesty," the Bonobo says. "A king cannot run a kingdom from the cloisters of a temple. If you came out of hiding, there would be no need for a regent."

Isa smiles back, then marks the Crocodile with her gaze. "If I came out of hiding, my family's assassins would dance over my corpse."

To his credit the Crocodile remains cool and composed on his throne. "But Your Majesty," he says, "from your tone one would almost think you were accusing me of something."

"The guilty are always quick to cry foul."

"And accusations against a headman must be founded on facts."

Isa walks toward him, feeling the train of her robe flow out behind her. He's in a glittering green robe that does little to hide the lithe muscles beneath, sitting in the throne facing the oceans—the place of honor. She feels Dino and Ijiro trail behind slowly. Such a scene has likely never played out in the Meeting Place. She stops at the foot of the throne, taking care to meet the Crocodile's fiery gaze with hers. "I made no accusations, did I? But here's a fact for you, Your Highness: you're sitting in my chair."

A deadly flame ignites in the Crocodile's eyes. Isa has to remind herself that she can't be harmed. This is why the king and the headmen will often meet here; the Meeting Place by the Sea suffers no violence on its shores. But the man's gaze still makes her shiver.

"Of course, Your Majesty," he says at last. "My apologies." And then he rises to his feet, strides down the steps, and walks to the vacant throne across the circle, retaining more dignity than Isa would have liked. His two escorts seethe visibly as they follow him.

She tempers her childish instinct to scold them and walks up the steps to her throne. Only once she's seated do the Lion and the Kestrel do the same. She nods at them in acknowledgment.

As Dino and Ijiro move to stand on either side of her, she wonders about the wisdom of bringing them here. They might be a reminder of the power she wields over the headmen, but that reminder might only encourage them to take that power away.

Her fears are validated as soon as the Bonobo opens his mouth to speak. "As I was saying before Her Majesty arrived, we will begin this Mkutano by deliberating the matter of the King's Sentinels, after which we will put the matter to a vote. The House of Law has given us the mandate to decide among ourselves whether to keep this oppressive system in place. Should we decide to abolish it, the Shirika will annul the sorcerous bonds that hold our sons and nephews prisoners—"

"Excuse me, Your Highness," Isa interrupts. "I must be dreaming because it seems to me like you're about to begin this Mkutano without giving me my due. Surely you wouldn't be so presumptuous as to assume that I have nothing to say to my subject princes."

The Bonobo lets his anger show on his mask, but only for a moment; just long enough for Isa to see the emotion yet fleeting enough to be deniable. "My apologies, Your Majesty. Yes, it is customary for the king to give a speech before we begin deliberation. I will yield the fire to you."

"Thank you, Great Bonobo." Isa interlocks her fingers and stares gravely at her headmen. "I'd like to take this opportunity to discuss something very important to me. Something so important it's been keeping me up at night these last few days. My beloved princes, I want to talk about colors."

The headmen trade baffled looks. The Bonobo is the first to speak. "What?"

"Colors," Isa says. "Are they not the most wonderful things in the world? Passionate reds, earthy browns, fertile yellows, mysterious grays, trusty blues"—here she looks across the circle—"treacherous greens. Could it be that the colors we're most drawn to say something about what kind of people we are?"

After another long silence, the Hare shakes his head. "Her Majesty makes a mockery of this sacred place."

"Her Majesty is the king," says the Kestrel. "And she is allowed to give a speech without interruptions."

"Thank you, Great Kestrel," Isa says. "Now, where was I? Oh yes, colors."

Mkutanos at the Meeting Place by the Sea are meant to last for two hours and not a second longer. The flames of the burning fire mark the passage of time; they grow weaker with each passing moment, dying out completely when the two hours have elapsed.

Isa has a whole speech prepared. While the fire wanes, she whiles away the time with several loosely related discussions, from the color spectrum to the capital's architectural history to the economic outlook of a kingdom at war with itself. She speaks until everyone knows that she will not let them do what they have come here to do, for she is king, and a king may speak for as long as she wishes.

She knows in her heart that this is weak power, but it is still power, so she will not shy away from using it.

The Bonobo's eyes gather rage until they burn brighter than the fire in the depression. The Hare and the Rhino begin to fidget. Across the circle, a slow smile of begrudging respect spreads across the Crocodile's face.

Isa doesn't stop talking until the fire goes out with a hiss, signaling the end of the meeting. She stifles the sigh of relief that builds up in her chest. "Oh, will you look at that. Our time is up. And I wasn't even close to finished! Perhaps I can give the rest of my speech next time."

When she rises to her feet, the Kestrel and the Lion do the same, though they appear a little more enthusiastic about it now. This time she lets the sigh out. She feared she would lose their respect with this move, but it seems the exact opposite is true.

"Mother's blessings upon you, Your Highnesses," she says. "Until next time." And then she descends the steps to her throne, heading for the stretch of beach they came from. She could just slip back to the temple from here, but she wants the satisfaction of a proper exit.

Dino and Ijiro follow quietly behind her. They didn't know what she was planning to do; if they think any less of her now, they aren't showing it.

Halfway there a voice calls out to her: "Your Majesty. A word, if you please."

Isa considers ignoring the request because she knows exactly whose it is. Curiosity wins out in the end, though, so she stops and turns around.

The Crocodile has taken off his mask. He's walking toward her alone, with what she might have considered a charming smile had its wearer not murdered her entire family.

How she wishes she could say he is hideous. Some vile, hollow-cheeked wraith with pustules swarming his face. Or perhaps a brute of monstrous girth, with blubbery breasts drooping down to his knees, the sweaty folds of his pendulous double chin rolling like the curds of rancid boar's milk.

But no. Kola Saai is quite easy on the eyes, if a little short for a man. He keeps his face clean shaven and his frizzy hair closely cropped. He's also fairly young for a headman; he can't be more than a decade older than Isa's seventeen years.

"A wonderful performance back there," he says. "Your knowledge of what goes on in the city's sewers is . . . enviable."

She suspects he's trying to rouse some kind of reaction from her. She tries not to give it to him, though it's incredibly hard to maintain her composure standing only a few feet from the man who took everything from her. "What do you want?"

"The answer to a simple question, Your Majesty: Why do you still cling to a crown you can no longer defend? It is futile."

At least he's direct. "You expect me to simply stand aside and let you have your way with my people? I think not."

"But I don't wish your people harm, Your Majesty. I'm only stepping in to fill a power vacuum that was torn into our society by the Royal Massacre." Kola Saai bows his head, tracing a solemn finger across his heart. "May the victims find peace on the Infinite Path."

Next to her, Dino and Ijiro repeat the gesture, perhaps without thought. She won't fault them—Kola Saai is a headman, after all—but she will not stand here and pretend that this man didn't murder her family. "There is no power vacuum," she says. "I am king."

Kola's sober expression melts into a crooked smile. "By what power do you make this claim? Your clan has no legion, and the Shirika, who granted your forefathers dominion over the other clans, have not recognized you. Meanwhile I carry their blessing as prince regent, and my clan has the most powerful legion in the kingdom. If that is not a power vacuum, then I'm afraid to say I do not know what is."

"I've been wondering how you managed to buy them off," Isa says. "Care to share?" It is extremely dangerous, even for a king, to accuse the

Shirika of corruption without evidence. But Isa didn't speak any names, so she has plausible deniability in her favor.

Kola's smile widens. "Be my wife, Isa. We would have such beautiful children, you and I, and we would rule the world as king and queen. There's no need for bloodshed."

Revulsion coils around Isa, but she lets her mask reveal no emotion. "Last I heard you already had a wife. A pretty young thing from the desert."

"Bah." Kola waves that away like it's a pesky little detail. "She's just a toy. You would be my first wife—my queen."

"Yes, except I wouldn't have any legitimate power because you want my mask destroyed."

The Crocodile stares at her mask with a hungry look in his eyes. "The Shirika cannot crown me so long as that mask exists. You know this."

"I do," Isa admits. "I also know that this mask is the most important symbol of my clan. Without it I cannot claim to represent them. We would become a clan with neither legion nor representative in the Mkutano. We would be at the complete mercy of all the other headmen and their whims."

"Another mask can be made if you're that attached to it," Kola says, like he thinks she might actually be that foolish or superficial. These masks are said to have been forged of gold that came from the moon itself; they can never be replaced.

Isa refrains from reacting to his condescension. "And what of my people? What will happen to them when you disband the Sentinels? Do you think the interclan hatreds you've stoked will just disappear? Who will defend them when the genocide begins? You said it yourself; my clan has no legion."

"Marry me, and my forces will step in to prevent any violence against your people."

"Or," Isa says, "you could just leave the Sentinels alone and let them do their job."

Kola feigns a sad smile. "The Sentinels will be disbanded, Your Majesty, one way or the other. They are a relic of a bygone age; it is time to let them go. Our sons and nephews cannot continue being your hostages." He glances briefly behind him, where the other headmen are talking in dispersed little groups. "You might have delayed the inevitable tonight, but that little trick you played won't work at the next Mkutano." A wicked gleam crosses his eyes. "Unless you choose to attend, of course."

The next Mkutano will be the first of the New Year and will therefore be held at the Summit, at the foot of the colossus. She would have to leave the temple's safety to be present. A veiled threat, though not a subtle one.

"You don't have much choice here, Your Majesty," Kola says. "I am giving you a way out, a way to save your people. Marry me, and I will ensure no Saire ever suffers ethnic violence. But the Sentinels cannot stand."

Fury boils in the pit of Isa's stomach. This man has taken her family. Now he wants to take her Sentinels, her crown, and her body. When she speaks, she makes sure her words are clear as a bell. "I'd sooner marry a devil-sent fiend."

To this, Kola Saai grins, showing that his teeth aren't entirely perfect—his canines are a little protuberant. "Observe true power." He turns to the headmen and shouts: "Your Highnesses. You are all invited to welcome the New Year's Comet at the Summit next Tensday night. I expect all of you to attend in person."

The headmen grumble, but none of them dare refuse the command.

Kola Saai turns back to Isa, his grin triumphant. "You are invited, too, of course."

"Maybe some other time," Isa says. *When you're dead.*

"Very well, then." He gives a gracious bow. "It was lovely to see you, Your Majesty. Until next time."

As he walks away, Isa glares at his back, feeling angry at herself and at how impotent she is. She is king, and yet she's powerless to mete out justice to her family's murderer. He should not be drawing breath while the ashes of her family litter the earth.

"One day I will kill that man," she whispers.

"Yeah. He's an asshole." Next to her, Dino places a gentle arm on hers. "Come, Your Majesty. Let's get out of here."

She reclaims her composure, considering the two warriors next to her. "Will you not speak to your fathers?"

They both shake their heads, Ijiro more forcefully than Dino. "No need," Ijiro says.

Dino shrugs. "I'll speak to him when he comes to the city for the New Year's Feast. Right now we should get you out of here."

She gives him a smile, grateful and relieved that she can still call him a friend, that she has not lost his respect. She feels like she's fumbling her way through the dark, but at least she's not making a mess of everything. It gives her hope.

After a deep breath she wills her mask to obey and whisks the three of them back to the temple.

PART 6

MUSALODI
*
ILAPARA
*
KELAFELO
*
THE MAIDSERVANT
*
ISA

Void craft—magic of space and time

Harnessing the moon's essence to exploit the many facets of the metadimension. The most versatile craft, though by far the least practiced. Kinetic barriers, telekinesis, shape-shifting, clairvoyance, teleportation, long-distance telepathy: all are possible through the Void. However, because of the vast differences in how they each use the converted arcane energy, specialization is required.

—excerpt from Kelafelo's notes

"Aba says I'm wise for my age but too curious for my own good. I think he's disappointed in me. Maybe we should stop with the lessons."

"But my child, don't you see? If you are wise, then you must be curious as well, for wisdom without curiosity is stagnant. It is curiosity that drives the explorer deeper into the abyss, where her wisdom is expanded once she sees what dwells there."

"What is the abyss, Aago?"

"It is everything we don't know, and it is larger than we can ever comprehend. But with wisdom and curiosity, we can make it that much smaller."

34: Musalodi

Lake Zivatuanu

A kiss like fire on his lips. A pair of the brownest eyes. A wicked smile. Strong arms pinning him down and a gentle nibble on his neck, teeth against skin, laughter like a feather tickling his ear. He arches his spine, breathless from the movement and the exquisite pressure, and in his core an electric heat builds. He doesn't know what it would feel like exactly, but in the quiet hours of dawn, when the possibilities of the day ahead still hang in the balance, Salo allows himself to imagine. Perhaps it would hurt at first, but then it would become . . . then it would feel . . .

Cold. Suffocating. Salo opens his eyes and takes an instinctive breath only for a torrent of water to pour into his mouth. He chokes, because somehow, inexplicably, he is now *underwater*. He tries to remember how he got here and sees images of an avian ship, of falling asleep on its main deck while he sailed across the longest lake in the world. Was there an accident? Did the ship sink?

Am I going to die here?

He thrashes violently, his lungs drowning in the water. The lake's cold embrace surrounds him on all sides, and it chokes him until he dies, or at least he thinks he dies, because for some reason his need for breath begins to subside, until he stops needing to breathe at all.

He blinks, ceasing his flailing. The water is cold and impenetrably dark, but a shimmer of dawn light dances on the surface above. He looks up and sees a looming shadow floating somewhere not far away. *The ship!*

But before he can swim up to his salvation, a presence reaches up from far, *far* below and coils around his shards. With it comes a great sense of age that presses down on his mind, along with the uneasy feeling that this presence has a message for him, a pivotal message he *needs* to see before the first sun crests the horizon and seals the day. The presence grows and becomes irresistible, snaking up his spine, begging him for permission to use his shards, to show him something. So he lets it, and he feels like he has touched electricity.

The skies above him ignite with red lightning. He looks up through the shimmer of the surface and sees within the lightning the contours of a great bird with its wings outstretched in flight. They extend from one edge of the sky to the other, dwarfing the world with their astonishing size, and when the bird looks down at him and he sees into its eyes, he immediately knows that what he is looking at is a sliver of the long-forgotten past and yet another affirmation that there are things far greater than he in this world.

The Lightning Bird of Lake Zivatuanu.

He was the Great Impundulu, king of a world whose people feared and worshipped him, and his story unfolds around Salo as brilliant mirages that swim in the water like memories, a story Salo both sees and feels as if he were there.

His essence was hedonism. He feasted on the blood of his enemies and seduced many women and men. His was an age of boundless wealth and hope, of grand cities and immortal empires, and though his domain was vast and splendid, it was but one of a multitude scattered across a milky, starry expanse.

From his throne he witnessed the turn of millennia and the birth and death of stars. He watched mountains rise from oceans and continents sink beneath the waves. He thought his rule would see no end, not until every soul to have ever lived had ventured into the infinity beyond the gates of heaven.

But then the extinctions began. A corruption rose from a far-flung arm of the milky expanse, determined to destroy the gates of heaven, and it waged a war unlike any ever fought, a war of shooting lights and fireflies zipping across empty black skies, stars blinking out of the cosmos in cataclysmic explosions. Death and loss on an untold scale, and the Impundulu's domain was not spared.

Helplessly, he witnessed its destruction, how his people were corrupted into vile parodies of what they once had been. He could not bear the sight, so when the chance came to escape, he took it.

He joined an immense convoy, a gathering of survivors who took the gates of heaven with them and fled toward a great princess of the stars, in whose arms they hoped to find refuge. But there were traitors in their midst, and their plans were given away.

The Great War resumed when the corruption gave chase, but this time there would be no winners. Curses were cast and Veils erected, and in the aftermath, the Great War was forgotten, and so was the Impundulu. Now he roams this lake restlessly, waiting to deliver a message no one can ever understand.

The visions in the water around Salo begin to cycle through different landscapes. A city in the jungle, where a red beacon flashes high above a citadel. Another city, this one preserved beneath glass domes and towers, sitting on the ocean floor. A truncated pyramid half-buried in the desert.

Then the visions hurtle up, up, up to the rock clusters in low orbit around the world, onward to Ama Vaziishe, pausing to look down at the blue-and-green marble the Yerezi call Meza, onward to the Morning Star, then the dancing suns, then the asteroids, then the four giant worlds of the deep black, and finally stop at the Star of Vigilance, also known as the fastest-moving object in the heavens, or the comet that marks the New Year when it slingshots around the world in a streak of blue fire.

It's a sleek pebble wrapped in a smoky shroud of ice, bright blue against the deep black like cobalt, or like a shard of the high summer skies, or like a blue flower on a quilt, blue like lapis lazuli. Salo wonders at it for several heartbeats before the bewildering visions wink out. In the ensuing darkness a voice reaches out to him from the lake's deepest crevice and says: *Listen, for the Veil shall be weakened until the rising of the second sun. Only those who remember the gifts given to them shall live to see its first ray.*

Then all goes silent. The presence retreats, and in the skies above him the red lightning fizzles and disappears.

Something is different, though. A vein of power has opened in his shards, a path that was previously inaccessible to him. He runs a little essence through it to probe its nature and is surprised when his Axiom responds not with Storm craft but with a different arcane energy altogether. Whatever it is, it makes him shiver like he's standing at the edge of an abyss, or maybe like there's an alternate dimension just out of focus, and if he tilts his gaze just so or leans a little closer, he'll see it.

He needs no one to tell him that this is his first taste of Void craft.

Even more, a cache of information now tickles the back of his mind, like a word on the tip of his tongue. He concentrates and is almost overwhelmed by the answering surge of cipher prose that floods his thoughts without warning.

A spell. An immense array of prose that marries Storm and Void craft to produce powerful lightning barriers. Such a thing would have taken him decades to compose on his own and months to learn from a spell book, but its secrets unfold to him in the twinkling of an eye. An explosion of knowledge so intense and unexpected he's left reeling.

Something moves in the water beneath him. No, to his far left. Or is it his right? He can almost taste it. A sorcerous rancidness grasping for him, inching closer by the second. In a blind panic he floods his right arm with essence and sinks it into the witchwood ring on his middle finger, activating its charm.

A sunrise in the lake. Salo has to turn his gaze away as the ring's citrine stone *flares* to life with a dazzling golden glow. Rays of Mirror light explode away from it and penetrate the lake's gloom farther than the eye can see, giving him perfect vision and a frighteningly vivid sense of the sheer depths beneath him.

And of the horde of pale figures swimming rapidly toward him from all sides.

They are a multitude, a sphere of grasping talons and empty eye sockets closing in, and they bring with them an unpleasant tingle that offends his shards, like a fetid wound or an oily rot.

Black magic.

Acute terror gets Salo moving. He kicks upward with as much power as his limbs will allow, and when his head finally breaches the surface, he gasps in his first breath in minutes. His arms flail as he tries to keep himself afloat. A thick layer of mist has blanketed the lake, and he can't see through it. "Help!"

"There he is!"

"Salo! Salo, over here!"

He quickly reorients himself toward the voices and launches into a powerful stroke. Soon the stalled waterbird appears out of the mists just ahead, and he sees Tuk and Ilapara gawking down at him from the main deck. Mukuni has his paws on the gunwale and is watching, too, his neon-blue eyes beaming like torches in the mists.

"Help!"

"Grab the rope, Salo!" Tuk shouts.

He has already thrown the lifeline overboard. Salo reaches it in several strokes and immediately tries to use the rope to climb up the hull, but his feet can't find purchase. "Pull me up!" he shouts. "Pull me up!"

"We're on it. Come on, Ilapara."

Around him the mists thicken, and the unpleasant thrum inside his shards grows stronger. He feels tension in the rope, and soon it starts to lift him out of the water. He uses his legs the moment his toes can grip onto the hull, until finally Tuk and Ilapara manage to haul him over the bulwarks and back onto the main deck.

He sprawls on his side, trying to catch his breath, trying not to vomit. Isiniso, the white sun, has just risen, and its rays make the mists enshrouding the waterbird appear incandescent. His traveling companions stare down at him, both worried, though Tuk appears confused while Ilapara is clearly furious.

"What the devil were you thinking?" she says.

"What actually happened?" Tuk says.

Salo tries to explain, but his lungs won't let him.

"I was sleeping," Ilapara says, "then I opened my eyes to see this *idiot* standing right over there. And then he jumped! I mean, who does that?"

"Danger!" Salo finally rasps, getting up to his hands and knees. "We're in danger! They're coming!"

"What's coming, Salo?" Tuk says, even more confused now.

"The . . . the things in the water. Look!"

At last they take their eyes off him and notice the shroud thickening around the ship. Tuk cranes his neck in a futile attempt to see better through it.

"I don't know about you, Ilapara," he says, "but I don't think this mist is a good thing."

"No kidding, Tuksaad." Somehow Ilapara has already found her spear. She turns her worried gaze toward the bow. "And what the devil happened to the sailors?"

"They weren't there when I woke up," Tuk says, then offers Salo a helping hand, his eyes blue and curious. "Were you communing with the Lightning Bird, perchance?"

Salo's hand trembles as he lets Tuk pull him up to his feet. "My staff. I need my staff."

"I'll get it for you," Ilapara says but stops before she goes too far. "Looks like Mukuni's already bringing it."

Indeed, the large cat pads over with the witchwood staff caught between his jaws. Salo could swear the cat's getting more autonomous by the day.

"Maybe you want to get behind us, Salo." Tuk's eyes are now pitch black as they settle on something in the mists. Salo sees it, too, a formless shadow drifting over the waters.

While he accepts his staff from Mukuni and moves as Tuk commanded, Ilapara grips her spear with both hands, stretching her neck muscles. "Any idea what we're facing here?"

"Not really," Salo says. "But I think we have to survive it until the second sunrise."

"You think, or you know?"

"It must be the test he needs to pass to prove himself worthy," Tuk says while he tracks the moving shadow. He clicks his tongue in a typically Yerezi expression of frustration. "I can't believe I missed your communion."

"They're here!" Salo shouts.

The first one appears on the aft deck. It coalesces from the white mists behind the vessel, nebulous at first but becoming more and more solid as it seeps onto the deck. Its skin is colorless, drawn taut over stringy limbs that mildly adhere to human proportions. Any pretense of humanity is further marred by the waterweeds mushrooming out of its bloated stomach and out of its head, as well as the fine gauze of white mist wafting around its form.

Salo has never seen such a creature before, but the fire that ignites in its empty eye sockets, bright as the white sun, is chillingly familiar. And there's no denying the Black magic emanating from it.

A tikoloshe, he realizes. Different in appearance from the ones that attacked his kraal—a creature of the water, not of the earth—but the power they draw from is the same.

Thoughtless panic makes him edge backward so he can put Tuk, Ilapara, and Mukuni between himself and the tikoloshe. The others stand their ground, their muscles tense and ready for anything.

"My goodness," Tuk breathes, watching the wraith with wide eyes. "Did you say there were *more* of these?"

The wraith springs forward with a limping gait that shouldn't be fast, and yet it closes the distance in a few strides, staggering toward them in a blur of mist and stringy limbs. Its growl is like a thousand bones breaking at once, its mouth a black horror of sharp, rotted teeth.

"Get behind me!" Ilapara is the first to move. She steps forward to meet the wraith with the cutting edge of her pole arm, swinging it in a wide arc.

The tikoloshe ducks, showing surprising speed, and Salo's heart stops beating for a terrifying moment. But Ilapara isn't cowed; she presses her advantage, seeking the creature's skull with her spearpoint. It lurches backward, but only to evade, because the next instant it's lunging at her with a clawed hand. Salo doesn't know how she does it, how she manages to move fast enough to sidestep such a lightning-quick blow, or how evasion quickly becomes counterattack, but somehow she's spinning on her feet to cut the thing down in a wide diagonal slash. Bones snap at the blow and explode into white mist, then dissipate into nothingness.

More shadows begin to coalesce all around the vessel, and a host of unnatural eyes starts to flicker in the mists like fireflies. Two wraiths lunge from the port side with open talons; Tuk barely has time to duck before they fly over him, landing on the deck just behind him.

"Tuk!" Salo shouts. "Watch out!"

Tuk's response is instant: the golden rings on his fingers flash like moonlight, and he pulls two blades *straight out of thin air*. They materialize in his hands in a brilliant shimmer, two finely crafted swords of a radiant golden metal, each with a single sharp edge. Salo recalls seeing such a blade in Seresa, though it was longer than either of these.

The delicate engravings on each flash with red lightning just as he ducks a swipe destined for his head. He leaves twin echoes of red light in the air as he retaliates, hacking into one of the tikoloshe with well-timed blows to the neck and head. His victim is still crumbling to white mist when he neatly dodges a sweeping attack from the second wraith; he swings his blade in a mesmerizing arc to decapitate this new enemy—even while the point of the other blade streaks toward a third tikoloshe's rib cage.

To Salo's horror, more and more of the things have made it onto the deck. They keep coming from the aft sections of the vessel, where the rigging and netting aren't dense enough to prove an obstacle to boarding.

Like the coward he knows he is, Salo backs farther and farther toward the bow, selfishly keeping Mukuni's growling form in front of him while Tuk and Ilapara fight for their lives.

And by Ama, fight they do.

Tuk's swift and relentless movements remind Salo of a three-eyed suricate of the southern savannas: small but quick, tenacious, and stupidly brave. The water wraiths slash at him like angry vipers, but he weaves his form among them with deft footwork, answering their lunges with quick one-twos, cutting through skulls, femurs, ribs, and backbones with his arcane swords.

Next to him Ilapara is like a dancer with her spear, and it baffles Salo that she can move as fast as she does when she carries no blessing in her bones. A ray of the risen sun pierces through the mists and glances off her silvery breastplate as she pivots to chop down a tikoloshe from skull to rib cage. It bursts into a cloud of mist, but more wraiths press toward her.

Salo holds on to his staff with a trembling hand, shamed by the bravery of his companions. *Get a grip! They can't keep fighting like this. You heard what the Lightning Bird said: use the gift he gave you to save yourself and everyone else.*

He slaps his face several times to wake himself up from his paralysis. Tuk and Ilapara are here because of him; they deserve better than a coward who won't even try to defend them.

The staff in his hands is like a lens; he directs his scattered thoughts into it, and they come out more focused. Only then does he probe his mammoth new spell. Nothing at all like his other spell of Storm craft, which he can cast instinctively, without prior calibration. This spell requires that he understand the exact nature of the lightning barrier he wishes to summon: how much space to bend, what shape to bend it into, how much lightning—a thousand other such parameters. In fact, it isn't so much a spell as a framework for *designing* spells; once he knows the parameters of the barrier he wishes to conjure, he could cast it at will just like any other spell.

But he's never reached into the Void before, and right now he feels like a child dipping his toes into a vast ocean. Surely he isn't expected to figure out how to use it to conjure space-bending barriers in the heat of battle? And surely he isn't expected to then electrify said barriers with lightning, is he? It would take him hours at least to come up with anything even remotely practical.

By Ama, we're going to die here.

Tuk spins away to evade the swipe of a claw even as he cuts into the clavicle of another wraith, his blade shattering bone and cutting through flesh across the chest. His other blade is already coming up to part yet another wraith from its head even before the first has crumbled to mist. Ilapara's red veil swells with the wind as she swivels yet again, the point of her weapon arcing through the air like a sliver of light. Two tikoloshe lose their heads in a single strike, only for more to take their place.

One of them slips past her and lurches toward the bow. Black leeches cling to its pallid skin, and the weeds boiling out of its stomach are almost long enough to touch its knees. The deck trembles as Mukuni roars and pounces, batting the wraith into the ship's netting with a fierce metal paw. But then another comes at him, and then another, and another. He tears them down with his teeth and paws and sweeps them away with his powerful tail. And still they keep coming.

Something moves behind Salo, and he looks. A tikoloshe with white fire in its eyes has slipped through the opening in the netting above the bowsprit. Salo's nostrils catch the unholy fetor wafting away from it, and he almost gags.

Tuk shouts his name in the background, but he barely hears the call. Without thinking, he fills his shards with essence and unleashes Storm craft into his surroundings, commanding the winds to obey him. But the magic curves away from the wraith, and the winds blow harmlessly around it, like it's cocooned in a bubble of space where the laws of nature will not obey Salo. Its white-hot gaze glows brighter as it moves closer, and Salo could swear the thing smiles at him.

He's not sure what comes over him—maybe he suddenly remembers that he has trained with spears and sticks before—but when the wraith gets close enough, he grips his witchwood staff with both hands and thrusts its bottom end with all his strength. He feels resistance, but the staff breaks into an eye socket and punches through something soft. The next thing he knows, he's standing in front of a haze of white mist.

"Salo!" Tuk shouts somewhere behind him. "Salo, are you all right?"

Wide eyed and terrified, Salo turns around in time to see Tuk pay for his moment of lapsed concentration. The young man cries out in pain as a tikoloshe catches him in the right arm with a claw, ripping a long gash that instantly pearls blood. He retaliates with a decapitating move and lets out a string of curses.

"We're not going to last much longer!" Ilapara shouts next to him. "There are too many of these damned things!"

Salo knows she's right. He can see a myriad of torch-like eyes drifting in the mists, slowly closing in on the vessel. But how the devil is he supposed to use his new spell to fend them off? The most useful barrier he can design at a moment's notice is nothing but a small and simple wafer-thin geometric shape, and that wouldn't even work as a protective shield unless . . .

Unless . . .

"I've got an idea!" he shouts as inspiration hits him like a lightning bolt. "Hold on just a while longer!"

Neither Tuk nor Ilapara has enough breath to reply, occupied as they are with stemming the tide of tikoloshe. Salo sinks his mind into his staff and lenses himself into focus. His thoughts accelerate. He awakens his talisman, closing his eyes to better interface telepathically with its high-speed core. Then he begins to string ciphers together faster than he has ever done in his life.

35: Ilapara

Lake Zivatuanu

Ilapara had heard that facing a Primeval Spirit entailed an element of danger. She'd heard that many a mystic who set forth to commune with one never returned.

But she did not know that it would be *this* dangerous.

Her aerosteel spear is a streak of silver in the air around her. The speed in her bones is a reserve she has nearly depleted, and yet she keeps pushing herself, diverting all her body's resources until the world closes in around her and all she can see and hear are the tikoloshe.

Tuksaad is a swiftly moving blur somewhere nearby. They have never fought together, but their bodies move in sync; he seems to know where she will strike, and she is able to read his cues even without looking at him. Tikoloshe fall to their blades one after the other.

But there is just no end to them.

She casts a fleeting glance at Salo and sees him standing in the dwindling pocket of safety they have carved for him, one hand wrapped tightly around his staff, the other raised. Magic is swirling away from the raised arm in a luminous grid, and the look on his face is pure concentration. *Whatever you're doing*, Ilapara prays, *do it quick.*

She begins to tire. Her spear grows heavy in her hands. Its charm of Storm craft has all but expended itself, and the red sparks that sputter along the blade are now largely harmless. She mistimes a swing, loses her footing, and rights herself in time to see a claw slashing toward her face. Her reflexes give her enough speed to dodge, but she puts too much into it and winds up falling on her back, hitting her head hard on the deck.

"Ilapara!"

While the skies spin above her, a group of wraiths gathers to look down at her, like they know she's finished. Her spear has rattled somewhere out of reach, so she is helpless as one of them raises its talons.

"Ilapara!"

I have given my all, she tells herself, bracing for what's coming.

A storm of feathers *erupts* onto the deck from somewhere above, sending a score of tikoloshe flying off in a shock wave. It should blast her away, too, but all she feels is a light prickling all over her skin. *Magic.*

When she lifts her head to look into the heart of the feathers—ravens, she realizes—she glimpses the faint outline of a young woman wielding knives that pulse visibly with shadows. As she watches, one of those knives whirls away from the stranger's hand and impales a tikoloshe across the deck right between its eye sockets. Another blade materializes in that same hand not a heartbeat later, and the stranger pivots to hew a second wraith's skull in half. Pale beads and red steel glitter in the maelstrom as she spins from one tikoloshe to another almost faster than Ilapara can track her, leaving only a trail of dissipating mist.

An Asazi.

For a moment, Ilapara isn't sure whether to be relieved or concerned. But she doesn't let that paralyze her for too long; the Asazi has given them some breathing room, and that's all that matters.

Drawing from a new fount of energy, Ilapara picks herself up from the deck and finds her spear before rejoining the battle with renewed zeal. Out of the corner of her eye she sees Tuk decapitating a wraith with his left blade. He looks pale now, and his right side is drenched in blood from a frightful wound, but he's still fighting with the viciousness of a red mamba. The deck shudders as the totem roars behind him, his metal claws slicing left and right with enough force to snap tree trunks. She thrusts her spear into a grinning skull and is satisfied to see it crumble into mist. They fight and fight and fight some more, until Ilapara starts to feel like her limbs are coming out of their sockets.

Only as the tide of tikoloshe starts to ebb does she notice the change in her surroundings: a barrier has slowly taken shape around the waterbird, visible only because of the arcs of crimson lightning that briefly and repeatedly spread along sections of its surface in tessellated hexagons. Like the barrier was built one invisible hexagon at a time, upward from the bottom of the hull, bulging outward to encompass the wing structures, and then curving inward high above the deck. The hexagons are all about a foot in width and are visible only when currents of electricity throb down their edges.

By Ama, he's casting a ward the size of a building.

She looks up just as the structure closes above them into a protective dome encompassing the entire vessel. It pulses regularly with currents that shimmer across its surface. A wraith caught outside claws at the ward and is instantly electrocuted, bursting into mist. More wraiths perish to the ward, sending off sparks of lightning every time they strike it.

Ilapara puts them out of her mind and moves to finish off the few tikoloshe caught within the ward. With Tuk, Mukuni, and the Asazi helping, it's not long before the deck is clear and they're all panting and staring at each other. Staring and panting.

The Asazi relinquishes her ravens and becomes corporeal, but she holds on to her Void weapons. Her pale beads and kitenges weave down her body in a manner that accentuates more than it clothes. She is dark skinned and bald, pretty like Asazi often are. A calculating gleam shows in her eyes as she watches Tuk, the totem, and then Ilapara.

Ilapara has never gotten along with Asazi, never liked their cunning and aloofly academic ways or their proclivity for deception, and she can tell straightaway that this Asazi fits that mold perfectly. For one thing, she's certain she's seen those ravens of hers stalking them several times over the last few days.

She holds her spear tightly in her hands, ready to move at the slightest provocation.

Tuk flashes the Asazi a grin, and the Asazi smiles back.

"Everything all right back there, Salo?" he says without ever glancing away from her. His right arm is bleeding, but Ilapara has seen him fight; she knows how quickly he could move if it became necessary.

The Asazi remains still, though she doesn't take her eyes off Tuk and Ilapara.

"Salo?" Tuk says again.

"I'm fine," comes Salo's reply. "I just need to concentrate if this ward is going to stay up." He's leaning on his staff with both hands, frowning in concentration. Ilapara suspects his eyes are closed behind his spectacles as he battles to repair the patterns of his ward faster than the wraiths can destroy them with their pummeling.

"We have an uninvited guest, if you haven't noticed," Tuk says, which makes the Asazi smile again.

"Oh, I noticed."

Tuk twists the shiny blades in his hands as he eyes the Asazi's knives. "It's just that I'd like to know if this is going to be another fight."

"Look, I need silence right now," Salo says. "Distract me, and we might all end up dead."

Tuk obeys, and the three continue to watch each other, at least until the Asazi seems to get bored and slowly starts to wander the deck, admiring Salo's ward. Beyond it the wraiths are a sea of pale limbs and waterweeds clamoring to break through, even though they keep bursting into mist every time they touch the ward.

Mindless creatures.

Even so, the ward is quite unusual to Ilapara. A physical barrier, so there must be space-bending magic involved, but the lightning means there's Storm craft as well. But how is Salo doing this so soon after his awakening? Shouldn't he be struggling with the most basic spells?

A flash as golden light washes across the world beyond the dome. The fog rapidly burns away, taking the horde of tikoloshe with it, and what was once an impenetrable blanket of mist gives way to a glittering lake that stretches toward an unbroken line of dense jungle.

"The second sunrise," Tuk says, glancing east, where Ishungu, the yellow sun, has just peeked over the horizon. The crescent moon is a thin red sliver not far above it. "Does that mean it's finally over?"

"Dear Ama, yes." Salo relinquishes his ward and puts more weight onto his staff, sighing with relief. His shards are still pulsing furiously with magic, though. "Is everyone all right?"

"Just a scratch," says Tuk.

"Do you know this Asazi?" Ilapara says, still watching the stranger.

"I do, actually." Salo straightens and drifts closer. He grimaces at the sight of Tuk's injury. "I'll need to dress that, Tuk. You might have been poisoned."

"I'm not worried about it." Tuk nods at the Asazi. "I'm worried about her."

The Asazi finally decides to break her silence. "I don't think I've ever heard more fluent Sirezi coming from a foreigner. That makes you very interesting."

"Interesting people make the world go round," Tuk says with a smile. His eyes, though, are still gloomy. "You say you know her, Salo?"

"Yes, so everyone can calm down." Salo puts himself in front of the Asazi with a raised palm. "I don't think she means us harm. She wouldn't have helped us if she did." He raises an eyebrow in the Asazi's direction. "Am I wrong?"

In answer, the Asazi returns her knives to the Void and clasps her hands demurely in front of her. "It is as you say, Yerezi-kin."

With those knives out of view, Ilapara allows herself to relax a little. Not that she thinks the Asazi means Salo harm, but something about her presence here smells wrong.

Salo seems to study the girl like he's thinking the same thing. "Tell me, Si Asazi, why are you spying on me?"

The Asazi raises a well-groomed eyebrow. "What makes you think I'm a spy?"

Ilapara cuts in before he can answer. "The fact that your ravens have been tailing us from Seresa, for starters." She looks curiously at Salo. "Doesn't the queen have a spell like that?"

"She does, in fact," he says, still staring at the Asazi. "And I'd recognize it anywhere. Not to sound ungrateful that you stepped in when you did, but did you really think you could follow me all the way up here without me noticing?"

The Asazi's sharp eyes briefly peer down at his arms, where his shards won't stop dancing with lights. A hint of *something* shimmers in her gaze, but she doesn't betray her secrets. "Maybe I let you notice me."

"Doubtful. If AmaYerezi wanted me to know about you, I think she'd have told me."

"Then why do you think I'm here?"

"She probably told you to reveal yourself only when necessary. My near death was probably a necessary condition. Clearly she wants me to get to Yonte Saire. But that begs the question . . . why didn't she just tell me about you? More to the point, why didn't she just send me with the protection I needed? Why all the secrecy?"

"Why do you think?"

"I think you're avoiding the question," he says, "but I'll take a guess. Either she mistrusts me, or there's something I haven't been told. Which one is it?"

Ilapara exchanges glances with Tuk, and he seems just as intrigued as she is. *Why does Salo think the queen would want to hide something from him? What's really going on here?*

"Do you think I'd tell you if I knew?" the Asazi says with a synthetic smile.

"I'd hope so," Salo replies. "The more I know, the better I'll do the job she sent me to do."

"Which is what, exactly?" Ilapara says, deciding she can't deny her curiosity. "I thought you were walking the Bloodway, but now it sounds like you have another agenda."

"You know everything you need to know," the Asazi says, and Ilapara gets the feeling those words are meant for her too. She looks at Salo, expecting an answer to her question, but he stares at the Asazi for a beat and then nods.

"I see. So what happens now? Do you disappear and stalk me from the Void, pretend I don't know you're there?"

"We all have our roles to play, don't we?"

"A suggestion, then," he says. "You want to spy on me, and I don't want a shadow, so why don't you just . . . travel with me? Stop being so mysterious. That way you can watch me as much as you want to, and I don't have to get nervous about it."

The Asazi's eyes glimmer with smothered laughter. "Knowing I'm watching you won't make you nervous?"

"Oh, it will," Salo admits, "but if you're with me, then I can watch you too. It's the unknowns I dislike."

The idea of traveling with the Asazi goes wrongly down Ilapara's throat. "Are you sure you want her with us?" she says to Salo, then looks the Asazi over with suspicious eyes. "I mean, how much can you really trust her? She's the queen's Asazi, for Ama's sake. An assassin to boot. Probably as devious as they come."

This only seems to amuse the Asazi. "Quite the team you've assembled. A she-warrior and an outworlder. I must say they have proven rather capable, but I wonder what your chief and clanspeople would make of them."

"Don't forget the big cat," Ilapara says, moving her weapon from one hand to the other. "And call me a she-warrior one more time, and I'll make you eat this spear."

"Wait, how do you know I'm an outworlder?" Tuk says.

Salo quickly intervenes. "I was given discretion to find my own traveling companions, Si Asazi. In fact, I was forced to do so. No one has any right to be upset about who I've chosen."

"Of course," the Asazi says. "I meant no offense."

"That's good to know. Now what will it be? I have nothing against you for doing your mystic's bidding, even if it's spying on me, but I'd rather you did your spying where I can keep an eye on you."

"And if I refuse?"

Salo smiles without humor. "That is your prerogative, of course. But remember: I wield the Void now. I may lack experience with it, but eventually I'll find ways of making your job very difficult. If you come with me, however, I'll cooperate; then we can both do our jobs quickly and return home. What do you say?"

Schemes and machinations glitter behind the Asazi's eyes as she considers the offer, but then she shrugs, like it all means nothing to her. "All right. I'll come with you." And then her voice sharpens. "So long as you remember that I'm not one of your guardians. I am an Asazi apprenticed—"

"Yes, yes, I know how this goes," Salo says. "You're an Asazi apprenticed to the queen, and you won't stoop so low as to serve one such as me, and so on and so forth. Let's pretend you've said all of that so we can get to patching our wounds." Salo shoots a worried look toward the ship's bow. "And looking for the sailors, who I think are hiding somewhere belowdecks."

This makes the Asazi chuckle a little. "As you wish, Yerezi-kin."

"Ah, a sense of humor," Tuk says, listing his head appraisingly. "I suppose I can learn to like her."

"You better watch yourself, Asazi," Ilapara tells the young woman. "Because I'll be watching you."

The Asazi shrugs again. "I expect no less from a pilgrim's guardian."

That response annoys Ilapara, but she bites her tongue.

"Now that we've cleared that up," Salo says with fake cheer, "allow me to formally introduce you to the team, Si Asazi." He goes on to do exactly that, and then he says, "As for me, you can call me Salo. And you are Si Alinata, are you not? I remember you from my awakening. You were one of the queen's honor guards."

"The most riveting awakening I have ever attended," she tells him. "Alinata is fine. You outrank me, after all."

"Old habits," Salo says. "All right, then. Welcome to the team, Alinata. Even though you're a spy and you're not really part of it. But welcome anyway."

The Asazi's presence will not be easy to tolerate, but Ilapara vows right then not to let it unsettle her.

But that doesn't mean I should let my guard down, she tells herself. *After all, if the queen's intentions are pure, why would she send an assassin to spy on us?*

36: Kelafelo

Akanwa is what she names the Faraswa girl. It means "she who was found" in Izumadi and is typically reserved for children abandoned when they are still too young to speak their own names.

Granted, the girl has seen six comets, so if she once had a name, it's likely she knows it, but a slave takes whatever name their new master gives to them, and the girl knows to accept hers without question.

In the first weeks after Akanwa's arrival, Kelafelo treats her as the Anchorite commanded. She makes sure the girl is fed and bathed. She sleeps next to her every night. She even grows to tolerate her quiet, lamblike presence and the way she's always looking down at her fidgeting hands. She is outwardly gentle and kindly with the slave girl, but deep in her heart she allows no true affection to bloom, because no one will ever replace her daughter.

Urura was a spirited and curious soul, always running her hands over everything as if she could understand the world only if she touched it. Kelafelo even had to scold her on several occasions for attempting to touch the embers of a crackling fire. She was everything good in Kelafelo's universe, the source of her joy, her purpose for living.

But Akanwa . . . the poor girl is almost a nonentity, quiet and unobtrusive to a fault, as if someone beat into her the compulsion to leave as little a footprint in the universe as possible. She plays no games, asks no questions, never speaks unless directly spoken to, and even then replies only with one-word answers.

She quietly shadows Kelafelo as she performs her chores, but not so close as to loom. When Kelafelo sits outside the hut with quills, gourds of ink, and sheaves of parchment, outlining her Axiom in carefully arranged ciphers, Akanwa lurks inconspicuously in the background. Kelafelo almost worries that the girl will trip and fall into some crevice in the fabric of space and disappear entirely.

Months after her arrival, on a rainy afternoon, Kelafelo finally glimpses the hint of a person buried somewhere inside the girl.

The Anchorite has left for the newly revived village of Namato to offer her healing services—as she used to do before the attack—and Kelafelo is seated by the table beneath the south-facing window, reading through one of the Anchorite's volumes of sorcery. She lifts her gaze and notices the girl sitting cross-legged by the door, watching as fat raindrops burst on the compound's barren earth.

Something in her crimson eyes catches Kelafelo's attention, a certain yearning she's never seen there before, as if the rain has taken the girl to some distant memory from a life she knows she'll never see again. That look breaks Kelafelo's heart.

"Do you want to go outside?" she says before she can think to leave things be.

The girl immediately withdraws into herself like a snail retreating into its shell, and whatever light Kelafelo saw dancing in her eyes snuffs itself out. Patent fear replaces it, like the girl thinks she's been caught doing something she shouldn't have been. "No," she says, shaking her head with force.

Kelafelo closes the book she was reading. "It's all right if you do. I used to dance in the rain as a child myself. It can be a lot of fun."

Akanwa's gaze slides back outside, a hint of the yearning returning to her eyes.

That decides things for Kelafelo. She stands up from the table. "Come. I'll go with you."

The girl's eyes widen. "But Mamakuru!" The Anchorite barely acknowledges the girl's existence; Akanwa is still terrified of her—understandably so, Kelafelo would say.

She puts on a reassuring smile. "Mamakuru isn't here, is she?" Kelafelo holds out her hand. "Come, before the rains decide to stop."

Akanwa regards the hand like it might turn into a viper and lunge, but slowly, she reaches out and takes it, and then together they go outside and let the rain soak them to the skin.

There is no drastic change in the girl's behavior, no sudden epiphany that makes her less timid, but in the rain the thick wall she hides behind cracks somewhat, and she even seems on the verge of smiling, though she doesn't quite get there. Her hands wander to her wet veil like she wants to lift it off her hair, but she hesitates.

"You don't have to wear it if you don't like it," Kelafelo says, and to prove her point she takes off her own patterned veil and lets her dreadlocks free. She laughs and tilts her head toward the rainy skies, checking herself when she realizes that this is the first time she's laughed since she lost everything.

Akanwa lifts her turquoise veil off her head, letting her hair fall in luxuriant curls. Were it not for the metallic hornlike appendages curling out of her temples, which shimmer now with raindrops, Kelafelo might have thought her pretty. As it is, they are too much of a reminder of the girl's otherness to simply ignore.

She almost changes her mind, however, when the girl finally lets herself smile as she spreads her hands to capture raindrops with her fingers. She sees something innocent in that smile, something pure, and so fragile Kelafelo knows she could crush it with a single harsh word, and it would never surface again.

In that moment, Kelafelo realizes something about herself: she will never love the girl, not like she did Urura. The part of her that could love—truly love—feels like a dead thing inside her chest, bloated and full of maggots, like her daughter's corpse on the day she finally had the strength to trek back to her old village and bury her. She will never love the girl, that much she knows, but she can certainly like her.

They stay together in the rain until it dies down, and from that day onward, caring for Akanwa is no longer a chore.

◆ ◆ ◆

She comes to discover that she is most comfortable with the branch of cipher prose dealing with Void craft. It intimidated her at first, but as she grapples with it, she comes to realize that the principles underpinning the craft are beautifully simple. Inevitably, this is where she decides to take her Axiom.

Despite the work she puts into the Axiom, however, the final result is never one she is satisfied with. For some reason she can't quite achieve a desirable rate of conversion. Her Axioms either rapidly convert a vanishingly thin stream of essence into Void craft or convert a thick stream at a dawdling pace. Neither type would allow her to perform the effortless spell casting she has seen the Anchorite perform on many occasions. She loses count of how many times she writes the last cipher of a new Axiom on a parchment only to throw its pages in the fire upon a thorough analysis. The task becomes a drain on her soul.

She doesn't allow herself to give up. She keeps wrestling with the problem, and only after many moons without a solution does she decide to approach the Anchorite for advice. She knows the old woman can't help her with the Axiom's specific architecture but wonders if there is something basic she's missing and if maybe the Anchorite can help her identify the problem.

She later wishes that she'd never asked.

"I was wondering when you'd decide to come to me." The Anchorite breathes out a cloud of smoke and shakes her head. She's smoking her calabash pipe beneath the knotted witchwood tree, watching Akanwa chase chickens around the compound. Kelafelo has seated herself on a mat in front of her with a quill and parchment in hand, in case she needs to take notes. "Why did it take you so long?" the Anchorite says.

"Devising an Axiom should be a lonely journey," Kelafelo says. "Isn't that what you said to me?"

The old woman grunts in contempt. "Don't go using my own words against me, young girl. I was beginning to grow impatient with you."

"I wanted to make sure I'd exhausted every option before approaching you, Mamakuru."

"And? Have you?"

Kelafelo looks down at the outline on the parchment. "I've tried everything I can think of, but I can't find a good balance between the flow speed and volume of conversion. I always have to sacrifice one for the other. It's almost as if . . ." Kelafelo tilts her head and taps her cheek with her quill.

"Yes?" the Anchorite prods her with obvious interest.

"I feel like there's a missing piece somehow, but I can't see it because I don't have the necessary framework to see it. Does that make sense?"

The Anchorite prolongs Kelafelo's suspense by dragging on her pipe, and when she exhales, a little smile lifts one side of her wrinkled face. "It makes perfect sense. You feel that way because there *is* something missing, and you *do* lack the necessary faculties to see it."

"But . . . why?"

"I once told you about spiritual insights of agony and how they enrich our understanding of Red magic, did I not? Well, my dear girl, you have reached the threshold of your spiritual insights. To achieve a higher level of understanding, you must subject yourself to more agony. Only then will your eyes be opened."

The first currents of discomfort roil in Kelafelo's belly, making her old scar throb. She knows of mystics who disfigure themselves in their search for power, some who gouge out their eyes, carve scars all over their bodies, or give themselves wounds that never heal. Is this what she must now do to herself?

Not long ago, she wouldn't have hesitated, but now the idea sends uneasy chills down her spine. "How far do I need to go?" she says, dreading the answer.

"A single brutal act of violence will do the job." The Anchorite speaks with such blatant callousness the air seems to freeze around her. She lifts an eyebrow upon seeing Kelafelo's startled look. "You thought I was going to ask you to mutilate yourself, didn't you?" She smiles, shaking her head. "No, dear girl. You've already suffered enough physical agony. The scar on your belly is proof of that. What you need now is to stain your soul so deeply the secrets of the moon will crack open right before your eyes. That is why you need your humanity; there has to be a soul to stain, otherwise no amount of agony will help you."

Kelafelo tries to remind herself that she came to this place for a reason, but right now that reason is hard to remember. "What sort of violence, Mamakuru?"

"The sort you would be incapable of perpetrating without help." The Anchorite's forehead creases with intent. "There is an elixir of Blood craft I will give you, born of the most powerful compulsion magic in existence. Before you drink it, you must think of the thing you wish to do but are incapable of doing because it is too heavy on your soul. Once you drink it, however, the elixir will take control of your body and compel you to do this thing anyway, and your mind will remain aware the entire time—this is important."

Kelafelo refrains from shivering. "But what will it make me do?"

"On the night of the full moon, you will sacrifice the Faraswa girl beneath the light of my Seal. Given how much you care for her, the act will agonize your soul so thoroughly no secret of the Void will remain hidden to you, and the Axiom you have been striving for will be yours."

For a full minute, Kelafelo sits there in silence, shocked, sickened, horrified by what she has heard. Then the horror mutates into a violent storm of anger that leaves her clutching her quill so tightly it breaks in half. "You heartless monster. This is why you bought her, isn't it? Why you had me grow attached to her? You knew what you'd ask of me."

The Anchorite gives her an ugly snarl. "I told you there would be a price to pay when you limped here with half your guts hanging out of your belly, didn't I? Well, the time for you to pay has come. But I don't see why you are so upset. This will ultimately benefit you more than it does me. You will add to my power through this sacrifice, but you will receive the greater gift."

Kelafelo knows she's not going to pay the Anchorite's price. She knows where that decision is going to take her, but she keeps it off her face. She has learned to hide her thoughts from the old woman, and she does not wish her to sense the half-formed plans already running through her mind. "I must think on this," she says. "You can't expect me to agree without thinking about such an act first."

The Anchorite gives a careless wave. "You'd be better served by not thinking about it at all, but be my guest. The full moon is two weeks away, in any event. You have until then to prepare yourself."

Without another word to the old mystic, Kelafelo rises from her mat, folds it, picks it up, and walks off. "Aka!"

"Yes, Mama?"

Akanwa has been running after the chickens all afternoon, and her bare feet are caked with dust. She's grown into her own over the months, and little by little she has carved herself a place in what remains of Kelafelo's heart. At the sound of her name, she stops running and beams at Kelafelo, clutching a wooden doll in her fidgety hands.

Kelafelo returns the girl's smile, wondering how she once struggled to see that she is beautiful. "Come, Aka. Let's warm some water for your bath."

"Okay. I'll get the firewood." And Akanwa bounces off merrily, wholly innocent of the evil that has been meticulously planned for her.

For the rest of the afternoon, Kelafelo is aware of the pair of milky eyes watching them from beneath the witchwood tree, but she pays no attention to them lest they see through her.

37: The Maidservant

Lake Zivatuanu

On a beach along the Zivatuanu's southeastern shores, the Maidservant quietly surveys what remains of the death squad she has just rescued from a heavily armed Tuanu patrol.

She was shadowing the Yerezi mystic's waterbird through the Void, matching, mile for mile, its progress deeper into the jungles of the Yontai, when she sensed a fierce battle raging southeast of her position. Upon drawing closer to investigate, she discovered that the death squad she'd sensed earlier, unlike the other groups who'd been pursuing the Yerezi boy, had not given up chase at the borderlands but had instead decided to follow him along the lake's eastern shore. A Tuanu patrol had intercepted them not long after.

Now they know why the other groups chose to turn back.

Before they were ambushed, they boasted one disciple and twenty men, each riding a giant kerit bear. The disciple is dead now, only a dozen of his men are still walking, and just one kerit came out unscathed. The rest are either dead or bleeding out on the beach.

By the red skulls on their faces, she knows the men are a squad of reavers—a militia pledged in service to the Dark Sun and currently under Sand Devil's command. Just the sight of them wearing those masks makes the Maidservant's blood boil with maddening anger, but she cools it with the knowledge that she has a greater aim to achieve. She is not here to kill them.

The stench of blood and offal swirls with the breeze. The lone unwounded kerit is feasting on a Tuanu corpse by the wash of waves on the sand while the surviving men nurse their wounds or finish off the animals too injured to be of further use.

The Maidservant picks her way across the bloodied beach and toward the squad's captain, who is at present kneeling next to a younger man lying supine on the sand. As she approaches, she notices the ghastly wound festering on the younger man's leg, wet with a black discharge. Given how he's shivering and drenched in sweat, she figures that whatever injured him was poisoned. He'll be dead inside of an hour.

"Captain," she says, coming to a stop nearby.

The captain raises his dirt-smeared face. He's taken off his mask, so she can clearly see the sorrow lining his heavy brow. He's holding the younger man's hands between his own like they're something precious, and there's a clear resemblance between them.

A father and son, most likely. Problematic. She wants the captain focused and useful.

"Those forsaken Tuanu used some kind of poisoned magic bow," the captain says in a gravelly voice. "One shot was enough to take down our beasts. If not for you, we'd all be dead."

And all she had to do was appear. The mystic-fearing Tuanu cowered into the jungles as soon as they saw her emerging from the Void in a chaotic vortex.

"Captain, you are alive because I have use for you," she says. "You serve me now. Understood?"

The captain's eyes fall to his shivering son, then come back up glistening with worry. "Yes, Maidservant. You are a chosen one of the Dark Sun, and we serve you in that capacity."

Not a very subtle way of saying: *We won't turn on our master for you even though you saved our lives.* Brave of him to say something she could easily take as an insult.

She chooses not to. "How many of your men are incapacitated?"

The captain searches the beach, his solemn gaze lingering on the bodies in red masks. "Five dead, three injured. My boy's the worst of them." He squeezes his son's hand when the young man starts coughing uncontrollably, and the Maidservant sees the spark of determination that comes alive in his eyes. "We'll send all three injured ahead on my beast. He's the only one they didn't hit. He'll get them home in time." The captain is about to get up when the Maidservant decides to douse that spark with ice-cold water.

"I'm afraid that won't do."

His voice hardens. "Why not?"

"We will leave the injured behind. I will take you, the surviving beast, and the men who can still fight. We will continue our pursuit of the Yerezi mystic through the Void."

His eyes widen with shock at first but quickly narrow in anger. "My son—"

"Is already dead, Captain," the Maidservant finishes. "The best you can do for him is end his suffering and go after the one who led you here. We have a mission, and it is pulling away from us as we speak. Can I count on you, or will you fail me and your lord?"

A war plays out in the captain's eyes, but he is a reaver, and he knows where his loyalties must lie. Eventually, the weight of resignation settles on his face, and he looks down at his son. His voice comes out like broken glass. "I am with you, Maidservant. Please give me a moment alone with my son."

Somewhere deep inside, a current of pity stirs, but she chokes it until it dies. "Very well," she says. "But we leave in five minutes. The Tuanu retreat was likely tactical. We need to be gone before they return with reinforcements." And then she walks toward the water to stare into the horizon.

Her thoughts have already left the beach and are many miles away, with the Yerezi boy. It'll be a risk to chase him deeper into the Yontai. The high mystics have coven acolytes spread across the kingdom, and one of them might detect her. Not to mention the boy's Void-wielding shadow, who she's certain is already aware of her.

She'll have to be cautious and patient. Bide her time.

"We are ready, Maidservant," comes a voice behind her. She turns around and sees the somber captain standing with his surviving men, the bloodlust still burning in their eyes despite their near brush with death—or perhaps because of it.

Something black and monstrous coils inside the Maidservant, a strong desire to shred these men into a red paste, but she diverts her hatred into her shards. They ignite with the moon's power, and she sends them all into the Void.

38: Isa

In a hallowed temple where rubies twinkle on every wall and gold gleams so abundantly as to be worthless, a king strides resolutely down a long hallway and knocks on a high priest's door.

She has worn one of her best garments—formfitting, strapless, and ivory as pearls, with delicate swirling patterns that shimmer like gold. Her hair has been plaited into thick braids interlaced with golden strands. An intricate gorget of colorful, concentrically arranged beads frames her face, which she has painted with the understated wickedness of a girl who knows things other girls do not.

She is a mortal king about to beg favor from a god, a young woman eager to take her destiny into her own hands, and she has tried her damned best to look the part.

The door opens to reveal Itani Faro's lanky form, dressed in a loose crimson boubou and soft slippers. With that smoking pipe pressed between his lips, he might have appeared benignly old, perhaps even grandfatherly, but the maze of scarified designs running across his face leaves no doubt as to what he truly is. It's also in his bearing and his dark, knowing eyes and the way they see past the material world to the truth hidden beneath.

She came here as a proud king, but the instant she looks into those eyes, she knows he sees her for what she truly is: a little girl, liar, pretender.

"My soul," she says to him. "I will offer you my soul if you help me banish the marks and end the clans."

A question has been plaguing her in her dreams of late: How can a game piece on a board ever claim to be powerful when it is but a slave to the hand that moves it? This morning she awoke with the answer: a game piece can never speak for itself, but a king can kneel before a god and beg for mercy.

The god before her gives her a hard, long look, then steps aside, gesturing into the room with his pipe. Suppressing a sigh of relief, Isa walks in and takes a moment to be surprised by her surroundings.

Instead of a barren chamber with ruby lights and impersonal golden ornamentation, the Arc's suite of rooms is rather cozy: warm crystal lamps like little drops of sunrise, Dulama rugs with thick piles, couches with plush upholstery, the sweet scent of incense coiling in the air. Not quite luxurious as much as it is comfortable. And surprisingly human.

She turns to face him and puts on a polite smile. "Your home is lovely, Your Worship."

The other six Faros have grand palaces in Skytown, but the Arc has lived in the Red Temple for as long as she can remember. These rooms are his home, and though she wasn't sure what she expected, this certainly wasn't it. *What does it mean that gods live as we do?*

"Take a seat, Your Majesty." The Arc motions her to the sofas, where he sits across from her and tortures her with a long silence while he smokes and stares at her. Finally he says, "Would you like something to drink?"

Isa clasps her hands together on her lap. She suddenly feels silly for dressing up so ostentatiously in these rather modest chambers. "I'm fine, Your Worship."

"I don't usually invite people in," he says. "Mostly because people don't usually come knocking."

She knows she should probably apologize, but what's done is done. "I wouldn't have come if I felt I had a choice."

"You would sacrifice eternity to save your people." Not a question. Not really. Simply an observation he's made, and if Itani Faro has seen it in her, then it must be true.

"Without hesitation, Your Worship."

"Then perhaps you are stronger than I thought."

Something cold wraps itself around her spine. "Will you accept my offer, then?"

"No."

The waterfall beneath them is a distant tumbling roar. For a second Isa wishes she could just hurl herself over the edge of the citadel and fall away from the world and all its worries. Then that thought turns to steel in her veins and becomes a searing question: *Why not?*

Why not risk everything right now, commit herself to this moment? And if she fails, she can at least say that she tried.

She rises to her feet, slowly. The Arc watches her, and she watches him right back. And slowly, she brings her knees to the floor, her hands pressed together in supplication. She, the King of Chains, the Great Elephant who straddles the center of the world and rules its beating heart, kneels on the floor and abases herself before a god. "You could be young again, Your Worship. I know you've done it before. I know it is why you have lived for so long. You could live longer still. Take my soul; help me help my people."

And what does the god do in the face of such a humble, desperate plea?

He laughs.

The Arc's hollow laugh fills the charmingly comfortable rooms, joining the tumbling waterfall to mock Isa for her foolishness, her sheer stupidity, that she could so openly accuse a Faro of partaking in such a revolting ritual.

She should know better. The things the Shirika do to prolong their lives might be open secrets, but no one, not even a king, should speak of them.

Isa's cheeks burn with shame, and her vision clouds over with tears.

"You are a brave woman, Your Majesty." And the tone of his voice says what he leaves unsaid: *I have killed many others for slights much less than this. You have no idea how close to death you came.* "But your offer is pointless."

"I understand."

"Because you will need your soul if this is going to work."

She looks up at him, confused. His eyes hold no malice but pleasant surprise.

"It seems I severely underestimated your resolve. Perhaps you are courageous enough to do what is necessary."

Tentatively, she dares to hope. "So . . . you will help me?"

"I will try," he says. "I have always wanted to help your people, Your Majesty. I just didn't think you could handle the responsibility, and I could not countenance forcing it upon you. But it is clear to me that I was mistaken." Setting his pipe on the low table between them, he rises to his feet and motions her to do the same. "Come. There is something I must show you."

Mechanically, detached from her reality, she does as she's told and follows him out the door.

What people call the Red Temple is actually a citadel with many buildings connected by a network of vaulted walkways. The true temple sits at the heart of the citadel, directly beneath the Ruby Paragon, and it is here that mystics come to commune with the Mother. As far as Isa knows, only mystics and votaries—folk who forsake their clans and dedicate their lives to the Mother—are allowed inside.

Which is why she stops when the Arc opens the temple's looming doors and walks in without a word.

He tosses back a questioning look when he notices she's not following.

"But Your Worship," she says. "I am unsanctified. I am neither mystic nor votary. I cannot walk through these doors."

The Arc smiles grimly. "I am the high priest of this temple, Your Majesty, and I say you are welcome. Now please follow me."

They say that death comes quickly to the unsanctified who linger in the Mother's presence, but Isa lacks the courage to disobey, so she runs a finger over her heart, mumbles a quick prayer, and steps gingerly across the threshold, following Itani Faro into the antechamber and down a dingy staircase.

They come to a floor whose high ceiling and walls of stone are tinged red by floating ruby lights caught in artistic wicker contraptions. Thick pillars and a low circular wall surround a pool of water several yards from the foot of the staircase. The Arc says nothing until they stop next to the pool. An eerie pink glow dances over the water, concealing its depths. A nervous shiver tells Isa it's probably much deeper than it looks.

"What do you know of the Covenant Diamond, Your Majesty?"

She pulls her gaze away from the pool, surprised by the unexpected question. "Only the stories I was told as a child, Your Worship. To become princes, eleven men sacrificed their kin to the Shirika—excuse me, to an ancient cabal of mystics." Isa looks away from the sorcerer. "They built a pyre so big it burned fiercely enough to compress everything into a single yellow diamond, and when all was said and done, their princedoms were sealed in blood. Is there any truth to the stories?"

If the Faro is offended by her slip of the tongue, there is no trace of disgust in his voice. "It is true that the Diamond was made from the ashes of the pyre, but that was many days after the fires were extinguished. But yes, the stories are unusually accurate given the fickle nature of legends."

Shock bleaches Isa's fear away, and she manages to meet his gaze again. "So the Covenant Diamond really exists? But . . . what is it, really? More importantly, *where* is it?"

"Both very important questions," the Arc says. "Possibly the two most important questions any KiYonte could ask. The Covenant Diamond holds the Blood curse that brands every child born to a KiYonte man with his clan mark. So long as the Diamond exists, the curse will carry on, and so will the marks."

"So the Diamond must be destroyed to get rid of the marks," Isa concludes.

"Precisely. Which brings us to your second question: Where is it? Let me ask *you* a question, Your Majesty: If you were a mystic and you were tasked with the Diamond's safekeeping, where would you put it?"

"Something so important . . ." Isa bites her lip while she thinks about it. "Somewhere no one can get to, perhaps even somewhere I myself couldn't get to once I put it there, in case I was later coerced into finding it."

The Arc offers her the ghost of an approving smile. "And that, Your Majesty, is precisely what happened. The young mystic who was given charge of the Diamond after its creation hid it in such a place as you've described, and you happen to be standing right next to it."

Isa's eyes fall to the water. "You mean this pool?"

"This isn't just a pool. This is a one-way portal to a chamber in the temple's innermost courtyard, a repository of powerful knowledge and artifacts that must remain hidden until such a time that they must be found—such a time when someone with the key to that chamber arrives."

The Arc begins to walk around the edges of the pool, dragging one scarified hand along the low wall and the pillars. His eyes gleam longingly in the water's pinkish glow. He stops and stares at Isa from across the pool.

"To destroy the curse, a mystic who holds this key must retrieve the Diamond from the chamber, but the rules are such that whoever this mystic is, they cannot be coerced into doing so. Retrieving the Diamond must be something they unquestionably want to do, or the chamber will not reveal it to them."

Isa braces herself, sensing she's about to learn what heavy price she will have to pay. "Do you possess this key, Your Worship?"

What do you want for it?

"I do not."

Confused, Isa frowns. "Oh?"

"But I know someone who does. The first part of your task will be . . . manipulating him into retrieving the Diamond for us."

Isa blinks. "Manipulating, Your Worship?"

"The inner sanctum contains millennia's worth of knowledge, Your Majesty," the Arc says, his eyes flashing. "*Dangerous* knowledge, and this individual holds the key to it. Our only advantage is that he is not aware of what he holds, because if he were, we would all be in grave danger. So yes, he must be handled deftly."

A game piece on a board can do nothing but accept what is given to it. *I came to him thinking I was taking control of my destiny, but what if I've been maneuvered here?* "And the second part of my task?" Isa says, so quietly she almost doesn't hear her own voice.

The Arc gazes at the pool for a good long while, and Isa could swear she can sense him convincing himself to say what he says next: "You will have to die, Your Majesty. It is the only way to destroy the Covenant Diamond."

39: Musalodi

On the Way to the World's Vein—Kingdom of the Yontai

Salo is rummaging through Mukuni's saddlebags for his medical supplies when the ferrywoman and her sons return from belowdecks looking rather peeved. While her sons set up their musical instruments, the ferrywoman scans the deck thoroughly, marks the new passenger with a hard gaze, and then frowns at Salo in a way that would have killed him were frowns given to such a thing.

She seems even more incensed as she glares at his shards, which are still making up for the large stream of processed arcane energy he borrowed from the future when he cast the lightning barrier.

He breathes a sigh of relief when all she does is shake her head resignedly and join her sons. Soon their music summons a waterbird spirit to power the ship into motion.

"Now I understand why they didn't want us around," Salo mutters as he crouches next to Tuk with his bag of medicines. "They probably knew what was coming."

Tuk has slumped against a crate on the main deck. He's trying to stanch his bleeding arm with the other hand, but it isn't quite working. A worrying pallor has washed over his skin. He gives a wan smile. "Meh, I don't pity them. They could have at least warned us." He glances at Salo's glowing shards with a questioning look. "Are you still casting spells?"

"Technically," Salo says as he wipes his hands with a moist disinfecting reedfiber cloth from the bag, "I'm drawing essence for spells I've already cast."

"I don't understand."

"I have one ring," Salo explains. "I couldn't have cast that barrier without accessing a larger pool of energy."

"So you took it from the future?" Tuk says, sounding incredulous. "That's actually possible?"

"If you build your Axiom right, it is. Gives you one devil of a headache, though. Also means I can't cast spells until the debt is paid." With his hands clean, Salo sets the cloth aside and leans to take a closer look at Tuk's injury. "I'm no healer, but I can dress it for you. I need to check for alchemical poison, though. Do you mind lifting your hand?"

Tuk shies away, still clutching his wound. "Don't worry. It'll heal. Atmechs are supposed to be weak, docile, and pretty, but we're built to recover quickly from abuse. That way our masters can knock us about if they like."

Salo holds his gaze for a long moment. "I'd rather treat it anyway."

At this Tuk smiles, but his eyes remain stormy and threatening. "But I'm *not* weak. Not anymore. I'm strong now."

"You're very strong, Tuksaad, maybe the strongest person I've ever met, but you're not indestructible. Let me dress that wound before it gets infected, all right? You might even be poisoned for all we know."

A startling flash of red visits Tuk's eyes for the briefest instant, but then he catches himself and shakes it off. His shoulders slump; he leans back against the crate and nods. "All right."

Salo begins by scanning the wound with his talisman. Tuk watches curiously as the red steel serpent rears its head and flashes its crystal eyes at the wound, subsequently producing a mirage of diagnostic information above Salo's wrist. Nimara would have known exactly how to interpret every line on the chart; Salo understands only those sections relating to infection and poisons.

At least he thought he did. Now he's not so sure.

"Let me know if you need help," comes Ilapara's voice.

Salo glances in her direction and sees her settling down on a crate nearby with a waterskin in one hand. A sheen of sweat slicks her forehead. One of her long red dreadlocks has peeked out of her veil—the first Salo has seen of her hair—and some of the kohl on her eyes has been smudged. Besides this, she got away from the battle with barely a scratch. Now her hawkish gaze won't stray from the newcomer. The Asazi, however, doesn't seem bothered at all as she strolls around the deck, studying the ship with visible curiosity.

"I think I'll manage," Salo says, returning to the mirage.

"If you say so," Ilapara replies distractedly.

Salo squints at the mirage, trying to make sense of what he's seeing. He thinks Tuk has been poisoned with a particularly virulent alchemical toxin, but the levels of toxicity seem to be ticking down quite rapidly, which shouldn't be possible without strong spells of Blood craft.

"I'm not sure what I'm looking at," he says. "Hang on a second." Following a hunch, Salo commands the talisman to scan the wound for active prose and is quite shocked when a window of rapidly shifting ciphers appears in front of him. "Dear Ama," he gasps.

"What is it?" Tuk says.

"You have *prose* running in your blood, Tuk, and it's . . . *purging* the poison on its own. This is the most beautiful thing I've ever seen."

Tuk flashes a sly grin. "Why, thank you. I get that a lot, actually."

Ilapara snorts. "You're so full of yourself."

"The universe is not kind to the timid, my dear Ilapara," he says with a smirk. "One must be confident in one's own assets."

"A big ego is one of yours, I see."

"Yes, and uncommon beauty is another," Tuk says, which makes Ilapara roll her eyes.

Still mesmerized by the ciphers displayed in the mirage, Salo shakes his head. "Your blood has so many built-in charms I'm not sure there's anything that could make you sick."

Tuk blinks at him with green eyes. "I did try to tell you."

"We'll dress the wound anyway," Salo decides and sends his talisman to sleep. He begins by wiping the gash with a cloth soaked in one of Nimara's antiseptic tinctures. Tuk hisses in pain the instant it touches him, which makes Salo smirk. "The pain will go away when I apply the flesh-knitting salve."

"That would be much appreciated," Tuk says and then sighs, stretching his feet out in front of him. "But I deserve this for letting myself get distracted."

Salo feels a blush spreading down his cheeks. "That was my fault. I shouldn't have . . . shrieked like that."

"No, *I* should have paid more attention to my surroundings. A mistake like that in the heat of battle can easily become the last you ever make. Unacceptable. I have to do better."

"You handled yourself well, in my opinion," Ilapara says, echoing Salo's thoughts. "You must have killed, what, twice as many of those things as I did? And your footwork is amazing. What kind of weapons are those swords of yours, anyway?"

"Flashbrands." Tuk splays his hands to show the fancy golden rings on his middle fingers. They are different from each other in design, though Salo senses magic-infused cores of moongold in both rings.

"They're Void weapons," Tuk says, "with a little illusion and lightning mixed in. They can take a range of different shapes, and the best part is they weigh almost nothing."

"More specimens of Higher technology, I presume," Salo says.

"Probably the most iconic," Tuk says. "Flashbrands are status symbols in the Enclave. You're not a proper aristocrat if you don't own one."

"If you don't mind, I'd like to take a look at them at some point." When Tuk's eyes dim somewhat, Salo begins to walk back his request. "It's fine if you don't—"

"No, it's not," Tuk cuts in. "You can look at them whenever you want. I insist."

Clearly there's a story there, but Salo decides not to pry, and so does Ilapara.

For a time, Tuk watches the Asazi as she inspects the vessel's wing structures across the deck, and then he says, "So you communed with the Lightning Bird, huh. How'd that go?"

Salo sets the bloodied cloth aside and starts applying the healing salve, smiling when Tuk releases an almost comical groan of relief. "I know how the waterbirds work now."

"You do?"

"There's an immensely powerful mind stone at the bottom of the lake. It's home to the Impundulu and many lesser waterbird spirits. Powerful enough to move ships even from hundreds of miles away."

"But what did you see?" Ilapara says, joining the conversation. "And why the devil did you jump?"

"I don't remember jumping," Salo says. "I remember falling asleep, and then I had this dream . . ." His cheeks flame at the memory of *that* dream. Was it why he jumped? "Anyway, I'm not exactly sure what I saw down there. It was a story about the Lightning Bird. He was a king, I think? And then there was a war and a princess of the stars—" He stops talking when he sees Tuk wincing and rubbing his temples with his good hand. "What is it? Is it the poison?"

Tuk shakes his head. "Just a headache. Sorry, were you saying something?"

"I was telling you about the visions I saw in the lake. There were stars and—Tuk? Are you sure you're all right?"

"I think I'm getting a migraine," he says.

"Ugh, me too." Ilapara tilts her head back, pressing the flats of her palms against her eyes. "By Ama, I can feel it throbbing behind my eyeballs."

"Must be an echo of what I'm feeling," Tuk complains. "Like someone's raping my skull or something."

"Not a pretty image, Tuk," Ilapara says.

"Not a pretty headache, Ilapara."

A familiar uncanny feeling sinks into Salo's bones. He stops tending to Tuk's injury and watches the others closely. "Do you recall what we were just talking about?"

They blink, both looking confused. "That's weird," Tuk says. "I must really be tired."

"What *were* we talking about, actually?" Ilapara asks.

"I don't remember either," Salo says, returning to the injury on Tuk's arm.

When he's done with the salve, Ilapara offers to wrap the dressing. He agrees and steps aside, and though he keeps it off his face, his thoughts are now troubled.

By now both suns have cleared the horizon. A new day in the same old world, and yet it has never felt more alien to Salo.

What does it mean that he can know things others can't? What is it that makes them forget? What did those visions mean?

"A question, Salo." Alinata has snuck up behind him.

He turns around, instantly held captive by her intense hazel gaze. "Go on," he says.

Alinata is the queen's apprentice, the envy of every Asazi her age, and she oozes it. Salo can feel just how deeply her bones draw from the queen—so deeply she's probably as powerful as any mystic of middling ability. She also has one of those faces no formula for beauty can conceive, only a happy accident of birth.

A weapon, that face of hers, designed to ensnare and disarm.

"I've seen the skill nexus you hid in your workshop," she says. "By all accounts it should have taken your mind the first time you used it. Why didn't it?"

An ambush. She wants to see how I react. "And how is it you were in my workshop, Si Alinata?"

"Please, Alinata will suffice. And I searched your workshop soon after your awakening. Queen's orders, of course."

"Of course." Salo considers his options and decides that being honest won't hurt. "I suppose the secret to the skill nexus is wanting what it offers so badly you're willing to die for it. Bit of a paradox in that way; you're less likely to die if you're willing to die."

"And therein lies my second question: *Why* were you so determined? I can't imagine it was the thirst for power. You don't seem the type."

This is probably the question Alinata wanted to ask all along, but Asazi are never straightforward. "Not power, just the answer to a question," Salo says.

"And what was that question?"

Salo's lips twitch at one corner. "That's a bit prying, don't you think?"

"At least tell me if you've found the answer."

Salo began his journey to understand why his ama cared more about her damned Axiom than she did about him. He thought he'd found the answer. But now . . .

"I thought I had," he says. "It turns out I'm still looking. If I find it, I'll be sure to let you know."

She studies him, calculation sparkling behind her hazel eyes, and then she smiles. "You do that."

Later that day, a bridle path through the jungles leads them away from the northernmost Tuanu village and into the Bonobo province of the

KiYonte Kingdom. Ilapara rides ahead while Alinata follows from above, and they race northeast toward the World's Vein, the roadway that will lead them safely across three provinces and into the city of Yonte Saire.

The jungles are so dense they feel to Salo like a vast green cocoon. At one point he and the others ride through a stretch where a thin haze drifts about the forest floor, shimmering in the streaks of sunlight lancing through the high canopy. Salo wonders at how it swirls and parts before Mukuni's paws like water before the prow of a ship, spreading away like a living thing.

A patrol of spear-wielding legionnaires in orange tunics stops them as they approach a bamboo village. Its buildings are nestled within the jungles so seamlessly Salo could almost believe they were grown rather than built. As for the legionnaires, they all bear the exact same tattoos on their necks—conspicuous lines and motifs of the jungle bonobo—markings Salo might have considered pretty were he not aware that they were born of a curse.

He is apprehensive at first, but the legionnaires leave him alone as soon as he flexes his KiYonte and explains that he is a pilgrim walking the Bloodway, showing them his queen's medallion as proof. The mystic Seal emblazoned on it seems to be all the proof they need.

So he rides onward with his companions until late afternoon, when the jungles come alive with the howl of chatting apes, the cackle of hunting birds, and the guttural rumble of something distant and probably monstrous. The sounds are a visceral anthem in homage to all that is bestial and untouched by humanity, and Salo finds it mildly unsettling. He is no stranger to the wild savannas, but a uniquely primal essence inhabits these jungles.

They set up camp in a semiclearing just off the path, which, judging by the charred signs of a campfire and the conveniently arranged logs around it, has seen much use by travelers. While the others tend to the animals, Salo wanders deeper into the jungles with his bow, his leather quiver slung over his back.

The lighting is poorer in these jungles, and there's a whole lot more cover than he's used to, but he knows to tread softly on his feet and to keep his eyes open. Easy to get lost in the wilds, and sometimes the hunter can become the hunted.

He soon spots a pair of game birds with colorful plumage foraging for grubs and insects in the thick layer of dead foliage on the forest floor. They are too conspicuous to be bush fowl, but he figures they'll still make a tasty meal. He spied an okapi among the trees earlier, but he let it go; it was a bit more than they could eat in one sitting, and the city isn't far away.

He goes down on one knee, hiding behind a mossy tree trunk. The raucous call of a parakeet can be heard coming from somewhere deeper in the jungles. Above him a boa constrictor coiled on a branch stirs. He ignores it.

An iron-tipped arrow is already nocked on his bow. He draws the bowstring to his ear and holds his breath. It's a secret he's never told anyone, but training his mind in ciphers drastically improved his archery. With the appropriate muscle memory, hitting a target became the simple matter of executing a calculation.

He's about to let loose when Alinata steps in front of Mukuni and claps her hands to catch Salo's attention, like she knows Salo can hear and see through the cat's eyes and ears if he wants to.

"Salo, come back to camp," she says to the cat. "Now. It's urgent."

He must betray his position to the game birds, because they squawk and flutter off in alarm. He utters a curse, slightly annoyed by Alinata for ruining what would have been an easy kill.

What is it now?

When he treks back into camp, he finds Tuk and Ilapara frowning at the Asazi, whose worried look is instantly sobering to Salo. His annoyance swiftly turns into burgeoning dread. "What is it? What's going on here?"

"That's what we'd like to know," Ilapara says as she glares at the Asazi. "Something's clearly spooked her, but she won't tell us what."

"You need to let me fly you to the city immediately," Alinata says to Salo. "We don't have much time."

He exchanges baffled glances with the others. "Explain yourself."

She appears to bite back an impatient reply. "Look, there was a disruption in the Void tailing you from the south before I joined you. I was keeping track of it, but it disappeared a while back, so I assumed it had given up chase. But whoever it is must have found a way to mask their advance from me. I can feel them now, and they're close."

A tremor of fear runs through Salo. "What disruption? What are you talking about?"

"People have been chasing you since you left Seresa," she explains. "You encountered one of them, but there were others. Two groups turned back after you crossed into the Tuanu borderlands; I dealt with a third, and a fourth chose to keep up at a distance. Now they are coming. If I don't get you out of here right now, we'll have a fight on our hands."

Ilapara searches the surrounding jungles with a grim expression. "The Dark Sun has only one disciple who can move through the Void, and you're acquainted with her, Salo."

"The Maidservant," he whispers and shivers at the name.

Tuk had also started roaming the trees with his eyes; now they snap to Salo. "You mean the same witch who—"

"Yes. She's the one. And now she's here for me."

Tuk glowers at Alinata. "Is there a reason you didn't mention this sooner?"

"I told you; I thought she'd given up chase," Alinata says. "It's virtually impossible to move through the Void without leaving a signature, and hers stopped approaching over a day ago."

"Or maybe your powers of observation just aren't as good as you think." Tuk shakes his head with his hands on his waist. "Honestly, Alinata. It was highly irresponsible of you not to warn us sooner."

"If not downright malicious," Ilapara adds with a dark look.

"There's no time for this." Alinata walks toward Salo and grabs hold of his forearm. "I can fly you to the city. She won't chase us there. She wouldn't risk drawing the ire of the high mystics."

"What about the others, Alinata?"

Her grip tightens. "I'm not a mystic. I can only take one other person with me into my Voidspace."

"Absolutely not." Salo jerks his hand free of her. "Out of the question."

From the corner of his eye he sees Tuk and Ilapara sharing a look, a silent conversation seeming to pass between them. On whatever is said, it seems they agree.

"You should go, Salo," Tuk says, his eyes somber. "We can take care of ourselves."

Salo clenches his fists and almost lashes out in an outburst, but he bites his words so that they are almost a whisper. "Is your opinion of me so low that you'd think I'd abandon you in the face of danger, to a witch who killed dozens of my people, no less, one of whom I loved like a brother? Have I so badly represented myself to you?"

Ilapara grimaces like the words have cut her somewhere unseen, but she remains adamant. "We're only looking out for you, Salo. That's how this is supposed to work, isn't it? If we're your guardians on this pilgrimage, then your safety must be our main concern."

"And yours must be mine," Salo says. "I can't let you risk your lives for me if I'm not willing to do the same for you. Maybe I'm a coward, but I'm not without honor. We will face this witch together."

Tuk regards him warily, but his eyes betray him by lightening just the slightest bit. A begrudging dimple shows on one cheek, and he nods. "All right, Salo. I follow your lead."

Ilapara frowns like she's conflicted, but she relents. "As do I, I guess. Even though I think you should take the Asazi's offer and get the devil out of here."

"That's not happening, Ilapara," Salo says, and next to him, Alinata opens her mouth to protest, but he cuts her off. "This is my pilgrimage. If you can't respect my decision, you are free to leave. Your choice."

She tries to stare him down, but a staring contest with someone in reflective spectacles is an exercise in futility. "Fine," she says. "How do we proceed, then?"

"How far away is she?"

Alinata closes her eyes briefly before she says, "We have an hour at best, and I sense she's not alone."

"If she wields Black magic, she could be bringing fell creatures from the underworld," Tuk says.

Alinata shakes her head. "That's not it. I mean, yes, that, too, but I can only sense what she moves through the Void, and the size of her signature tells me she's bringing others with her. A squad of men, perhaps, and something bulky . . ." A thought seems to strike the Asazi. "Another group was in pursuit just before I joined you, but they were intercepted by a Tuanu patrol. Men wearing red skulls on their faces riding the largest kerit bears I've ever seen. She must have intervened."

"Red skulls?" Ilapara fails to restrain her alarm. "They could be reavers. The Dark Sun's personal cadre of elite raiders and assassins."

Tuk shoots the Asazi another moody glare. "You really should have said something, Alinata."

"I had no reason to suspect I was being duped by Black magic," she says rather defensively. "And the last thing I wanted was to worry you for no reason. It was a mistake; I see that now."

"What's done is done." Salo walks toward Mukuni's saddle, where he sets his bow and quiver down and reaches for his staff. His mind is already racing with ways to counter what he thinks they're all about to face, how to best deploy the weapons in his arsenal.

"When the so-called Maidservant attacked my kraal and killed my people," he says, "I was weak, defenseless, and unprepared." With a gesture he summons essence into his shards. Red sparks activate around the tip of his staff. "This time things will be different. This time she will find that I am ready for her."

♦   ♦   ♦

He begins by carving up a little kingdom for himself.

While the others stand guard rather nervously, watching the surrounding trees for any sign of movement, Salo sits down on a log by the dying fire Ilapara lit and commands his talisman to perform a continuous scan of everything in a two-hundred-yard radius. Such a feat demands more raw essence than the talisman has in its stores, so he feeds essence into it directly from his shards.

The talisman doesn't produce a mirage; instead, he closes his eyes so that he interfaces with it telepathically. Soon it offers him a circular domain in which he has near-perfect information and spatial awareness, even though his eyes are closed.

For minutes on end, with his focus lensed through his staff, he devises parameters for his lightning-barrier spell. The tessellated hexagons worked well on the waterbird, so he uses them as the building blocks for larger barriers.

In the background Alinata keeps flexing her fingers as she watches the trees, occasionally throwing him impatient glances. Then her shoulders tense up, and Salo feels a ripple of cold energy as she wraps the Void around herself like a cloak. She appears to blur out of sight just the slightest bit while ghosts of fluttering ravens start swirling around her.

"She's near. And she has company." Something hardens in Alinata's eyes, and she seems to come to some hidden decision. "I'll distract her so you can deal with the others."

Salo gets up to his feet before she does something foolish. "Don't try facing her alone, Alinata. She's too powerful."

"We need to separate her from her forces if we want any chance of surviving this. I'm the best person for the job, and it'll give you time to deal with whomever or *whatever* she's here with."

He doesn't argue with her because he knows she's right. "Are you sure about this?"

She nods, then seems to consider her words. "But if I get trapped in the Void, can I trust that you'll get me out?"

Salo studies her face for a beat, and he thinks he sees the dimmest specter of fear hiding beneath her otherwise calm appearance. "I'll do my best, Alinata," he says, which gets her to tilt her head and smile.

"Your best has done great thus far, so it'll have to do. See you on the other side of this." And then she turns into a flock of ravens and flutters away into the trees.

40: Ilapara

Bonobo Province—Kingdom of the Yontai

Ilapara has never been one for patience in the face of impending danger. If she knows an attack is coming and she can't escape, she prefers to meet it head-on. Take control of the situation, drive the enemy out into the open, never let them gain a foothold.

Probably why she starts growing impatient as she waits in the camp clearing for the Maidservant and her forces to ambush them. She taps into her training to sharpen her senses and quicken her reflexes but ends up too alert, picking up on even the softest hiss of the wind and the quietest chirping of bugs in the earth and trees around her. Maddening.

Several times she glares down at Salo while she paces restlessly with her spear locked in a tight grip. The boy is back to sitting motionless on a tree stump with his staff balanced on one end between his legs, while the red serpent on his left wrist shoots out regular arcs of light from its crystal eyes. She saw him cast spells of lightning earlier, but now he's just sitting there like a wooden carving, waiting.

He should have left when he had the chance.

Tuksaad is almost her mirror opposite, facing the bridle path beyond the clearing with his shoulders free of tension, his face calm and serene like he's basking in a pretty sunset. She would think him wholly unprepared for what's coming were his eyes not as inky as the night sky on a new moon. There's also the long blade dangling from his good hand, a sleek-looking thing of gold with a slight curve, chased with esoteric scripts that give off a red glow.

At last, Ilapara loses her patience. "Alinata's been gone for minutes now. Where is she?" *And why the devil are we not already under attack?*

Salo responds without moving to face her. "She's locked in battle with the Maidservant in the Void. It'll be some time before it ends one way or the other." And then, almost as an afterthought, he tilts his head slightly and says, "A large beast is approaching from the west. I'm sending Mukuni to intercept."

The cat is on his feet instantly, his mane of metal spines rattling like peals of thunder, and with a fierce growl he makes for the bridle path and bounds west. Long seconds pass before the ground trembles under the weight of violent roars. Trees snap with loud cracks in the distance as the battling beasts tumble between them.

Ilapara shares a tense look with Tuksaad. At the same time Ingacha lets out a nervous grunt where she tethered him next to the abada.

"We're surrounded," Salo says rather distantly, like he might not be fully in his body. "About a dozen men armed with machetes. All wearing red skulls on their faces."

"Definitely reavers." Ilapara scans the trees, then twists to look over her shoulder at Salo. *Dear Ama, I wish I had a soul charm right now.* "A dozen, you said?"

"If there are more, they haven't entered my field of view." He tilts his head like he's trying to get a better view of something in front of him. "Well, that's a pity."

"What is it?" Ilapara and Tuk say at the same time.

"Their garments have powerful protective charms," he says. "I won't be able to incapacitate them as I'd hoped."

As if they can read each other's minds, Ilapara and Tuk both move into vanguard positions, putting Salo's seated form between them.

"Whatever happens," Salo says to them, "I want you both to know that you've been good friends to me in the short time we've known each other."

"Then let's make sure we live long enough to become even better friends," Tuk says. "I don't intend for any of us to die today."

They say reavers have no souls and are incapable of feeling pain or mercy. Beneath the terrific roars coming from the west, Ilapara tries to pick up the rustle of leaves and the crunch of footfalls, but if the reavers are coming, they aren't making much noise.

Salo speaks, once more in a strangely detached voice. "I've warded the clearing. Stay within two hundred yards of this position. And don't worry about me; I'll be fine."

She looks around, searching for signs of the ward, but sees nothing. Before she can ask, multiple flashes of movement appear in the trees around the camp. Shadows subsequently materialize and resolve into bare-chested men in black kikois, aerosteel vambraces, and hide skins hanging over their fronts. Red skulls cover the upper halves of their faces, making their heads look misshapen and protuberant from a distance. Their machetes are crusted with dried blood, and their leering grins are each and every one of them dental horrors of blackened teeth filed to spikes.

No one faces a dozen reavers and walks away with their head still intact. Ilapara knows this, but as she falls deeper into her conditioning, everything becomes a remote consideration, everything but the here and now, the spear in her hand, the breath in her lungs.

Survive this second and get to the next.

The reavers close in on the camp almost leisurely, like a pack of hyenas moving in on wounded prey. Ilapara readies herself for an attack, but the men all stop at some hidden cue, and then the tallest of them speaks in a deep, gravelly voice. "You have made us chase you a long way, sorcerer. That's going to cost you dearly in blood and guts."

Battle scars striate his entire torso, and a necklace of bones rests around his neck. Ilapara is taken aback by the sheer murder burning openly in his bloodshot eyes, like Salo is the bane of his existence.

Without moving an inch from where he's sitting, Salo answers the man in Izumadi. "We have never met. I have not wronged you in any way. Why do you pursue me?"

"We serve a master," the reaver snarls, "and when he says kill, that's what we do. But you we will kill with extra relish for making us chase you this far. I've lost good men because of you."

Ilapara feels rather than sees Tuk smirk. "Perhaps you should take better care of your men," he says. "That way you won't have to blame other people for getting them killed."

"Is there no arrangement we can come to?" Salo asks.

The lead reaver bares his teeth. "None that involves you leaving this place with your head still attached to your body."

All right. That's it. No use in delaying the inevitable. "Then why are we even talking?" Ilapara says.

The lead reaver's glare slides to her and intensifies. "Boys," he says to his men, "take your time."

And then everything happens very quickly after that.

Your body is a cage into which you are born a slave, her uncle would tell her as he taught her his secrets in the privacy of the open wilds, with nothing but the sky above and the savannas below to listen. *Heartbeat, coordination, speed, pain, breath, fear; most of the body's workings are naturally inaccessible to you. They control you, dictate the terms, and you either sink or swim. It is up to you to break out of your cage and take control of it, and the first step is recognizing the power of your mind.*

A trio of reavers descends upon her all at once. A blood-spattered machete darts for her head. She sees it in time to sway away, using her momentum to whip her spear around, but these are reavers, high on tonics and the thirst for blood: her spear cuts through nothing but air.

They give her no room to breathe. A machete comes for her belly. Another comes from behind, destined for her left shoulder. She spins away yet again—and straight into the path of a third blade already halfway to her face. The man wielding it is the same reaver who spoke, promising evil things to come. Here he is now about to kill her, because even in her accelerated state, she is only human, and this man is a reaver; she could never be fast enough to evade a blow already so close, only fast enough to see it and to register that this is the blade that will end her.

Except something curious happens, so quickly she almost misses it: a delicate field of red lightning arcs right before her eyes and *deflects* the reaver's blow with a resonant peal, as though it has struck a shield of unbreakable glass. They all pause battle in surprise, and the reaver in question inspects his machete like he thinks it might be defective.

A proud enemy is an enemy set in his ways. His victory is assured; the laws of nature are on his side. It is why, when he is suddenly confronted with a creature that fails to conform to these laws, he will sooner question his reality than accept it and adapt. Punish him.

Ilapara doesn't let the reaver make another mistake. She erupts forward with her spear and sinks it into the soft flesh at the base of his neck. His shocked face will haunt her in her sleep if she survives this, and so will the gurgling noise of blood gushing out of his mortal wound, but the nightmares will come later. Now she twists her spear to bring his life to a swift and permanent end and lets the body crumple to the ground.

Light flashes and a crack thunders as a blow that would have cut into her right flank is deflected away before she has reoriented herself. She moves to evade a little too late, and another peal sounds behind her, another blow that should kill her, but she remains unharmed.

In the face of her seeming invulnerability, the reavers attacking her grow wary, which gives her just enough room to maneuver herself out of their immediate reach for a precious split second and finally take stock of her environment. Out of the corner of her eye she sees that Salo hasn't moved from his seated position, though he's cocooned himself in a rather intimidating whirlwind of leaves and loose earth. The reavers are ignoring him for the more immediate threats, thinking perhaps that they'll save him for last. *Good.*

Tuk is tangled in a knot of reavers, not even trying to evade them. Bolts of lightning keep arcing around his form as the reavers unleash blow after blow onto his body only to strike a luminescent specter that disappears as soon as it appears. His flashbrand, meanwhile, cuts through the air unhindered, leaving ghosts of red light where he swings it. With his recovering arm and the exhaustion of a day's travel weighing down on him, he's far from the clinical swordsman Ilapara saw on the waterbird, but three reavers are already lying dead on the ground by his feet.

The split second of peace ends, and Ilapara sidesteps a hacking strike to her neck. A loud crack behind her tells her she just survived yet another lethal blow. *Is this what cheating death sounds like?*

She punctures a reaver in the stomach, retracts, swings her spear so forcefully the reaver's mask gets chopped in half when the blow connects. He falls, his face a bloody ruin. She ducks—a peal as the machete behind her hits anyway, but it doesn't touch her, so she shifts on her feet, pivots, and thrusts.

One by one the reavers fall to her spear. Men who are feared across the vast savannas of Umadiland, men who have raped and pillaged and killed for their mystic warlord; they prove no match for a girl they can't hit.

"Kill the sorcerer!" At last one of them figures out that the real threat in this battle has thus far gone unmolested, but Tuk performs a dexterous twisting leap and cuts him down before he can test the winds blowing around Salo.

At this point, most reasonable people would recognize that the tide of battle hasn't been in their favor for a while now, that perhaps it never was, and they would flee, but the three remaining reavers only grow more rabid, as if they have tapped into some previously sealed reserve of rage. Ilapara's phantom shield cracks several times under heavy blows before she and Tuksaad whittle down the reavers and she impales the last one in the heart and watches his murderous fervor bleed out of his blackened mouth.

Abruptly the whirlwind gusting around Salo dies out, and he rises to his feet, anxiety showing in the high arch of his eyebrows. "Are you all right? I'm sorry I wasn't much more help."

Breathing heavily, Ilapara surveys the bodies strewed around what used to be their camp. The fetid reek of voided bowels is thickening in the air. She feels a stirring of nausea but fights it off. "We killed a dozen reavers without suffering a single scratch," she says, panting. "I think you helped us plenty."

"That ward of yours, Salo." Tuk picks his way over a dead reaver lying facedown in the dirt. By the awe in his blue eyes, one would almost think he doesn't even see the bodies. "A dynamic, self-activating kinetic barrier. Did you come up with that just now? And how is it so precise?"

Tuk's enthusiasm fails to steal Salo's attention away from the blood and bodies around him. For a while he stands motionless, taking in the carnage like he can't quite believe his eyes. Ilapara sees signs of growing panic in the way his hands start to tremble. "Did we just kill twelve men?"

"Now's not the time to think about it, Salo," Ilapara tells him in a firm voice. "We're not out of the woods yet. Survive first; panic later."

"Not to mention the fact that *they* were trying to kill *us*," Tuk adds.

"Right." Salo takes a moment to process this before he nods. "Right," he says again. Absently, he walks off and starts searching for something in the canopy beyond the clearing. Ilapara follows the line of his gaze but sees nothing there.

"I can't sense Alinata anymore." Salo turns around to face the bridle way. "I can't even sense . . . oh no."

Ilapara gives in to a surge of worry and steps closer to him. "What is it?" But before he can answer, something casts a shadow over them, and when they look up, they see it seeping through the high canopy like grains through a sieve. Then it swoops down faster than any of them can react.

"Watch out!" Salo cries.

Too late. While the main cloud of darkness veers away, a thin stream—flies, Ilapara notices after the fact—reaches out like a tentacle and wraps itself around Tuksaad, whisking him off the ground. She has just enough time to shout his name before she suffers the same fate, and the last thing she sees as an invisible force pulls her out of reality and into a horribly empty chasm is a face painted black with arcane ciphers.

41: Kelafelo

Namato—Umadiland

As the full moon approaches, each day counting down to Akanwa's scheduled sacrifice at the Anchorite's altar, Kelafelo finalizes her plans for escape.

Despite Kelafelo's vow never to see the slave girl as her daughter, the Anchorite's revelation about her malicious plans for the girl opened her eyes to the simple fact that she isn't as empty as she thought she was. Moreover, that being empty isn't what she wants for herself anymore.

If Urura's death stripped her of her humanity, Akanwa's arrival returned a small piece of it. She is not Urura and will never be, but she returned a modicum of color and laughter to Kelafelo's life, and for that reason alone, Kelafelo loves her.

She makes no changes to her routine or preparations that will give her away to the Anchorite. She continues to work on her Axiom. She rereads every book on the Anchorite's shelf, treatises on poisons, alchemy, and soul charm creation. She does her best to appear the hard-working apprentice resigned to a difficult task.

But in the privacy of her own mind, she makes plans for a life away from her master. She will disappear with Akanwa in the night while the old woman sleeps, and then they will take a boat and sail upstream, perhaps make their way to a town along the World's Artery.

She won't even need to awaken and become a mystic. She already knows enough about mind stones, soul charms, and healing elixirs to earn a decent wage. She will be free to live as she chooses, with no parent or husband or sister-wife to answer to. She will build a new life for herself and Akanwa.

On the eve before their intended escape, however, three days before the full moon, Kelafelo returns to the hut from laundering clothes by the river to find Akanwa missing.

At first she figures the young girl has gone chasing after the bronze-furred monkeys that sometimes come to scavenge through their rubbish pit or steal fruit from the Anchorite's garden. But as the hours progress and the suns dip lower without any sign of her, a sick worry begins to twist her stomach into knots.

She walks over to the garden to find out if the Anchorite has seen the girl, but the old woman isn't there either. She walks down to the river, calling out Akanwa's name. Not finding her there, she trots back and searches the hut just in case she's missed her, but the girl is nowhere in sight.

She searches the compound again, the chicken coop, the garden for a second time. She runs along the path to the village of Namato, the same path she used when she first stumbled here in search of vengeance over a comet ago now, but Akanwa isn't there either.

When she is out of breath, she stops and shades her eyes with a hand, searching the flat savannas for any sign of movement. Did they go somewhere together? But where would the Anchorite take the girl, and why?

Kelafelo calls Akanwa's name until her throat feels raw; then she runs back to the hut and searches it again. She looks everywhere twice and then thrice. She looks until she realizes that her whole body is shaking. Eventually she leans against the hut and waits, convincing herself that the Anchorite wouldn't do anything to the girl. It is Kelafelo who is meant to perform the sacrifice, not the old woman.

When the Anchorite finally appears in the compound later that evening, however, Kelafelo takes one look at her and knows. She *knows* it in her bones and in her soul, and the knowledge breaks her.

Still, her trembling lips have to ask. "Where is Akanwa?"

"I sold her off." The Anchorite stops and leans on her staff with both hands. She might as well be giving a lecture on magical theory or announcing what she wants to eat for dinner. "It was a bad idea in retrospect. I underestimated how strong a bond you'd form with the girl."

"Where is she?" Kelafelo asks again.

"You will never see her again. You'd have either tried to escape with her, or if you'd gone through with it, it would have destroyed what little humanity you have left, which is worse. We shall have to purchase a different slave. Perhaps an older man. Someone you won't get too attached to."

For the first time Kelafelo realizes that she can tell when the Anchorite is lying to her. It's in the way her fingers keep tapping her staff. *She cares what I think of her.* A measure of cold clarity comes to Kelafelo's vision. "You didn't sell her off, did you."

The Anchorite frowns. "It doesn't matter. The girl is gone, and you should get over it. Need I remind you why you limped here begging for my teachings? Have you lost sight of what you are here for?"

On the contrary, things are suddenly very clear to Kelafelo. The Anchorite is absolutely right: she came here for a reason, but Akanwa took her away from that path. The time has come for her to return to it.

She lets tears fall down her cheeks and wipes her eyes. "I'm sorry, Mamakuru. You are right. I wasn't going to do it. It would have been too hard."

The Anchorite waits for her to compose herself before she speaks again, this time in a mild voice. "I should apologize for putting you in this position. Living alone for so long has made me a stranger to human compassion, but I should have known better. Sometimes we simply aren't strong enough to go against our most powerful human instincts, and none is more powerful than the love of a mother. But don't worry; I am committed to making sure you reach your potential. I have taught other students before, but you have been the most promising."

Deeply grateful that the Anchorite has restored her vision, Kelafelo wipes her eyes one last time and says, "I thank you, Mamakuru. I will try not to fail you."

And in a way, this is entirely true.

◆ ◆ ◆

For a plan she never intended to put into motion, Kelafelo executes it flawlessly. On the night of the full moon, the Anchorite sits up in her pallet to find Kelafelo watching her from the table across the hut. Straining for breath, she presses a hand against her chest.

The hut is lit only by the moon's crimson light, which lances through the shutters, but Kelafelo can clearly see the moment the old woman realizes what's happening. It's right when she gasps and turns her head toward the table.

To her credit, her voice is free of panic. "What have you done?"

"I mixed up a concoction from your poison vials," Kelafelo answers, also calm. "Bloodrose essence to mute your sorcery, a slow-acting paralyzing agent, something to sharpen your senses so that you feel everything. And in case you get any ideas, your little centipede can't save you. I trapped it in an urn and buried it just before you woke up."

"How? I would have detected the poison in my food."

"I smeared it onto your hoe. A day never passes without you using that thing."

The Anchorite processes this and then grows visibly angry. "You would kill *me* for a Faraswa slave?"

"I'm merely following your teachings, Mamakuru," Kelafelo says. "You told me I need to stain my soul if I'm ever going to reach my best

Axiom, so that's what I'm doing. It just so happens there's no one else to sacrifice but you."

The Anchorite gasps again. "You won't do it."

"You're right. Not without help." Kelafelo picks up the vial on the table next to her and holds it for the old woman to see. "Fortunately, you made this elixir of compulsion for me. Once I drink it, I won't be able to stop myself until you're dead. You taught me well, Mamakuru."

"Perhaps too well." The Anchorite begins to sink back onto her pallet, the poisons starting to debilitate her body. Her eyes remain wide open, though; Kelafelo made sure she'd be awake until the end.

"For what it's worth, I wouldn't be doing this if you hadn't killed Akanwa. I'd have run off with her. I was actually considering giving up magic and my quest for revenge, if you'll believe it, but you set me straight. I owe you for that."

The Anchorite is wheezing now. "If you do this, the underworld's darkness will consume you. You're not strong enough to resist its call. I can see it in you. Why do you think I sent the girl away?"

An unexpected bolt of searing anger comes from nowhere, and Kelafelo almost shoots up to her feet. She holds it in, however, turning it into the hatred she'll need to continue with her plans. "You killed her, Mamakuru. Let's not beat around the bush."

"Curse you, girl. Curse you and everything you touch." By now the Anchorite's tongue is numbing and her speech is slurring, but the rage seething off the old woman is almost tactile.

Kelafelo's task will only be easier.

Without a second thought she reaches for the compulsion vial and downs its bitter contents, thinking about the thing she knows she needs to do. A witchwood knife rests on the table; she picks it up, gets up from the chair, and slowly approaches her immobilized mentor. "A glimmer of light had returned to my life," she says, "but you snuffed it out, Mamakuru. Now darkness is all I have left. I am a monster of your making."

Suddenly the Anchorite laughs.

The compulsion has yet to take Kelafelo, so she still has the sense to pause and be wary. Paralyzed and helpless on her pallet, the old woman somehow manages to summon the will to look up at her. "Foolish girl. Do you really think I am powerless over an elixir *I* made?"

Dread cools Kelafelo's skin. "What are you talking about?"

"I am no bumbling amateur. I knew I couldn't trust you, so I took precautions. You now have the most powerful compulsion magic in existence flowing in your veins—magic *I* created. You are completely at my mercy."

"Lies." But Kelafelo instantly knows it is true. She can already feel the stirring of magic inside her, twisting her thoughts, realigning her will.

The Anchorite wheezes and coughs. "Perhaps it is fitting that I die now. But you, oh, you will rue this night forever." She gasps and her eyes go wild, and Kelafelo stands helpless as she utters one last malediction, a hateful curse that will echo into the future, long after she is dead. "You will be a slave to the one you hate the most."

"No."

"Upon my death he will know of you," the Anchorite continues, "and he will come for you, and you will serve him as you would a god."

Kelafelo takes a step forward, the compulsion taking root. She wanted this just a second ago, but now she tries to fight it. Her legs move forward anyway. "No."

"Your thirst for vengeance will consume you, you will hate your enemy, you will wish him evil even as you stare at him, and yet you will lack the strength to lift a finger against him."

"Stop!"

"The darkness will take you, my dear girl. You will lose yourself to it."

In a wild rage Kelafelo rushes forward and gives in to the compulsion, screaming as she lifts and thrusts her knife over and over again, its blade flinging a rain of dark droplets. The world goes crimson with warm blood and rage and moonlight, but Kelafelo doesn't stop, not until she has cried herself hoarse and the blood has soaked her to the skin.

That night, Kelafelo dies for the second time in her life, although this time, there will be no way back for her.

Two full moons later she journeys a hundred miles upstream to an old altar at the top of a lonely mountain and calls down her redhawk from the heavens. She feels no fear as the arcane bird descends before her wreathed in a firestorm, and she does not tremble when it touches their heads together and brands her arms with cosmic shards.

The contact brings with it an explosion that splits her mind *open*, as if a great chasm has been dug into the foundations of space and time and she can suddenly see what was hidden inside. A culmination of over a comet's worth of tears, sweat, and endless hard work, and yet she knows this is only the beginning.

If she is ever going to break the Anchorite's dying curse and accomplish what she vowed to accomplish on the day Urura was taken from her, then she has more to do.

She begins by digging out the mind stone from the dead tronic centipede; she has no doubt that the key to breaking the curse will be hidden within its lattices. To her mild annoyance, she finds that the mind stone is now locked behind a wall of protective charms, but this does not trouble her too much. She will find a way to break through the wall in time. How hard could it be?

In the quiet isolation of the Anchorite's hut, she puts her ancestral talent to use for the first time, rooting her shards to the Anchorite's old domain. She finds that she can't spread herself far in any direction before she encounters other powers rippling like currents in the land—in effect, boxing her in—but the little there is adds a second ring to her shards.

She commits all the old woman's tomes to memory, building up her arsenal of spells and rituals.

She learns how to anchor herself to the Void by bonding her soul to a secondary vessel; changing forms becomes the simple matter of switching vessels, bringing one into the world while sending the other into the Void. For a secondary vessel she chooses the plague of blackflies that invades the Anchorite's overgrown garden, where she disposed of the old woman's corpse.

She learns to tap into physical agony to improve the potency of her sorcery, beginning the process of marking her flesh with ciphers of Blood craft so painful she has to abandon clothes altogether. The pain is a price she is willing to pay, a constant reminder of why she is still alive and not with her daughter on the Infinite Path, why Akanwa had to die.

The mind stone proves to be more challenging than she anticipated, and she grows more frantic in her attempts to break through the charms protecting it, knowing that it holds the key to her freedom.

Such is her state of mind when, on one rain-soaked afternoon, an unusually tall man veiled in shadows rides into the hut's compound on a great sable antelope and waits beneath the witchwood tree. She feels him before she sees him, a presence that seems to shift the earth beneath her feet and coil wrongly inside her mind, compelling her to go outside and meet him.

A single eye shines scarlet through the darkness swirling around his face, and even in the rain his tronic mount releases tendrils of black smoke from angry, flaring nostrils. He is armed with a long black spear that also emits shadows and wears a robe the color of a starless night.

She recognizes him. She has never seen him before, but she recognizes beyond a doubt that here stands her enemy, the warlord whose men stormed her village and killed Urura, the focus of all her murderous intent. A profoundly venomous sort of rage burns beneath her newly scourged skin, and her shards crackle with power as she prepares to attack, but her limbs refuse to move. She calls on the deadliest spell she knows, a spear carved entirely from Void craft, but it fizzles out in her hands before she can strike.

By the way his head tilts to one side in apparent amusement, he must understand what is happening.

"I sensed my old mentor's death," he says in a voice like rumbling thunder. "Even from miles away I sensed her power exerting itself one last time, searching, reaching out to me. Do you want to know what it told me before it vanished?"

That this warlord was a student of the Anchorite's is a deep betrayal she feels like a knife twisting inside her guts. *All this time, she knew and said nothing.* "You're not welcome here. Leave."

"It told me that she had left a parting gift of a sort, the most promising student she had ever taught, handed to me on a platter." The red eye strobes in the rain. "You must be truly remarkable if you could inspire such emotion in her."

"I will never serve you."

"Kneel."

An irresistible force pulls her down to the earth, and she sinks to her knees before the warlord. She roars in hatred, fighting her own body from the inside. It refuses to obey.

The warlord watches silently until she stops struggling against herself. "I am here to offer you a position, maidservant of the Anchorite, a position in the fief I'm building."

"I'm not interested," she spits.

The warlord is unruffled by her flat rejection. "You may have survived out here beneath our old mentor's shadow—after all, she was deeply respected and feared, even by the most hardened of us. But she's gone now, by your own hand. You will soon find that you are defenseless."

"I can protect myself."

"Perhaps I misspoke. I tolerated the Anchorite's presence out of respect for her, and so did those who ruled this land before me. But now that she is gone, I am here to claim what is mine. I would be glad to share it with you, of course, and if you prove as useful as I think you are, I will share much, much more. But only if you come under my wing."

"Why the devil don't you just compel me?"

"I would rather you served me willingly, knowing that if I had to compel you, I would make you do terrible, terrible things. I lose nothing either way, but the cost of disobedience to you would be great."

Still on her knees, she forces herself to think rationally, to see through the thick mist of hatred fighting against her body. *You will lose yourself to it.*

No. She refuses this. Her dead mentor will not win. She will act the thrall to this man, serve him as a loyal disciple, but she will look for a way to break this vile curse and free herself. And then, when he least expects, she will have her vengeance. "I don't have much of a choice." She lets her head hang. "I will serve you."

Whatever expression steals across the warlord's face is hidden behind his veil of shadows, but she senses that he is satisfied. "A wise decision. What shall we call you, then, maidservant of the Anchorite?"

She thinks for a second, and the answer comes to her as if it were whispered into her ear by a breeze. "You shall call me precisely that. I am the Maidservant."

"Once our old mentor's helper, soon to be mine. A fitting name."

In her heart she thinks: *And I shall stand over your corpse just as I stood over hers, even if I have to call on the powers of hell.*

42: Musalodi

The ground seems to go out from under him, and Salo almost collapses, his ears ringing with Tuk's and Ilapara's screams as they fell into the Void.

Across the clearing a cloud of flies drops to the forest floor like a solid weight and congregates into a woman with black markings covering the entire expanse of her body. Her hair stands wild like horns on either side of her head, and there is a hungry look in her eyes.

The Maidservant.

At the sight of her, rage clouds Salo's vision, and he grips his staff so tightly he feels the blood leave his knuckles. He was afraid before, and he still is, but anger and vengeance have set his mind on fire and outshine everything else. This is the woman who killed Monti. This is the woman he hates more than anything in the world, and now she has taken his friends from him.

"Your quarrel is with me," he says in her forsaken tongue. "Fight me and leave my companions out of it."

The Maidservant tilts her head curiously and starts to edge along the clearing's perimeter on lissome legs. "I remember you," she says, her filed teeth glistening as she speaks. "I saw you that day. You really are newly awoken, aren't you?"

Salo starts to move, too, matching the Maidservant's progress around the clearing's perimeter. "I'm not afraid of you, witch. You will pay for what you did to my people."

"Perhaps I will," she says. "But first, you will tell me about this power you wield, this . . . Elusive Cube. I had my doubts, but I have seen that yours is no ordinary Axiom. How did you know to build it?"

Salo can't help his surprise. "How do you—" he starts but immediately cuts himself off. "I will tell you nothing!"

The Umadi witch keeps walking. "Believe it or not, but I don't want to hurt you. This isn't personal. If you force my hand, however, you will regret it. All I want is information. Tell me how you knew to build that Axiom of yours, and maybe I'll let you go."

"I will die before I confess anything to you."

The witch's eyes flash threateningly. "I don't need your consent to get what I want, but have it your way." In the next split second, magic crackles in the air, her shards flare with power, and from the Void she launches a spear of warped space in his direction.

Salo doesn't flinch. His mind is still connected to his talisman, which sees the projectile even before it has covered half the distance, judging it hostile to him based on its trajectory. Through its vastly accelerated logic, he is able to know precisely how much Storm and Void craft to draw and where to cast a simple barrier of tessellated hexagons that winks out of existence as soon as the spear crashes against it.

A loud peal and a flash of red lightning, and then the spear flakes away into nothing.

"Impressive," the Maidservant says. She keeps moving around the clearing, and so does he.

Then her eyes incandesce with moonlight, and she spreads her arms wide. When she slams her palms together with a loud clap, a hundred Void arrows fly out of thin air and converge upon him.

He lenses his mind with his staff, letting his talisman guide his release of magic. An instant later a half dome of Void hexagons and lightning takes shape from the ground up and covers him like a giant parasol tipped on its side. The hail of arrows shatters on its surface with sparks of lightning, and the shield blinks away a heartbeat later, replenishing his flow of magic.

"You Yerezi are very talented," the Maidservant says. "I have always envied and respected your depth of knowledge." Finally coming to a stop, she considers him with interest. "I'm going to give you one last chance to tell me what I want to know. No one has to get hurt. I'll even return your friends to you unharmed."

That last part makes Salo second-guess himself, but he doesn't take the bait. To expect the witch to keep her word would be foolish. He firms his voice. "I won't bargain with a mass murderer."

"Then you give me no choice."

He knows what's coming even before he feels the corruption stirring in the air, an unpleasant oiliness that inspires an opposing surge in his shards.

The first time he watched her use Black magic, summoning tikoloshe from the underworld to kill his people, he saw nothing but plumes of dust that appeared from nowhere and coalesced into the fell beasts. But now that he can sense magic with his shards, he sees the horrid truth as it unfolds: her mind is connected through the Void to the devil's domain, and this connection manifests itself as a portal she can open whenever she wishes to summon spirits from the other side.

He senses her open this portal and summon a tikoloshe, not a hulking skeleton this time but a spirit in the form of pitch-black slime. With a thrust of her hands the slime leaps onto his face much faster than he can react. It instantly starts crawling beneath his glasses and into his eyes, his nostrils, and even his ears, burrowing into his head.

He tries to summon power into his shards, but it's like they've been poisoned or disengaged from the source, leaving him defenseless. Dropping his staff, he falls to his knees with a silent cry, scratching at the profane webs infesting his face, but they only dig deeper into him, somehow melding with his thoughts, stealing them. He chokes as they enter his mouth and curl themselves around his throat, then falls to his side, gasping for breath.

Footfalls sound nearby. To Salo it feels like there's a long tendril of black ooze leading straight from his mind and into hers, continuing deep beyond the profane portal.

"I used to believe that Yerezi supremacy in magic was due to your virtuousness as a tribe," she says, "how you worked together despite your clans, how you were better than us." She crouches next to Salo's choking form. "Imagine my disappointment when I learned that you're no different. That in fact you are possibly worse. At least we know what we are and don't pretend otherwise. You smile at each other and act like one people while plotting each other's destruction. Hypocrites."

The slimy webs infiltrate his mind. Their corrupted ciphers shift and multiply at the speed of his thoughts, too fast for him to neutralize.

"Don't fight it," the witch whispers. "It'll only prolong your suffering."

As he lies on the forest floor, some part of him notices how hard she's straining to keep the mind-stealing tikoloshe under her control. In fact, the more he pays attention, the more he realizes that her hold on her own power is tenuous at best.

He could tip the balance, turn her Black magic against her . . .

Salo tries harder to draw power from his shards, but the profane spirit tightens its grip around his throat, cutting off what little breath he had left. His back arches involuntarily; his fingers curl into his palms, grasping fistfuls of wet earth. He wheezes in desperation, feeling consciousness begin to slip away from him, and yet he redoubles his efforts to reach for his shards, expending all the willpower he has left. He reaches and reaches until something *breaks*—

Power comes surging back into his arms, and the witch loses complete control of the tikoloshe, falling back with a cry.

With nothing to stop it, the spirit draws more power from beyond the portal, deepens its hold around Salo's mind, and *pulls*.

43: The Maidservant

Bonobo Province—Kingdom of the Yontai

When she first knocked on the door to hell, it was because she was curious.

The door had been a wound whose silent presence had always haunted her in the Void, an ancient malignance carved forcefully into the metadimension by something unfriendly to the moon—and she could tell this because the power that seethed off it was nothing at all like the moon's power. It was colder, darker somehow, *wrong*, and it promised her great things if she just opened the door, made her wonder if maybe the key to her freedom didn't lie beyond.

It did not, as it turned out, but the power that rushed out from the other side was great nonetheless.

Now she feels it turn against her. The spirit she used to steal the boy's thoughts entangles his mind with hers and *pulls*, and the connection forged between them is so total it's as if his soul has been laid bare before her so that he has no secrets left to her. She sees every facet of him so that she knows him as well as she knows herself. She sees his life the way he lived it, the scars he survived, the horrors he's endured.

She sees it all, and so does he.

◆ ◆ ◆

For Musalodi, it began shortly after his seventh comet, on the night his ama poured acid onto his eyes, making them melt right out of their sockets.

That night she locked him in her drystone hut and told anyone who came inquiring about the screams that he'd contracted a rare infection and she was trying her best to treat it. In truth, she was torturing herself by watching her beloved son writhe on the floor in pain from something she had deliberately caused.

The act was a ritual, the first of many she planned to perform, in which she caused herself great spiritual pain by tormenting him, the one she loved most in the world, thereby forging the deepest connection possible to the source. The rituals would grow in intensity until they culminated with his violent sacrifice at the altar of her spiritual agony, and this would grant her the insights she needed to build the thing that was her obsession: the All Axiom.

She already wielded the power of the moon and served her clanspeople as their mystic, but she would face the redhawk again, for the All Axiom was the most important thing in the world.

That night, however, as she watched her son toss and turn on the floor of her hut, screaming her name and clawing in agony at his bleeding eyes, as the guilt of the crime ate away at her soul and she wept inconsolably, she realized that her carefully laid-out plans had turned against her. The boy she had conceived *precisely* to love and coddle before sacrificing him to her All Axiom had grown too dear to her. She could not bring herself to hurt him any further.

Instead, she used her sorcery to replace his devoured eyes with unnatural ones, whose interiors were faceted and multicolored, like opals in the sunlight. She convinced everyone, even her son, that what had happened had truly been the result of a rare disease. Years passed before the boy would come to terms with the truth.

Even so, his mother continued her work, for it was far too important to set aside. The object of her efforts would be different now, however, and who better to wield the All Axiom on her behalf than the one whose blood had been shed for it?

In a way, she had already begun to prepare him for the role. His ordeal with the eyes, though it had been meant to provide her insights of spiritual agony, had done the same to him, too, priming him for the ciphers of Red magic. If she paved his way to the All Axiom, then his pain wouldn't have been for nothing. It would be her penance for the crime she had committed.

Knowing that she couldn't be discovered teaching a boy the secrets of magic, she did just enough to stoke his interest in the mystic arts, securing all the things he would need to teach himself when he was old enough. He was his mother's son, clever and curious, so she knew he would prevail so long as he asked himself the right questions. All he needed was a push in the right direction.

And so, when it was time to give him this push, her last gift to him, the agony that would open his eyes to the greatest secrets of Red magic, when it was time to give her life to the cause, she did not hesitate. His victory would be hers. What would have been a mother's betrayal would become the greatest gift she could ever give him, the crown he would wear on her behalf.

The Maidservant sees how, on the night Musalodi would have died beneath his mother's blade, it was she who bled instead, victorious in the knowledge that her son would complete her life's work.

The Maidservant sees it all.

She sees how he killed his own mother.

They appear standing side by side in a stone hut lit by luminous vines, a construct of a memory he's buried so deep it surfaces only in his nightmares. In front of them a beautiful woman gives a much-younger version of the boy a choice in the form of a witchwood blade.

Next to the Maidservant, the older boy watches his younger self shake his head with force. "No, Ama. Please. I can't."

In the background, two younger boys are huddled together in a corner, identical twins, it seems. By the way they are leaning against each other and the threads of drool hanging from their mouths, the Maidservant can tell that they have both been bewitched into insensate stupors. A large feline shadow looms over them, its teeth bared in menace. It growls, making the walls shudder.

"Do you love me, my sweet?"

"You know I do, Ama."

"That is why you must do it. This isn't just for you. I am sick, you see. I'm in so much pain. I need you to help me stop the pain."

"But you can be healed!"

"I can't. It's too late. But Salo, if you don't help me, my sickness, my pain, it will make Mukuni kill and eat your brothers. You don't want that, do you?"

The shadow growls again, and the boy starts to cry.

"Take the knife. Use it many times—that's important, Salo. Many times, or Mukuni will do it. You must not stop until he leaves. Do you understand? Please. Help me. Stop the pain."

In front of them, the younger version of the boy the Maidservant came to kill cries in a pool of his mother's blood while his insensible younger brothers watch with glazed eyes. Their father is the one who finds them like this.

"I killed her," the older boy says while he watches his father pry the witchwood blade from his younger hands. Later, the man will conceal the truth of what transpired here to protect his children. "I remember now."

The Maidservant sees how the trauma of the memory comes to overshadow the memory itself, so much so that it blurs and becomes an indistinct but painful wound in his soul, a wound that will never heal. It comes to haunt and define every minute of his life, and she sees how his agony draws him to all things magic, fueling his quest to understand his mother's actions.

She sees how his memory of slaughtering the person he loved most becomes a deeply crippling fear of violence and confrontation, leading him to shirk the warrior's path and become an outcast among his tribespeople. She sees how he wilts under their jeers, how he finds refuge in the study of magic, how the thing his mother tortured him for becomes his obsession, and how, altogether, these were the secrets that led him to his power. A power he still doesn't understand.

"I killed her," the boy says again, and the Maidservant wants to tell him that it wasn't his fault, that he wasn't given a choice, just like she wasn't given a choice, but the memories shift before she can open her mouth, and they prove her wrong.

She did have a choice.

◆ ◆ ◆

She sees herself.

On the day she attacked his kraal, a dark vortex of mindless hate. She feels the boy's confusion as he heard the first screams, then his fear when he spotted the Seal in the skies, then his shock when he witnessed her fell spirits slaughter his people. She feels his devastation at the senselessness of it, that such cruelty could come to them unprovoked.

She sees Monti. The young boy he wished were his brother. He saw a lot of himself in the boy and secretly entertained notions of teaching him everything he knew about magic. She feels the heartrending loss of him, the debilitating guilt of failing to protect him, the hatred of his murderer, and all of it echoes the things she felt on that rainy night as she lay by her hut's threshold with her belly sliced open, back when she went by another name.

She sees all this, and it is a damning, inescapable mirror showing her a truth she has known for some time but refused to acknowledge: That she long ago became the very thing she set out to destroy. That she is no different from the men who slaughtered Urura.

That in fact, she is worse.

She sees this, truly sees it, and it breaks her.

But she is not alone in her visions. In the fleeting moment during which she sees his life, the boy sees hers too.

Her love for Urura, her devouring hatred when she was violently taken away from her. He sees her journey to the Anchorite's hut, her lessons in the mystic arts, her brief second chance with Akanwa, and her eventual fall into darkness when she murdered her mentor and cursed herself with a compulsion that would bind her to her enemy.

He sees how she lost herself to killing for the Dark Sun, how each kill became easier and weighed less on her soul, until she could burn down entire villages without a second thought. He sees how her quest for freedom from the curse made her hungry for power, how she convinced herself that the only way she could find this freedom was if she gave herself entirely to the underworld. He sees how she lost herself to it, all of her crimes, all of her atrocities, all the blood she spilled and the suffering she wrought.

He sees her down to her rotten core.

This is who I am.

I am evil.

I am irredeemable.

I am lost.

I am unworthy of Urura's love.

The thought is a scream echoing into the deepest fissures of her blackened soul. It is a wave that swells and roils inside her until she is drowning. She thinks it will consume her, choke her, dash her against the jagged edges of her guilt, but then another wave crests over the first, foreign and intrusive like a burst of sunlight in a universe that has never known a star. It says: *You don't have to be.*

The Maidservant screams. She harnesses all her will, all her strength, and with the entire stream of magic she can summon, she pushes against the portal in her mind and severs the connection to it.

She feels the boy's mind wrenching free of hers, and then she's back in the glade, lying on the forest floor not far from him. Her limbs trembling with grief, she crawls away, trying to escape his merciful words. She climbs to her feet, and there is a moment in which she looks down at him and he looks up at her, and where she saw hate and fear not long ago, she sees confusion, pity, and even mercy.

You don't have to be.

The words torture her with their hopefulness; they sting and burn her because she knows she doesn't deserve hope. How could she, after all she has done?

And yet she felt him look at her soul and see something worth saving.

Tears blur her eyes. She backs away from him, this boy who would feel pity for her despite what she did to him. She discorporates into a thousand flies and hurtles away from the clearing.

The words follow her. Well into the twilight skies and beyond. They follow her, and they stay with her.

44: Musalodi

The world sways on its axis.

A cloud of flies surges away. Ravens burst out of thin air, and two bodies come tumbling to the ground, instantly curling into shivering balls. In his disoriented state, Salo takes a while to realize that the bodies are Tuk and Ilapara.

Almost passing out from the wave of relief that washes over him, he gathers himself up and staggers toward them, calling their names. By the time he gets to them, Ilapara is on all fours, while Tuk has sprawled on his back like he doesn't ever intend to get up. Alinata materializes next to him, hugging herself and looking mildly peeved.

He searches the trees but sees no sign of the Maidservant. He felt her pull away from him after her life flashed before his eyes; now she's already far enough that he can't sense her with his shards. "Are you all right?" He extends a hand to help Ilapara up to her feet. Her hand is cold to the touch but not cold enough to warrant shivering.

"Peachy," Tuk answers from the ground. "Just reeling from the most disturbing experience of my life."

A relieved chuckle escapes Salo's lips. To the Asazi he says, "You held up longer than I expected. I was worried you'd been hurt."

She frowns like she's tasted something bad and turns her face away. "Not hurt. Just imprisoned. A hazard of the trade, I suppose."

Knowing Asazi and their perfectionism, he's certain this will be a big slight to her pride. At least that's the worst of her injuries.

He looks about the clearing, noting Mukuni sitting on his haunches protectively next to the other warmounts. The cat has a few scratches on his spotted coat but is otherwise unharmed.

"Where's the witch?" Alinata says, searching the trees with a wary look. "I assume you defeated her, given we're all still alive."

You don't have to be, he said to her after he saw her torment and felt the force of her guilt. *It's not your fault,* is what she said to him when she saw what he did to his mother.

In some ways Salo always knew. At least he suspected, but his memories of that night felt so unreal he couldn't be sure what actually happened.

How he willingly and consciously killed his mother.

Even now his mind recoils from the memory, rejecting it. But he saw the truth with his own eyes, and there's no denying how much it all makes sense.

It wasn't your fault.

He hated the Maidservant for what she'd done to Monti. He wished her all the evil in the world . . . and yet, what he saw, the things that had been done to her . . . *How can I still hate her now?*

"She's gone," he says.

Alinata studies him. "Are you sure?"

"She's no longer a threat to me or any of us." Of this he is absolutely sure. "I appreciate your help, by the way. I'd probably be dead without you."

"Think nothing of it," Alinata says, and an amused light enters her eyes. "All things considered, I think you handled yourself rather well."

Ilapara has ventured off to find her spear; she returns with it, looking at Alinata like she's seeing her through new eyes. "Is the Void . . . always like that?"

The corners of Alinata's mouth lift ever so slightly. "You get used to it."

"Respect, Ali," Tuk says. "I seriously don't know how you do it." He finally forces himself up, springing off the ground with unexpected energy. He attempts to dust himself down, but the mud won't budge. He sighs. "I suppose the campsite's ruined now. Perhaps we should find somewhere close to a river? A bath and a change of clothes might be in order."

Salo's gorge rises as he takes in the remains of the dozen men he helped kill, strewed about the forest floor. He tears his eyes away before the queasiness can set in. "What do we do about the bodies? I don't know any spells for funeral rites."

"We leave them," Ilapara says.

Tuk nods in agreement. "I have no problem with that. Do you?" He looks at Alinata, who shakes her head quietly, then at Salo.

When he communed with the Lightning Bird, Salo felt a new vein of power opening in his shards, almost as if his communion had broken through some barrier of ignorance and deepened his connection to the moon.

Now he feels the same stirring again, a new aspect of his Axiom opening up to him, an arcane energy with power over the patterns of light. *Mirror craft.*

He stares at his glowing arms as his shards adjust to this new sensation, wondering if the memory of his own hand driving a blade into his mother's belly broke through yet another barrier of ignorance.

But why? he thinks. *Are my own memories and knowledge keeping the other crafts from me?*

What else is he supposed to remember?

Noticing that Tuk and the others are still waiting for him to respond, he lowers his arms and shakes his head. "We don't owe them anything, we don't have the time, and I'm tired." He exhales loud and long. "Let's just get out of here."

As they pack up and leave, Salo's thoughts drift back to the Maidservant and the brief experience they shared when their minds entangled in the Void.

He thinks about how much he hates her for what she did to Monti, for unearthing that horrible memory. He thinks about the change he felt in her just before they were severed, the feeling that beneath all that hatred was a woman desperate to find peace. He also thinks about how there may still be hope for her and how this makes him want to forgive her despite everything.

All of it makes him weary to the bone.

45: Isa

The old stories say that the foot of the city's colossus is where the first Saire king made a covenant with the Shirika by sacrificing his beloved firstborn son to them. It is said they drank his blood and feasted on his flesh, keeping him alive with spells, that he lay screaming in agony for days on end with his guts exposed to the sky, his torment paid in exchange for Saire supremacy over the rest of the Yontai.

It is said that afterward, the new king dug a grave with his bare hands, wearing them down to shredded stumps, softening the earth with his blood and tears, and upon his son's grave he built a gilded monument so that no one would ever forget the terrible price he had paid.

Isa never gave much thought to the legend, never wondered about what had been done to put her dynasty in power, but now it's all she can think about.

She stares at the colossus across the city from her chamber in the Red Temple, wondering what the young man was thinking as they tore the flesh off his bones. Did he appreciate the sacrifice he was making for his clan and family? Or did he curse them all and curse his father? What would she have thought?

Behind her, a knock comes on the door, two quick raps, then four, then three.

"Come in," she says without turning away from the city.

A draft of wind rushes in through the window when the door opens, and then there's a sharp intake of breath. "I apologize, Your Majesty. I'll wait outside until you're . . . er, decent."

Isa turns to face her guest, somewhat annoyed by his prudishness. "This is who I am, Obe. No lies, no chains, no frills. This is all I have left of myself. And it's nothing you haven't seen before, so come in and shut the door."

The young warrior hesitates and takes a peek down the corridor. Eventually he slips in, shutting the door so gently she barely hears it click. He leans against it, folding his arms as he takes her in, and for the longest moment he speaks with nothing but those intense eyes of his, caressing her body with them, and it's enough to make her shiver.

"I hate this, Isa," he says. "I hate seeing you so unhappy. It kills me that I can't do anything about it."

Bars of light from the adjacent blinds stripe his face, showing it to be creased with worry.

She looks out the window. The gilded colossus across the city looks back at her, judging her. "You being here is enough," she says.

"I feel like a better man would do more."

"And a better king wouldn't need you to."

Obe Saai lets out a long breath. She hears him walk toward the bed, then feels him come closer. Gently, lovingly, he drapes a silken gown around her naked back, letting his hands linger on her shoulders, thumbs rubbing idle circles on her nape. His breath is warm against her cool skin, and right now it's the only thing that's real to her.

"You're wrong, you know," he says.

She feels his voice ripple down her spine. "Oh? How so?"

"You're not all you have left. You have me too."

"I know," she says.

"You have your cousin."

"That's true."

"And many others who would gladly give their lives for you, for their king."

Slowly, she untangles herself from him, wrapping the gown around her body. She drifts to the foot of the large bed taking up much of the chamber, and there she sits like she's carrying the weight of a mountain. "I know, Obe; I know these things, and I'm not ungrateful, but it's not enough. I'm sorry, but it isn't."

You will have to die, Your Majesty. You will have to play games, and eventually, you will have to be the piece sacrificed for the greater good.

He looks down at her like he's sad she can't see how wrong she is. Obe is not simple by any means, but his world is painted in stark colors, with no room for ambiguity. He proceeds to pace the width of her chamber, his hands on his waist. "I used to look up to him, you know? My uncle. But now . . ." Obe shakes his head, pausing to look down at Isa, his hurt and confusion written in the lines of his face. "He shames me, Isa. He's a disgrace to every Saai in the kingdom, and his scheming will be the death of us all."

A reckless impulse veers into Isa right then. Knowing she is stoking a fire, she says, "He's still your uncle."

His eyes spark with strong emotions, and he seems to loom taller in the room. "He is *nothing* to me, and if he thinks the Sentinels will just lay down our arms and let him butcher innocents in this city, then he's in for a surprise—bond or no bond. I've been talking to my comrades, and there's a real"—Obe brings his fingers together as he thinks of the appropriate word—"cohesion, you know? We're all fired up, for you, for our king. We're not going anywhere, not even if the motherdamned Shirika threaten to rain fire down on us."

She's witnessing the hubris of youth, passion yet to be tempered by experience and disappointment. She takes it anyway, because it's hers and hers alone.

Isa leans back onto her elbows and brings one foot onto the bed, leisurely, parting her legs, letting the silken gown slip down her body.

Obe is a fire, but he can burn hotter still. "You'll have to obey them," she says. "The gods must not be defied."

He wears the light-green tunic of the King's Sentinels, but the insignia on his breast and the marks on his neck are those of the Saai clan. He slips out of the tunic now and stands naked before her, a strong, powerful, striking silhouette against the sunlight flooding in through the open windows. "For you, Isa, I would declare war on heaven," he says, and she knows he means it. At least right now.

But she needs to hear more.

Make me feel alive, she says with her eyes. *Remind me I am young and beautiful.*

He comes toward her, answering her silent request. He smells like the earth, like the lush jungles of her kingdom, like the roaring waterfall gushing beneath them. He leans closer, pushing her flat onto her back. "For you I would align my soul with the powers of hell." His voice is dusky; his eyes blaze with fervid reverence. "For you I would storm the golden gates of the Infinite Path and raze its ivory walls to the ground." He kisses her neck, scorching her skin, singeing her, making her shudder. "I would do these things for you, or I would die trying, because no heaven is heaven without you in it."

And at last, he captures her lips in a possessive kiss, this Saai warrior, the blood of her mortal enemy, her lover. She is an empty shell, but Obe is life and energy. He is hope, the only thing she knows to be true in the universe, and so she yields to his fire and his zealous worship, and she burns in it.

She burns, and she says to herself, *I am powerful, I am adored, I am absolute, a king, a goddess, and nothing on this earth can touch me.*

Isa knows she's a liar, but lies are all she has left.

When Obe leaves, she begins to play the game that has been set for her.

She summons Jomo's clerk to her chambers and has him sit while she paces nervously, gathering her courage. She can't see all the pieces on the game board just yet, nor read the moves that have been made, but she can see that she has been maneuvered. That much is clear to her now.

She just can't do anything about it.

The irony. To be a king, and yet to be powerless.

"I have a message I need you to send via mirrorscope," she tells the clerk at last. The young votary already has a pen and a pad in hand. He looks up when she makes a cutting gesture. "I don't want anyone finding out about this just yet, so nothing on paper."

"Of course, Your Majesty." The votary puts his pen down and then asks, politely, "To whom will this message be sent?"

She inhales deeply, thinks before she lets it out, and then decides to take the plunge. "The prince regent," she says. "Tell him that I accept his proposal and that he can start preparing for bride-price negotiations with my cousin."

The votary manages to keep his expression unchanged, but the way he falls very still betrays his surprise. "Will that be all, Your Majesty?"

"Don't tell my cousin. I will let him know myself."

"Yes, Your Majesty."

As the votary leaves to deliver her message, Isa walks to stare out the window at the gilded warrior who's been taking up much of her thoughts lately. *I will play this game for now,* she tells herself, *because I have no choice. But I must find a way to make the game end on my own terms.*

46: Ilapara

Ilapara leads the way east along the World's Vein as they race toward the Jungle City.

Her buck has grown so confident in his newfound power it's almost a chore to restrain him from going too fast, but the thrill of edging him to the limits of her strength has become addictive to her, so much so that she doesn't mind the gradual burn she's developed in her thighs and in her arms and in her—by Ama, her entire body is sore. Whenever this journey ends, she'll collapse into a heap of bones and sleep for a week, bed or no bed.

The traffic begins to thicken as they race toward the city. The World's Vein becomes somewhat wider and paved with red bricks. Even so, they are forced to slow down due to the sheer volume of riders, beast-drawn carriages, and clunky spirit-powered carts clogging the road.

Ilapara has never been to the Yontai before, but something tells her that this kind of traffic isn't the norm. Not even for the Vein.

Bamboo villages on either side of the road, some empty, others bustling with activity; no discernable reason for this difference. Men and women walking along the edges of the road, many balancing heavy loads on their heads, babies slung on their backs, young children trailing behind—entire families, perhaps. Why the mass movement? And yet farmers in straw hats look on from their fields, so not everyone is on the move, but they're watching because this kind of movement isn't normal, else they'd be beating back the encroaching jungles with their machetes like they're supposed to be.

Ilapara can't pinpoint exactly what it is about this picture that's not sitting quite well with her. She feels the itch to stop one of these people and ask what they are running from, but she knows that asking the wrong questions—more precisely, being seen asking the wrong questions—can get a person killed. So she decides to keep her eyes open for now and ask questions later.

She rides abreast of Salo the whole time, while Tuk trails behind with the Asazi riding pillion on his abada. Salo doesn't notice her stealing glances at him now and then because he's locked inside his own head, more so than usual, at least. The little crease on his forehead tells her he's trying to solve a puzzle that both troubles and intrigues him. Makes her wish she could pry open that inscrutable head of his and find out what he's thinking.

They should have never made it anywhere near the Jungle City given the forces that rose against them. More to the point, those dangers could hardly be the result of Salo stepping in to save a Faraswa thief from execution. Clearly something else about him caught the Dark Sun's attention, something compelling enough for his lieutenants to pursue him well out of Umadiland.

The thoughts have been sending uneasy shivers down Ilapara's spine. *Who are you, Salo, and why am I here with you?*

The city of Yonte Saire comes into view when the World's Vein rounds a peaked hill and the jungles fall away on one side, becoming a sprawling vista of towering gilded statues, landscaped gardens, and latticed bamboo domes both large and small, some paneled with glass, others with gilded struts and shingles, all of them gleaming like precious stones in the afternoon sunlight.

So much to gape at, and though it all siphons the wind from her humbled lungs, leaving nothing there but breathless awe, Ilapara's eyes are drawn to the twin waterfalls hung like drapes of fine gossamer on the city's eastern rock face, so tall they seem to dwarf everything beneath them.

Really it's one waterfall, but it's sheared in half at the top by the improbable: a citadel of stone and bamboo perched at the lip of the precipice like a naturally occurring feature of the river—because how could human hands have built such a thing?

What's more, two thin spires rise from within the citadel to soar high above its walls, and between them hangs a red gemstone of mammoth proportions, so immense she can almost see its gleaming facets even from miles away, and it hangs in thin air, perhaps held in place by its sheer magnificence, or by some other force Ilapara cannot begin to comprehend.

"The Ruby Paragon," she murmurs. "The Shrouded Pylon, the Red Temple; it's all real."

She thought the stories she'd heard about them were lies. Now she knows she was right; they were lies, but only because they didn't do the truth any justice at all.

She realizes she's stopped when Salo brings Mukuni to a halt next to Ingacha. He takes in the city with speechless wonder, as if words would only be a travesty of what he truly feels. Then some hidden realization slowly dawns on his face, and he gapes at the distant Paragon like it has enchanted him.

"What is it?" Ilapara asks impatiently.

"Along a scarlet road," he says in a near whisper, "past a gateway beneath a red star. It shines far beyond your horizons." He slowly shakes his head. "I can't believe I didn't figure it out before."

Moments like these make her wonder if Salo is truly sane. "Figure what out?"

And just like that, the enchanted look turns into a sad smile. "Nothing. Tell me, my friend: Do you believe in fate?"

He says *friend*, but she isn't sure that's what they are.

Why am I here?

"I believe in the consequences of the choices we make," she says. "I believe in accountability. Why, do you?"

"I don't know." He looks toward the Red Temple. "But . . . I think I've been brought here, somehow."

"You're here because the queen allowed you to awaken and commanded you to walk the Bloodway," Ilapara says. "A consequence of the choices you both made."

"But what if she commanded me to walk the Bloodway because I'm *meant* to be here?"

"Then she acted without choice," Ilapara says. "She was compelled by forces unseen, like a pebble on a matje board, which means she can't be held accountable for her actions—in which case no one can. Are you willing to accept that?"

She knows where his mind goes when his face hardens. "I think she still had to make the choice," he says. "She could have decided not to."

"Then it's not fate."

"No, but maybe something put the choice in her hands."

"Something like what?"

He smiles like he knows something she doesn't and nudges Mukuni into motion. "That's the question, isn't it?"

Tuk and Alinata finally catch up to them. Ilapara's disquiet must be evident on her face, because Tuk studies her and says, "All right there, Ilapara?"

Alinata says nothing, but amusement dances in her eyes.

"I'm good." Ilapara prods her kudu into following Salo.

Why am I here?

Her whole body is still thrumming with the excitement of the battles she fought along the way. Hard for her to admit, but she's never felt so full of life. This is why she left home. For adventure, and to make her own path and become her own woman.

And yet . . . it rankles to have to depend on someone else. She knows she's stuck with Salo and Tuksaad and now this Asazi spy. She can't turn around and go back to Umadiland.

Thinking about the life she left behind floods her with conflicting emotions. On one hand, she'd eked out a life for herself back there, made useful contacts, built up a reputation. Another month, and she might have finally made it onto a caravan. But on the other hand . . .

What she saw at the boneyards still flits across her vision whenever she closes her eyes.

Heads rotting on pikes. A burning wagon in the distance. The silent horror on Salo's face . . .

I don't really want to go back to that, do I? And Salo did say he'd pay me handsomely, didn't he?

So maybe she can stay here with him. Or maybe once she makes enough money, she can go back to Umadiland and pay whatever life debt she might owe.

The possibilities unfold in her mind like branches, and as they ride toward the glistening city at the heart of the Redlands, the conflux of the World's Vein and the World's Artery, one thought rings louder than the others.

For now. I'll stay with him for now.

47: Musalodi

Riding down the World's Vein into the continent's beating heart, Salo concludes that the city was built specifically to leave visitors and passersby with an overwhelming impression of the Yontai's wealth and power.

The redbrick road enters the city from the west so that the waterfalls and their impossible temple loom directly ahead, drawing attention and due reverence to the Shrouded Pylon and its giant ruby. There, the eyes will naturally progress to the gilded warrior west of the waterfalls, a colossal statue with a shield and spear standing at one corner of a flat-topped hill, almost level with the temple. Grand palaces of bamboo, glass, and gold descend from the colossus, peeking through a canopy of lush terraced gardens as if to gloat over their magnificence and taunt onlookers with splendor they will never know.

Then, as the road touches the valley floor, the view slowly vanishes behind dense, living walls of bamboo and towering trees, doubtless grown into such a state by powerful Earth craft, leaving only a tantalizing glimpse through the open city gates. The gates themselves are an imposing latticed sculpture of bamboo struts and gilded effigies, the most prominent of which are the heads of eleven beasts arrayed in a line above the gates, where the four-tusked elephant takes the place of honor. They look down on the road from their lofty perches as if to say: *Here is power, if you have never seen it.*

To have the gates rising in front of him is almost like a dream to Salo. They are visual proof of just how far from home he's traveled, so far that home might as well be a figment of his imagination.

What is Nimara doing right now? Does Niko think of me? Why am I here, so far from everything I know and love?

An unexpected tide of emotions floods his eyes with tears, and he has to take a deep breath. *The world is a big place,* he tells himself. *It is an old place. What are my sorrow and guilt to such a world? Who am I to the spirits who roam its lakes, who have seen the stars with their own eyes and have seen the rise and fall of immortal empires? My pain is insignificant, and I should not let it control me.*

When they arrive at the gates, the two guards inspecting incoming traffic gape at Mukuni, seeming more impressed than frightened. They are both in brown tunics and aerosteel armor, with scimitars hanging from leather shoulder belts. Like all KiYonte tribespeople Salo has seen thus far, their necks are branded with dark tattoos, though Salo can't quite make them out from atop his mount.

He presents the queen's medallion so that they see its Seal. Both guards stiffen at the sight of it. "Allow me to accept that, honored one," says the taller guard, and then he runs with the medallion to the bamboo shed nearby and emerges a minute later with a light-skinned, barefoot young man in an aerosteel breastplate and robes of crimson brocade. Instead of regular clan marks, he has thin white lines running down his neck. His eyes are cool and distant.

"He must be a Jasiri," Ilapara whispers with a note of awe in her voice.

Tuk leans closer from his abada, watching the Jasiri approach. "There aren't many around, but you don't ever want to get one angry."

From behind him, Alinata says, "They don't anger easily, though. Just be respectful, and you'll be fine."

Salo has heard of the Jasiri before, and he read about them in the reports the emissary gave him. He appreciates just how feared they are. Apparently, even the most powerful Umadi warlords will hesitate before provoking their ire.

He steels himself, forcing calm into his bones. Thus far his encounters with foreign mystics have not gone well, so he has to be careful about this one.

The Jasiri stops next to Mukuni, proffers the medallion to Salo, and bows his head respectfully. "Welcome to Yonte Saire, Honored Emissary Musalodi Deitari Siningwe. I am Acolyte Kamali Jasiri of the Fractal. We have been expecting your arrival."

He is statuesque, and he must be in his early twenties, but his elaborately braided beard falls thickly down his chin, making him look somewhat older. Salo is a little taken aback by his politeness as he accepts the medallion.

"Thank you, Red-kin," he says in thickly accented KiYonte, "though this is the first time I have answered to that title."

A polite, unreadable smile parts the Jasiri's beard. "Do you wish to be called something else?"

"I usually go by Salo."

The smile becomes a slight grimace, like the word tastes bad in the Jasiri's mouth. "That's a diminutive of your given name, is it not?"

"It is."

"Then I'm afraid I cannot comply with your request, Emissary Siningwe. In this city, sorcerers and diplomats will be shown due respect at all times, and you are both." He looks to his side and beckons a guard mounted on a striped antelope. "This guardsman will guide you to your leased residence in Skytown. I have messaged ahead, so your steward will be waiting to receive you." The Jasiri bows his head. "Welcome once again, Honored Emissary. I wish you a prosperous pilgrimage and a pleasant stay in the city."

"Thank you, Acolyte Kamali Jasiri of the Fractal." Salo isn't sure what that title means, but he says it in full to avoid accusations of disrespect.

The Jasiri nods and steps aside, letting Salo follow the mounted guard into the city.

"That went rather well," Ilapara says. "For once."

Tuk quickly spurs Wakii to catch up to them, surprise brightening his face. "You leased a residence in *Skytown*?" He tilts his head back and lets out an incredulous laugh. "Oh, my friend. Bumping into you in Seresa is turning out to be the best thing that has ever happened to me."

"What's Skytown?" Ilapara asks, and Salo shakes his head, staring at the city ahead of him, no longer a distant dream but a close reality.

"I can't say I know," he says.

Tuk's eyes twinkle like jades in the sunlight, and he smiles. "Well. I suppose you're about to find out."

Yonte Saire. The Jungle City. The world's beating heart. The red star shining beyond his horizons. He will find answers here; Salo is certain of this. Answers to the questions that now plague his thoughts. What is not so certain, however, is whether those answers will kill him.

In the distance, the Paragon strobes once, twice, and three more times after that. And then it stills.

Black magic—magic of the underworld

Breaching the Void to summon creatures from the devil's domain. Not considered a craft of Red magic but a foreign corruption. Reviled throughout the Redlands.

—excerpt from Kelafelo's notes

Epilogue

Somewhere in the gloomy labyrinths beneath the world's beating heart, where the suns never shine and reptilian monsters prowl unseen, the Enchantress enters a subterranean sanctuary, where she has come to visit the apostate sibyl who calls it home.

Attar of bloodroses trails behind her as she walks, the heels of her gold-encrusted shoes clicking on the wet floors. She has covered her face in a diaphanous scarlet veil and clothed her hands in matching gloves. Dirt will not cling to her robes of violet Dulama silk, nor will the stench of sewage pervading the tunnels overpower her perfumes.

To the pair of masked Jasiri guardians walking two steps behind her—they are her escorts, courtesy of one of her Faro friends—she is an oasis of glamour in the foulness of the undercity. They perceive her as fragile, a delicate flower in need of their protection; the Enchantress knows this because she made it so.

What they don't know—indeed, what she will never let them know—is that she is a mystic herself, whose power is hidden beneath a field generated by her metaformic jewel. They don't know that her perfumes, grace, poise, beauty, and allure are in fact specialized spells of a kind. Like a spider hidden in the shadows, she has woven them surreptitiously around their minds, ensnaring them in fervent loyalty to her. Their devotion is so complete they would slit their own throats if she only commanded it.

The Enchantress smiles at the thought. Jasiri guardians, arguably the world's deadliest warrior mystics, and she has them wrapped around her little finger like twine.

She has come a long way from the sniveling victim she once was.

They enter a dimly lit chamber within the sanctuary, a shrine of sorts, with the stone carving of a stylized eye ensconced within a niche on one wall, candles arrayed beneath it so that it seems to move in the wavering light, like it's alive. The Enchantress lifts her veil and studies the blue hieroglyphs painted onto the wall behind the statue. They all bear the faded quality of age.

This sanctuary is old. It's been here for decades at least.

She purses her lips, displeased. Damn these cultists. Like cockroaches, they spread everywhere no matter how many you crush beneath your boot. How in the world did they infiltrate the Red Wilds without anyone noticing until now? The Enchantress would shed much blood to know the answer to that question.

"Welcome to the Sanctuary of Vigilance, Your Highness." A bright-eyed woman of middle age has materialized next to her, dressed in a patterned blue caftan and a matching head wrap, no trace of fear in the depths of her gaze, only mild curiosity.

A mystic, no doubt, though not a powerful one. Probably one of those pesky independents who run around "helping" the poor with their magic. The Enchantress wonders why the Faros tolerate them at all. This woman alone has likely proselytized many converts into her cult.

"You draw power from the Mother," the Enchantress says and gestures at the carved eye with a gloved hand, "yet you insult her by bowing to false idols. Do you not fear her retribution for such flagrant apostasy?"

The woman remains calmly impassive. "I do not reject the Mother, Your Highness. I only accept that she is merely one of many expressions of the greater good and that there are other expressions that can work through us just as well. If the Mother did not approve, I doubt I could still call upon her benevolence."

"I wonder if you'd say the same thing about mystics who consort with the devil. The Mother allows them to keep drawing from her, does she not? Even after they've sullied their souls. Do you mean to tell me that she approves?"

"I wouldn't know, Your Highness. Would you?"

Silence falls between them and thickens as they stare at each other, and to her credit, the woman remains cool as frost. *Such composure when I could have your head with the snap of a finger.* The Enchantress ends the staring contest with a smile. "I have come to consult with the Sibyl Underground. Is she free to see me?"

"As a matter of fact, she is. I can take you to her now."

"Excellent."

"If you would please follow me, Your Highness."

The apostate mystic proceeds to lead her down dingy tunnels with wall-mounted crystal lamps barely bright enough to illuminate the many figures milling about. The Enchantress frowns in distaste when a little Faraswa girl in a dirty blue tunic almost bumps into her as she scurries after her friends.

They have children here. And Faraswa living among them. This isn't just a cultist sanctuary; it's a thriving community.

They have grown far too comfortable in this city.

The Jasiri cause quite the stir as they follow her deeper into the sanctuary. Cultists blanch and turn around; children huddle together in the corners, pointing and whispering. Their reaction doesn't surprise the Enchantress; the eyeless masks of the Jasiri—fashioned to resemble weeping skulls with horns—are never welcome sights to those who have cause to fear the authorities.

The apostate mystic leads her into a chamber lit by so many candles the walls seem on fire. Wax flows thickly down the candlesticks, and a flowery aroma pervades the air, a change the Enchantress welcomes with a relieved breath.

Like well-trained pets, the Jasiri do not enter; they stand guard by the door outside, arms folded over broad chests, enchanted spears balanced on their ends.

Beyond the door, a girl not yet old enough to sprout breasts sits on a grass mat in the center of the chamber, her shaved head bowed, her chest encumbered by beaded necklaces, folded legs hidden beneath a voluminous layered skirt. Bones and other mysterious articles are strewed on the mat around her. A table and a wicker chair sit in one corner.

"Your guest has arrived, Reverence," the mystic announces, and the Enchantress fails to conceal her surprise.

"You were expecting me?"

"I expected someone," comes the sibyl's juvenile voice. She still hasn't raised her head. "Please, sit. Have some tea."

The woman motions the Enchantress to sit by the table and then proceeds to serve her aromatic spiced shaah in a porcelain cup. She has an inscrutable expression as she sets the teakettle back onto the table. The Enchantress notices with a quirked eyebrow that the tea is still hot enough to steam.

"I'll be right outside if you need me," the woman says and then glides out of the chamber.

While she takes off her gloves and sets them on the table, the Enchantress studies the so-called Sibyl Underground. She knows that her gift of foresight is an ancestral talent unique to Void mystics of a now-extinct tribe of hunter-gatherers who lived in the Umadi savannas. Hard to imagine that this girl is the last of them, the world's last soothsayer. A child. She must be something truly extraordinary to have built an Axiom and faced a redhawk at her age. A pity she had to go and entangle herself with cultists.

The Enchantress lifts her cup and takes a sip. *Perfect.* "You knew this was my favorite tea, didn't you," she says, breaking the long silence.

"I knew only that my guest would appreciate it," the sibyl replies without lifting her head.

"I do. Thank you."

"You are welcome."

The Enchantress wonders briefly how to extract the information she has come for. Her Faro accomplice wouldn't give her the full picture of what's going on, wouldn't say anything about the key or where to watch out for it, expected her to simply trust that things were under control. But she'll be damned if she lets herself sit in the dark. If the Faro won't tell her, she'll have to find out for herself.

She sips from her cup. "Do you really see the future, Reverence?"

"But how could I?" the girl says. "One cannot see that which is not set in stone. I see only possibilities, and even then, small fragments. The future is an infinite number of threads branching away from a single continuously moving point: the present. Through the Void I see many more threads than you do at any given time, so I am able to tell which ones are thicker. That is not the same as prophecy."

"So you do guesswork, essentially."

"Exceptional guesswork, Your Highness."

"Can you guess why I'm here, then?"

"You are here to help me, of course."

The Enchantress feels a mirthless smile breaking on her face and sits back in her chair. "Am I, now."

"I believe so, yes," the sibyl says. "There is a great disturbance in the threads of time. Something is in motion, but there are too many threads affected for me to pinpoint where the disturbance is coming from. I need a piece of information, a trail or a scent—something that will help me focus. You are about to give that to me."

For a moment the Enchantress wonders if this girl is truly as young as she looks. "Perhaps I am." She gazes into her tea while she orders her thoughts. It would not be wise to reveal too much, at least not before she has pried the answers she seeks from the girl. Then it won't matter what she sees. "Someone with a key to something old and very powerful is approaching this city. I need to know everything you can tell me about them, if they really exist, anything to help me identify them when they arrive."

The sibyl finally raises her head, and all the light in the chamber *flees*, pooling at the edges and corners as if a tangible cloud of darkness has materialized to push it away. At the center of it the sibyl's eyes are impossibly black windows into the Void, bordered by weak halos of light.

The Enchantress shivers despite herself.

"A key . . ." In the unsettling gloom the sibyl turns her head like she's tracking movement in the chamber, and the Enchantress thinks she sees mounting awe in the child's expression. "Yes, a key is the source of the disturbance. Although . . . it is only part of it. A small part. A vital part." She gasps, her soulless eyes fixing on something in blank space. "Oh, these are ancient threads."

The Enchantress frowns as a prickle of anxiety turns to impatience. She needs her answers before the sibyl sees too much. "Tell me what you see, Reverence. Tell me about the one who brings this key."

The sibyl pries her gaze away from whatever she was looking at and picks up the bones on the mat. The Enchantress watches her rattle them between her cupped palms only to scatter them in front of her. She is quiet for a long time as she peruses the bones, a spread hand moving over them with its palm facing downward.

Finally the Enchantress loses her patience. "What are you doing?"

"Do you know of the Great Forgetting?" the sibyl says, and the Enchantress has to struggle to hide her alarm.

What has she seen?

"I know of the legend. Supposedly there was a night several thousand years ago when all history was erased from the minds of every human being alive. Why do you ask?"

"It is no legend but truth." The sibyl keeps moving her hand over the bones. "These bone fragments belong to an ancient queen, a woman of great consequence who lived before the Great Forgetting. Though her deeds are lost to us, they touched so many threads of time that she serves as a lodestar to those of us with the dark sight."

The sibyl's hand stops when the halos around her eyes brighten. And then, with a bloodcurdling voice as old as she is young, a voice that seems to transcend time itself, she says: "I see a prince with a bow, riding a terrible beast of the wild with fur as white as sap. A warrior cloaked in blood follows him, then a seeker of justice shrouded in the night, then a maiden of death who wields the Void . . ."

Before the Enchantress can puzzle out what this means, the sibyl withdraws her hand like it has been scorched by fire. "Oh no."

The Enchantress edges forward in her chair. "What is it? Tell me."

"So much death . . . so many threads crumbling to ash . . . the riders bring doom upon this city."

A thrill of fear and excitement runs through the Enchantress. She traces a lacquered nail over the rim of her teacup, feeling it tremble in her hand. *So it's true. The key to the Ascendancy's power has been found.* "Is that all you see?"

Now the sibyl looks straight at her with those horrific eyes of hers, and the Enchantress burns with the sudden desire to know exactly what she sees. "You must not let the prince pass through the gates. You must stop him. Save this city!"

The Enchantress decides that it is time to leave. Clearly she has extracted as much use from the young sibyl as she ever will. She places her teacup on the table and picks up her gloves. "You have been most helpful, Reverence. And thanks for the tea." And then she rises from her chair and makes for the exit, only to stop at the sibyl's desperate pleas.

"You don't understand the scale of the destruction we face, Your Highness," the child cries. "You must stop the prince before he brings ruin upon us all. Surely it is why you are here."

With a chilled smile the Enchantress turns around, and she lets a morsel of her power peek through the veil she hides it under. "But ruin is exactly what I seek, my dear sibyl."

The sibyl stares in shock. If she could not see the threads of time that touched the Enchantress before, she can certainly see them now. "You," she whispers.

"Indeed."

The Enchantress leaves the chamber without another word, and just before they reach the portal to the undercity, she turns to her masked Jasiri and whispers, "Put spies near the city gates. I want to know the moment someone rides in on a white beast, something sizable and likely predatory. He will be traveling with three companions."

"As you wish, Your Highness," says one of her masked guardians, and his voice comes out with a harsh metallic edge.

"And one last thing." The Enchantress casts a glance down the tunnel, where the hum of voices can be heard, the sounds of cultists living their lives and raising families in these sewers like rats. "Purge the sanctuary. No one gets out of here alive."

A brief silence as the two Jasiri share a look. "What of the sibyl, Your Highness?" says the one who spoke before, and the Enchantress lets a silent gaze answer his question. His fiendish mask conceals his face, but the hesitation is clear in his voice when he speaks. "But she is the last soothsayer. The late king consulted with her regularly. She was under his protection."

"Am I flinching?"

After a pause, the Jasiri nods. "It will be done."

And it will; of this she is certain. The Jasiri will not fail to carry out her orders to the fullest extent, and the Cult of Vigilance will be wiped from this city once and for all.

A smile stretches her lips as she leaves the sanctuary. It falters, though, when she hears the first screams behind her, but she forces it to hold.